COBRA Z

BOOK 1 OF THE NECROPOLIS TRILOGY

SEAN DEVILLE

SEVERED PRESS

COBRA Z

www.severedpress.com

ISBN: 978-1-925493-40-5

"If thou openest not the gate to let me enter, I will break the door, I will wrench the lock, I will smash the door-posts, I will force the doors. I will bring up the dead to eat the living. And the dead will outnumber the living."

— The Epic of Gilgamesh

Important Characters

British Government

David Osbourne MP – Prime Minister
Arnold Craver – Head of the Centre for the Protection of National Infrastructure (MI5)
Bill Dodson – Prime Minister's Private Secretary
Mitchell Tanner MP – Chancellor of the Exchequer
Sir Peter Milnes – Metropolitan Police Commissioner
Claire Miles MP – Home Secretary
Sir Nicholas Martin – Chief of the Defence Staff
Sir Michael Young – Head of MI5
Sir Stuart Watkins – Head of MI6
'Davina' – Interrogator MI6
Jeremy Smith – Sergeant, Metropolitan Police

British Military

Major David Croft – Investigating Officer for the Centre for the Protection of National Infrastructure
Captain Lucy Savage – Head of Biomedical Science, Porton Down Research Centre
Captain Mark Grainger – Grenadier Guards
Captain Lewis Hudson – SAS
Sergeant Craig O'Sullivan – SAS

US Government

General Roberts – Head of the Joint Chiefs of Staff
Ben Silver – White House Chief of Staff
Keith Johnson – CIA Director
Damian Rodney – President of the United States

The Sons of the Resurrection Cult

James Jones – The Chief Cleric
Abraham – Cult Leader
Fabrice Chevalier – Warrior of Truth

British Civilians

Jack Nathan
Gavin Hemsworth
Owen Patterson
Elizabeth Holden

The Daily N

Sunday, May 11, 2014

Esteemed Professor Found D

Yesterday, Professor Clive Cook, Nobel Prize winner and Visiting Professor at Oxford University was found dead near his holiday home in Dunvegan Scotland. The esteemed geneticist, who in 2003 was awarded the Nobel prize for his revolutionary research in Recombinant DNA, was reported missing three days ago by his wife.

Police have yet to release the details of his death, but it is thought the 38 year old Professor took his own life. The scientific community across the UK and the world has reacted with shock at the news. The death of a man who many have labelled "a genius to rival Einstein" will be seen as a significant set back to the revolutionary field of cancer research he founded

Rer
foll
imp

The
that
rela
the
beh
of a
exp
in l
its
beh

Ref: FGu5867th

Top Secret

The Civil Contingencies Committee Command Structure Platinum
Eyes Only

WARNING

Unauthorised reproduction/viewing/ distribution of this document will result in prosecution under the Treason Act 1695 and may carry a penalty of life imprisonment under the Crime and Disorder Act 1998

Confidential Report on Project Z43851-5

Report by the Joint Intelligence Organisation

Ref: FGu5867th
Date: 21.04.14

At roughly 8PM on the 17th of April 2014, there was a containment breach at the BSL-4 genetic laboratory facility at the Hirta Island Research Complex, designation RESURRECTION. Although the breach was ultimately contained, 17 people lost their lives, including facility director Professor Clive Cook and head of security Stewart Goldsmith. It is as yet not known where a pathogen this virulent came from, how it escaped containment into the general facility, how it spread so rapidly, or why those infected manifested the symptoms that resulted in the tragedy. What is known is that the security lockdown prevented the contagion from escaping into the outside environment, and that the incident has now been deemed to be contained.

The following is a transcript of the final video log of Professor Clive Cook. This was sent via Intranet to the secure server at the facility where it was retrieved after the event, along with the video logs of the surveillance cameras. Many of Professor Cook's words were inaudible due to the background noise. Some of the details have also been redacted as they fall outside the security clearance of many on the Civil Contingencies Committee.

"The virus got out [INAUDIBLE] know how. I've barricaded myself in [INAUDIBLE] not hold for long. Their strength is incredible. We never imagined [REDACTED] beyond all recognised scientific norms [INAUDIBLE] … and most of my research team are dead. Oh God, what have we done? How did this happen? You must not open up the facility. The lockdown must stay in place. All my research has been uploaded to the central server, but please, I implore you, this research must be abandoned. I was wrong, I was so very wrong. [INAUDIBLE] cannot be repeated. [REDACTED] ignored my advice. I told him we were rushing this, and I told him [REDACTED] would be a disaster. Oh God, they are breaking through; I can hear them … I can feel them. I was bit … I can feel them in my mind. Why does this itch so bad? In my head … they are in my head. They are so hungry. Why is my mind on fire? Fire, yes, fire, that's what I meant to say. I tried to activate the fire sterilisation system, but it malfunctioned. Activate it from the outside, cremate everything in here [INAUDIBLE] … I can see them. They are [REDACTED].”

After analysis of the situation, Major Croft has stated he is in agreement with the position put forward by Professor Cook, and as the surveillance feed showed no uninfected survivors, the sealed-off sections of RESURRECTION were fire sterilised as per SOP on his orders. It is the government’s position that research into project Z43851-5 be terminated due to the unexpected nature of the outcome and the potentially catastrophic infectious nature of what occurred. It is notable that none of the research data on the official server shows any indication that this was a result of the research officially being performed at the facility.

Video feeds of the event as it transpired have been uploaded and will be available during the briefing. Attached, you will find summary data on the reasons for the research and the results Professor Cook had hoped to achieve. You will also find the report by Major Croft, which details the events that occurred and the steps he felt necessary to secure the situation.

Yours Sincerely,

James Flynn, Prime Minister’s National Security Advisor

Report on the 17.04.2014 containment breach at the BSL-4 genetic laboratory facility at the Hirta Island Research Complex, designation RESURRECTION

Ref: FGu5867th
Date: 19.04.14

Upon arrival at the facility, I found the lower-level laboratory area sealed and intact. Due to the nature of the apparent contagion, and the fact that all personnel in the quarantined zone were verified (via biometric data transmitted from their implanted microchips) as being either dead or "infected" (I use this word as an assumption as to the cause of the incident), I ordered immediate thermal sterilisation of the laboratory area on my authorisation as granted by s.5(1c) of The Civil Contingency Act 2004. As you are aware, the laboratory is supplied by two filtered positive pressure air vents and one access door. All three were sealed prior to sterilisation, and action is underway to permanently block off these potential access points with concrete, as whatever occurred is deemed too dangerous to risk exposure to the outside world. It is my recommendation that this facility never be re-opened, and a quarantine zone is being erected around the facility that supplies the laboratory under my authorisation as granted by s.5(1b) of The Civil Contingency Act 2004. The four-level subterranean structure above the laboratory is planned for controlled implosion to ensure nobody can access the sealed area in the future.

Through analysis of the surveillance feeds and the biometric readouts, I have not ascertained the source of the outbreak. It does not pertain to any of the research recorded in the official logs. I, therefore, suspect and deduce that there was unsanctioned research being done. I have, however, been able to ascertain patient zero. Dr. Johansson, the senior virologist at the facility, was the first to experience visible symptoms of the virus. His biometric readings show a spike in blood pressure and temperature, followed by a massive breakdown at the genetic level, with a rapid and violent expulsion of bodily fluids. He was seen on surveillance in the canteen area drinking coffee several minutes before he underwent seizure. Dr. Smith and Dr. Carter, along with three junior scientists, were all present when this occurred and went to his aid. The seizures stopped and then Dr. Johansson attacked his colleagues, biting three of them. The time stamp showed that they too underwent seizure within 5-10 minutes, indicating a virulent pathogen with a very short gestation period. They each went on to attack multiple individuals. The ensuing chaos saw the facility overrun. The video of Professor Cook shows compelling evidence that we are indeed dealing with a new form of pathogen.

Those affected show very specific symptoms of uncontrolled rage, increased strength, and an almost insatiable desire to attack other species, not just humans. One of the affected individuals was seen on video attacking the caged rhesus monkeys. He was able to rip the locked cage door from its hinges, losing a finger in the process, indicating they have a negligible reaction to pain stimulus. These symptoms follow a brief period of illness, including vomiting, abdominal and head pain, with diarrhoea and loss of bladder control. As witnessed on the various videos taken by the CCTV, those affected also have distinctly bloodshot eyes that seem to bulge out.

There is nothing in the computer logs to indicate what this potential pathogen is. The facility was reportedly working on the early stages of the Methuselah cure, an artificially manufactured gene coding virus that it was hoped could slow the ageing process. None of the test animals showed similar symptoms, and there is no indication in any of the research that this eventuality could occur, and as already stated, I believe this was either unsanctioned research or research sanctioned outside the normal chain of command that was being done in secret. Even so, it is unknown how any manufactured pathogens could escape the BSL-4 containment protocols set up at the facility. Fortunately, the quick acting nature and the virulence of the pathogen meant its affects became apparent before it could escape the BSL-4 lab. The control computer designated TRQ did what it was designed to do and sealed the facility.

As reported in my last briefing, I strongly suspect that this is another act of deliberate sabotage. I believe persons unknown have used this facility as a production site and/or a test ground for a new bio-weapon. I have no information on how this could occur. Close inspection of the computer log shows voids in the data, suggesting manipulation and deletion of files. I would advise a thorough re-vetting of all staff at similar government facilities, and immediate investigation of all staff employed at this facility since its conception, by the intelligence service MI5. One thing of note, the number of bodies in the BSL-4 lab is one short of the designation for that facility. There is no record of any other individuals working there, but the facility is definitely one personnel member short, and there are indications of manipulation of the employee files, the entry and exit logs, and the data files themselves. This suggests to me that somebody left the facility prior to the event occurring. This might very well explain the disappearance of the transport helicopter from the island the day before. Search and rescue has not located it, the assumption being made that it crashed into the Atlantic.

It is not beyond the realms of possibility that whoever this was sent a blueprint for the pathogen electronically via what might well be a compromised network. I do not believe they would have been able to smuggle a physical sample out – not with the security procedures in place. As you are aware, transport from the BSL-4 laboratory level requires the discarding of all clothing, and the full body scans would have detected a foreign object, even if in a body cavity. On sight interviews with surviving facility personnel has not shone any light into the identity of this unknown individual, although there are some who do remember a Caucasian male who is not on the list of the dead. An artist's impression has been attached.

A full diagnostic examination of the operating systems of all facility command and control computers is now warranted, and I ask the home secretary to authorise this.

Major David Croft, investigating officer

Analysis of the cause of the 17.04.2014 containment breach at the BSL-4 genetic laboratory facility at the Hirta Island Research Complex, designation RESURRECTION

Ref: FGu5867th
Date: 20.04.14

This is a preliminary analysis of the data collected by Major David Croft and from the servers of the TRQ computer. Conclusions may be subject to change.

A full audit of the biological material stored and used at the facility does not correlate with the symptoms that manifested at the facility. There are to date no known natural or artificial pathogens that create these symptoms in a human host, and there is no indication that the manipulations of the test strains for the Methuselah cure resulted in this. Indeed, the viral strains being investigated were still only in the computer-modelling stage and had yet to undergo fabrication. The biological data collected from the implanted microchips prove that this was not a psychosomatic event and that some sort of infection was involved. We believe that, whatever the cause, it was created (or at the very least perfected) on site and in secret. This would require several personnel to be involved. I can only, therefore, assume that it was done with Professor Cook's knowledge, which does seem to correlate with his last video entry. This does also implicate someone in the upper echelons of either government or the country's security apparatus.

The pathogen itself seems highly contagious, although we do not believe it to be airborne. More likely it is spread by direct physical contact with body fluids, definitely through bites and blood-to-blood transmission, but also probably by getting bodily secretions on the skin and mucous membranes, such as the mouth and the eyes. Although direct analysis of the pathogen would have been preferable, I totally support the decision to sterilise the site. Better to eradicate the unknown than face this in the outside world.

It is my contention that patient zero was deliberately infected, most likely via his insulin which would have been freely available in the medicines fridge. I suspect the person responsible left the facility several days prior. Supply logs show Dr. Johansson only had two days of insulin left on his prescription and would have had to leave the BSL-4 level to retrieve more from the facility's pharmacy. His microchip recorded him taking his insulin 10 minutes before the symptoms developed.

With my knowledge of contagious disease, I believe this to be an artificially created pathogen and that the Hirta Island incident was a covertly ordered test run of what can only be a weaponised virus. This poses a very real threat to the stability and the security of this country.

Captain Lucy Savage, Head of Biomedical Science, the Defence Science and Technology Laboratory, Porton Down

PROLOGUE

6.02PM, 16th April 2014. Hirta Island Research Facility, BSL-4 Containment level access tunnel

It really shouldn't be this easy. It shouldn't be this easy to kill 17 people and get away with it. Setting his bags down for a moment, he took something out of his inner pocket and zipped up his weatherproof overcoat. He pulled up the hood, tying its laces tight around his face, bracing himself for the icy Atlantic that waited outside. Placing his travel bag over his shoulder, he held his ID badge with his right hand and picked up his suitcase again with his left. The corridor ahead turned left, and he walked along it towards the secure exit. As usual, there were no guards present, and he stepped up to the door, placing his ID badge against the reader. Hidden cameras scrutinised his biometrics, ensuring he was actually the owner of the card. After a moment, the reader flashed green, and the door unlocked itself, his departure authorised by the central computer. Putting the ID in one of the coat's outer pockets, he pushed the door open with his shoulder. Deep within the facility's computer system, a Trojan virus began to eradicate all data related to the card and its owner. By the time the door closed behind him, it was as if he hadn't even existed.

He walked out of the research facility, into the driving rain that some might think was sent as a divine force to drive him back within the building that was soon to become an illustration of hell. God it was cold up here, and he pulled his weatherproof overcoat tighter. Cold it might be, but better to be up here than to fall victim to the heat that would incinerate the whole lower level several hours from now. If he was honest with himself, he didn't want to do this. They were his friends down there, his co-workers, people he had known for years. But none of them were true believers; none of them felt the spirit of the One True God in their hearts. Most of them were atheists, and deep down, he knew that ending their sin now would only lessen their torment in the afterlife. So in a sense he was, some could argue, doing them a favour. He still struggled with the logic of that one.

The helicopter was already landing, unsteady in its descent as the wind relentlessly buffeted it. But it was not to be defeated, and it finally landed. The side door opened, ready to embark its three passengers; the other two already stood patiently at the heliport's edge. Of course, the computer logs and the transport logs had already been doctored. By whom he didn't know, but he had faith in Brother Abraham. Brother

Abraham had powerful followers, true believers in the One True God, hiding deep in the heart of government. The travel log would say there were two passengers, but of course, the helicopter would never reach its destination, so there would be no witnesses to his travel. Running over to the helicopter, hand on his hat to stop the Atlantic from stealing it, he glanced back at what had been his home for the last three years, unaware of the merciless death that awaited him less than thirty minutes from now. He paused. He realised he was going to miss the people down there, but he had trust in the word of the Lord. For as Brother Abraham always said, God came first.

8.45PM, 17th April 2014. Hirta Island Research Facility, BSL-4 Containment level access tunnel

He ran. He ran and he bled. Bathed in the hypnotic orange flashing emergency lights, he propelled himself down the subterranean corridor, the howls of the damned echoing all around him. He didn't dare look back, didn't dare risk seeing what he knew was relentlessly pursuing him, the insane eyes and the blood-stained mouths. And he bled, oh how he bled. His once white, pristine lab coat was now soiled, thick with the crimson artwork that seeped from the wound on his torn and lacerated neck. He stumbled and almost fell, a wave of dizziness and nausea crashing over him, and he knew that it wasn't just from the loss of blood. He could feel it, feel it working away inside his mind. The virus was in him, ravaging and raping his cells. But still he ran, because what else was he to do with the insanity that pursued him?

He was running with such determination, fuelled by masses of adrenalin, that he couldn't slow himself down in time, and he hit the door at the end of the corridor with panicked force. He almost didn't feel the impact. Behind him, the racing footsteps of his tormentors could be heard getting ever closer. On the edge of losing what little sanity was left to him, his blood-slicked hand tried to punch in the door's access code on the control panel illuminated blue at the side of it.

"Come on, come on." The panel flashed red in response, making what on an ordinary day would be an irritating error noise and an annoying wait for technical support. Today, that noise was a death sentence, and a calm, almost reassuring computer voice spoke to him from the access panel

Security Lockdown
Access denied

"Fuck, fuck..." He tried his code again, only to get the same response, his hands now slick with sweat as well as his own blood. And the blood of others. His mind still had difficulty registering the mass of guts and flesh he had fallen into when he had fought off the woman who had attacked him, the one who had bitten him ... the one who had infected him. Was that how it spread?

The door mocked him; there was no way through it. It was designed for one purpose, to stop what was coming from escaping into the outside world, to keep the population safe from the mistakes made down in this once sterile and ordered environment. He should know – he helped design the security protocols, insisting that multiple layers of security be put in place to prevent the unthinkable.

It was at that moment all hope left him, and he did the only thing left to him. He turned, putting his back to the door he had walked through hundreds of times before. And then he saw his true reality. There were dozens of them, and seconds away from what he knew to be one of the worst fates imaginable, his bladder opened, and his lungs exploded in a scream that mingled with the hungry roar of the damned. Then they were upon him, and his last minutes became a savage torture of teeth, of gouging fingers, of kicks and of punches, and he collapsed to the floor, insanity mercifully stripping what was left of his scientific, logical mind. Their brutality and their viciousness were matched by only one thing: their insatiable hunger for human flesh.

8.52PM, 17th April 2014. Hirta Island Research Facility, BSL-4 Containment level. Office B7

Quiet, don't make a sound. If they can't hear you, they can't find you. If they can't find you, maybe they will just leave you alone. Locked in her office, cowering in the corner on the plush carpet she had demanded be installed just a month earlier, she let fear overwhelm her. This wasn't supposed to happen. This was the thing of movies and TV – this wasn't real life. How was this even possible? She could hear them now, their howls far off in the facility. They were searching, running ... hunting.

She could feel their anger, their desire, their hunger. Wait, that didn't make any sense; how could she know these things? Looking at her hand, she saw the teeth marks that bled and throbbed and ... no, it couldn't be that. This was madness, her scientist's mind told her. But the little girl inside her knew the truth. The child who had escaped a life of emotional abuse into the maze-like wonder of the library, who had devoured any book she could find knew the truth that logic failed to admit.

Something twitched in her mind. Something pulled her, dulled her, seduced her. Despite her fear, she realised she didn't want to be alone. She had witnessed what the others had done, had witnessed them attack, rip, bite and scream. Witnessed them kill those who she classed as friends, and yet she felt drawn to them. There was a pain behind her eyes that grew with every passing moment. Was pain the right word? Perhaps not; it was more a feeling of pressure that seemed to block out her thoughts, her reasoning. Then she vomited, and her bowels opened. And the pain hit her anew in ever-increasing waves.

Something thumped onto the outside of the door to her office, and she jumped in terror, despite the agony that coursed through her system. She could almost picture the crazed maniac on the other side, blood-smeared hands clawing at the wood that was her only barrier. The sight in her left eye blurred, and she gasped as her stomach suddenly churned, threatening to expel its contents all over her once again.

"*Join us.*" Who said that? The voice, more a collection of voices, seemed to come from inside her head.

"*Join us, feed with us, kill with us.*" No, I won't, I won't. But despite her protestations, she found herself standing up. Staggering to her feet, using the wall for balance, she felt a part of her die. The pain in her hand was being replaced by a warmth, a warmth spreading throughout her body, and as the warmth spread, pieces of who she was simply slipped away – it happened that quickly. A spasm rocked through her, nearly sending her back to the floor, and her head twisted to the side as the muscles of her neck contracted violently. The warmth grew, and with it came the hunger. She had never felt anything like it. She knew it would be insatiable; she knew it would be relentless. As the last of her human mind evaporated, as the last of her independence was burned away by the virus, her mouth drooled, and her body shook with the urgency of what she had to do.

"*Join us.*"

"Yes, yes I am yours," she said. Did she say that out loud? She didn't know; she didn't care. All she cared about was the hunger, and she scrambled to the door, unlocking it and sending it wide. Three of them were waiting for her on the other side. They did not attack, but they embraced her, pulling her into the corridor.

"*Feed with us,*" the voices in her head demanded.

"Yes, yes I will feed." And, those being the last words she would ever utter, she joined them in their hunt for the living.

8.35PM, 17th April 2014. Hirta Island Research Facility, Security Command Room

He watched them die. Standing with the three men tasked with monitoring the evening security of one of the country's most secure and secret biological research facilities, he watched and listened to the dying minutes of the people they knew and worked with. At least the alarm claxon had been shut off.

It happened so quickly. One minute, he was sat at his desk going over the latest scheduling report, the next he was running from his office as the worst sound in the world bellowed in his ears. Why the hell had he decided to pull another all-nighter? Why hadn't he just listened to his wife for once and left early instead of deciding to burn the midnight oil? He could have been out there, in the cool night's breeze, breathing unfiltered air. And without the dread that within hours he might be burned alive.

"Attention! Biological hazard detected. Containment lockdown initiated."

Right now, he was utterly helpless, helpless to help those in the lower level. Powerless to help anyone else in the facility should the lockdown spread. Powerless to help himself. The computer would determine everything. It would collect and collate all the data, the very data it had used to initiate the lockdown, and determine its recommendation for who lived and who died.

"We'll be okay. Whatever it is, it hasn't breached containment. We should be okay." He said this to nobody in particular, perhaps trying to convince himself more than anything. They were on the ground level, and the lab was now completely contained. The computer monitored everything, scanning for deadly microbes in the filtration systems and in the bodies of the people who worked throughout the facility. They called the computer TRQ, which stood for "The Red Queen" after the homicidal computer in the film *Resident Evil.* He didn't feel that joke was so funny now.

"Sir, TRQ reports no sign of contagion outside the BSL-4 containment level," one of the security officers stated as he typed furiously on his computer. "Filters are clean, biologicals for all personnel outside the lab level green."

He didn't respond. It was a waiting game now. Each self-contained level was isolated from the next. The computer, based on the algorithms programmed into its software, would determine who would be released from the facility. On the large screen, he watched one of the lab technicians being chased down by three of her former colleagues. The video feed, in full colour, showed them ripping her apart, her white blouse turning crimson, arterial spray actually hitting the lens of the camera.

"Sir, confirmation Whitehall has been informed." He knew what that meant. Within hours, a helicopter would descend upon this small island, and the man it brought would have a decision to make. Although TRQ could seal off the facility, it had not been given the power of life or death unless there was a breach of the outer doors. As long as the facility remained contained, the fate of those inside would be determined by one man, a man with a chequered past. A merciless man, a man who could make the decisions normal men could not. Until that man arrived, all he could do was wait. He didn't like it, but he knew the risks when he took this assignment. But how the hell had this happened? There was nothing down in that lab that could cause this. The worst they had down there was bloody Ebola.

"Turn those monitors off. I don't want to see any more of this."

1.30AM, 18th April 2014, Waterloo Rd, London

Always the same fucking dream. The relentless heart-rending screaming of his men, the tearing physical pain and the blood and the flames. The complete feeling of failure and helplessness and the smell of the dead and the dying and the burning of flesh. Always the same dream that mutated into night terrors that woke him, drenched in sweat, his heart pounding, his mouth dry and his mind ripped open by fear and the blackness of the souls lost on his watch.

The psychiatrist told him it wasn't his fault, and he knew that on a logical level, she was correct. It was a mechanical failure in the helicopter, the brutal irony of that fact not lost on him. Half his men lost, men who had survived nine months unscathed in one of the most hostile military environments known to man. Half his men killed because the bloody helicopter that was transporting them decided to give up the ghost and fall from the sky with them on board. Even though he was an officer, the men he had lost were friends. Sergeant O'Brian, who had saved his life twice in the field, who could drink any man under the table and still be there for the five-mile run in the morning. Corporal Hillier who had the gift of "feeling" when those Taliban scum were skulking in ambush at the side of the road, and had once pulled Croft away just as he had been about to step on a mine. Two short seconds later, and the pair of them would have been scattered in bits across the roadside, balls and legs shredded and useless. Seven heroes dead; seven men he had fought with, lived with, trained with and who he watched die through a haze of semi-unconsciousness, flames and agony. And the worst thing of all? He had lived to remember it all.

That had been eight years ago. The dreams came less frequently now, less than once a month. "Your mind will heal," they had told him. "It will adjust as it processes the trauma you went through," they said. And they were right; he no longer jumped half out of his skin at loud noises. He no longer broke down in tears for no apparent reason, or felt his heart pounding in his chest from some random stimulus. He was functional, effective and useful once again. No longer broken, but far from fixed. But the dreams still came. And invariably they were portents of doom, messengers of danger to come.

Sitting up, alone in his bed, he breathed slowly and let the terror subside, soaking in the normality of the darkness around him. He ran a scarred and calloused hand over his shaved head and sighed deeply. Alone he sat, the almost hypnotic thrum of London traffic the only noise audible in the bedroom air. No lover by his side, no children sleeping in the next room. Not even a cat to wake him in the morning. Why risk such loss again?

He didn't even jump when the telephone at the side of his bed rang. Part of him was almost expecting it. Here it was again, the call in the dead of night. The insistent voice stating that he must be dressed and packed in 10 minutes so as to be ready for the government car to pick him up. The call to duty. No time to shower, the overnight bag already prepared and sat by the side of his front door. His HK P8 pistol loaded and holstered, easily accessible in the gun safe, stripped and cleaned five hours before. Again, thought Croft. Here we go again. This was the sixth time in two years. What were these idiots doing now? What horrors had they unwittingly unleashed this time? Were they so intent on opening Pandora's Box, on destroying the world? But this is what they paid him to do, and so he went where they sent him. Although he was now a soldier in rank only, he still knew how to follow orders. After all, what else was there for him to do? Besides, somebody had to be there to clean up the mess those incompetent criminals in Whitehall created. It might as well be him.

Croft picked up the phone and listened. "I'll be ready," he said to the faceless voice on the other end of the secure landline. Placing the phone back in the receiver, he stood from his bed and walked into the bathroom, the pain in his right knee a constant reminder of that fateful day in Afghanistan, the day he and his men were being shipped home. They all went home, just some went home in pieces, wrapped in a flag that now really had no meaning, dying for a dream of England that never really existed.

8.30AM, 18th April 2014, Hirta Island Research Facility

Yep, another goddamn mess for him to clean up. Another fuck up by genius scientists who lacked the common sense to know they shouldn't meddle with the forces of nature. Scientists who could calculate the nature of the universe but probably needed help to cross the road and tie a shoelace. There was a reason evolution occurred over millions of years, why nature made changes gradually and methodically. Why couldn't these idiots understand this? Just because you could do something, didn't mean that you should. And so here he was again, dragged out of his slumber to go to wherever the government needed him. And it seemed they needed him more and more these days.

David Croft felt his stomach lurch as the SA 330 Ouma military transport helicopter was buffeted by the winds coming off the merciless Atlantic Ocean. At least this facility wasn't on the bloody mainland, and at least this time, the incident had been contained quickly. That was what the emergency dossier on his secure tablet told him. Now stored away in his bag, it had briefed him on everything he needed to know to make the decisions those in power paid him to make. His job held no title and was unknown to all but a select few. This was what the Yanks called "Black Work". Dirty, unpleasant, and sometimes far from legal. But it was necessary, and he was needed so as to give those in power a sense of deniability. His job was to protect the clamouring, selfish and hypocritical masses from the inevitable mistakes his government and their minions made. This wasn't a job; it was a way of life, and he knew the very people he protected would scream for his incarceration if they learnt of the things he had been forced to do for their protection. They wouldn't understand, and they would turn on him and those who made him like a rabid dog turns on its owner. Sometimes, he wondered if the masses actually deserved saving, but he knew that this was not a decision for him to make. He was merely the hired help. And yet the price he paid for their safety was the soiling of his very soul.

Looking out of the window, he saw Hirta Island drawing closer. Another godforsaken rock. The helicopter buffeted again, and rain started to impact on the outside, obscuring the view of his destination, which got ever closer. Croft hated helicopters – understandable really, considering. It had been two years before he had been able to get near one without suffering chaotic palpitations and anxiety. And now all he seemed to do was fly about in the things.

"One minute to landing, Major," the voice of the co-pilot stated over the intercom. Thank Christ. Croft grabbed hold of the door handle and readied himself for touch down. Even a cold, wet, barren rock in the Atlantic was better than this.

There were people waiting for him at the helipad … but then there were always people waiting for him. That was his life now it seemed. Some carried worried faces, others had defiant eyes. Some even reeked of resentment, as if Croft's presence was an insult to their existence, to their competence. And in fairness, in a way it was. If he was anywhere on orders of Whitehall, it meant that someone or something had failed. Despite the safeguards, despite the systems, and despite the training, human error always crept in. That was one of the first things they taught him at Sandhurst, a message battered home in his SBS training.

"All plans fall apart upon engagement with the enemy."

And didn't he know that all too well. Hadn't he experienced that very thing time and time again? He held his breath as the helicopter touched down, and sighed internally as the motion stopped and the ground became his new home. Another bullet dodged. Another day to carry on living.

"You are safe to disembark, Major." Croft didn't respond; he undid his seat harness and opened the door, mindful of the rotors that were still spinning as they slowed their rotation. There were three people there this time, two struggling with umbrellas as the wind buffeted them, toyed with them. Grabbing his bag, he stepped from the helicopter and made his way over to where they stood anxiously. One of them saluted – the one who stood in the rain without protection, the soldier and the driver of the car that waited to take Croft to his latest massacre. He saw the hint of fear in the man's eyes, the look that told him the man had seen something no human being should ever see but lived to talk about it. Not that the man would ever speak a word of what he had seen here. That was what the Official Secrets Act was for. Croft saluted back, gave the man a nod that relayed respect. Nobody spoke for there was nothing that needed to be said, and they retreated quickly to the relative warmth of the car. The next 30 minutes would determine whether 47 people got to live or die. *All in a day's work*, thought Croft.

12.47PM, 23rd April 2014, Hyde Park, London

The bench was bitterly cold, but Bill sat there nonetheless, his back resting firmly against the ancient wood. He was far from comfortable, but he ignored that as best he could. Seated, seemingly oblivious to the world around him, he pretended to read the newspaper on what many would assume to be a lunch break for one of London's many white collar employees. This was, of course, not the case. A gentle breeze flirted with the newspaper, and the trees behind him whispered their secrets to each other, laughing at the stupidity of the fleshy creatures that dwelled around them. *Look at how important these pathetic monkeys think they are*, said the trees. *Look at how they run about their lives as if their lives actually mattered.*

He had done this numerous times before, but still he was nervous. No, that was the wrong word. He was almost sick to his stomach. He was risking so much for what amounted to little in the way of personal gain. He knew that at any moment a hand could drop on his shoulder, the agents dressed in black with well-oiled machine guns could pick him up off the street, or more likely from the illusory safety of his home in the dead of night. One minute, he would be safe in his own self-indulgence, the next, he would find himself trussed up in the back of a black van with a bag over his head and a boot on his throat. But still, he did what needed to be done because it was what the Lord demanded. And the Lord it seemed resorted to blackmail these days.

His instructions were clear, and he knew he was never to again meet the man who had given them to him. The man who Bill knew would give his life for his God. The thought depressed him, for Bill had never found such passion in life for anything, had never found a cause worth fighting for. No, but he had found frailty and weakness, which had allowed them to get leverage over him. So he had submitted, pledging his allegiance and his soul, prepared to betray his country and the man he worked for, the man who trusted him with the safety of these sacred isles, with the secrets that could bring governments down. Bill sat here, as he did every month, pretending to be mesmerised by the propaganda that the British Press called "News", pretending to be one of the sheep, one of the drones that worked the gears and oiled the machine that allowed society to run. He was trapped. If the secret of his affliction came out, he'd be ruined, most likely imprisoned. And if the secret of his betrayal did not come out, the same was likely to happen. There was nothing for him to do but do as he was told and hope, just hope that they would tire of him. He sat and he waited until the time his contact had given him.

He paid attention to those around him, every stranger scrutinised, mindful of the risks he was running and mindful of the forces lined up against him. He had to remember that he lived in a surveillance state that not even George Orwell could have imagined. Even here, in the heart of Hyde Park, there would be cameras and agents watching for those who went against the order of society. All wrapped up in the soft, loving blanket of safety and security. It was for the children after all; it was for the next generation that the present surrendered their liberty to the ever-pervasive glare of the state. And most of them did it willingly, giving the agents of oppression the information they craved through their smartphones and social media. There was no denying what the country had become; he worked at its very heart after all. He saw how the people went about their daily lives under the illusion of some mystical freedom that they believed existed. Democracy, what a fucking joke. And deep down, they knew they were watched, they knew that data was being collected and stored, but there seemed to be some form of mass social dissonance that hid the truth from their eyes. So every day, the people of this country woke up and ignored the elephant in their living room. They went to work, they watched TV, and they paid their taxes. They drank their beer, raised what they thought were their children and groaned about how this incompetent government was ruining the country. If only he could shout to them that the government knew exactly what it was doing, that it was slowly stripping away their liberties to serve the vile forces of the Son of Perdition. The Devil dwelled below the surface of this warped and fetid society and shaped the living world to create his master plan. And by their acquiescence, they had all become his willing servants. But not Bill – no, he was apparently now a warrior of truth. Why did it have to be religious nutters who had discovered his secret?

Bill looked at his three thousand pound watch, and seeing the allotted time stood, folding the newspaper he had never actually read. Discarding it in the almost empty park bin that lived beside the bench he had briefly dwelled on, he picked up his black leather briefcase and walked away towards the nearest park exit. He didn't look back, didn't rush, and did nothing to draw attention to himself. But nor did he linger. That was how he lived his life. He did his official job to the best of his abilities, and then shared the secrets he learned from his job with God's right-hand man. It was not treachery he had been told, for how can the war against Satan be anything but just?

Bill Dodson, Private Secretary to the prime minister of Great Britain and Northern Ireland, did not see the park employee with the cart come along a minute later to empty the bin. He did not see the park employee pick out the newspaper, which contained taped to its inner pages a micro simcard. A micro simcard with photographs of everything that had crossed his desk in the previous month, courtesy of the smartphone Bill carried around with him. He didn't see the park employee place the newspaper in a separate part of his cart, before emptying the bin. And neither did anyone else of consequence. Another act of rebellion perpetrated right under the very nose of the state. But what was just another day's disloyalty when viewed against the months of sedition already committed?

PRESENT DAY

8.54AM, 14th September 2015, Hounslow Primary School, Hounslow, London

The roar of another plane taking off from Heathrow Airport was always present during the day, and often late into the night. But when you lived with the noise most of your life, you tended to block it out. It just became part of the environment you lived in, part of the pollution of everyday existence. Jack Nathan did that now, hardly registering the roar of the huge airbus as it streaked across the sky. He had other things on his mind, and he stepped off the dirty, litter-strewn bus outside his sister's dilapidated primary school. A moment later, she joined him on the pavement, carrying her frozen bag like her life depended on it. They were the last people to get off, and the doors closed behind them with a mechanical hiss. The bus juddered and moved forward, merging back into traffic.

"Is Mum going to be okay?" Amy Nathan asked her older brother, looking up at him with worried eyes. At six foot one inch, he towered above her, and he put a reassuring hand on her head.

"Of course she is, sis. She's just a bit sad at the moment."

"She's always sad. I don't want her to be sad anymore." She suddenly clung onto her brother, giving him a tear-filled hug.

"Hey. Where's this all coming from?" He disengaged and crouched down so he was on her eye level. "I told you, she'll be fine." He looked over to the school gate and saw a smiling teacher waiting for her pupil. "Now come on, you'll be late for class." Amy sniffed and wiped tears from her eyes. Jack stood and gently pushed her towards the school gates, hand behind her head. Reluctantly, Amy went where her brother guided.

Of course their mother wasn't okay, hadn't been for several months. Depression was a horrible disease for those who suffered it, and for those who witnessed it. And the doctors were about as much use as a condom machine in the Vatican. Why didn't they help her? They just gave her pills – pills that didn't work, pills that just turned their once loving and bubbly mother into a bloody zombie. She wandered around the house almost in a daze, ate very little and spent most of her time watching daytime TV. And, of course, then there was the alcohol. The gift that kept on giving, the slow little death that promised so much but delivered nothing but disease and death. Jack knew she would already be drinking now, and by the time he returned to the school to bring his eight-year-old sister home, their mother would often be completely inebriated. There was always a smile there for her children though, and Jack was starting to learn that everyone handled loss differently. He just wished his mum could pull herself out of the black hole she had fallen into. They needed her. He needed her. And a part of him was even starting to resent her for her illness.

Six months ago, things had been different. Six months ago, his father had been alive, Jack had been ready to go to medical school and life had been good. He'd even had a girlfriend. And then one night on his walk home from his job at the airport, Benjamin Nathan had been mugged in the middle of the street, beaten senseless despite fighting back valiantly, and had died three days later from the head injuries sustained as he'd collapsed to the ground. Despite there being dozens of people around, nobody had stepped in to help. And nobody had stepped forward as a witness to the events that seemed more and more common on London's streets. Nobody had been arrested for the crime. As far as Jack was aware, nobody had even been questioned. Robbed of his father and mentor, Jack had been forced to take on the role of surrogate parent, putting his life on hold for the people he loved, forced into it by a sense of duty. His job at the fast food joint was his way of topping up the benefits his family now needed to survive.

He watched his sister walk slowly onto the school ground, and he gave the teacher a friendly wave. He was well known to the teaching staff now, having had to explain to the Head Master the problems his family now faced. He really wasn't sure he was ready to be a parent. But as his father had always said, you played the cards you were dealt in life. That was what a man did. And like it or not, he was now a man. Life would give him further opportunities to prove that over the coming days.

9.34AM, 14th September 2015, Brookwood Cemetery, Woking

How vulnerable this all was. Life was so brutally fleeting, so exquisitely brittle. For some, it was a precious gift; for others, an endless torture, punctuated by moments of clarity. And for many (perhaps most), it wasn't even life, their existence almost eternally machine-like as they went about their daily business, never contemplating the mystery and the wonder of the universe around them. Their lives lived vacuously through the experiences of others. Did the bulk of humanity deserve what he did for them?

Standing over the grave of Sergeant John O'Brian, the morning sun failing to warm his chilled heart, Carter thought back to that devastating moment several years ago that ended his last tour in Afghanistan. It was a moment rarely from his thoughts. He came to this cemetery once a month to pay his respects, never wanting to forget the man who shouldn't have even been his friend. After all, it was not deemed proper for the ranks to mingle like that, not proper for an enlisted man to be on first name terms with an officer. But that was the regular army, the so-called "Lions led by Donkeys". Those conventions ended when you stepped through the gates of Hamworthy barracks. When a man wants to put on the insignia of the Special Boat Service, rank becomes almost obsolete. Proving yourself and beating the gruelling selection process meant more than a few bars on your shoulder. The significance of rank came in second place to the significance of working with the best in the business, to prove you were worthy of their respect. Rank meant nothing in selection. Just because the sergeant major who was taunting you on your 40-mile forced hike across the Brecon Beacons called you sir, well that did nothing to dispel the reality that you had a long way to go to cancel out the man's obvious disdain for your abilities. Until you earnt that respect, you were just another bloody nugget Rupert.

Croft knelt down and touched his calloused palm to the chilled gravestone, running his fingertips over the engraving. "We saw some shit mate," he said to the cold marble. "We saw some shit, and we nearly made it out. And now here we are. They put you in the ground, and they made me a fucking major." Croft stood, his knee groaning. "With the shit I've seen recently, I think you might have got the better end of the deal, my friend." As if on cue, the sun disappeared behind a blanket of cloud and he shivered, more from memory than the drop in temperature.

Shaking his head, he turned and walked away across the grass towards Long Avenue, one of the many footpaths in the cemetery. He always got to walk away whilst those around him seemed to die or get maimed. He always got to watch whilst those he cared for suffered and died. Was that a blessing or a curse? Perhaps it was both. As he walked, he couldn't help but notice the solitude and the calmness around him, representing a complete contradiction to his present life and to the deaths that many buried beneath this ground had experienced. From above, a crow landed on the ground to the side of him and observed Croft almost dismissively. Nature was foolish to lose its fear of man, Croft thought, and his sombre form made its way along the avenue of the dead. But then, likewise, man was foolish to lose his fear of nature.

Perhaps vulnerable wasn't the correct word. Perhaps fragile was better. Society was just a thin veneer, a patchwork plaster cast that stopped everything from falling into chaos. The chaos was there, waiting to be unleashed, waiting to force itself onto the world, to let loose its fury, its vengeance, its power, its anger for being locked up and contained. It wanted to be free, and Croft knew, with what he had seen in the last few years, that chaos would get its wish. It was only a matter of time. It was coming, and it would rip this placid city, this island, this world asunder. A student of history, Croft was well aware that all civilisations had a tendency to collapse from within. The barbarians at the gates of Rome were not the cause but a symptom of the collapse. And humanity was nothing if not consistent in the mistakes it liked to make.

Croft's phone vibrated in his pocket. Withdrawing I, he stopped walking and read the message that had come over the encrypted network.

Civil Contingencies Committee meeting today at 2PM, Conference Room A, 70 Whitehall. Top Priority

That was unusual. His paymasters rarely met with him in person, but if he was honest, he wasn't surprised. His last briefing paper had really put the cat amongst the pigeons. Telling the government there was an impending risk of a full scale biological attack had not put him on anyone's Christmas card list. And telling them someone high up in the security structure of government was directly involved made him even less friends. They had listened though. They always listened, because his track record spoke volumes. They paid him to do the job he did because he was good at it.

Putting his phone away, he continued walking. The path took him beneath a small roof of trees, past an empty bench where a lone grey squirrel sat nervously, looking at him with quizzical, worried eyes. As Croft walked closer, the squirrel panicked and darted off, disappearing into the uncut undergrowth with nimble agility. Croft smiled at the sight of it, his smile however faltering as he turned his head back in the direction he was heading. Sixty metres ahead, a couple came into view, walking towards him in a lovers' embrace. The blonde-haired woman was carrying a large bouquet of flowers, a common occurrence in any graveyard across the country. She laughed in response to something the man said and clung to his left arm, the flowers obscuring her right arm and most of her torso. So why did Croft suddenly feel alarmed? Why was there a claxon going off in his head, warning him of impending danger? Why were his adrenal glands firing up?

Slowing his pace, he did a casual 360 look around him and noticed a third individual closing in behind at a similar distance. Croft did not make eye contact with him but noticed his lean, muscular physique hidden from the world by jeans and a heavy sweater. Something wasn't right here. He didn't know what it was that first alarmed him, but he saw the tell-tale signs of the man walking behind him. The guy probably had a concealed weapon on his right hip; he could tell by the way the man moved, by the way he swung his arms differently. Croft's training was kicking in, and when that happened, he listened.

Croft stopped and pulled out his Bluetooth from the inside pocket of his black suit, placing it behind his ear. He pretended to activate it with an exaggerated motion.

"John, good to hear from you." There was, of course, nobody on the phone; he just needed a plausible excuse to stop, and he spoke loudly, the words puncturing the quiet bubble he had been dwelling in. Wandering off the path, Croft went over to a large oak tree and placed his back to it, his right hand slipping onto the gun holstered to the left of his spine. To the unsuspecting it looked like he was perhaps merely scratching himself, but the HK P8 felt reassuring in his hand. There was a calmness in him, and he felt time almost slowing down. Three targets, 15 rounds, plus a further 15 in the other magazine on his belt. Thirty metres out.

"No, I hadn't heard that, could you forward that to me, please? Great." The three people grew closer, and neither of them looked at him, despite him directing his gaze at them in turn. They were avoiding eye contact. An innocent passer-by would have been drawn to the volume of his voice, would have noticed him staring at them, maybe even given him a disapproving look. He sidestepped the tree, moving backwards a few steps ready to use it as a shield, the gun now free, held behind him, safety off, finger on the guard. Never point a gun at anything unless you are prepared to shoot it. Never put your finger on the trigger unless you intend to fire. "How's the wife?" he asked the ether. The question came up now, should he flee or stand his ground and prepare to fight? Obviously, he couldn't just start shooting. These might still be just regular passers-by; there was still a strong chance of that. Despite his training, he might just be riddled with paranoia. So what was it that had triggered his alarm? Whatever it was, and perhaps he would never know, he didn't run. If they were here for him, he wanted to know why. Ten metres out now and the woman stumbled and dropped the flowers. Croft tensed, his gun moving.

And then it happened. The flowers were an illusion to hide the fact she was holding a gun. The stumble to distract him from the man coming in the other direction who reached to his hip. The woman's partner threw himself sideways off the path. Her gun came up, and Croft dropped sideways, throwing himself behind the tree. In the emptiness of the cemetery, the noise of her gun was deafening, and he heard several rounds impact the oak. Then he was on his knee, gun up, aiming at the man who he was not shielded from, saw the gun pulled free, coming up, aiming.

Croft put three in the guy's chest right over the heart, saw the guy's arm jerk up and fire off wildly. As he fell, Croft put another towards the legs and saw it enter just above the right knee. Even with chest armour, the pain from that leg wound would give Croft time, especially as the man lost the grip on his gun as he fell to the floor. He heard the other two moving. They would try and flank him, coming at him from both sides of the tree, so he moved. He fired another shot at the fallen man, heard the impact and the cry and stepped out from behind the tree towards the other threat, gun up, firing as he went … 11 shots left, 10. He felt a round hit his right ear, ignored it, found his targets, centred on the first. One was running, panicking; the other, the woman, was the one firing at him, a look of surprise and shock in her eyes. They hadn't expected things to go down like this; they hadn't expected him to come out shooting. They had underestimated him. Her stance was off, she didn't have control, her shots not accurate. Croft was the trained one, the professional, the man who had killed before and who would kill again. He was the man who could outshoot any of the men who had served under him, who had faced enemy fire and who knew what to expect when the bullets started flying. So barring the miraculous, there was really only one outcome from all this. And so, without a moment's hesitation, he put one round straight into the woman's forehead. The impact sent her backwards, the front of the skull cratering from the impact, the back of the head exploding as the round exited, taking much of her brain with it. She was dead almost instantly, and he moved forward as he aimed at the last attacker.

"Stop, don't make me shoot you in the back," Croft shouted, looking left, seeing the lone man moaning, gun out of arm's reach behind him on the path. The remaining man stopped and turned, fear riddled across his face. "Hands on your head, palms up." The man did what he was told, visibly shaking with fear. "Interlock your fingers." Croft walked around the man so that he could see all three without turning his head, then came up behind the guy and kicked out his legs, sending him painfully to the floor. This was definitely no professional hit. These guys were amateurs. What the hell was this? Nobody got mugged at gunpoint in a cemetery at ten in the morning.

"What have you done?" the man cried. "How could you do this?"

"What have I done? I defended myself, you wanker." With that, he holstered his weapon and took the man from behind in a rear naked choke, his strong arm constricting the carotid arteries. Ten seconds of struggling and the man was out cold. A quick pat down revealed no weapons and no ID. Why would only two of them be armed?

Croft stood up and looked around. He heard nothing moving – the noise of the fire fight would have scared off most of the wildlife. How many people even heard the commotion? This time, he did turn on his Bluetooth as he walked over to the shot man.

"Call Control," he said to the Bluetooth. There was a beep and the phone rang for two cycles.

"Control here."

"Control, this is Croft, voice recognition, please."

"Voice recognition accepted. Verification code required."

"Alpha, Gamma, Foxtrot, 154783, Lima, Echo."

"Thank you, Major Croft," said the unseen female. "What do you need?"

"GPS on my location. Get GCHQ on the line; I need video feed surveillance checked for the last hour around Brookwood Cemetery and railway station. I have been targeted by armed attackers and have had to use lethal force. I have three suspects down, one certainly dead." Croft gave the woman a description of the three people and knelt down by the first man. Knee shot, groin shot and a hell of a lot of blood. The bullet had probably ripped open the femoral artery. He patted the man down, noticed the chest Kevlar. Again there was no ID. Amateurs with body armour? That made even less sense.

"Please hold."

One dead, one dying, one unconscious. This one would likely bleed out before the emergency services got here, and Croft decided not to do anything to alter that fact. He was not a forgiving sort at the best of times. Taking out his phone, he switched it to the camera feature and held the man's head as he took two close ups. Running a final check for weapons, he stood up and retrieved the discarded gun and walked over to the woman. Checking her pulse to confirm her death, he looked into her lifeless eyes.

"Who the hell are you?" It was a question that needed answering, and he took two more photos. The voice came into his ear again

"Three suspects matching your descriptions were seen exiting a car in the cemetery car park 40 minutes ago. There were four people in the car. I have GCHQ running their biometrics through Mother." Mother, the core of the UK intelligence infrastructure. A vast central database, a super computer that could track virtually every human being through every transport hub, along every street, anywhere it was connected to the CCTV network. All those facial images stored, all that biometric data collected and collated. And virtually nobody knew the damned thing existed.

"I'm sending you pictures, should help speed up Mother's recognition. Get the local police out here to seal off the area. I've got a live one here, so I'll need MI5 on scene." The police would arrive, their superintendent having been phoned directly. They would seal off the area, and then the questions would probably start. Croft would be patient, would explain that this was now an MI5 matter, that he would only discuss the matter with their superior officers. He would show them his official ID. Major David Croft, Military Police of her Majesty's armed forces. If the officer was clued up, the questions would stop there. If not, if the person speaking to him persisted, it would not be great for that individual's career prospects.

"Do we have eyes on the fourth assailant?"

"Yes. GCHQ report he has left the scene. Two SCO19 units have been sent to intercept. We have a helicopter unit en-route." SCO19 designation, the firearms units of the Metropolitan police. If these had been trained killers, he would have advised against that. But his analysis at the scene suggested these weren't experts.

"Control, you better let Whitehall know I'm probably going to be late for that meeting."

10AM, 17th February, 2008, Whitehall, London

He had been waiting for thirty minutes, which was about right. This was generally how it always was. How many times had he sat outside offices like this, either government or his senior commanders? When you sat with nothing to preoccupy your time, you tended to notice things. Decorated probably a hundred years ago, the room's ornate nature a façade of greatness long since faded. He looked around, noticed the signs of decay, the signs of an empire that now existed only in the history books. A bit of peeling wallpaper here, a chipped skirting board there. Threadbare, stained carpets and windows that could really do with some double glazing and a lick of paint. The whole of Parliament was like this. Old, unrepaired, and in need of a damned good clean. Rumour had it that there was an electrician on site to deal with all the electrical fires that kept breaking out from the ageing wiring that the taxpayers didn't seem to have the money to replace. And yet, despite letting their own home rot under their very feet, the government still had the money for war, still had money to keep the Parliamentary wine cellar well stocked. Croft could have laughed at the ridiculousness of it all; after all, there wasn't much else in his life to laugh about these days.

Croft shifted nervously on his chair, its wooden carved arms unpadded and uncomfortable, probably deliberately so. His right knee throbbed as it often did at this time of year, the cold no good for his apparently healed injuries. Despite being inside, it was as if someone had forgotten to turn on the central heating, and he kept his winter coat on. Admittedly, these were all minor discomforts compared to what he had endured so far in his life. Still, it would have been nice if someone had at least brought him a cup of tea.

There was a sound, and the door to the inner sanctum opened. Out stepped the thin and gaunt humourless woman who had led him to this waiting area from the front desk of the building when he had arrived. "Captain Croft, they are ready for you now." Croft nodded his agreement and stood, his right knee cracking loudly. He took the four steps over to where she waited and stepped through the threshold. The woman remained outside and closed the door behind him.

"Captain, apologies for keeping you waiting. Affairs of state and all that." Croft recognised the elderly man who strode towards him, the present Home Secretary David Pendlebury. He walked further into the room and shook the proffered hand. There were two other men in the room with them, both seated, neither of them Croft knew. "This is Arnold Craver, Head of the Centre for the Protection of National Infrastructure."

"MI5?" Croft asked, knowing the answer. Craver nodded in agreement.

"This is Sir Peter Milnes, Commissioner of the Police of the Metropolis." Neither of the seated men stood or offered their hand. "Please, Captain, have a seat."

"I presume this is where I learn why I have been trundled into a car and brought to London, sir?" Croft sat down, this leather seat infinitely more comfortable than the one outside.

"Yes, sorry about that, old boy," Pendlebury said. "Secrecy and all that. So let's get to it. Craver?" Craver lifted a briefcase off the floor and placed it on his lap; opening it, he withdrew a thick folder and set the briefcase back down. He looked at Croft for a second and then opened the folder.

"Captain Croft of Her Majesty's Royal Military Police, age 38. Formerly a commissioned officer in the Black Watch and the Special Boat Service. Graduated top of his class at Sandhurst. Two tours of Afghanistan. Three Tours of Northern Ireland. Saw action in Iraq and various other theatres that remain classified. Winner of two Military

Crosses and the Conspicuous Gallantry Cross. Mentioned in Dispatches countless times. Presently with the Royal Military Police at Regimental headquarters." Craver closed the folder. "Quite an impressive CV, Captain."

"I do what I can, sir. But I suspect we aren't here to talk about my service record."

"No, Captain, we aren't," said Milnes. "You are here because someone thinks you are the man for a job we require filling." Milnes stood up and walked over to a decanter set on a sideboard. "Drink, Captain?"

"No, thank you, sir, never touch the stuff." Especially not before lunch time.

"Well, I trust you won't mind if I indulge," Milne said as he poured himself a short measure. Ice followed. At the side of the decanter was a clipboard which Milne picked up. He took a sip of his precious drink, savouring its texture for a brief moment. He brought the clipboard over to Croft. "Before we continue, you need to read this, and if you agree to it, sign it." Croft took the clipboard and took off the attached pen. He started to read it.

I agree that the information I am about to receive is Top Secret...
Official Secret Act blah blah blah
Disclosure will result in life imprisonment, etc., etc.

Croft sighed to himself and skipped to the last page, leaving the bulk of the document unread. He signed it and handed it back to Milne, pen attached. There were undoubtedly over a dozen similar documents with his signature on it lurking in filing cabinets in the bowels of some secure office somewhere. One more wouldn't make any difference.

"Very good, Captain," said Pendlebury. "Now to business. We need a job doing, one that you and several others like you are eminently qualified for. Did you ever wonder why you were pushed into joining the military police?"

"Yes, to be honest. After Afghanistan, I was expecting to be asked to resign my commission due to the ... medical issues I had." That had been a surprise when it didn't happen. He'd been kept on in an administration role after his release from the German hospital and had received intense counselling above what was normally provided. The physical injuries had been the least of it; it had been the trauma to his mind that had nearly ended him. Then a job offer at the Royal Military Police had been pushed upon him, which he had accepted on the advice of several senior officers who he knew and respected, and who had each visited him personally.

"You were being groomed, Major," said Craver.

"I'm a captain, sir."

"Not if you accept the job, Croft," said Pendlebury.

"So this isn't an interview then?"

"No, Croft, it's an offer. Let me tell you what will be expected of you," said Pendlebury with a smile. "And we will need your answer before you leave this room."

Croft had left the room a major, on a much higher salary, far in excess of what the army usually paid for the rank. He was to be given a residence in Waterloo so he would be close to Whitehall. He would retain his military police position but would probably never set foot in a uniform again. Croft and four others like him had been chosen to be the trouble shooters, the fixers. They would be the ones who got the phone call in the dead of night. They would be the ones who would deal with the things the conventional emergency services didn't even know about. Croft presumed there had been others before him, others tasked with the job he now had. He didn't ask what happened to them. Croft was a soldier; he knew what happened to them. They either died, or they became obsolete, a fate he himself would face at some point in the future. But what the hell, he had nothing better to do.

10.54AM, 14th September 2015, Hounslow, London

Jack didn't mind working in the fast food establishment. It had been his weekend job since he was sixteen (his father had insisted on it), and his manager allowed him flexibility with his hours. His manager had known Jack's dad and had wanted to help the family out as best he could, which Jack had obviously appreciated. Although working at the tills or in the kitchen could be mind-numbing, it was sometimes just what he needed to anaesthetise his brain and give him a reason for being out of the house. Plus, he had friends here, and the money helped keep his sister in her precious Disney paraphernalia.

"I'll have a burger with medium fries and a large full-fat coke please," the umpteenth customer of the day said. Although the grossly obese customer looked like he really should be eating salad rather than food riddled with fructose and trans fatty acids, Jack just went through the motions, smiling a repetitive smile, laying out the tray, taking the customer's money. When he eventually presented the food, the customer thanked him and moved away to one of the tables to enjoy his most splendid feast that would probably harden his arteries just by touching it. It was then that Jack saw trouble come in.

The three teenagers that entered were well known in the locality, and not for their humanitarian activities. They were also barred from the restaurant, for very good reasons. And if they hadn't been barred, the fact that they had all walked in smoking would have seen to that in an instant. Jack wasn't the only one to have spotted them – his manager had too.

"Oh for fucks sake," Clive the manager said under his breath. Clive was as tall as Jack, but where Jack was slim, Clive was built like a brick shit house. But as Jack knew, he also had a heart condition brought on by years of smoking, unhealthy eating and his advanced years. Although in his mid-fifties, and although Clive now smoked only electronic cigs, his angina seemed to get worse as the months progressed. As physically imposing as he was on the outside, the organs on the inside were weak and failing. He was no longer a force to be reckoned with. "Oy you lot, I've told you, you're barred," the manager shouted at the new arrivals. They swaggered forward anyway.

"That's no way to treat a customer," the leader of the gang said. Owen Patterson was a nasty piece of work. Dripping the arrogance of youth and wrapped up in the blanket of sociopathy, Owen did not seem intimidated by Clive's obvious size advantage.

"Out, or we call the police," Clive said stepping from around the counter. He bunched his fists together, trying to ignore the gnawing pain that was threatening to stab into his chest. The three white yobs stood inside the entrance to the establishment, one even leering at a female customer, and Clive took another step towards them. Jack followed him from out behind the counter, backing him up. There were only five other customers present, and they eyed the developing situation nervously.

"Well, will you look at these two black bastards," Owen said. It was obvious to Jack that he was trying to goad Clive, and Jack put a restraining hand on his boss' arm. Clive looked back at him and seemed to physically calm. He nodded to Jack and shouted for one of the other staff members who appeared from out of the kitchen.

"Beth, code seven." Beth nodded and dipped her hand under the counter by one of the cash registers. Clive turned to Owen. "So do you want to leave now, or be dragged away by the cops when they arrive? It's your choice."

Owen looked back at his two lieutenants and smiled. He turned back to Clive, gave a resigned shrug and then looked at Jack. Pointing a finger at him he said, "I'll be seeing you later, cunt." He flicked his cigarette at Jack's head, which Jack dodged easily.

"Out," Clive said, pointing to the door. Owen looked up at the ceiling, snorted a large wodge of phlegm into his throat and spat it at Clive's feet. Backing up, he collected his minions, and with an exaggerated display of his middle finger, he and his warriors left the building. When they were out of sight, Clive pulled out his spray from his back pocket and gave himself two shots under the tongue. The angina began to subside, much to his and Jack's relief.

"I'll clean this up, Clive," Jack said. Clive smiled and put a fatherly hand on his shoulder.

"You watch out for those three tonight, Jack," Clive said, with a worried expression. "There's evil in that boy's heart."

11.35AM, 14th September 2015, Thames House, Millbank, London

Croft sat in an empty grey room without windows or anything but the most basic of drab furnishings. The table in the centre of the room was metal, bolted to the ground, a steel ring welded to the top obviously for the securing of handcuffs, which he fortunately did not wear. The room was featureless except for its fluorescents and its utter grey blandness. A solitary CCTV camera watched him from the corner by the room's only door, its red dot winking occasionally. Croft resisted the temptation to look into it. He wasn't in any trouble; this was just somewhere to put him. The door was unlocked, but that's only because this was the headquarters of MI5, so saying he wasn't going anywhere until dismissed was an understatement. Besides, there was no handle on his side of the door, and he knew that it opened inwards. He had been in rooms like this many times in his life, only on those occasions he hadn't generally been sat on this side of the table.

This was the home of what he knew as Control. Although not a member of MI5, Croft worked under the supervision of the Centre for the Protection of National Infrastructure, an MI5 branch. He ultimately reported to the home secretary and the prime minister, but for now, it would be MI5 who would be doing the inevitable de-briefing of the morning's events. And as expected, they had taken his firearm. Understandable really – he had just killed three people on UK soil, and his story needed to be verified. This wasn't America. This wasn't a country where you could own a host of weapons and in some areas carry them freely. No, this was a land of Queen and Country, and despite popular belief, the agents of government did not have a licence to kill.

The first responders to the scene, two veteran police constables, had been cautious but mindful of the instructions given to their superiors. They had sealed off the entrance to the cemetery and waited for backup, as was their instructions. MI5 had arrived seven minutes later, and the PC's knew better than to try and pull some jurisdiction crap. They never got to speak to the blood-soaked man in the Saville Row suit who was quickly whisked away from the scene, nor the man the MI5 agents carried away in handcuffs. What happened that morning in the cemetery would forever be a mystery to them, and would be whispered about in their precinct for the days to come. At least that was until other events sent the world around them insane.

The door opened and Craver walked in, a concerned and harassed look on his face. "You're as good a shot as you've always been I see, David," he said, sitting down opposite Croft. "And I see the doctor has patched you up." The bullet had only grazed his ear, which didn't faze Croft. He'd suffered much worse than that in his time, as the story of the scars and sealed holes in his body could declare. He was, however, pissed that one of his favourite shirts was probably ruined. The suit he could probably get away with because it was black, but he doubted the shirt could be salvaged.

"Has the prisoner said anything?" Croft asked.

"No, nothing of note, hasn't even asked for a lawyer. Not that he would get one of course." Craver smiled thinly. "The statement you made on the helicopter ride over here made interesting reading though. You're right about them being amateurs. Second-hand, poorly maintained guns in the wrong kind of holsters. They were most likely bought off the Deep Web with Bitcoin, probably at the last minute, which might explain why our guest wasn't armed."

"Do you want me to have a crack at him?" Croft said with a smile. "I'm sure I could get him to talk."

"Yes, I'm sure you could," Craver said disapprovingly, "but I think not. We aren't bloody Americans now, are we? The man still has rights. He'll talk; they always do. He's presently enjoying an endless loop of Barney the Dinosaur. He'll be singing a different tune soon enough."

"I think this means I'm close though. It also means we definitely have a mole in the organisation. I wasn't followed – I can assure you of that – so someone told them I was going to be there."

"Yes, I believe you," said Craver. "And I think you might be right. We need to find out who this group is and what it is they are planning."

"Are you sure you don't want me to have a crack at him?" Craver stood from the table and walked over to the door, which opened for him.

"Julia will be along shortly with the paperwork. I'll let you know when the guy cracks." And with that Craver left, the door closing behind him.

2PM, 14th September 2015, Conference Room A, 70 Whitehall, London

He wasn't late after all. COBRA, that's what the press called it. The bloody leech-like press, how they liked their acronyms and their cloak and dagger and their misinformation. COBRA, the Civil Contingencies Committee, held in the Cabinet Office Briefing Room A. He didn't normally attend these briefings in person, but today was a notable exception. When his masters called, he attended. There were twelve people in the room, including Prime Minister David Osbourne and Home Secretary Claire Miles. Of course, a different Home Secretary to the person who had offered him the job under the last administration, that man now sitting on the back benches of the opposition. Probably just counting the days so he could retire on a big, fat government pension.

Whilst the politicians came and went, the civil servants always stayed the same. Milnes and Craver were both there, as well as the present heads of MI5 and MI6. Impressive, Croft thought, it seemed somebody had actually listened to him. Christ, even Sir Nick Marston, the Chief of the Defence Staff, was here. Croft didn't salute because technically he wasn't in the army anymore, and besides, the general wasn't wearing his hat.

"Prime Minister, General," Croft said, indicating the two senior people in the room. He took his place at the table and sat down.

"You've had an interesting day," the PM said. "Any word on who it was that attacked you?" Croft was going to answer, but the MI5 head, Sir Michael Young, spoke up instead.

"We don't know who they are as they aren't in any of our databases. Even the passport database is clean. The one the major captured is refusing to talk, hasn't even demanded a lawyer. The suspect driving the car got away. We found the car abandoned, burned to a crisp."

"They were amateurs, Prime Minister. If they had been professionals, I probably wouldn't be here. Three against one is never good odds. It would, however, be interesting to know how they knew where to target me and why." That was something Croft was itching to know.

"This does add extra fuel to the intelligence chatter we have been receiving," said Stuart Watkins, the head of MI6. He looked like he had just walked straight out of the 1950's with his tweed suit and his waxed moustache. "It can't be coincidence that Croft was attacked. As you know, Prime Minister, his investigations have uncovered some very disturbing possibilities."

"That there is a traitor or traitors in government?" the PM asked.

"I believe so," answered Croft. "And I believe it is related to the Hirta Island incident." As he had expected, there was an agitated murmuring from the room.

"I believe that's why you're here, Captain Savage." The PM turned his attention to a woman sat three chairs away from him. She was tall and slender, but Croft could tell there was muscle there. She was in civilian clothing, but she was no civilian. She just screamed military.

"Major, I believe you know Captain Savage?" said General Marston. Indeed he did. That was one of the fuck ups he'd had to deal with two years ago. Head of Biomedical Science at the Defence Science and Technology Laboratory at Porton Down, she had been there when he arrived one dark and wintery morning to find that a very nasty strain of Foot and Mouth had escaped into the surrounding environment. His report didn't blame her, however – she had only been in the job a day and hadn't even unpacked. Even so, she had almost lost her job due to the public, media-induced uproar when all the hooved cattle in a 10-mile radius were slaughtered. The picture of them being burnt in the middle of a field even made the front page of several newspapers.

"Good to see you again, Major. Prime Minister, may I?" The PM nodded in agreement. Savage picked up a remote off the table and pressed it. The large screen at the end of the conference room came to light, displaying several files. Heads turned towards it. "We ran analysis of the incident at Hirta Island and came to several disturbing conclusions, which concur with the major's analysis of the event…"

Croft filtered it all out. He'd heard it all before, written most of it. Instead, he watched the faces around him. Someone in this room was dirty, he was sure of it. He just didn't know who, and he didn't know why. It wasn't motivated by profit, of that he was sure. Having millions in the bank meant little if the world was dead, and dead was really the only end game for the Hirta virus. Croft looked for guilt, for deception, but saw nothing but arrogance and genuine concern. Savage was telling them a tale to chill the hearts of men, a tale that even Croft had found difficult to believe even as he was typing it into his computer. He concentrated on Savage, noticed the pulled-back hair, the determination in her face, the line of her neck. The tight, conservative skirt and the white blouse didn't for a minute disguise a figure that Croft found appealing. Croft briefly felt something in his mind he hadn't felt for.... well, years. Lust.

"It is our conclusion that the Hirta Island incident was the result of a deliberate viral attack. The virus, we believe, was manufactured at the facility with the full knowledge of the now deceased Professor Cook. Whether he thought he was working under official sanction, we will never know. We believe the person or persons unknown contaminated the insulin dose of one of the facility's senior staff, and then left by helicopter. That helicopter was never found, and we have never been able to ascertain the identity of our saboteur."

Croft believed the helicopter was at the bottom of the Atlantic, along with everyone on board. Whoever had organised the Hirta incident had decided to make sure there were no loose ends left. Savage continued. "We believe the data on the virus was transmitted offsite, despite the facility's firewalls, and that there is now, at the very least, the blueprint for a devastating biological weapon in the hands of some very dangerous people. Whoever they are, they have money and influence."

"You think they have a working form of the virus?" asked General Marston. Savage looked at Croft.

"I do, yes, General. And both myself and Major Croft have come to a similar conclusion that someone high up in our chain of command is complicit." That was a surprise; Croft hadn't expected her to back him up on that aspect. *Hmm, I think I like this woman*, thought Croft.

3.00PM, 14th September 2015, Hotel Suite, Hilton Hotel, Heathrow Airport, Hounslow, London

"The Lord is most displeased with you, Ahab. He trembles with disbelief at your incompetence." Brother Abraham sat by the window, watching as planes came and went through the sky, catching an occasional glimpse of his reflection in the glass. Inside, he was burning with rage. He did not look at the man who his fury was aimed at, and he showed no external signs of his anger. But the anger was there, and it was only by power of will that he did not let the mask slip.

"I am sorry, Brother Abraham," Ahab said, a slender man in his forties, prostrate on his knees. "I thought I was doing the Lord's will." Abraham closed his eyes and pinched the bridge of his elderly nose. Such audacity.

"The Lord Our God would not send sheep to kill a rabid wolf. Now we have two brethren dead, Brother Eli sat in the bowels of Satan himself, and another cowering before me trying to repent his most egregious error. Whatever possessed you to think that you could kill this man?" Abraham looked away from the window and scanned the room, looking at the three other men who stood silently behind Ahab. He looked each in the eye, seeing the devotion and the selflessness there. These men he could trust unquestioningly. Each of them he knew would die for him without a second thought. "You were only supposed to follow the man, using the drone the Lord provided you."

"Croft is a threat; I saw a chance to eliminate that threat," Ahab said defensively. His chest almost puffed up with pride when he said it.

"Indeed, he is a threat, more so now thanks to your stupidity. You thought you could kill him, using guns … bought off the internet. The man you tried to end is a trained killer, a warrior of countless wars. You …" Abraham held his hands up in exasperation, "you were a fucking accountant until you found the true faith. But we are where we are, and our enemy will undoubtedly redouble his efforts now. You have given the Wolf a taste of the flesh he craves." Abraham shook his head in frustration. The man before him was pious, that much was true. But he was incompetent like many of the Lord's followers. Still, you had to take what the Lord gave you. One had to trust that you followed the true path. "Fortunately, we are mere days away from the cleansing. The world will see the penalty for their wickedness, and they will know the purity and the vengeance of the Lord Our God. But you, my friend," Abraham nodded to one of his followers, "you will be spared any more toil in the field of the Lord." Abraham reached down from where he sat and took Ahab's face in his hands. "I release you from your penance, and bless you to eternal bliss." He released the cowering figure. Ahab's face showed shock realisation, and then the garrotte passed over his eyes and tightened onto his neck. As the man bucked and fought, Abraham stood and walked into the bathroom. Such unpleasantness on such a beautiful day was distressing but necessary. Washing his bearded face, the 72 year old looked at his wrinkled reflection in the mirror.

"How many more years will your servant have to do thy bidding, oh Lord?" he whispered under his breath. "How many more years before you gather me up to be by your side?" Abraham grabbed a towel hanging by the side of the sink and dried himself. Noticing that the sounds of struggle next door had ended, he discarded it and walked back into the bedroom.

"Someone dispose of that," he said pointing at the now dead Ahab. "And pack my bags. I have a plane to catch." Yes, it was time he left the Devil's playground. Fifteen hours from now, he would be safely back home in America, safe to continue the Lord's work if his message went unheeded. So much to do, so many sinners to free from their worldly bondage, so many converts to welcome. He turned to the man who had killed the foolish Ahab. "Did you do what I asked of you?"

"Yes, Brother. We have ensured the apartments where they stayed have all been sterilised by the Lord's fire. There will be no trace of them left; it will take weeks for our enemies to find their identities … So long as Eli doesn't talk."

"Don't worry," Abraham said with a smile, "Eli will be dead before the day is over. The man is a true believer." Abraham sat back down as his men busied themselves with the Lord's work. Soon, 7 billion souls would witness the truth about the world, and the Lord would weep in the heavens at the manifestation of his justice.

3.30PM 14th September 2015, Thames House, Millbank, London

Brother Eli held his hands over his ears and tried to keep out the relentless noise. When he had come to, he had been strapped down unable to move and hooded. There was white noise filling his ears, and he suspected from the motion that he was in a helicopter. A moment of panic filled him as he realised he was in the hands of the enemy. It was not panic regarding what would become of him – no, he had already accepted that he was already dead. His concern was aimed at what he might reveal about the Lord's vengeance. Sooner or later, he would break. If not from the psychological torture, then from the drugs that would inevitably be placed into his system. Brother Abraham had told them all well how the Devil's foot soldiers would look to use the imperfection of their own bodies against them. And now he was here, amongst them, captive to the agents of evil.

Now he was in a bright room, the lights so bright he could see the veins in his closed eyelids. A toilet and a mattress were his only companion…..apart from the noise that was the unbearable cacophony that went on relentlessly. He had been subjected to it for several hours now. "So the agents of Satan have learnt to use the Lord's own weapons against the faithful," Eli said to himself, although Joshua would never resort to this torture.

They had questioned him at first. There was no 'Good Cop, Bad Cop' routine. They had simply asked him what they wanted to know. He had been quite animated in his response, and had almost told them to suck their Devil's cock like the whores they were. But he kept that comment to himself. Now, in a disposable boiler suit, his clothes stripped from him before the interrogation, his hands still handcuffed, he considered his predicament. Ahab had been wrong to order them to try and kill the man. Eli had said as much, but the other two had been all for it. They had shown him the guns they had bought illegally and assured Eli that the job would be done quick and fast. For was not the Lord their Shepherd? Eli wished he had said what was in his heart, that the Lord would not protect those whose arrogance made them foolish. But he had not, and had seen his friend and his lover gunned down by a warrior who served the lord of lies. Eli also felt ashamed. In that brief moment where his friends had been gunned down before him, fear had won over, and he had turned and ran. Could he have helped? Could he have somehow turned the tide to bring down the enemy?

And now he was in their lair, helpless and vulnerable, subject to their whims. There was, it seemed, only one thing for him to do, one final defining act to show his defiance to the defiler that ruled the world. To show his faith, his true devotion. Eli uncovered his ears and opened his eyes, despite the bright pain from the light. Standing unsteadily on his feet, he propped himself up with his back against the wall. Praying silently to God and casting his hands behind his head, he placed his tongue out as far as it would go, holding it there firmly in-between his teeth. He paused, savouring the last moments life had to offer him. And then he let himself fall forwards, resisting the temptation to break his descent. The impact not only broke his jaw but also severed his tongue, cutting both lingual arteries. In a haze of pain and light and sound, his mouth quickly filled with blood, and as he lapsed steadily into unconsciousness, he inhaled his own life force and died before medical teams could be dispatched to save him.

4.30PM 14th September 2015, Hounslow, London

He was already well on the way to getting nicely drunk. And he was still angry, very angry. Owen sat on a less than clean sofa in the abandoned flat that he had acquired for himself. The council's attempt to board it up had lasted less than ten minutes when faced with an onslaught of crowbars and the well-placed boots of his gang. To be honest, it wasn't much of a gang. It was just him and four others who only really stayed around because it was beneficial to them. They were also afraid of him. Owen wasn't big, but he was vicious, and didn't seem to have any fear whatsoever. He was well known for his ability to lash out with unrestrained violence at any provocation.

At the moment, he was alone, which was probably for the best. Now was not the time for others to be around him. Yes, Owen was feared by those in his gang and by those his gang harassed. The people around him learnt quickly to make themselves scarce when he got into one of his moods, because those moods always ended in violence. Today was one of those times, and the two young men who had been with him in Clive's fast food joint that morning had quickly made themselves scarce when they had seen Owen start drinking about lunchtime. They suddenly found they had errands to run.

Deep down, Owen knew what brought on the anger. It was his own self-loathing that spurred it on. Truth be told, he hated himself, hated what he had become, hated the world he had created around him. But he only knew one way to react to those feelings. So he bottled them up, denied their existence and did his best to wash them in a sea of alcohol whenever they dared make themselves known. Of course, the alcohol fuelled his anger, which made him self-destruct even more, which made him commit more acts which scarred and damaged his psyche even more. The bravado he displayed was merely an act, the act of a boy growing into a man who was not the sociopath he pretended to be. He was just a broken child who didn't know how to fix himself. So he lashed out at the world that he blamed for the gnawing pit of despair that burned within his very soul. Unfortunately, the more he let his anger run wild, the more the fires of sociopathy grew within him.

His mother saw the truth of him, saw the pain and the anguish that he tried to hide. She had been there listening to him weep in the early hours. But she knew she couldn't help him, knew she couldn't fix the train wreck that his life was becoming. How could she? She hadn't been able to salvage her own life. She had lost any chance when he first manifested these traits, when she first saw him commit an act of wanton violence. She should have gone to the police, turned witness against him, let the law of the land bring down its justice so that it could also bring down its mercy. But she hadn't, not because she loved him, but because she too was broken and wanted nothing to do with the scum that wore the blue uniform. And with no father figure to enforce any kind of discipline, she did the worst thing any mother could do – she let him go down his own path with no guidance and no hindrance. And now her son was a killer. And she lived inside a bottle, a further example for her precious son to follow.

Owen had not meant to kill the man – at least that was what he said to himself. To those who followed him, however, he showed no self-doubt, had merely shrugged when the stupid bastard had smashed his skull on the pavement. Owen didn't think he had even hit the guy that hard, but his anger had exploded when the black fool had fought back. It was a mugging for Christ sake. You didn't fight back when you were outnumbered – everyone knew that. But the man had, and had landed some pretty decisive blows on two of his attackers before Owen's fist had slammed into the side of his jaw. Owen had looked down at the semi-conscious, groaning figure and had looked around at the group with him. He winked at one, a smile forming on his lips. And then he had kicked the prone figure of Jack Nathan's father in the head with his steel-capped boot. Inside a little voice was screaming, but the ego knew the show of force was demanded, was expected. A short piece about the victim's subsequent death had appeared in one of the free newspapers, and on reading it, Owen's blood had turned to ice, and a little bit more of his humanity had died. They always say the first kill is the hardest, that it becomes easier after that. Owen didn't know who "they" were, but he figured they were probably right. And over the next few days, he would get to test that theory out in abundance.

5.34PM, 19th November 2014, Hayton Vale, Devon, UK

To those who routinely drank in the Rock Inn Pub, the lone man who arrived at the same time every day was a curious fellow. He was always polite, he always seemed to wear the same tailored suit, and always ordered the same meal. His hair and beard were always well groomed, although he never availed himself of the local hair salon. He never spoke more than he needed to, and he always washed down the food with the same two pints of beer. Attempts to engage him in conversation, to explain the mystery of the man, had always been politely rebuffed. Nobody even knew his name or why he had suddenly appeared and chosen to live here for nearly a year.

Word had also gotten around about the sale of the old farmhouse years prior, and of the building work that had gone on, mostly unseen due to the farmhouse only being reached by a long and winding private road that was now secured by security cameras and a formidable electronic gate. The twenty acres of land that the farm covered quickly became encircled by sturdy eight-foot Barbican fencing, topped with fresh and gleaming razor wire. Earlier attempts by the few neighbours to welcome the new owners to the locality had been unsuccessful, nobody answering the electronic gate intercom, and after the construction was complete, nobody was ever seen using the gate to enter or exit. Soon enough, people had given up trying. It was thought that the quiet man lived in what the locals now called "The Fortress", although nobody really knew for sure. And due to the man's thin frame, scarred face and meek demeanour, they labelled him as a harmless eccentric and left him to his own devices. Eventually, like everything else familiar, his presence amongst them faded into indifference.

In reality, he was a devout man with a genius IQ. Devout to science, not religion. If the drinkers in the Rock Inn Pub had been avid readers of the more obscure scientific journals, they might have recognised his face, but only if they had read those journals twenty years ago. A brilliant virologist, he had, at one time, had it all. A beautiful wife and three children who he had adored more than life. On the very cusp of becoming the head of Virology at Cambridge University, his life had been stripped from him one vicious evening. Driving carefully home from a day out – the wife in the passenger seat, the children playing kids' games in the back – he had seen the Ford Escort two seconds before it ploughed through a red light, sending his car and his life into a burning hell.

The victim of a drunk driver who ironically had escaped virtually unscathed, Professor James Jones, one of the most brilliant minds the country had to offer, awoke to find his legs broken, a tube sticking out of his chest to deal with the collapsed lung, and the sight in his right eye gone due to the flames that had licked at his features. He also found his wife and two of his children dead. The third was in a coma and held on for another two days before nature took her to where all living things go eventually. The nurses and doctors had struggled to know how to break this further news to him, a man who no longer had any living relatives of note, and whose friends seemed noticeably absent, despite this being the time he needed them the most. The doctor who finally told him felt a little piece of her die when her words visibly destroyed what was left of the man who had already been on the brink.

That brilliant mind, a mind that was destined to cure disease and to help the lives of millions, simply snapped. Something inside it just broke, and after his initial uncontrolled despair, Jones descended into a catatonic state that medical science was unable to rouse him from. As his physical injuries healed, his mind closed down, and now unable to be released into the world he had retreated from, he was hospitalised and diagnosed with Schizophrenic Catatonia. His burns healed with little in the way of visible scarring, but the sight in the dead eye never returned, and he dwelled in an internal world of peace, oblivious to everything that made him human.

When the catatonia broke four years later, he returned to the world with a different perspective than the one he had held before the accident. When he turned his head and asked for water, frightening the life out of the care assistant who had been giving him a sponge bath, he felt something dwelling in the forefront of his mind that he had rarely experienced before:

Rage

It was there all the time; it was all he had. There wasn't even any room for grief. The psychiatrists sympathised with him, said they understood the way he felt. He spat their words back in their faces. How could they know? How could they understand such loss? Not just the loss of his family, but the loss of his hope, the loss of his belief about the world, the loss of such perfection. The rage became all consuming, and it wasn't helped with the knowledge that the man who had killed his family had served less than three years at her Majesty's Pleasure. Three years? Where was the justice there? Jones railed against society, hurled venom and verbal abuse at those whose job it was to try and help him. He would not be consoled, and he would not forgive a world that allowed such pain and suffering to dwell at its very core. Even worse, he would not forgive the people who created it, who helped oil the wheels of its systems and governments. He quickly learnt to loathe humanity, because they had such potential, and yet they let themselves be corrupted by weakness and selfishness. In his weakened state, muscles atrophied, he was no real physical threat, not to those trained in how to deal with such cases. But his obvious hatred for the world and subsequent attempts at suicide saw him sectioned to a secure psychiatric facility.

That was time passed. Now he sat, passing the half-filled glass to his lips, listening to the inane chatter in the pub around him, his burns mostly healed, but having sight still in only one eye. Those around him would claim they were good people, that they deserved the life they held so dear. But how often did he see them consume four, maybe five pints before venturing outside to drive their chariots of death home? How often did their bigotry and their racism escape the confines of their hearts through the words they expressed, through their actions? He truly despised them all. Including the children that often ran laughing through the pub. As innocent as they were, they were slowly being filled with hatred and poison by the corrupted adults who surrounded them.

Even now, many years on, utter hatred filled his heart for the human race. But long ago he had learnt to contain his rage, to bottle it and channel it to where it needed to be, to show the psychiatrists what they wanted to see. It was the only way to escape their clutches. So he wore the mask of meek compliance and pretended to enjoy the simple pleasures that life offered whilst rejecting the blanket of comfort that society claimed to provide.

He was able to perform this masquerade because he believed he had been shown a truth about the world, and had learnt that he had an important place in it. In the psychiatric facility, he quickly learnt to tell the head shrinkers what they wanted to hear. He showed pain at his loss, and slowly "learnt" the lessons they tried to teach him, taking his medication as ordered, but discarding the pills whenever he could. When he was released, he gave the illusion of working with the medical professionals and the social workers, but deep in his heart, his hostility to the human race grew, dark thoughts beginning to fester in his mind in those dark moments before sleep. The thoughts became plans, and the plans searched for a way to manifest themselves.

Money was of little concern to him. His parents had been rich when they had died, and a large trust fund was there for his every whim. He did not, therefore, seek employment, but embraced a new technology that was revolutionising the world … the internet. And through this he found the writings of a controversial American professor whose latest book *The Plague of Man* was causing quite a stir in the scientific community. Jones realised that the author was a glorified Eugenicist, but the basic premise that man was a cancer that needed eradicating to save the Earth took root in his already diseased mind.

When the author came to speak in London, Jones attended. Sat in the audience, he grew tired of the author's talk, which was more of an elitist rant than a true understanding of the virus that humankind represented. Halfway through the lecture, Jones put his hand up. At first, he was ignored, but he persisted. Then he stood up, causing a murmur around him.

"A question from the audience?" the author said. "I don't normally answer questions."

"Is that because you are afraid what you might get asked?" Jones said.

"Of course not," the author said defensively.

"Good. I've been listening to you, and I hear your message that the herd should be culled. But I also hear your other message, that the elite should be spared. Am I hearing that correctly?"

"Yes, I believe the best and the brightest should be left to inherit the Earth."

"Would those be the best and brightest who developed nuclear weapons? Who developed technology that allowed humanity to grow from hundreds of millions to billions and thus create the very overpopulation we now face? Who developed vaccines and medicine and sanitation? Are those the best and brightest you refer to?" Jones was animated now, and there was a noticeable shift in the audience.

"I don't think you quite understand ..."

"Oh, I understand more than you could possibly imagine. You don't believe in saving the Earth. You believe in your own superiority over everyone in this room. Tell me, what gives you the right to pick who lives and who dies? If you believe in your mission so much, will you be the first to lay down your life? Will your sons and your daughter join you in your sacrifice?"

That had caused an uproar, and some of the audience even rallied to the truth in his interruption. Jones had still been escorted out, but not before the room had descended into anarchy. With one false prophet slain, Jones had continued his quest. He went to similar lectures, and through other such meetings, he discovered a secretive network of like-minded people who wanted nothing more than to see the human race if not wiped out completely, then at least reduced to a manageable level. It was through this group that he met and befriended an elderly man called Zachariah. Or was it more truthful to say that Zachariah found and befriended him? Then came the fateful day when, attending a meeting with his new mentor (at least that was what Zachariah considered himself to Jones' inner amusement), he was introduced to a man called Abraham.

To this day, Jones knew little about the person known only to him as Brother Abraham. What he did know was that his wealth seemed limitless, that he had power normal people couldn't even imagine, and that his belief in a vengeful God seemed unshakeable, almost infectious. This was not the God of the Bible, although selective Bible texts were used to justify various belief systems that Abraham would spout with such passion. Like the belief that the End Times were coming, and that it was God's will that his agents on Earth would need to be the catalyst for Armageddon. Jones always wondered why God needed people to work his miracles for him. He didn't remember the Great Flood being outsourced.

Jones knew full well that he was joining a cult, and although he wasn't impressed by the religious aspect of it, the resources that were offered and subsequently made available to him were more than he could ever hope. The professor's original plan was to create a virus so infectious, so contagious, and so lethal that the planet would be stripped bare of the majority of human life. Some would survive, but the festering, bloated system that allowed his family's murderer to walk free would be brought to its knees. That was his vision, that was his purpose, his identity. That's what kept him awake at night, the possibilities churning through his head as his imagination watched a civilisation die.

But Abraham had other plans, and he slowly and methodically worked his warped influence on a mind that could not admit that it was broken.

"I know not where the quote comes from," Abraham had said, "but I think it reflects the Godliness and the wickedness of the planet we live on. The words as I remember them are 'When there is no more room in hell, the dead will walk the Earth.'" Abraham had gripped the professor's head between his surprisingly powerful hands. "This is the Lord's vengeance I want to bring to the world. But the Lord is merciful, so we must give his children the chance to repent. Can you do this for me?" Jones believed he could. There was something gnawing at the back of his mind, some knowledge that he felt could give Abraham exactly what he wanted. And so he worked.

For years, he toiled to develop an infectious agent that could bring Abraham the world he desired. Helped by other scientists who also believed the virus of humanity needed addressing, protected by an unknown agent at the heart of the British government, they experimented and failed numerous times. But they persevered and eventually the breakthrough came. A new virus was created, and countless test subjects died in agony to create it. Jones didn't even blink when he injected their bound forms; it was all for the greater good. It wasn't perfect though – it was contagious enough, but it quickly killed the host. He needed access to the infectious agents that only governments had stored deep in their vaults. So another mind, almost as brilliant as Jones' and just as disillusioned with the human race, was engaged. Deep within the Hirta Island Research Facility, Professor Cook created Abraham's vision.

The virus underwent its final transformation and first live field test at the RESURRECTION research facility, and Abraham passed it as God's true vengeance. On the day of that successful test, Jones gained another name amongst the followers. The Grand Cleric.

Abraham gave him an unexpected reward for his success. Returning to his laboratory one morning, he entered to find the chained, naked and unconscious body of the man who had killed his family. For the first time since his release from the mental health facility, Jones cried. But these, these were tears of joy. These were tears of vengeance. The man who once prided himself on his humanity and his civility, the man who would trap and release a spider rather than kill it, took his time with the man who had stripped his family and his life from him. The man had taken five months to die, and every minute he was conscious had been unspeakable agony. This was the gift Abraham had promised, and Abraham always followed through on his promises. Any last vestiges of sanity that Jones possessed died along with his victim. And as he sliced the flesh from the man's bones, as he tortured him with acids and cold and heat, he knew that Abraham's plan was not enough. He needed to sit and watch the whole world burn.

8.25PM, 14th September 2015, The King's Head pub, Waterloo, London

He had been given the night off. Tonight, he wasn't on call; someone in another paid for government house would have to deal with the end of all things should it occur tonight. Whilst it wasn't often he got woken in the dead of night, he had to be available, which meant behaving himself, meant being there when the call came. Which meant little in the way of a social life. There were no worries on that regard tonight though, and he sat with his second pint of the night. Although this could be classed as his local pub, he hadn't actually ever been in it. Looking around when he had entered, he quickly realised he hadn't been missing much.

It was a lonely job. Yes, there were briefings and assignments, but his work never actually allowed him the opportunity to talk to people in a social setting. Croft wasn't sure if he was bothered by that or not. Most of his friends had been in the military, and only God and government knew where half of them were now. The others ...well, they were six feet under or scattered on some field somewhere, their families left with sorrow and a pitiful military pension. And a part of him didn't want that connection anymore, didn't want to feel that pain, that gut-wrenching loss ever again. Not again, it was too much. So in a way, this job was ideal for him. He told himself it was all part of the healing process, but perhaps the mental scars had formed too thick. Perhaps he was dead inside.

There were moments when he thought about these things, and it was frightening just how empty his life actually was, filled with his routine of government work and exercise. Lifting the glass to his lips, Croft took a big swallow. He had to admit, he'd missed this. The pub was quiet, not surprising considering the fucking price they were charging for beer, and he pretended to watch the football match on one of several screens scattered around the establishment. But he didn't really care about football, never had. It was just good to sit amongst humanity. That being said, he certainly didn't entertain the concept of sitting with his back to any entrance, and he positioned himself to see every way in. There was no way he was going to ignore his training. He had his gun on him, and who could blame him following the day's events? It wasn't every day someone took shots at you. And he was going to limit himself to three pints. Getting drunk was tempting, but it wasn't an option, which was why he wasn't drinking at home. He had a strange feeling that if he let that cat out of that bag, he might not be able to put it back in. He was in no way an alcoholic, but there had been moments where he had let alcohol gain control of him, and the results had been less than pleasant. Not the thing to do when you had a loaded gun with fifteen loaded rounds and two extra clips.

The old ornate wooden door to the pub opened, and Croft raised his eyebrows in surprise and recognition. Craver walked in and went straight to the bar where he was served almost instantly. Croft watched the man. In his fifties, he had the bearing of competence and confidence. He looked like a pen-pusher, but Croft saw the signs, saw the training, saw the killer that lurked in him. The man had slain at least half a dozen people. Anyone who chose to mug him mistaking him for some city banker or accountant would be in for a nasty surprise. He didn't know the MI5 man's past, but Croft presumed it was as colourful as his own.

Craver gathered his drinks and walked over to Croft's table. Placing one of them before Croft, Craver sat down next to him, also keeping his back to the wall.

"Quiet night for it, David."

"Best way. I'm too old for nightclubs and disco music. Should you be drinking on a school night?"

"Every night is a school night for me, old chap," Craver said. He took a sip of his whiskey and placed it on the table in front of him. The men didn't look at each other, but stared out at the clientele. "I presume you heard?"

"What, that our captive killed himself? Yes, I was informed." That had taken everyone by surprise. Not even the Jihadists they caught did that.

"Damn poor show if you ask me. Someone's going to get a bollocking for letting that happen." Craver swished the ice around in his glass, took another sip.

"Are we any closer to finding out who they were?"

"Not really," Craver said. "The chap's history didn't really point to anything. 'Mother' is still looking for connections, but he wasn't on any of our watch lists."

"He didn't strike me as a ghost. He seemed quite amateurish. Is this a new organisation we're dealing with?"

"It would appear so," Craver said. On the other side of the pub, a drunk man leapt from his chair and waved his fist in celebration at the TV screen. It would seem someone had kicked a ball into a goal. How the plebs loved to roar at such trivialities.

"Yes, you fucking beauty," the man roared.

"Oy, what have I told you about bloody swearing in my gaff? Any more of that and you're out," the landlord said from behind the bar.

"Sometimes makes you wonder why we bother, doesn't it?" Craver said, indicating the drunk. "The people, the society that surrounds us. It's broken, sick. This country is not what it was."

"Not my job to comment," Croft said. He finished off his pint and picked up the one Craver had bought for him. "Cheers," he said and he raised his pint to his companion.

"Good health." Craver finished off his whiskey and slammed it down on the table. "Have to admit, this place is a bit low class for me. I'm worried I might have to dry clean my suit just sitting here."

"I doubt you'll get fleas," Croft said with a smile. He could see the idea hadn't even occurred to the MI5 man.

"Oh Christ, now you've made me itch." Croft took another swallow.

"Why are you here, Arnold?"

"Because you killed two people today. Despite your training and despite your past, there's no escaping that. And as I'm not one who believes in those bloody mind rapists, I figured you could do with someone to talk to. And I figured you could do with getting drunk."

"You think you can outlast me, do you?" Croft said wearing the first smile of the evening. He was now looking at Craver.

"Oh undoubtedly – I used to drink for Eton. But not here. That shit was barely drinkable," he said pointing to his empty glass. "I require a much more superior vintage if I'm going to damage my liver. I have standards."

"Where did you have in mind?" Croft said, downing his pint.

"My driver's waiting outside, and my club is only a ten minutes' drive away." Craver stood. "Coming?"

"Why the fuck not."

9.00PM, 14th September 2015, Hayton Vale, Devon, UK

Jones stood in the doorway, watching the black Land Rover approach the house along the gravel road. The last visitor of the night. The gate in the distance had closed automatically as soon as the car was through. He stood with his arms crossed, inhaling the fresh autumnal air. It could get stuffy in his laboratory, despite the powerful extractor fans and the air conditioning. It wasn't natural to be cooped up like that. It wasn't how mankind was supposed to live, and what was he doing all this for if not to remind mankind of how far they had fallen from the Grace of God?

At least that's what he told the likes of Brother Abraham. God? Really? People still believed in the concept of an invisible friend, living in the sky? Did they really think there was some entity up there judging them, creating them? That there was some blissful afterlife for them to go to when they died? What on earth would be the point of that? It was weak, and it was pathetic. Ironically, Jones knew that the events over the coming days were going to send billions of them hurtling into the arms of their false prophets, begging him for forgiveness and salvation. Humanity, such potential, but such a disappointment. Better to just end it all quickly and let the planet reset. He bent to pick up the case as the car stopped several metres from him and smiled. There was no turning back now. The car door opened, and an elderly man stepped out. The man's tailored suit was immaculate.

"Brother Zachariah, how is God's servant this evening?" Jones said to the newcomer. Jones displayed an aura of friendship and respect, but really he felt neither for the man.

"The Lord Our God keeps me busy. His children are aimless and corrupted by the pleasures of the flesh." Walking forwards, he pointed at the case Jones held. "I presume this is the last of it?" The man's accent was from the American Deep South. And although he hid it well, Jones truly despised him.

"Yes, you are the last emissary to pick up the Lord's message," Jones said. He couldn't believe how easy it was for him to spout this bullshit. These were not the words of a scientist, but of an actor, playing a part to fulfil his own agenda. "This is the last of it," he said, gently patting the case. Zachariah held out his hand, and Jones passed the case over.

"The Lord thanks you," Zachariah said. Jones watched him turn around and get back into the car. That was it – that was his part in all this done. He had been offered a flight out of the country, but Jones had declined. As the car moved away, it's blacked out windows obscuring most of its occupants, Jones felt no relief from the excitement he had been feeling over the last couple of weeks. Brother Abraham and his little death cult had their plan, and Jones had his. Standing there, the wind gently playing with the trees far off behind the perimeter fence, he realised he had gotten away with it. Now he just had to sit back, put his feet up and watch the world burn.

10.03PM, 14th September 2015, White's Private Members Club, London

So this is how the other half lives, thought Croft. He had never been in White's before; he never even knew it existed. He sat in a dining area more opulent than he had ever experienced, eating quail. Who the fuck ate quail? The dining area had a low murmur to it, important people talking about important things with the security that everyone would respect the privacy of those around them. There was a feeling of calmness, of order about the room, and Croft felt strangely comfortable here.

"I don't get to come here as much as I like," Craver said slicing into his steak. "It's a treat I like to give myself at least two or three times a month."

"I see your job has more perks than mine," Croft said. He lifted up his glass still amused at the waiter's face when he had asked for a beer. Craver had laughed, not at him but with him. Apparently, the only thing more heinous would be picking something off the vegetarian part of the menu. Allegedly, that was only there to weed out undesirables in the membership. Members of White's were carnivores through and through.

"Oh heavens no, old chap; this has nothing to do with work. Family connections and family money. Silver spoon and all that."

"And yet you still run around playing spies," Croft said. "Worried you'll get bored?" Craver took the steak and carefully placed it in his mouth. He let it sit there for several seconds and then delicately chewed the morsel, abject pleasure adorning his face.

"Oh absolutely, old boy. When you grow up being given everything, you soon realise that wealth has its limitations. And MI5 seemed the natural thing to do after leaving the Army. The old Etonian network saw to all that." Craver attacked his steak again, and Croft looked at the man's plate, a look of regret spreading across his face. "Anything wrong, old chap?"

"As nice as this is," he said indicating the plate of quail, "I'm kind of wishing I'd chosen what you're eating."

"Happens all the time in here. The food's so good it risks being made illegal." The waiter passed the table and poured more red wine into both the men's glasses. Croft felt the urge to order another beer, pictured the swearing and muttering waiter having to disappear into a dark cellar where he would scavenge for a dust-covered bottle that had been bought just in case any philistines found their way onto the premises. He resisted the temptation and thanked the waiter.

"A good red this," Croft said.

"Of course it's bloody good. That, my friend, is 1957 Chateau Lafite Rothschild, the best of the last century." Craver picked up the glass and held it up to his nose, taking a long, slow inhale. He then took a sip and seemed to melt with the pleasure he was experiencing.

"Sounds expensive," Croft answered.

"Very."

"Isn't this wasted on me? My palate rarely experiences anything better than a cheap supermarket merlot."

"Oh dear boy," Craver chuckled. "This isn't for you; this meal and this red are purely for my enjoyment. And a good meal with good wine is never a waste of time. Even a condemned man is allowed one last meal." Craver picked up another piece of steak with his fork and consumed it. "Which kind of feels like what this is." The two men looked at each other.

"That sounds a tad ominous," Croft quizzed.

"Chatter old boy, intelligence chatter. The last few days, 'Mother' has been throwing a hissy fit. Something big is about to hit."

"How big?" Croft finished his beer; he was now well on the way to inebriation.

"Bigger than 911, bigger than the 77 bombings. Bigger than Madrid. Big, and it's happening soon. So you see, I had a feeling I wouldn't be able to come here for the foreseeable future, and I really hate to dine alone."

"Well, I'm flattered you thought to invite me," Croft said.

"Don't be," Craver said with a mischievous smile. "Nobody else was free."

10.09PM, 14th September 2015, Hounslow, London

Jack Nathan sat half watching the TV program, half thinking about where his life was going. He looked over again at his sleeping mother, collapsed in the armchair she always occupied at this time. She wouldn't be waking up in a hurry, and with his sister asleep upstairs, he basically had the house to himself. Picking up the remote, he changed the channel to the news.

He felt trapped. His obligations lay on his shoulders like a weight, slowly crushing the air out of him. Jack knew he needed to get out of here, needed to forge on with his life, but he didn't know how he could achieve that. If only his mother could regain control, if only she could climb out of the bottle she craved and realised she still had responsibilities to be a parent. And although Jake hated to admit it and tried to hide the realisation deep within him, he knew he resented her. Yes, it wasn't her fault Father had been killed, but it wasn't Jake's either. He needed to do something about all this, but he just didn't know what.

Would he still be here if not for his sister? Probably. He loved them both – there was no denying that. But he also hated them both in a way, hated that he was being tied down, his dreams and ambitions castrated just as he was on his way to achieve them. Jake didn't want to be stuck here any longer than he had to be, stuck on this estate working a shit job for shit pay, never knowing when violence would descend as it had descended on his father. And he was also afraid, afraid that things would get worse, afraid of what the future held and what it didn't hold. And it was painful to live in fear, because that meant he wasn't in control.

10.54PM, 14th September 2015, White's Private Members Club, London

Croft didn't normally eat dessert, but by the time the offer had been made, he was drunk and had decided to throw caution to the wind. And he freely admitted that it was the best thing he ever tasted, the waiter pleased at his obvious delight, but also a tad annoyed at the volume with which he had expressed it.

The two men now sat away from the dining area, facing each other across a small table, sat in plush high-backed leather chairs. So Croft said to himself, *Now we learn what this is all about.* A different waiter delivered their drinks, scotch for Craver, mineral water for Croft.

"Are you sure, old boy?" Craver protested when the drink was delivered. "The night is still young."

"Oh I'm sure; I've had more than enough. I may not be on duty, but the days when I let myself lose control are long gone. And besides, I notice you aren't even close to being drunk."

"Cast iron constitution, my friend." Craver winked. "I suspect you've seen through my little ruse." Croft nodded at him seriously.

"Why am I here, Arnold?" Croft asked. Craver picked his drink up, swirled the ice around the glass twice and took a small sip. He placed the glass back on the table.

"I want to know who you think the mole is."

"You've read my reports," Croft answered.

"Yes, and I've seen enough reports in my time to know you're holding something back."

"I don't have any evidence. I don't have any confirmed leads. All I have is guess work and conjecture." Croft had suspected this was where the evening had been heading. It was either that or Craver had taken a fancy to him. Neither prospects were particularly palatable to him.

"Sod the evidence. I want to know what your gut tells you. It's usually right."

"Yes, it is," Croft said. "And my gut also tells me when I should keep things to myself until I'm sure. Needless to say, it's not a politician. They come and go. It's likely not someone in the civil service either. The mole is either high-ranking Army brass or top -level intelligence. It might even be you."

"Crikey, didn't see that one coming," Craver said defensively. "Is that a serious suspicion?"

"No," Croft said in response. "But whoever it is, I will find out."

"Could be embarrassing for Whitehall," Craver wagered. He finished off his drink, safe in the knowledge that a waiter would be along shortly to refill it for him.

"You know that's not the case. If I find out who allowed Hirta to happen, there won't be any arrest. There won't be any trial. That individual or individuals will simply disappear into a hole that no lawyer will ever be able to save them from."

"Good," Craver said. "Ah waiter," he said as the man appeared as if called by telepathy. "Another round, please, and water for my sensible friend."

"I've actually narrowed it down to four people," Croft said out of the blue. "You get a lot of free time in my job, so I've been poking my nose in where it's not wanted. I think that was what the attempted hit on me today was about, although I'm not convinced whoever is organising all this officially sanctioned it. I've heard things – rumours and whispers that make me think there is definitely a large organisation at play here."

"But surely if that was the case, we would have heard the same rumours."

"Not if there were traitors high up the chain. Not if the rotten apple sat right at the top of the barrel." The waiter arrived putting the drinks on the table between the two men.

7.55AM, 15th September 2015, Canary Wharf, London

Fabrice awoke one minute before the alarm was due to go off and switched it off before its noise intruded on his thoughts. He lay there, staring at the ceiling, fully at peace with where he was in the world. The bed almost felt like a womb, and he was loathe to leave its confines despite the pressure on his bladder and the knowledge of the days ahead. This would be the last full day he would ever spend in this blighted country, and he was eager for it to end so that he could get on with tomorrow's task.

There was little in the way of sound in his bedroom; all was quiet. Despite living in a city of almost ten million people, the penthouse he occupied provided him with luxury and seclusion most Londoners could only dream of. Of course, the penthouse wasn't his, but having lived here for only three months, it felt more of a home than many of his past residences. And the fact that he shared it with two others did nothing to spoil that. This was where he belonged, this was his path, and every day he felt blessed that God had chosen him to do his ultimate bidding.

People often questioned why God had to work through the hands and actions of man instead of blatantly displaying his omnipotence, but that was only the confusion of the uninitiated speaking. God had given dominion of the Earth to his children, and so, whilst he could guide them, the ultimate decision on their fate had to be down to what mankind chose to do with that wisdom. And if God chose only to speak to a select few, to make them his emissaries, then so be it. Only those worthy of his blessing would hear his word, and they would be the ones chosen to determine the fate of the world.

He pushed the duvet back and stepped naked from the bed. The en-suite beckoned, and he walked barefoot across heated tiles to the shower it contained. As the en-suite was a wet room, there was no shower door to open, and he soon had the water running at the correct temperature. Stepping under the downfall, almost moaning with pleasure at the force of the water on his back, he released his bladder, watching the water carry the yellow urine down the drain. It all went to the same place, and twenty-four hours from now, it wouldn't matter if the whole apartment was smeared with his excrement. This was his last day here. Tomorrow, he would be in France, with his feet up, a beer in his hand. The God he believed in allowed the faithful their worldly pleasures.

9.55AM, 15th September 2015, London City Airport, London

"Enjoy your trip, sir," the check in agent said.

"Why thank you. You have a good day." A smiling Sir Michael Young took his passport and boarding pass and slipped them into the inside pocket of his overcoat. Picking up his carry-on bag, he turned and followed the concierge who had greeted him when his car had dropped him off at the airport. His security detail followed him, having checked in first, and he walked in the direction of passport control, his smile slipping. The day was finally here. The day for him to leave this godforsaken country and never come back.

With his free hand, he pulled out the prepaid burner phone. It was untraceable and encrypted. The last thing he wanted was for those eavesdroppers at GCHQ to listen in on his conversation. He brought up his contacts and dialled the number under the heading 'car'.

"Hello," he said, "I enquired about possibly test driving the BMW Z4 you had on your website, but I didn't hear anything. Is it still available?"

"I'm sorry, sir, that car has already been sold. It is being picked up tomorrow. Are there any other cars you are interested in?"

"Not at the moment, thanks. I'll get back to you if I see anything, though; right now I'm leaving the country on business." Young disconnected the call, confident that even if anyone had overheard him or recorded the conversation, it would have meant nothing to them. There was no turning back now. The conversation had been all code of course. The plan was going ahead tomorrow, and he had confirmed to his handler that he was leaving the country. It was hoped that as the head of MI5, he would continue to be of use to the Western intelligence operation, worming his way into it, secreting himself away so as to be further use for his master. And to think he had once been an atheist, but that had all changed ten years ago when his wife had died so violently at the hands of the cancer that had claimed her. Young would swear he had actually seen her body waste away before his eyes as the disease ate her alive. Many people turned away from religion at the death of loved ones, but he went the other way. Because of his position, he was privy to all sorts of information, and months later his discovery of compelling evidence that the international pharmaceutical companies were suppressing natural cancer cures so as to push their expensive and toxic alternatives had pushed him over the edge. The evidence wasn't strong enough for him, a part of the system that had killed his wife, to take action. Not in a legitimate manner at least. But the man who came to him months later showed him a way he could avenge her – and all those like her – to bring the whole system down. To bring justice to the people who were torn up and destroyed by the system that was supposed to protect them.

And now he secretly worked against Queen and Country, serving a God who had become tired of humanity's frailties, of its greed and stupidity. He didn't know exactly what was planned, although he had ideas. And yes, he was scared. Scared of being discovered, scared of what was about to happen, but above all else, scared of failing his God. Because it was a vengeful God; Abraham had assured him of that.

10.28AM, 15th September 2015, Waterloo Rd, London

Croft lay in bed looking up at the ceiling. Five names. That was what he had it pinned down to, all of them way up in the chain of command. He didn't even have any proof, just a feeling. Croft had, however, learnt to trust his feelings because thinking from his head usually got him into trouble. There were only so many people who could have arranged the chaos of Hirta. Hirta, there was so much that stank about that, so much that didn't fit. The fact that nobody could tell him how the pathogen had been manufactured there under everyone's noses made him suspicious as fuck. Even with the access to government intelligence, he knew he wasn't being told everything. And when a man in his position was kept out of the loop something was deeply wrong.

Sitting up, he swung his legs out of bed and sat on the edge a moment. Pain again, worse today, probably from the alcohol last night. It lived with him constantly, a companion he could push away but never remove entirely. The doctors had told him that it would worsen with age. "Thanks for that," he had told them. "Thanks for sticking that little gem into my mind." He'd seen that before, thoughts actually becoming reality. Seen men a few days from being rotated back home become convinced they were going home in a body bag, only for that belief to almost magically manifest as reality. He was of the belief that the mind had an incredible ability to heal so long as you didn't feed it full of toxins, both nutritional and psychological. But then he wasn't a doctor, so what the fuck did he know?

7.25AM, 16th September 2015, Coffee Shop, King's Cross, London

The city of sin teemed with the unworthy, fruitless lives of the wicked. Brother Fabrice patted the precious steel box that rested by his side as the black Land Rover he was in pulled over to the side of the busy London street. His companion in the back of the car exited, closing the door behind him. Fabrice closed his eyes for a moment, relishing the task that was to come, feeling the rush of knowing that he was finally doing God's work. The Lord Our God, merciful and also relentless in his disappointment. And God was indeed disappointed. Billions didn't even believe in him. Even worse, some worshipped false gods and prophets, false idols that were tearing the world apart with hate and bigotry and greed. It was time for the Lord's cleansing hand to descend, as it had so many times before, to wipe away the stain of humanity so that the righteous and the worthy could step forth and take claim to the world that was rightfully theirs. And where better to start than in the city at the very heart of all of it? London.

He gave it several moments, and then stepping out of the back of the car, he inhaled deeply. He could smell it. He could smell the evil all around him. Mankind didn't know it, but they worshipped the Devil as he danced his way through the lives of the hapless. All around him the intoxicated sheep milled in the early morning rush hour breathing in Satan's intoxication. Yes, God had given his creation free will, but it was the job of the chosen to be God's warrior when the children abandoned him.

Brother Fabrice smiled at the thought of what was to come, of the judgement that was about to befall humanity. Standing by the car, he made eye contact with those around him. An attractive blonde smiled back at him as she walked past, mistakenly thinking he was somehow desirous of her. So foolish. As handsome as he was, she would have run wildly in terror if she had known what he had planned for this day, for this city, for this world. Fabrice smiled back, but there was no flirtation there, just deep satisfaction. Deep inside, he almost felt pity for them. Almost. For how could you pity those who worshiped false gods? Or even worse, worshipped no gods at all. Who surrendered to the illusion of a reality created by Satan himself? Surrounded by heathens and the Godless, a shiver went down his spine. Looking back briefly at the car whose engine was still idling, he stepped forward through the throng and walked into the coffee shop that was his third of the day. He knew he had to work quickly, for already God's vengeance was unleashing itself on the unsuspecting city.

Heads turned, as they often did when he walked in an establishment. Tall and well-built, his chiselled features held longing for some and envy for others. He cared not, and he let himself drown in the noise of the coffee shop as he stepped to the end of the line that led to the checkout. He ignored those around him and set his eyes on the order board up on the wall. He ignored the two middle-aged women that sat at the corner table who were eyeing him up and down, no doubt fantasising about what times they could have with "their" Adonis in the Saville Row suit. Their fantasies would shortly be forgotten in the terror that was to come, and he hoped that God would judge them harshly. He ignored the family of five, whose children, loud and uncontrolled, had obviously never felt the Lord's discipline. And he ignored the impatient man behind him, muttering under his breath at how long it was all taking to get served. Everyone he knew he could kill, here and now, with his bare hands had he wished it. But no, they were to be God's messengers. They were to be the chosen, to spread his word across this vile, festering carbuncle of a city. They would all soon meet the Lord's justice, and if they were fortunate, would feel the Lord's mercy.

Finally, it was his turn to be served, and his smile almost melted the heart of the woman behind the counter. "A tall tea please, to go."

He could tell she wished to flirt, but he had little time for that, so he paid and stepped aside to await his order. He knew that her eyes would follow him, if only briefly. Let them. There was a time when he had used his charismatic presence to engage in the pleasures of the flesh, to lie with sinners and the wretched, to be one of the fallen. He had been a player, a seducer, perhaps one of the greatest who had ever lived, and he had suffered greatly because of that. And that time was long past now; he had repented and been purged of his unholy desires. The scars on his back, on his thighs, were testament to that. There was only one focus for his desire now.

The Lord Our God

Brother Fabrice collected his order and stepped up to the milk station, where he proceeded to pour some into his tea. Good, the milk container was full. If it hadn't been, he would have asked for a refill. Placing the milk back on the side, he joined it with his cup. He then reached into his inner jacket pocket and withdrew a nitrile glove which he donned. His hand returned to the same pocket and removed a small vial. Fabrice stood and waited for the words that Brother Zachariah had already said several times today. Behind him, one of the coffee shop's customers slowly stood at his table, pushing the chair to one side. Three loud slaps to the table with the palm of his hand resonated across the room. Everyone turned their attention as his voice boomed out the message.

"Children of the Lord, the Day of Judgment is at hand. The signs are there for you to see, but you are blinded by your accursed greed and your fornication. You worship the gold in your pocket when you should be worshipping the word of the Lord Our God."

Fabrice nodded his approval of the words and glanced quickly around him to confirm he was unobserved. Unscrewing the lid to the semi-skimmed milk, he poured in half the contents of the vial, doing the same for the skimmed milk. With the lids closed, he then wrapped the now empty container in his glove as he removed it. The glove went into the bin.

"I see the evil in your hearts, and I see the Devil in your eyes," Zachariah shouted.

"Shut up and sit down, you bloody nutter," responded a man standing in line. Zachariah turned to him and pointed an old, wrinkled finger at him.

"You see, you see how you deny the truth of the Lord Our God. The mark of the beast is all over your face, my brother. Your sins will see you burn in the pit of hell for all eternity." The man rolled his eyes at Zachariah's words and flipped him his middle finger. Zachariah just smiled and turned his attention back to his audience.

"I have seen the signs; I have seen the fourth seal broken. And when the Lamb broke the fourth seal, I heard the voice of the fourth living creature saying, 'Come and see.'" Zachariah carried on talking as Fabrice walked past him, tea forgotten where he had left it, seemingly ignoring the man in his religious frenzy. Fabrice looked back once at the room he was leaving, and then pushed the door and exited onto the street. Exhilaration filled his heart.

"And I looked, and behold, an ashen horse; and he who sat on it had the name Death; and Hades followed with him. Authority was given to them over a fourth of the earth, to kill with sword and with famine and with pestilence and by the wild beasts of the earth." Zachariah looked at the snickering faces of those around him and felt that he could almost weep. He had tried. Again, he had been the messenger of God's word, and they had rejected him. Seeing this, he turned and walked towards the door. As his hand grasped the door handle, he half turned his body and looked at those around him. If only some had shown their piety to him, then they could have been saved. But none did, none before him listened to the words or heard the message within them.

"God's vengeance is upon you all. By nightfall, you will all be dead." With that, he left to the sound of disbelief and mockery.

Outside, Fabrice held open the rear door of the same Land Rover that had brought him here. Guiding Zachariah into the car, Fabrice followed his brethren. They both relaxed back into the plush leather seats, and Fabrice told the driver to go onto the next and last target. There was a brief pause as the car waited for a black cab to pass, and then the car moved carefully and pulled out into the orderly traffic.

"I don't think they appreciated the truth of our Lord," said Zachariah, looking out the window as a red London bus passed them in the opposite direction, its side adorned with an advert displaying flesh and perversion. As the bus passed, Fabrice noticed the satanic eyesore that was the country's biggest library, and he smiled at the knowledge that nothing would ever be read from its inhuman interior again. Fabrice turned back to look at his companion.

"Fear not, Brother, they will witness his wrath soon enough. His fire is already raining down upon them; they just do not have the eyes or the will to see," said Fabrice. He picked up the small metal box and opened it. Inside were three identical vials of clear liquid like the one discarded in the coffee shop, held securely in black foam. Fabrice placed his index finger in one of the two holes that once held further vials, feeling the texture of the foam. Withdrawing his finger, he pulled out another vial and placed it in his inner suit pocket. In the lid of the box was a laminated card with five addresses written down.

Vial 1 - Canary Wharf
Vial 2 - King's Cross
Vial 3 - Paddington
Vial 4 - Waterloo
Vial 5 - Clapham Junction

Fabrice knew there were five other such cars performing the same mission in Manchester, Leeds, Birmingham, Nottingham and Glasgow. Each with five targets, each with five vials, each vital to God's work.

"It is a shame that the Grand Cleric could not cultivate more of God's fury. There are so many sinners in the world," said Zachariah.

"Do not fear, my brother. Our job is almost done. What we have delivered will be more than sufficient to send a message to the world. Within the hour, the first infections will be taking hold. And after that, the subsequent infections will take mere minutes. Within hours, this city will be a charred Sodom. Within days, the whole country will be dead. The reaping has begun," Fabrice said, placing the box back on the seat next to him.

"In his name," said Zachariah
"In his name," said the man driving the car.
"In his name," said Fabrice.

8.36AM, 16th September 2015, Westminster, London

Sergeant Jeremy Smith of the Diplomatic Protection Group (known as SO6) was late due to the bloody tube again. It was all very well working in London, but the rental cost meant he had to live out in the sticks, and that meant commuting every day by the less than reliable London Underground. Still, it wouldn't matter if he was a few minutes late. That was the name of the game with London these days. He didn't have the luxury of staying in a Section House; that wouldn't go down too well with the wife and two kids after all. They expected him back every day, even if it was late into the night. Those who knew him were of the opinion he considered himself a father first and a police officer second, despite the importance of his job. The only time forty-five year olds tended to stay in section houses was when divorce hit, which had happened to quite a few of his fellow coppers over the years. But not to Smith. His wife had gone into the marriage with her eyes wide open. She had known from the start what being married to a policeman entailed and never complained because she also knew that he would be there for her when she needed him. Or at least that was what she believed. If she truly knew the man she had married, if she knew the darkness that had wormed its way into his soul of late, she probably would have been clamouring for divorce. But he hid the darkness well, those around him oblivious to the danger he now represented.

Having exited the chaotic and bustling Westminster tube station, he walked up Whitehall through the rush hour throng of tourists, Londoners and Ministerial staff. The road was clogged with the usual traffic, and he found it easy to cross the road. Arriving at Downing Street, he gave an embarrassed shrug to the subordinates on duty at the Downing Street gate.

"Late again, Sarge?" one of the men said jokingly.

"Blame Transport for London. The sooner they sack the lot of them and replace everything with robots, the better I will be." The subordinate gave a respectful laugh. Smith handed over his ID and allowed it to be scanned whilst the gate computer matched it to the biometrics he was displaying to several cameras. The turnstile light turned green, allowing him access to one of the most secure locations in England. The first time he had passed through that gate, he felt a sense of honour and pride that somebody had trusted him enough to give him that level of responsibility. Now, it was no different than walking into Tesco's. He went through a side door, saying hello to various staff members, and made his way into the locker room where he changed into his uniform and then donned his ballistic vest. Popping into the canteen, he passed a female PC who winked at him, and he found his mug filled with a very welcome brew of builder's tea. That's what you needed to survive in this city, a regular well-made cup of tea.

"Bless your heart, love." Smith took a sip, deciding it needed a bit to cool down first. Taking his mug with him, he went to the operations room, where he found his inspector looking distracted and harassed, but generally, that's how he always looked.

"Cutting that a bit fine, aren't you, Sergeant?"

"Sorry, sir, won't happen again."

"That's what you said the last time," Smith's superior said with a wry smile. The inspector turned to a large array of television monitors all displaying CCTV images of the areas around Downing Street. "Could be a busy day today. We have word from MI5, lots of chatter out there. We have a very plausible threat, so I want the barricades out to keep the public away from the gate. I'm told a Battalion of the Grenadiers is on standby. We may also be seeing mechanised troops deployed."

"Is it that bad?"

"MI5 seem to think so, which means the PM seems to think so. So that means I think so. I've doubled the sniper detail. Let's see if we can go a day without having to use them, shall we?"

"Yes, sir." Smith paused to view the various scenes displayed on the monitors, and then left. He made his way to the armoury where he was issued with his side arm and semi-automatic rifle. As a specialist firearms officer, he had intense training in the use of both and was renowned for being one of the best shots on the force. Not as good as the snipers positioned on the rooftops surrounding Parliament, but good enough. A veteran on the force, he had never fired his gun in the field. That was all about to change in a few hours' time. By the end of the day, he would have fired off a full magazine.

8.38AM, 16th September 2015, Waterloo Rd, London

Croft locked the door to his terraced house and walked down the front steps into the rush hour throng. His was probably the only terraced on the entire street that hadn't been split up into flats, and that's only because the government owned it. The exterior needed a lick of paint, but Croft didn't care – it was all part of the cover. The dilapidated-looking blue door with its pick-proof lock was in fact steel reinforced, and would have taken either an acetylene torch or a significant amount of C4 to get through. The walls of the terraced themselves had been also reinforced and fireproofed. The peeling paint on the window frames hid the truth behind the glass' ballistic resistant nature, the same as that in all government secure facilities. Nobody was getting in who shouldn't be, which was, after all, kind of the idea. It was a miniature fortress, one of many owned by MI5 across the city. And it was Croft's home for as long as he was needed, mainly because it was the closest thing available to Whitehall.

London seemed busier than usual, and he had to pause before joining the pavement crowd. There really were too many people in this city, especially so close to the heart of government. Fortunately, his plans for the day could be done solely on foot, and he made his way up Waterloo Road, the cool, polluted morning air heavy in his lungs.

He noticed the limo with the blacked-out windows as it went past him, but thought little of it, and he carried on his way somewhat amused that he was progressing faster than most of the traffic heading in his direction. Cars were an expensive and inefficient way to travel around London, which is why he didn't bother with one of his own. If he needed to go somewhere, the transport would either be provided for him, or the city's transport network was more than adequate for the task. A car would be nothing more than a burden.

So no, there was no need for a government car for this journey, not with Whitehall twenty minutes by foot, and besides, he wanted a drink from his favourite coffee shop, which slowly came into view. He avoided the corporate chains, preferring instead to frequent an establishment where he was now known and greeted. He had always liked to spend his money with the small business, where the heart and soul of the owner was often on display. He despised the uniform, polished corporate machines who spent millions on the facilities whilst forgetting the importance of passion, something only motivated and empowered staff could deliver.

He walked in, letting two severely overweight Americans exit first. Christ, they were big, and it offended Croft that someone could do that to their body. He just didn't understand it, didn't understand how a person could hate themselves so much. Croft shook his head, more through pity than anything, and briefly watched as they painfully walked away from him, their limbs and joints obviously struggling under the unnatural weight.

With the door now clear, he added himself onto the back of the queue, exchanging a wave and a smile with the Italian owner who was looking harassed, but at the same time satisfied by the extent of the morning's custom. The corporate chain coffee shop that Fabrice had left the Lord's Fury in was twenty metres down the road.

9.05AM, 16th September 2015, HSBC Building, Canary Wharf, London

He really didn't need this, not today of all days. John really didn't feel well, hadn't for the last ten minutes, and that wasn't like him. It wasn't like him at all. He was renowned for having the constitution of an ox. But that wasn't the case now, and whilst he often felt that people tended to exaggerate their symptoms when they were ill, John wasn't embellishing the facts when he said his guts truly were on fire. He picked up a napkin and dabbed at his brow, which was decorated in sweat. Nausea grew inside him, and he reached over and poured himself a glass of water with what he noticed was a trembling hand. Whatever this was, it was hitting him like a goddamn tsunami. Please, let me just keep it together so I can get through this bloody meeting.

"The projected profit for the next quarter is up due to higher mortgage acquisitions ..." John had stopped listening to the presentation; they were just words now, their meaning pointless compared to what was happening within his body. He took a sip on the water from the table in front of him and almost gagged. Somebody turned to look at him, and he heard a voice speak to him, but it sounded muffled.

"John, are you alright?"

"I just feel ... oh God." Panic suddenly overcame him as his body revealed to him a new level of urgency. All his adult life, he had been meticulous about the image he presented to the world around him, fearing ridicule and scorn above all other things. That was why he had worked tirelessly and methodically to rise up the hierarchy of his chosen profession, and his soul had celebrated when he had been headhunted not once, but twice in his career. Those fears were forgotten now. John hurled himself to his feet, the dozen other people in the room suddenly staring at him in disbelief as he rushed from the room, not even able to express an excuse. He had intended to make a quiet "be back in a moment" exit, but a sudden uncontrolled need to purge was now upon him, and this display of chaos was far preferable to throwing up all over the conference table. Lurching almost drunkenly from the room, he hit and rebounded off the corridor wall. The toilets were only ten metres away down the corridor, but he didn't even get half the distance before his stomach finally exploded, and he fell to his knees, vomit pouring from his mouth and nostrils. John almost blacked out, a thick dampness spreading across his body. And then he saw the blood, and vomited again.

"Somebody call an ambulance," he half heard someone shout. John collapsed fully to the floor, his face smearing itself in his own excretion, his mind encased with pain, pain that was spreading throughout his whole body. A pitiful whimper escaped him. He felt his bladder give way, and then he soiled himself, bringing forth a godawful stench that contaminated the air around him. A thought briefly popped into his head that he would never be able to work here again, and then the violent convulsions started. He vaguely felt arms restraining him, and he felt his forehead impact on the carpeted floor several times.

If there had been an analyses of the outbreak, John Gibbons would have been given the grand title of patient zero, the very first patient to display the disease that was about to ravage an entire country and infect over fifty million people. But there would never be such an investigation, because there would not be anyone left on the ground to investigate.

He felt hands grab him, turning him onto his side, putting him into the recovery position. He vomited again, destroying someone's expensive suede shoes. Trying to mumble an apology, he belched loudly, and that's when the real pain hit. It blocked out everything. He stopped being a conscious human being and was merely a receptacle for agony. Someone had wrapped his brain in a blanket of fire and began poking it with red hot kebab skewers. He had never experienced anything like it.

John screamed, somebody else screamed. And then as quickly as it came, the pain went. His body shook one final time and was then still, a strange warmth starting to spread from his fingertips upwards. "Is he still breathing?" someone asked far away. "Has someone phoned an ambulance?" John opened his eyes and looked around him, a red tint masking his vision. "My God, look at his eyes," he heard someone gasp, but the words were strange, almost like a foreign language. He tried to sit himself up, but he was too shaky at first. A pair of hands helped him, and he propped himself up against the wall, sitting in his own filth, dripping with his own filth. For some reason, he didn't care. John's head twitched, and a new sound came to his ears. A rhythmic sound, mesmerising, seductive. His mind, blurry and confused, focused in on that noise.

"John, are you okay?" Was that his boss?

"Hung …" John answered in a whisper

"What was that, John?" In his blurred vision, he saw a head come close, trying to hear what he had to say. But John had nothing really to say; he only had one thing to do.

"Hungry … so hungry." He needed to eat. There was no resisting it, no fighting it. It was all consuming. There was no John Gibbons anymore; there was just the craving, the hunger. The all-engulfing, all-encompassing, insatiable hunger. It was now all he was, and all he would ever be. His possessions, his wife, his children, his bank accounts and his stock portfolio were all forgotten. His hopes, his desires, and his dreams were now reduced to one thing.

"Help, I need some help over here," said a voice at the other end of the hall, and then he heard the voice in his mind, a voice that spoke to him not so much in words, but in desires. The owner of that voice was hungry too. And angry. John turned his head to the person close to him, and with movement so swift he didn't think it was possible, he grabbed the man's head and sunk his teeth deep into the guy's neck. He bit down, ignoring the man's wails and his flailing fists.

I must feed, the voice in his head said. And then it was joined by another voice, and then another. *We must feed. We must feed, and we must spread. Yes*, John thought, *yes, we must*, as he ripped flesh away with his teeth. He had bitten down so hard that two of his porcelain veneers had fractured. Arterial spray from a ruptured carotid hit a horrified secretary in the face, and she screamed as John turned his face towards her. And thus the infection began, all played to the rhythm of the beat of terrified human hearts. Within five minutes, the being that had once answered to the name John Gibbons had infected fourteen people. He would go on to infect over a hundred before the day was out.

9.07AM, 16th September 2015, 999 Call Centre, London

"999, which emergency service do you require?"

"Ambulance, my boss is really sick."

"Please hold, I'm redirecting you."

"London Ambulance Service, what is your emergency?" Helen preferred the morning shift. There were fewer drunks on the line, and thus fewer idiots to deal with. Plus, her husband could drop the kids off at school, and she could pick them up in the afternoon and spend some quality time with them. Her kids were important to her, and if the ability to spend time with them had been removed, she would have quit the job in an instant. But she was fortunate that she had a flexible employer, and that the twenty-four-hour nature of the day meant that there were shifts to choose from.

Mornings were usually a quiet affair, but that was certainly not to be the case today. This was the busiest she had ever seen the call centre. "My boss just collapsed in the corridor....oh my God, there's vomit everywhere." The caller sounded distressed, and it was difficult to hear him due to the background noise.

"Where are you calling from?" Helen asked

"I'm on the fifth floor of the Canary Wharf HSBC building."

"Okay, I'll need you to stay on the line whilst I dispatch paramedics. Do you know if your boss is still breathing?"

"I think so. We were just talking and he collapsed. He said he wasn't feeling well." The sound on the phone became muffled, and Helen could tell the caller was talking to somebody else. Somebody screamed. "He's started fitting; what do I do?"

"Paramedics are on the way. Try and stop him from hurting himself –"

"He's stopped," the caller interrupted.

"What's your boss' name?" Helen asked

"Trevor Brooke … oh wait, he's sitting up." More indistinct chatter … then someone screamed. The line went dead. Helen looked around her and saw the room had suddenly become pandemonium.

9.12AM, 16th September 2015, Waterloo Rd, London

Croft enjoyed people watching. Sat outside the coffee shop, he finished the rest of his drink and folded up the newspaper that he had taken from inside, but which he hadn't really read. An attractive blonde walked past and gave him a brief IOI, as she sipped on her logo coffee. An Indicator of Interest, as the now deceased Corporal Hillier used to call it. A self-proclaimed "player", Croft had to admit he had never actually seen the man talk to a woman who wasn't giving him orders. Hillier had been well known as a complete bull-shitter, but nobody ever held it against him. In fact, Hillier had seemed to revel in his reputation. Croft still missed the man, but he drowned the thought out with the view of the blonde's rear end as her shapely figured made its way down the street. That was the problem with spending almost half his adult life in a war zone. He'd spent most of his time surrounded by hairy, uncouth men.

But because of that, and because they fought together, they formed bonds of friendship that could never be matched by civilians. Even though he had been an officer, the men under him were his responsibility, his family, and even now it wrenched at him to know some of them were no longer alive. He in turn had proved his worth to his men, and they treated him with a level of respect that was unusual in Special Forces. Croft had not been a "Rupert" to them; he had been seen as a competent officer, who could out run, out drink and out shoot most of the men under him. He had earned the respect that others demanded just because they held rank. He smiled at the memories, one in particular coming to mind. 2003 on the road to Baghdad. He and his SBS troop had been ahead of a convoy of American grunts, most of them in open top trucks. It was hot, and sat in the military Land Rover, Croft had been startled by an explosion that erupted several meters to the right of him, peppering his armoured vehicle with shrapnel.

"Contact, do we have contact?" Croft had shouted into his radio. Several minutes of chaos ensued as troops dismounted to protect the column from attack. Only there hadn't been an attack. One of the American soldiers had unwittingly fired his M203 grenade launcher, the projectile rocketing into the air at an angle, only to land and almost hit Croft's vehicle. An unsecured weapon in the hands of a tired private on a bumpy road was not a great combination. When the truth of this had come out over the coms, Hillier had gone ballistic.

"Fucking Yanks trying to kill us again," he said referring to a previous incident where American artillery had landed dangerously close to their forward observation post. He had grabbed his sidearm out of its holster and was halfway out of the Land Rover before Croft grabbed him. Hillier had looked back, saw the look in Croft's eyes, and had sat back down. Croft had been the one to go over to the Americans. Walking casually over to the American commanding officer, he withdrew a cigar from his top pocket and lit it with his lighter. "Colonel, I want the bloody idiot who failed to control his weapon under arrest."

"I'm not sure I like your tone, Captain," the colonel had stated, puffing his chest out. The Americans knew they were with British Special Forces, and knew the reputation the men had, but still the colonel's ego was being attacked. "I will deal with him when we get to camp."

"Colonel, you don't understand. He almost killed me, and more importantly, he almost killed my men. And my tone should be the least of your concerns." Croft took a deep inhale and blew it into the desert wind that whipped at his uniform, fluttering the stained and tattered British flag that flew from the back of his Land Rover. "There are ten men over there," Hillier cocked the hand with the cigar behind him, "who are just as pissed off about that as I am. In fact, probably more so. And if they don't see that incompetent cunt in cuffs within the next minute, they will deal with the matter in THEIR way." Croft put the cigar back in his mouth and put his hands on his hips. He waited for the colonel's reaction. Croft, fortunately, got his way.

Croft stood up and stepped inside to return the newspaper to the wall rack in the cafe. Waving goodbye to the proprietor who reciprocated animatedly, he stepped back out and stood to the side of the door, watching the people go by. What would most of them make of him if they knew the things he had seen, the things he had done? What would the people do if they knew there were plots within plots uncovered every day to reduce this city, this nation, to a charred, radioactive remnant? That there were schemes and agents who would think nothing of releasing Sarin gas in the London Underground, or sprinkling Ricin onto the Queen's cornflakes. This is what the government had to deal with every day, all the while keeping the frail sensibilities of an easily offended and easily outraged population in check. The populace – the Proles as George Orwell had so rightly called them – just couldn't be trusted with the decisions that really mattered. Croft sometimes felt like a tiger walking amongst lemmings. When the shit really hit the fan, most of the people around him would be dead within a week. They would beg him to help save their lives, but they would also be the first in line to see him hang.

He looked at his watch and sighed. Okay, another meeting to get through. And then lunch with Captain Savage. He couldn't believe he'd asked her out. Noticing the lack of wedding ring after the briefing, he'd had a sudden impulse that he just hadn't wanted to resist, despite how nervous he felt. He could face armed insurgents and issue orders that could result in countless deaths, and yet asking a beautiful woman out to lunch made him feel almost nauseous. Surprise was actually his genuine response when she said, "Yes, I'd love to go to lunch." Croft hadn't been out with a woman since his wife had divorced him six months before the helicopter crash that had temporarily wrecked his life. Mostly because he was either wrapped up in a cloak of despair, or else living the life that wasn't really conducive to dating a civilian. But of course, Savage wasn't a civilian, and asking her out had just seemed right. Croft surprised himself by actually finding himself looking forward to something. For years, he had simply been going through the motions, almost machine-like, and now here he was excited about going on a date.

Croft made his way towards York Road and Westminster Bridge. He wasn't witness to the free newspaper vendor behind him collapsing on the street, his armful of newspapers scattering to the ground. He wasn't witness to the blonde he had found so attractive staggering in the street and falling to her knees. He left before all that.

9.21AM, 16th September 2015, St Pancras Train Station, London

Jesus, he had almost missed his train. Holding the precious laptop case to the side of his body with his right hand, Carl walked quickly to the departure area, finishing what was left of the day's second cup of coffee. He'd spent the last hour and a half in the coffee shop with his business partner going over the final battle plan for his business meeting up North. Carl had even been there to witness some religious nutter make a fool of himself. There were some strange people in London, there really were.

He paused briefly to leave the empty paper cup on a table due to there not being any bins, and looked up at the train time's display. The departure board showed he had minutes to spare, and he weaved his way through the people awaiting other trains and slipped his ticket through the gate. He hated travelling, always had. It was a noisy, dirty business, and every time he ventured up North, he seemed to catch some sort of disease. Even thinking this, he realised his throat was starting to itch. Goddamnit, next time Jeremy could go and make the bloody presentation.

Carl bundled himself onto the train and found his designated seat in First Class. At least now he could relax and be by himself, even if just for an hour or so. It was these precious moments that made life worth living, he thought. He would sit down, switch off his phone, and hopefully finish the book he had been "reading" for the last month. Taking the book from his case, he dropped it on the seat next to the one that displayed his reservation. Carl always preferred an aisle seat; he didn't like being hemmed in, didn't like to feel contained. Placing the case on the overhead shelf, he sat, and as he did so, his guts suddenly did a cartwheel. He almost fell into his seat so surprised was he by the pain.

"Oh great," he said to himself, believing this was most likely the first signs of food poisoning. Oh, that was just what he needed.

"Good morning, ladies and gentlemen, we would like to welcome you on board this nine twenty-five Midlands Mainline train to Leeds. Calling at Derby, Sheffield and arriving in Leeds at eleven forty-two." The voice over the tannoy continued with the mandatory messages to the passengers who were quickly filling up the compartment. Carl felt pain again and wondered how long it would be before he would be forced to run to the toilet. Sweat began to break out on his face, and he reached up and delved back into his case, taking out a half-filled bottle of water. With that in hand, he sat, wincing as another spasm shot through his intestines.

Drinking the water made him feel a little better, and the pain began to subside. Taking deep breaths, he closed his eyes just as the train began to pull out of the station. His symptoms began to improve, and he sighed with relief. That was until three minutes later, when he released a godawful fart that stank like the arse of a hellhound. There were muttered complaints from his fellow passengers, and some looked at him in disgust. Carl's stomach tied itself in a knot, and he cried out in agony. He farted again, even louder.

"I'm sorr …" he tried to say, but more gas escaped, only this time the horror of him soiling himself occurred. "Oh no, oh God," Carl said, and he tried to stand, only to fall into the aisle, as his legs failed him. He vomited, and people moved away from him with mutterings of dismay and disgust.

"Someone had a bad night," he thought he heard someone say, and then the fire started in his head. But over all that, deep within his mind, he thought he heard a voice asking him….he couldn't quite hear it. What was it saying?

"Someone better go and get the conductor," a far-off voice said.

Feed with us. Carl sat up and looked to the nearest person. He was drenched with sweat.

Will you feed with us? Will you spread with us? The voice, inside him, became part of him.

Carl looked around, no longer looking through the eyes of human consciousnesses. All he felt was pain and a burning hunger, a ravaging craving that ripped his innards out and demanded satiating. And he knew, just knew that the cure for the pain was to surrender to the hunger.

Will you feed with us? the voice from within said, voices now, dozens of them, stronger, louder, more demanding.

Carl blinked, confusion draining from his mind. And then he said the last words his mouth would ever utter. "Oh yes, yes I will feed."

9.25AM 16th September 2015, Pentonville Rd, King's Cross, London

The end of the world would, it seemed, be televised. Despite the plethora of 24-hour news channels and internet bloggers, it was not the conventional media that first broke the story of the end. The first recorded case of the infection hit YouTube at 9.47AM London time. The video, taken outside the second coffee house visited by Brother Fabrice, showed utter mayhem. Taken from the perspective of a cyclist's head camera, the jerky, often out-of-focus video showed about a dozen people fighting. The video showed an average London rush hour street as the cyclist weaved in and out of the gridlocked cars. He turned a corner, and the mini riot came instantly into view. The cyclist (Jez453Ihatecars as his 240 YouTube subscribers knew him) positioned himself in the centre of the road to get past the bedlam. As he passed, there was the sound of glass breaking, and his head panned round to see someone landing on the pavement, having been apparently thrown through the front window of the coffee shop. A teenage girl jumped through the window and onto the man sprawled on the floor, tearing into him with her fingers and teeth. The two wrestled on the ground, the teenager winning the battle.

"Holy fuck!" the cyclist's voice exclaimed over the general traffic noise and the screams. He stopped and the camera centred on two men on the floor. The one on top was biting down and ripped an ear from the side of his victim's head, blood smearing his face. His eyes were seen to light up at the morsel in his mouth, and he thrashed his head from side to side, blood flying off. Then he started to chew whilst the violated beneath him wailed in agony. The cannibal's eyes locked onto the camera, seeming to break the fourth wall, and then the assailant looked back down at the meat suit he was astride and began punching the man beneath him relentlessly.

"Fuck me." Again the cyclist, who obviously decided caution was the ruler of the day, cycled off, cutting through a red light. In the distance, a police siren could be heard, and the video ended with his panicked breath as he cycled fast to get away from a brief glimpse of chaos. The time stamp on the video said 9.25AM. In days, it would become one of the most viewed videos in the history of YouTube, reaching into the billions. Seeded relentlessly, it would be the starting point for the end of over fifty million lives.

9.28AM 16th September 2015, Claremont Primary School, near King's Cross, London

Wendy looked up from her drawing as Miss Scott rose from her desk and left the classroom. Wendy liked Miss Scott; she was funny and made her laugh. She looked at the door a moment longer, and then looked down at her picture and picked up a blue crayon. Unicorns should be blue—everyone knew that—and she began to colour it in, her tongue stuck out from the corner of her mouth. Miss Baker said something, but Wendy didn't hear it because Miss Baker was talking to Gavin. Wendy didn't like Gavin. He picked on her and pulled her hair when Miss Scott wasn't looking. She didn't really like Miss Baker either because she smelt funny and sometimes got angry when Miss Scott wasn't around. Miss Scott never got angry, so it was a good thing Miss Baker was only the teacher's helper. Wendy realised there was something missing from her picture, and she picked up the yellow crayon to add some flowers. You couldn't have unicorns without flowers, everyone knew that.

Rachel Scott had started to feel unwell within the first half hour of class. She tried to ignore it, but very quickly she realised that that just wasn't going to cut it, and she had to excuse herself. Fortunately, the female toilets were just across the hall from her classroom, and she rushed in just in time. Throwing herself into a cubicle, the morning's breakfast erupted into the toilet bowl, some even coming out of her nose. She threw up again, and almost blacked out with the force of it. She tried to reach up to flush the cistern, but the strength just wasn't there. She vomited a third time, a sharp pain erupting in her neck as if something had ripped open, and then everything went black.

She must have passed out, she realised. Lying on the floor, she picked her head up off the tiles and noticed the smell. Her trousers were damp, and her hair and face felt sticky. Sitting up, she propped her back up against the cubicle wall, wincing as someone drove a nail between her eyes. At least that was what she imagined it felt like. The nail was hot, and it was being pounded in by a sledgehammer wielded by a professional weightlifter who had that very day overdosed on steroids. The pain hit again, and this time, she cried out. Rachel panicked, and she tried to stand, but the invisible nails suddenly embedded themselves in her stomach, and she collapsed back to the floor. She'd never felt pain like it, and there was something else there, forming in the back of her thoughts. Her vision blurred, and a shiver ran through her entire body. The thing in her mind grew, and she began to drool.

The door opened, and Wendy looked up as Miss Scott walked in. Oh no, she looked terrible. Her hair was all over the place, and her blouse was all stained. And she smelt, she smelt worse than Miss Baker.

"Rachel, my God what happened?" Wendy heard Miss Baker ask. Miss Scott kind of gurgled and took another step into the room, the door closing behind her. Miss Scott said something that nobody could hear. All thirty children were looking at her now, their classwork no longer of interest. Wendy heard someone crying and looked behind her to see Claire in tears. Claire was always in tears. That was when everyone but Wendy jumped. Wendy looked back, and she saw something she had never seen before. Miss Scott was fighting with Miss Baker. Why were they fighting? And why was Miss Scott biting her? Adults didn't bite each other.

"We feed!" shouted Miss Scott, and bit into Miss Baker's neck this time. All the children screamed, and some jumped from their chairs and ran to the back of the class. *Don't hurt her, Miss Scott*, Wendy said in her head. *Please, look I've drawn you a nice unicorn.* That was when

Miss Scott pushed Miss Baker to the floor and turned to look Wendy right in the eyes.

"WE SPREAD!" Miss Scott shouted, and by the time the screams brought other teachers to the classroom, half the children had already been infected. Within fifteen minutes, fifteen turned to over a hundred.

9.31AM, 16th September 2015, Kings Cross Train Station, London

The last thing he needed on a Wednesday morning was to have to deal with a fucking riot. I mean, who rioted at nine o'clock in the bloody morning for Christ's sake? Any self-respecting scrote would still be in bed at this hour. Pulling up outside the front of King's Cross Station, Police Constable Fred Aycoth watched the panicked masses as they ran away from what to him looked like a mass brawl.

"Can you believe this shit?" Aycoth said to the man sharing his car. He put on the hand brake and spoke into his radio. "EO47 to control, looks like we'll need back-up here. Definitely looks like this is getting out of hand."

"Wilco EO47. Additional units have already been dispatched to your location. Be advised, SO19 units are already on scene." Over the police radio, a call went out to his fellow officers. Aycoth removed his seatbelt and opened the car door. A hand grabbed his shoulder.

"I don't like this, Fred. This doesn't look right."

"We don't get paid to like it, mate. Besides, you heard her, SO19 are here. Who's going to try and fuck with someone wielding a fucking great machine gun?" The hand on his shoulder retreated. Aycoth stepped out of the car, placing his cap over his neatly cropped ginger hair, then removing his baton from his utility belt. He could see there were people fighting on the Pentonville Road. Looking around, he saw two armed officers, what control had called SO19, standing outside the main entrance to King's Cross. The two new arrivals made their way over to them, knowing there was safety in numbers. A woman ran past them, bleeding from her left ear, part of which was missing. Aycoth tried to stop her, but she dodged him in what was obviously total terror. In the distance, more sirens could be heard as reinforcements arrived. They walked quickly over to the armed officers, both of whom were known to Aycoth.

"Morning, lads. What kicked this all off then?"

"Fucked if I know, Fred. But if this carries on, we'll have to close down the station. Riot police are already en route."

"The mayor's not going to like that," said the other armed officer. Aycoth shook his head and was about to say something when his attention was drawn to a man stumbling towards them. He had no physical injuries, but his skin was deathly pale, and he obviously had difficulty keeping himself upright. An ambulance pulled up behind Aycoth's police car

"Officers, I need …" The guy coughed violently and fell to his knee.

"Sir, are you alright?" Aycoth's partner asked, moving to help the man. *Bloody stupid question*, thought Aycoth. *Did the guy look alright?* He didn't really get on with the man he was assigned with this morning if he was honest, but you went where they put you.

"I don't feel …" The man heaved, and Aycoth stepped back. *I'm not having someone vomit on me twice in one week*, he thought. And then the man started to retch, and within seconds, he projectile vomited all over the legs of Aycoth's three fellow officers. Aycoth stood there surprisingly unscathed.

"For fucks sake," someone said as the ill man collapsed in front of them. His body began to twitch, going into full spasm. Aycoth's partner tried to hold him steady, not knowing the ultimate fate that now awaited him due to his humanitarian act.

9.32AM, 16th September 2015, Paddington Train Station, London

The Hilton staff member serving drinks in the dining area of the Hilton Hotel had been a tad irked at the nine Japanese tourists who had sat down only to be joined by a tenth a moment later. He was annoyed because the tenth was carrying carry out cups from the local corporate chain "coffee" house. Luke considered making an issue of it, but he had seen them coming and going from the lifts, and as they were undoubtedly paying a small fortune to stay here, he let it go and concentrated on the myriad of customers vying for his attention: the paying customers, the ones that would give him his much-needed tips. The Japanese tourists had followed exactly the same routine for two days in a row. They would arrive early, sit and drink coffee not purchased from the hotel, and talk about whatever Japanese tourists in London talked about. He seriously suspected none of them even spoke any English

That had been over an hour ago, and they were still chattering away when one of them cried out. Luke glanced over annoyingly and turned back to the customer who was trying to order a gin and tonic. Luke smiled outwardly and asked if there was anything else the woman wanted. Inside, he was amazed that someone could even consider drinking alcohol at this hour in the morning. But it wasn't his place to judge – that was the lesson taught to him by the mentor assigned to him when he had first gotten work in the hotel. "It doesn't matter what you see, or what you hear. Just smile and act like it's an everyday occurrence. People are entitled to their quirks, and they are entitled to their privacy – remember that."

He was about to walk over to the bar to collect the lady's order when there was another cry of pain, and one of the members of the Japanese party fell forward off the sofa she was sitting on. She began to writhe on the floor, legs knocking against the glass table at her side. Luke turned, watching the spectacle for a second, only to see another of the Japanese lunge backwards in a cry of pain. There were panicked mutterings from the other Japanese tourists, and Luke did what he was trained to do. Quickly moving to the bar, he stepped behind it and picked up the walkie-talkie.

"Code 99 in the lounge area, code 99 in the lounge area." It was eerie to hear his voice booming out from the surroundings, and within seconds other, more senior staff members arrived on the scene. Code 99, possible medical emergency. They trained regularly for this eventuality, as tourists had a tendency to be an unwell bunch, suffering from a host of afflictions that could leave them near death's door at any minute. Either that, or they tended to be very drunk. Especially with a clientele that seemed to feel comfortable drinking gin and tonics for breakfast. As the three extra staff members arrived, another of the Japanese tourists cried out in pain. Then the first – the one still lying on the floor – vomited all over the carpet. Luke closed his eyes and shook his head in frustration. *I'm likely going to have to clean that shit up*, he thought to himself.

The most senior staff member reached into a pack on his belt and withdrew a set of Nitrile gloves. Donning them, he bent down to the stricken woman, who was now shaking violently. He was about to try and hold her steady, when the nearest Japanese still seated vomited all over him. Luke almost laughed, but the scene quickly descended into chaos as one by one the tourists all began to convulse and expel whatever bodily fluids their orifices held. "Jesus Christ," the Samaritan cried as he tried to wipe blood-stained vomit out of his hair and off his face. He stood up and made to step back only for a hand to shoot out and grab him by the ankle. Luke saw him stagger for a second and then fall, smashing the back of his skull open against the edge of a glass table. Someone screamed. One of the Japanese laughed.

The woman on the floor slowly stood and looked at her fellow travellers. Only three of them now seemed unaffected by the sickness that was spreading through their ranks, and she rushed to them, sniffing their odour deeply, pawing their faces as they cowered at the slime that was dribbling from her mouth and nostrils. She examined them one by one, then turned to the fallen hotel staff member, who was moaning and trying to right himself. Luke heard her shout something in Japanese and then she pounced, landing on him, biting straight into his neck.

Luke panicked. He wasn't trained for this, and he certainly wasn't paid enough for this. He rushed from behind the bar towards the back entrance to the lounge, which also led to the toilets. Backpedalling, he didn't see the huge bulk of a man stagger out from the gents, and Luke ploughed right into him. Both of them fell to the lushly carpeted floor, Luke landing face down. Spread-eagled on his front, Luke tried to get up, but he felt hands on him, then a weight on his back holding him to the ground. Someone crawled up his back, and Luke felt fingers grabbing onto his hair. Then there was warmth on his ear as someone exhaled. And then a voice came.

"*We feed, we spread*," said the voice. The same words were shouted from another part of the hotel, and then something bit into him. As he felt his ear being ripped from his body, Luke put all his effort into escape. Just as he thought pain and his assailant would have him, the weight lifted, and Luke was able to scramble forwards, escaping the clutches of the madman. He turned onto his back and used his hands and his legs to scoot away from the giant who now stood looking at him. Luke found his progress stopped by a wall, and he clutched the side of his damaged face, the pain flowing through his body. The attacker suddenly moved towards him with inhuman speed and spat into Luke's face, half-chewed ear landing in his lap.

"*We feed, we spread*," the man said, and with that, he was away with an agility a man of his bulk should not have possessed. Luke watched him go, bile rising up into his mouth as shock took him. Before he lost consciousness, he heard the howl that chilled his soul.

9.36AM, 16th September 2015, 10 Downing Street, London

Croft waited whilst the officer checked his name and his ID off on the roster. Sergeant Smith wandered over, a playful grin on his face.

"Twice in one week, you're getting popular, Major," Smith said jokingly.

"Hello, Sarge. That wife of yours still feeding you then?" Croft said, indicating Smith's somewhat enlarged belly that was only partially hidden by the man's body armour.

"Bloody woman's got me on a diet. She says she's fed up sharing a bed with a bloated whale. Says if I don't start looking after myself, she's going to restrict me to bread and water. And she doesn't just mean in the food department." Croft laughed, and was ushered through the gate by the police constable. Smith was going to say something more, but he was distracted by a voice in his left ear.

"Be advised, we have reports of a live fire incident involving SO16 officers in Canary Wharf. All SO6 officers are advised we are at Amber Alert." Sergeant Smith listened to the voice. Standing outside the gates to 10 Downing Street, he saw that his lads had received the same instructions.

"Lock her down, boys," Smith said. The three other officers outside the gate with him withdrew and one by one passed through until they were all behind the protection offered by the reinforced black gate. Once upon a time, the public had been free to walk up and down 10 Downing Street as if it were just another street. But the multiple threats from the IRA and the more recent Jihadist threats made that now an impossible dream. With the pavement barricades still out, nobody could approach the gates directly.

Now on the other side, Smith saw Croft looking at him concerned.

"Trouble?" Croft asked.

"I don't think so, Major. Just another day in London." Croft nodded and turned, walking down Downing Street towards the entrance that would allow him access to the Cabinet Offices. Smith watched him go for several seconds then turned to look back out at the world outside their protected fortress.

"CW23 to control, any word on what's going on?" Smith said into his shoulder radio.

"Negative CW23. So far just sporadic reports of rioting." Smith's eyebrows raised in surprise – rare to have an officer-involved shooting. And if it was riots, were they a result of the shooting, or the cause? Further up Whitehall, Smith didn't see the man fall down in the street outside the Household Cavalry Museum. But the CCTV did; the CCTV saw everything.

9.40AM, 16th September 2015, Hounslow, London

It was unusually quiet for this time of morning. Okay, the rush hour was over, but the fast food restaurant was on a major road, and they still had the breakfast menu on. There were only two customers sat in the restaurant, and Jack stood at the tills, found himself staring into space.

Noticing the traffic passing by outside the establishments' windows, he found himself thinking back to the other day. He hadn't seen any more of that cunt Owen Patterson, but it was only a matter of time. Whilst Jack could handle himself, he wasn't sure of how he was going to deal with someone who was probably packing. Jack was confident he could deal with it though. He was well built, and – unbeknownst to many – he had been undergoing training in a rare form of Russian martial arts for three years now. Systema they called it, and it was absolutely incredible. Jack just hoped he would never have to try it out in a real live situation, because that's the first thing they taught you. If running away was the safest thing to do, then that's what you should do. No question about it. There were plenty of egos lying dead in cemeteries.

"Woah, check this out." Jack found himself pulled out of his dream world by one of his fellow workers. She was holding up her smartphone, which displayed Facebook, and a smile was adorning her Goth visage.

"Chris, you know you shouldn't be on your phone. If Clive catches you, he'll do his nut."

"Chill dude," Chris said. "What Clive doesn't know won't hurt him, and he won't be back for an hour yet. But check it out, there's a riot in Canary Wharf." She showed him the various Facebook threads, some displaying pictures, others video.

"Good," said Jack. "It's about time those rich fuckers realised how the other 99% live." Jack didn't actually believe that, but he felt it was the response the people around him would want to hear. Although Clive had left him "in charge", he knew he wasn't. The people he worked with would do the bare minimum to keep their jobs even when Clive was around. They weren't going to show respect for some eighteen year old who started trying to throw his weight around. So Jack did the wise thing and didn't even try.

"True dat," Chris said with a grin, and she wondered off to join her fellow employees in the kitchens.

9.41AM, 16th September 2015, University College Hospital Accident and Emergency, Euston Rd, London

"We've got more coming in," the face said as it popped into the door of her office. The face didn't stay long enough for her to give a response, and Dr. Simone Holden realised she was in for another busy morning. She let out a sigh, massaging the bridge of her nose, hoping that the two Aspirin would hurry up and kick in. She had drunk too much last night, and although she wasn't suffering a full-blown hangover, she was still definitely suffering from an alcohol-induced headache. Holden knew she was drinking too much, and even felt the urge coming on her during the day sometimes. So far she had resisted that, but the lure of the wine bottle seemed too powerful when the end of her shift came. There had even been a few mornings when she had thought about rehydrating herself by the use of a saline drip. Things hadn't quite come to that yet, fortunately.

As one of the A&E consultants, she not only had to help run the department but also deal with the cases as and when they came in. Ten years she had been doing this – ten years of heart attacks, strokes, poisonings and even the occasional gunshot victim. The stress of the job was definitely having a toll on her health, and she knew at some point she would have to consider her career choice. She wasn't cut out for this anymore. For fucks sake, things were supposed to get easier when she became a consultant. But they didn't; if anything, the stress increased. And today looked like it would be even worse, the hospital was already running out of beds due to the rioting.

She got up from her chair and left her, quite frankly inadequate, office. Closing and locking the door behind her, she made her way towards the main treatment area. It wasn't right that she had to lock her door, but the problem with hospitals was they attracted all manner of lowlife as well as the normal decent human beings that she wished were the norm in her department. Unfortunately, it wasn't, and much of her time was spent dealing with drug users and those intent on killing themselves either through suicide, alcohol or stupidity. The fact that she kept seeing the same faces on a regular basis had reinforced her opinion that alcoholism was just a drawn out form of suicide.

The hospital sounded busy, and she heard running feet behind her, but didn't turn. Two security guards moved past her, one brushing her arm roughly. She thought she heard a faint "sorry" uttered, and the guards both ran around the corner ahead. She followed them and saw (as well as heard) that there was a commotion in one of the treatment cubicles. The guards had obviously been summoned there by panic alarms, and they both ran into the cubicle.

"Now what?" Holden said under her breath. It was too early for this kind of shit – it really was, even for London. She walked two more steps only to stop dead when one of the guards was flung back out into the corridor, hitting a cart of medical equipment, which spilled noisily to the ground. He collapsed to the floor and lay there apparently stunned. More bodies appeared around her drawn by the noise and the impending drama, but Holden's attention was pulled to a cubicle to her right where a nurse was trying to hold down a young girl who was thrashing about on the bed, vomit spraying everywhere. Who Holden assumed to be the child's mother was in hysterics.

"*Feeeeed,*" a voice roared, and the second security guard staggered back out into the corridor, a hand up to his head. He was bleeding, and a nurse ran from the cubicle, obviously distressed and in tears. Holden saw a blood-stained hand grab the cubicle curtain, and the curtain was pulled from its runners onto the floor as a man in police uniform staggered out in front of Holden. That was probably what surprised her the most, not the bloodshot eyes and the face of madness, but the fact the man was a police officer. The first security guard had already picked himself up and was backing away, hands up defensively.

"I don't want any trouble, mate," the guard said. Holden felt herself taking the same action, putting distance between her and the officer, but slowly so as hopefully not to attract his attention. He didn't see her, his concentration briefly on the guard. The policeman hissed violently, and then took off in the same direction as the nurse who had just fled.

There was a scream from her right, and Holden looked to see the nurse with the previously convulsing child clinging to her. The girl was clawing at the nurse's face. Then Holden saw the blood and witnessed the nurse try and fling the child off her with frantic hands. But the child dug its fingers into her hair and bit down hard onto her face, just under the left eye. The whole accident and emergency department just seemed to erupt around her, and for probably only the second time in her life, Dr. Simone Holden panicked. The first had been when she had witnessed the death of her mother through cancer at the age of nine. The woman who could intubate a fitting child, who could re-inflate a lung, who could suture a spurting femoral artery, felt her sanity slip. As the world around her descended into anarchy, she did the only thing her brain allowed. She ran.

Others ran also. Some fled, some chased, and the wails of a fearful and endangered humanity began to fill the hospital. And as the minutes ticked by, the predators grew in number, infected by bites and scratches and bodily fluids that were more infectious than Ebola. Their ranks swelled, finding easy pickings amongst the hallowed halls of medical science. Doctors, nurses, patients and other hospital staff all were worthy targets of the infection. Holden, close to exhaustion, staggered on, the disease strangely ignoring her. Several infected passed her by chasing other prey, and soon she found herself wandering the hospital almost in a daze, her body shaking as the initial adrenaline of her panic began to wear off.

With no real plan for where she was going, she moved at random and eventually she found herself in the reception area of a part of the hospital distant to where she normally worked. It was deserted, or so she thought, and with sanity beginning to take hold of her again, she went to the nurse's station to try and find a phone. Get control, she had to get control. Walking around the desk so she was behind the nurse's station, she picked up the first one she saw and dialled 999, but the loud crash made her drop it, and she spun round to see what had made the noise. Out of sight, she heard what sounded like shuffling feet, and the panic began to build again. Looking around, she noticed an alcove under the main reception desk, and she threw herself there as quietly as she could. Hidden by the bulk of the nurse's station, she at first couldn't see, but she could hear.

Shifting her position slightly, Holden noticed light coming through a thin seam at the back of the alcove, and putting her eye to it allowed her to see the reception she had been standing in seconds before. To her horror, she saw the source of the crash. A dead reanimated obese woman turned the corner into the maternity ward reception. She was naked save for a pair of soiled knickers and an assortment of tortuous medical devices. Her chest displayed a gaping wound, held open by rib retractors where the doctors had been previously trying to repair her damaged heart. A bite mark was obvious on her right breast, and a long piece of intubation tubing dangled from her mouth. The woman had obviously been attacked whilst on the operating table, and she moved with drunken randomness. Of course, Holden didn't know the woman was dead, and her medical mind struggled with what she was looking at. How could what she was looking at be possible?

The zombie's head spun sharply to the left, the intubation tube whipping like some deformed elephant's trunk, and the zombie's body lurched in the same direction. Lacking coordination, it fell, sprawling across the now blood-stained floor and writhed about for several seconds as if trying to swim across the linoleum, its torso propped off the floor by the once sterile rib retractor. Holden watched in awe and disgust as the body started to crawl away from her, attracted by some unknown delight. It scrambled to its feet, the right hand catching on the tube, yanking it from the zombie's windpipe, bringing forth a gush of foul air and bile. Now standing, the zombie meandered unsteadily off around another corner. And then Holden saw the sign on the wall with the arrow pointing to the way the zombie was heading, and her stomach lurched into her mouth and terror seized her very soul. Maternity Ward. Oh God no.

9.42AM, 16th September 2015, St Pancras train station, London

The road outside was awash with blue lights and the sounds of slaughter. PC Fred Aycoth joined the line of riot police that had formed outside the British Library. Nobody knew what the fuck was going on, and his head ached from where something had hit him in the temple.

He had seen his partner of the day have his throat ripped out, had seen a crowd of around thirty charge at the two armed officers he was with. They had issued warnings, but still the crowd ran, blood-stained, with hell in their eyes. Then the shot rang out. Then another, and still the crowd came. Two semi-automatic machine guns against a crowd of thirty was a close run thing, but the machine guns had won out. But preoccupied, they hadn't seen the others coming out of the station, not until it was too late. Aycoth had seen them, and he had fled, abandoning his fellow officers because he knew it was the only thing he could do. And looking back, he had seen the bullet-felled bodies slowly rise up and continue with the carnage. Although they moved slower and less coordinated, move they did despite their bodies being riddled with bullet holes. Now he stood, part of the thin blue line, cleared by the paramedic who was needed for more serious injuries. Just as he left Aycoth to be scrutinised by an inspector, the paramedic mentioned he had never before seen so many bite injuries. He was having to deal with dozens of them. The inspector had arrived minutes before and was trying to ascertain what the hell was going on.

"Surely you're mistaken, Constable," the inspector said.

"I saw my partner have his throat ripped out by someone using his fucking teeth. And I saw them, sir. I saw them get up after our boys had emptied whole clips into them. They just kept coming, even after the warnings, even after the shots ripped into them." A fellow PC was stood to the side listening, face blanched, holding a bandaged hand from where she had been bitten.

"You can't be seriously telling me they were zombies, because that's what you are describing. They must have had some sort of body armour. That's the only logical explanation." Aycoth grabbed him and almost dragged him to the police riot line, the inspector surprised by the ferocity and the fear in his subordinate's face. Aycoth pointed at the massing throng of infected some thirty metres away.

"Then why are there people in police uniform getting ready to attack us?"

St. Pancras International Railway Station was the main station for trains to the Northeast of the country, and also the primary UK hub for the Eurostar train, bringing passengers through the Channel Tunnel from mainland Europe. Its layout was a lower level of shops and restaurants, with an upper-mezzanine style level that held more bars and restaurants. Deep within its bowels, the news of the battle outside had shot through the thousands of commuters. It was too late to seal off the station, not that it could be sealed off because there were already infected within it. Wounded and scared, they had fled to what they thought was relative safety, thinking this was only a riot. But it wasn't a riot, and they brought the infection with them. Shutting the fire doors on the lower level slowed the advance, but more infected just got in through the upper entrance with its direct street access, and through the attached hotel. As people ran, the howls came from the upper level as infected hurled themselves down upon the compressed and panicked collection of humanity in the stations shopping concourse. Other infected vomited down upon the masses, infecting hundreds without the need for teeth.

It was a slaughter.

Ryan had experienced the closest thing to hell he thought he could possibly imagine. The urgency to use the bathroom hit him quickly just as he passed through the barriers to the St. Pancras underground station, and he half-ran, half-walked to where he knew the gent's toilet was in the main train station. Concentrating on keeping his sphincter closed, he tried to ignore the stabbing pains in his abdomen that threatened to send him double. The pressure built up to intolerable levels just as he seated his scrawny arse down on the porcelain throne and let loose a torrent of vile smelling waste, obviously a result of something dodgy he had eaten the night before. God that was truly unpleasant, and he whimpered as another purge made its way to the watery depths below.

It had taken a good twenty minutes for him to compose himself and to be sure nothing else was following. Using multiple sheets of toilet paper, he cleaned himself up as best he could, wiping the sweat on his forehead with his sleeve. Food poisoning, great. Just what he needed. Absolutely terrific. Exiting the stall, a vile odour following him out, he washed his hands and made his way to the exit. Things had changed in the twenty minutes he had been otherwise engaged. Walking out of the gent's toilets, he saw people running. He heard their obvious terror. Edging towards the main shopping concourse, three women ran past him the way he had just come. One of them looked at him almost pleadingly, but she was dragged onwards by one of the other women. Why was she bleeding? He moved his head to follow them and turned back just as the thing chasing them rounded the corner appeared. Thing was as good a description as any to use for what he saw, and its eyes bulged red, blood dripping from its chin, staining its white shirt with a deathly map. Part of its scalp flopped down uselessly above one eye. It didn't seem to care. Ryan hesitated, stepping backwards, and the thing stopped and hissed at him. He saw the crimson on its teeth, and it spasmed as it seemed to look him up and down with almost erotic delight.

"*Spreeead,*" the thing said, taking a step towards him, then another. Behind it, a body dropped from the floor above, landing almost gracefully on both feet, before it ran off out of sight. The thing in front of Ryan raised a hand in front of it and pointed at Ryan. Then with an ungodly howl, it charged at him, quickly bringing Ryan to the floor. Ryan was not a powerfully built man, and he felt himself easily pinned by his adversary. The thing brought its face close and belched into his face, making Ryan gag from the putrid stench that was almost visible. If Ryan hadn't already evacuated his bowels, he would have done do then and there.

A soiled hand grabbed him by the neck, turning his head from side to side, and then the other hand grabbed him by the hair, restraining his head even as Ryan struggled beneath it. Then the thing lunged its head forward and bit off Ryan's nose. It was not a clean removal, but took several seconds, and the jaws worked and mashed the teeth through flesh and cartilage. Ryan bucked, screaming in pain and terror, his hand hitting out against the cannibalistic attacker weakly, only for the thing to release him. It looked down at him for a moment, chewing its prize with obvious relish, and then swallowed. Almost smiling, the thing stood and turned to walk away, only to stop. It looked back at Ryan, still prostrate on the floor. It pointed at him again.

"*Spreaaad.*" Then it ran off, disappearing from his sight. Ryan tried to get to his feet, but only managed to stumble to his knees. Turning, he half crawled, half stumbled back to the gent's toilets, and made it several metres before he felt himself grabbed from behind. Another creature grabbed him, twisting his now helpless body around, and it sniffed him. The new infected – a black man with half his left hand missing – licked Ryan's face, and seemed to nod his approval.

"*Goooood,*" the creature said, and it dropped him from its grasp, obviously satisfied with whatever it was he was looking for, and made its way off into the ladies' toilets. More screams ensued. Ryan touched his face gingerly and wept at the obvious damage. He got back to his knees and then to his feet and staggered back to the gents.

There were grown men crying in here, banging on the toilet stalls, demanding entry in the hope of some sort of protection from what was occurring in the station. Ryan didn't know it, but the stall next to him had accommodated an infected, who had attacked those present just as

Ryan had encountered the three women. Ryan ignored his fellow collateral and meandered over to the mirror, shock and pain bringing him to the edge of consciousness. Grabbing the edge of one of the sinks, he felt his legs buckle, and he came down smashing his chin onto the porcelain, blackness taking him to the floor. Nobody tried to help him. There were no heroes here. No good Samaritans. The only thing here was survival, and that was in very short supply today.

It was several minutes before Ryan came round. Another "thing" stalked past him leaving the toilets, paying him no attention. The thing only had one arm, and it left a trail of red ooze behind it. Its gait was somewhat uncoordinated, and it bounced off the wall several times. Ryan looked around to see a half-dozen men either dead or collapsed on the ground. One was moaning on the tiled floor, which was a lake of bodily fluids. All around him the walls were an artist's gallery, as if Jackson Pollock himself had come in to paint his masterpiece with the spray from his own severed arteries.

His mind buzzed with confusion as he pulled himself up off the floor. Looking at himself in the mirror, he almost laughed as he saw his shattered face. His jaw was fractured and dislocated, and pain pounded through him. But the worst pain was not from his head, but from his stomach, and it grew like a furnace. He had no choice but to collapse back to the floor, and he curled up foetal style as bile began to churn towards his mouth. As the vomit expelled itself, it seemed to take his consciousness with it, and the mind that was Ryan quickly died, only to be replaced by a burning desire to seek out and feed. Before being shot in the head thirty minutes later by a grenadier guard, Ryan would go on to directly infect thirteen people.

9.43AM, 16th September 2015, Piccadilly Train Station, Manchester

Brian Pickering stepped out of the black cab and rushed to the railway station entrance so as to get out of the pouring rain. The sooner he got on that plane and away from this damp-ridden shit hole, the better he would feel. This would be his last time in the UK for quite a while, and he wasn't going to miss the place, not for one second. Especially in this damp, rain-sodden city. Every second he spent here was a second too long as far as he was concerned.

He didn't hear the scream that came from the road behind him, didn't see the pack of seven children that ran feral towards the rank of taxis and bus stops. Out of the rain, he walked towards the packed escalator, dragging his wheeled black travel bag behind him, indigestion gurgling into his chest. He hadn't even had time to have breakfast. He'd changed the time of the alarm on his smartphone to make sure he got up early enough to catch his flight, but had forgotten to press the save button. So he'd woken late and pissed off at his own stupidity.

As he stepped on to the escalator, there was another scream; this one he heard, and he turned his head as he began to ascend. There was a woman in the doorway behind him with two small children clinging to her arms. She was evidently trying to fight them off, but they clung on clawing at her, their jaws clamped into her.

"What the hell?" he heard someone say. Two more children ran into the station, wrapping themselves around the legs of an elderly railway employee, and he fell. One of the children sank its teeth into him, and the other got up and attacked a good Samaritan that had come to help. Chaos just blossomed at that very moment. Then the escalator stopped with a jolt. Someone had clearly pressed the emergency stop.

Brian looked up and saw four more children at the top of the escalator. They couldn't have been more than seven years old, but with their bleeding eyes and devil's blood stained faces, Brian felt fear float into his consciousness. The veneer of reality slipped. An elderly man at the top was the first to be bit, and as the reality of the situation began to dawn and the children began to descend, those at the top began to push their way back down. Only there were children at the bottom. An elbow caught Brian in the face, sending his glasses flying, and he felt himself lose balance. One of the children leapt from the top of the escalator and landed on the back of someone who was obviously a body builder, what were once small, fragile fingers clawing into the man's hair. Catching the hand rail, Brian steadied himself, his nose bleeding. Someone began to push up against him, and stuck in the middle as he was, he began to get squashed. Then he heard the chorus of what were once children's voices as in unison they all shouted the same thing.

"*We will spread!*"

9.44AM, 16th September 2015, Paddington Train Station, London

The voice told them what to do. The voice always told them what to do. The voice was them, and they were the voice. The whisper, the seductive words that flowed through their once-human minds like a lover's seductive promise. The voice was them, and they were the voice, and every moment the numbers speaking grew. The voice grew louder, more insistent, more demanding as more infected minds joined the viral collective.

"*We will feed, we will spread.*" But the voice came from the remnants of human consciousness, and in those thoughts there remained a concept only basically understood by those who now yearned to feed their growing hunger. Strategy.

Yes, they would feed. Yes, they would spread, but they were not the mindless animals of horror lore. Something deep within told them to kill only the dangerous, to infect the rest. Of course, those they killed magically came back to life. Whilst some spread through the streets randomly, scattering the seed of the deadly infection throughout the city, others grouped together, concentrating on specific targets, areas of high human density. The contaminated milk at the Paddington Coffee House had infected about sixty people. Within minutes of their symptoms becoming fully expressed, each one of them had infected another dozen people via exposure to bodily fluids and through direct bites. Fifteen minutes after, each of these new infected had spread their gift to dozens more. And so the infection progressed, almost doubling every couple of minutes as the ticking time bomb of the infection rolled through the bodies of the exposed, steamrolling to those who were blissfully unaware.

And then the infected began to get smart, descending on the underground stations en masse. Over fifty forced their way down the steps of the Paddington tube station, into the main concourse, biting and clawing as they went. Those travellers at the bottom of the escalators faced a wall of panic as people tried to descend against the upward flow, trying to escape the terror that washed over them like a wave. In fact, that was exactly what the infected acted like, a wave, hurling themselves down upon the people below them, some sliding down the partitions between escalators. The civilians they infected, the underground employees they killed, tearing their throats out, leaving them to resurrect as the slower but no less deadly undead. "*We will feed, but for now, we spread.*" Stood at the top of the escalator some of the infected attacked directly, others vomited, raining contagion down upon the masses.

The Circle Line train was just pulling in when the panic hit the platform. With little room to move, the chaos pushed people against the side of the now stationary train, and the doors opened on those cramped inside. Some people died in the crush, others fainted. The driver, witnessing the chaos, had no idea what was going on. He couldn't go anywhere; it would be too dangerous to those trapped against the side of his train. He tried to close the doors, but the safety mechanism prevented it, which meant he couldn't go anywhere even if he wanted to.

It was the infected seven-year-old child that made it onto the train first. Once known as Chloe, loved by her parents who both now fought to bite and devour the flesh of the living, the tiny infected creature used her small size to her ultimate advantage. Crawling through the legs of those on the platform, biting and gouging all those she came across, she slithered onto the tube train, her face and clothes painted in blood. Several people had kicked out at her attacks, but she felt no pain, the broken nose and the gashed scalp of no consequence to her. The fact she was missing an ear didn't even seem to register. Once on the train, she attacked in earnest. She thrashed and cut and clawed her way down the carriage, jumping along the back of seats and traversing monkey-like by the hand rails suspended from the ceiling. She took fingers and ears and flesh with her as she went, pausing on occasion to vomit her pestilence over the trapped masses. She directly infected over two hundred people on the train, the rest trapped on there whilst those around them quickly turned.

That one attack resulted in the infection of over five thousand people. And it wasn't even ten o'clock yet. Some of the infected even squeezed themselves past the train to get to the tunnels, even the rats fleeing from them as they spread almost unhindered through the tube network. The driver, sat safe behind his locked door, saw it all, although he wouldn't survive to tell anyone about the sights he had seen. Although the infected never got to him, he likewise was unable to leave and he ended up dying of thirst. The train cabin became his tomb.

9.45AM, 16th September 2015, Euston Underground Station, London

"I hope Grandad likes the present I made him," Stephanie said, clutching the wrapped parcel like her life depended on it. She held it to her chest with one hand, the other holding tight onto the guiding and protective hand of her mother. At just seven years old, she was still nervous about the bustling city she found herself in. It was much different to the sleepy little village she had lived all her life in. It was noisy, and it smelt. Sometimes it smelt bad.

"I know for a fact he will love it," her mother Rachel said, guiding her onto the escalator that led up to their ultimate destination.

"Mummy, is Grandad very sick?" They both stepped onto the moving staircase and began to ascend. Rachel looked down at her daughter and gave her a reassuring smile.

"Yes, he is, rabbit. But the doctors are looking after him." Stephanie scrunched her face indicating her displeasure. "What's that face all about?"

"I don't like doctors. They stick needles in you." Her mother chuckled and gave her a playful hug.

"Yes, they do, but only when they need to make you better." Rachel had always been honest with her daughter. It was the only way she knew how to raise the child. With the father dead in a war that never should have been fought five years ago, it was important to her that Stephanie realised there were good and bad things in the world. And she would have preferred to keep her away from the throngs of humanity that London so ridiculously represented, but her father's heart attack had put those plans on hold. "Can you come, Rachel? The doctors don't know if he will make it," her mother had asked. Estranged from her parents, who had all but disowned her for marrying a black man, she hadn't wanted to have anything more to do with them. She knew it was her father rather than her mother, but she also knew her mother would cower down to the whims of the domineering man. So no, she could have happily gone years without seeing or hearing from them. But death changes all that.

Holding the top of the escalator, holding her daughter tightly, she guided the girl off the moving steps towards the ticket barriers.

"Go on, rabbit, you can put your own ticket through." She showed her where the slot was and watched amused as the small fingers struggled with the ticket. It eventually went in, and the child passed through, Rachel following in her wake.

"What if I didn't have a ticket?" Stephanie asked.

"Then that man over there would come over," Rachel said grabbing her child under the arms, "and he'd tickle, tickle, tickle you." Stephanie squealed with delight as her mother tormented her, and an elderly woman passed by beaming with delight at the sight of the laughing child.

"Mummy, stop," Stephanie giggled, "people are watching."

The exit from the Euston Underground Station they chose was right near the hospital on Euston Road. It was busy, even for London. Two police cars with their lights and sirens going were trying to traverse the packed traffic. Stephanie stared mesmerised at the sight. She felt her mother grip her hand harder, and she looked up. Her mother looked troubled.

"Mummy, what's up?"

"Nothing rabbit. You just stay close to me." They stepped into the street and joined the crowd that seemed to Rachel strangely agitated. Gingerly, stepping between people, they made their way to the hospital entrance.

Rachel didn't know when the panic started. But start it did. There was a shout from somewhere behind her, followed by a loud scream, and she turned her head in what she thought was the direction of the source. Someone with wild eyes ran past them on the actual road, followed by a second pedestrian.

"Who's screaming, Mummy?" a timid voice said, barely audible. Rachel looked down and saw fear brewing in her daughter's eyes. Looking hastily around, Stephanie quickly dragged her daughter over to the side of the pavement into an inset doorway. That was when the ripple spread through the crowd, as more shouts erupted. Heads turned, voices were raised, and packed together the realisation that danger was close caused terror and chaos to erupt. The people began to flee. What the hell was going on?

"I'm frightened, Mummy." Stephanie knelt down in front of her daughter and looked into her eyes.

"It's ok, rabbit. You're okay. We're just going to wait here until this crowd settles. You remember how the chickens on Bob's farm can sometimes get frightened and run all over the place?" Her child nodded sceptically. "Well, people can be like that too. Especially the silly people who live in big cities like this." Stephanie picked her daughter up and turned to look at the bedlam. Everyone was now running in one direction, and she popped her head out from the door recess to see what the cause was.

She didn't see it at first; there were too many people. But through a brief break in the crowd, she saw people fighting about fifteen metres away in the middle of the road. There was something about it that wasn't right. Her intuition told her this was more than just a street brawl. One of the combatants jumped off the person they were fighting and ran up the street towards Rachel. It was then she saw the blood.

"Come on, baby," Rachel said, stepping out of the alcove and moving with the crowd away from the obvious maniacs. Panic skipped into her heart, and she clutched her now terrified child close to her. She heard Stephanie whimper, her face pressed tight into her mother's neck. "It'll be okay, rabbit," she said reassuringly, but she was far from reassured herself. Within a few dozen steps, she turned onto the main road and continued towards the hospital entrance. Car horns were blaring all around, and both carriages of the road were gridlocked.

"Move your fucking arse!" she heard someone shout. An obese man in a white van was leaning out of his window screaming in futility at the people ahead. He clocked Stephanie looking at him, appraised her momentarily, and then leaned back into his van, slamming his fist down on the horn. The police cars from earlier could be seen trying to weave through hopeless traffic. Then she noticed something else. The crowd she was in was heading east, but there were people running towards them in the opposite direction. There was a scream behind her. She knew she had to get off the street, and the main door to the hospital finally became visible on her right. She rushed to it, muted apologies uttered as she squeezed her way through the crowd. The automatic doors opened, and she stepped through backwards into what she hoped would be normality.

It wasn't. As the door closed behind her, the noise of the street diminished only to be replaced by a more primal sound. Rachel turned around to see an empty waiting area, empty except for the three bodies lying on the ground by the reception desk. There were more screams from outside.

Rachel did a full turn surveying the surroundings. What the fuck?

"Mummy?"

"Shhhh rabbit, it's okay. But I need to put you down now. Mummy's arms are tired." She lowered the reluctant child to the floor, only to have her clutch tightly to her leg. "Hold my hand, rabbit." With her free hand, Rachel pulled out her mobile phone and tried to ring her mother.

"Your call cannot be answered. Please try again later." Rachel looked at her phone, the worst thoughts imaginable creeping into her head. She tried to ring 999.

"We are experiencing high call volume. Please hold the line and the first available operator will answer your call," the automated recording said. Rachel almost flung her phone across the room, and if it wasn't for the frightened child depending on her, she would have. But she knew she had to show a brave face.

"Come on honey, let's find Grandad." The child clung to her leg, making it difficult to move. "Stephanie, we have to go."

"I'm scared, Mummy." Lifting her head up with her free hand, she looked into her daughter's soul.

"I'm scared too, sweet pea, but we have to go." It was then she heard the running, and she turned to where the sound was coming from. A nurse barrelled around the corner and came straight at them.

"RUN!" the woman shouted and went straight past them. Seconds later, a second nurse came round the corner, but this one was not like her fellow sister. Her uniform was torn and bloodied, and one arm hung uselessly, swaying with whatever motion the body gave to it. The second nurse glared at Rachel but ran right past, intent on who she was originally chasing. There was no mistaking that this was a pursuit. Rachel's head followed the nurse in bewilderment and alarm, only to spin back to where they had originally appeared from. A third person ran around the corner, and hell came with him.

The infected, seeing Rachel, went straight for her. Pushing her daughter away, she readied herself to meet the assault, dropping her bag that had been on her shoulder all this time. The man tried to grab her, but Rachel – a third dan in Aikido – spun the man away using his own momentum. She'd almost abandoned the martial art when the man from the military had arrived to tell her James had been killed by a sniper in that far-flung hell hole. Her husband, the man she loved almost more than life itself, the father of the most beautiful child that had ever entered the world, had been murdered. Not so much by some animal in a pointless conflict but by the political scum who had sent him there for their misguided and, as she personally felt, their criminal agenda. They thought they still had an empire to protect. At least in the times of empire, the elite were there on the front line leading the soldiers into battle, not sat in luxury whilst others died for their actions.

But she hadn't abandoned it. Aikido was one of only two things that had kept her sane. That and her daughter. That was all that stood between her and a razor blade in a hot bath. The nights she had wanted to just lie back and let the life flow out of her were too many to count. But she chose instead to fight and to live, just as she did now.

The infected slid across the floor, and with amazing agility, leapt to its feet again. It hissed at her. "*Feeeeeed.*" Its bloodshot eyes stared at her, and it took several steps towards the protective mother. Rachel backed up.

"Get behind me, Stephanie." The creature came at her again with speed she had never seen before. The man was about her height, and in bad shape, but he moved with power and grace that surprised her. Lunging at her, he grabbed her throat, and she felt a vice-like grip descend on her. Her training kicked in again. Bringing her hands down onto the insides of his elbows, she broke his hold and, pushing his head down, she brought her knee up into his face. He staggered back and flung his head from side to side, keeping his balance, droplets of blood flying away. Stephanie stepped into him and planted the same knee into his groin, expecting him to double over. But the man merely grunted and grabbed her neck again. This time, she gouged his eyes, feeling their softness start to give under the pressure of her thumbs. She saw the madness in him and knew she had no choice, not with her child at risk. She blinded him. That got his attention, and he released her to grab his face, howling in pain and anger, even his infected mind unable to ignore the trauma. As he staggered, Stephanie swept his legs out from under him. He collapsed to the ground, striking his head hard on the floor, a strange groan escaping him.

Rachel reached to grab her daughter, but she saw the blood on her hands and stopped herself. Best to clean herself up first. She bent down to pick up her bag and ushered her daughter away from the lobby, towards the sign for the ladies' toilets. She didn't know that the virus was already eating itself into her through the blood on her hands and the blood on the denim covering her knee. She didn't know that her life as a loving mother would be over in around ten minutes' time.

9.49AM, 16th September 2015, Euston Train Station, London

"*We must feed, but we must spread. We must spread.*" The twenty infected used a similar strategy to those in the underground. Avoiding the main Euston Road, they had taken back streets, guided by some natural inner cunning, attacking only those who didn't get out of their way, which most people did. They arrived at Euston unobserved by the security services, and divided into three groups, joined by others who swarmed out of the now overrun hospital. And then they began to herd their human prey. Those who later viewed the CCTV footage would swear the hunters had some form of telepathic form of communication to go with their howls and their snarls. Like sheepdogs, they corralled those amassed outside the station so as to spread Abraham's gift to as many as possible.

The crowd in Euston Station that sat outside on the array of tables didn't see the danger until it was too late. Although they had witnessed the blue-light spectacle that flowed back and forth to Kings Cross Station, most of those in Euston were slow to recognise the threat posed to them. Packed in, distracted by social media, by conversation, and by the inevitable wait for train information, those on the periphery were taken unawares by the attack, which ripped through them. As inefficient as an attack with human teeth was, the increased agility and strength of the infected made short work of the helpless commuters. Within the first minute, two hundred people had been bitten or exposed to various bodily secretions, causing a cascading stampede away from the planet's latest predator.

Two armed police officers patrolling the station tried to intervene, but neither of them had a chance to even fire their weapons, as they were pounced on by multiple targets from multiple directions. These the infected killed. By the end of five minutes, over four hundred people were infected. The panic spread from the station to the underground, which was now becoming one of the infected's prime hunting grounds. The two officers, their guns still around their necks, slowly picked themselves up from the ground. Their undead bodies, no longer bleeding, sniffed the air, and now showing a distinct lack of coordination, ambled towards where they suspected more prey resided.

9.57AM, 16th September 2015, London Eye Pier, London

The Thames Clipper pulled away from the pier with roughly 200 passengers on board. Very few of them wanted to be there. Most of them were going to jobs they despised, in a city they hated, just so they could put food in the mouths of themselves, their loved ones, as well as people they found themselves living with who were now almost strangers. Slavery had never been abolished; it had just been wrapped up in a fancy package and had its name changed to employment. Daniel, one of the oppressed and depressed masses, sat amongst them, his head starting to pound. He felt suddenly weak, and he was definitely breaking a sweat. The elderly Afro-Caribbean lady sat next to him looked at him, a concerned look in her eyes. A retired nurse, she knew when someone wasn't well.

"Child, are you okay?" she asked, putting a hand on his arm. The heat coming off him was extraordinary, and she recoiled away, suddenly fearful that he might be a carrier of something contagious. He looked at her, looked at those others who were now curious about him, and felt the pain hit him right in the appendix. It took his breath away, and he curled forward, smacking his head on the hand railing, his bladder letting as he screamed.

"What the fuck!" someone deep at the back exclaimed. Daniel looked at the nurse through clenched eyes and felt the fluid rush up his throat. He tried to hold it back, he really did, and he even managed to avert his head to the floor just as the contents of his stomach erupted in a foul-smelling torrent. Not a single person on the boat would escape infection.

10.01AM, 16th September 2015, University College Hospital Accident and Emergency, Euston Rd, London

Joanne felt no pain, and there was no emotion within her anymore. Somewhere deep within her decaying cortex, there was a realisation that she was dead, but it meant nothing to her. All that mattered was the burning, aching, churning hunger that gnawed at her like a rabid rat trying to chew its way out of her stomach. That was her life; that was now her existence. It was her everything, and her only desire now was the need to feed. She didn't even seem to register the metal surgical device protruding from her chest or the fact that she was all but naked.

She staggered sideways, her motor controls slowly deteriorating as the nerves that carried the impulses quickly degraded. There was no longer any oxygen getting to them, and the cells, although dying, were being changed and mutated by the virus that infested her. Still, she managed to wander forward, her dry eyes scanning for what she craved … food, her ears searching for the unmistakeable heartbeat of her prey.

There was a sound that she would have once recognised as a baby crying, but that noise now only meant sustenance to her, and she sped up slightly, making her way towards the noise that was as sweet as the sound of a ribeye steak sizzling in a frying pan had once been before her death. She had been a woman who had certainly enjoyed her food.

The noise came from behind a door, and she banged up against it, not able to fathom how it operated. It felt different though; it felt like she was meant to go through it, and she raised a fist and banged against its wooden structure. Her attempts were feeble at first, her brain seeming to learn a new skill. But her pounding became more forceful, more concentrated. She wanted entry. From within, another sound escaped its vessel, and she banged even harder against the door. Vaguely, she recognised the sound as something she had once made, something she had done to communicate with others of her kind. But the words were just noise now, the noise of something she could eat.

The door opened, and a woman in a dressing gown stood in shock at the vision before her. The woman backed away, mesmerised by the naked, obese corpse that stood before her. Joanne swayed in the doorway, the remnants of her salivary glands still able to propel liquid into her mouth, and a sliver of drool escaped, running down her uncovered and sagging breasts. She took a step forward, and the woman in the room made more noise, and so did the smaller human that shared the room with her. Joanne moaned and rushed into the room as fast as her uncoordinated limbs could go, falling upon the woman, who fell to the floor under the undead weight. The need for fuel grew, and Joanne's once immaculate teeth began to snap towards the flesh that waited just inches away. But the prey held her off, her hands holding the bloated face away from its ultimate destiny. Joanne roared in what she once would have described as frustration and tried to push her mouth down onto the squirming meal.

That was when the crushing impact hit Joanne on the back of the head, and she fell sideways off the woman she was trying to consume. There was another impact – this time to the side of her head – and she found what was left of her consciousness drifting towards blackness. A final impact and the skull caved in. All life finally left the dead woman, and she was not there to witness Dr. Holden help the woman off the floor, who then picked up her crying baby.

"We've got to get out of here," Holden said to the woman. "And you've got to keep that baby quiet." The mother grabbed her child, and the three of them left the room where the dead woman now stayed dead, the virus unable to reanimate the corpse with the brain stem crushed. It was Holden who heard the voice.

"Help me?" She turned to the sobbing child that stood at the end of the corridor. Holden went over to her, noticing the tears falling, the shuddering shoulders as the terrified child was wracked with sobs.

It was about five minutes after fending off the maniac and fleeing into the interior of the hospital before Rachel began to feel unwell. It began as an itching in her hands and her knee, and at first she thought it must be a reaction to the soap she had used in the bathroom. But she soon realised that wasn't the case, as the itching began to spread relentlessly up her arms and around her knee, like thousands of small biting insects relentlessly feasting off her. Mild at first, but growing ever more insistent, it soon began to consume the entirety of her flesh. And with the itching grew the nausea, and the heat that began to sprout sweat from all over her body. Soon her clothes were wet through, and she was having to wipe moisture out of her eyes just to be able to see. With her eyes stinging, she staggered on regardless, passed puddles of blood, passed motionless bodies searching for somewhere safe to hold up and look after her child. A child so precious to her, almost equal to life itself, but also a child that instinct told her not to touch. Her instincts were right in that regards, for the sweat-drenched skin now carried the contagion that would send her daughter down the same road Rachel now found herself on. Protect Stephanie – that was her job now, her only job. Her own wellbeing was secondary, and she would fight a thousand of those maniacs before she would let one of them lay a finger on her baby. At least, that had been the plan.

But the pain and discomfort weren't the worst of it. The worst part came after the gut-wrenching spasms that stopped her in her tracks, causing her to double over and almost collapse on the floor. It came after the feeling of hopelessness when after several valiant attempts to stay upright, she finally collapsed, the agony blocking out almost everything around her, even the concerned and uncontrolled crying of a seven year old who she had held in her arms as a baby, who she had nursed and held close as they together stood over the grave of the man they both loved. No, the worst of it was the growing insistence within her fevered mind to turn on that child. Her motherly instinct wanted to protect, but something more primal within her, more powerful, wanted to consume, to feed. Rachel tried to raise her head up off the floor, to try and warn her beautiful Stephanie that she needed to get away, to run and hide, but the words wouldn't come. She couldn't remember how to form them; her whole neural cortex began to revolt, overtaken by something much more alien, much more savage.

Lying on the floor, she heard voices. The words meant nothing to her, but she knew what the sounds represented. The true voices in her head told her all she needed to know. The person she had been just moments before was quickly slipping away. No, that wasn't right. Pushed away, that was more realistic. What remained of her could feel something evil pushing her into the darkest recesses of her brain, a more powerful and violent entity taking up residence. As this new being slowly took over her body, it almost mocked her by letting her last vestiges witness the final transformation, letting her witness her world slowly going to black. As everything that was Rachel winked out of existence, her body went into a final convulsion, and the creature she now became heard the pitiful whimper of what was now her prey.

"Help me."

The woman formally known as Rachel lifted her head up off the cold floor and sat up. Looking around, she looked at the direction the voice had come from, just around the corner from where she now resided. Raising to her feet, unsteady at first as the new her gained full control over the muscles and the bones and the ligaments, she staggered almost drunkenly towards the voice.

"Are you alone, little lady?" Rachel heard a voice say. There were several of them, several victims for her to infect. That was what the collective voices in her head were urging her to do, and as she listened, she found her individuality merging with the collective herd. The internal voices grew louder, more insistent. There was no denying their commands. She would infect as many as she could, although the concept of infection was unknown to her. She would kill those who threatened the collective. Rachel, gurgling softly to herself as bile rose in her throat, turned the corner. Eyes turned to her. In the darkest hole within her withering soul, a faint voice cried 'NO, please NO'. But the other voices drowned it out. They would not be denied.

"Mummy?" the small human said. Rachel looked down at her, the closest target, the easiest foe to defeat. So weak, so vulnerable. Rachel knew she had the strength to snap the little human in half. Rachel knelt down, opening her arms sluggishly, and the child rushed into them, all trust and memory and fear. How easily the world ended.

"No, get away from her," one of the bigger humans said, the one wielding the fire extinguisher. Rachel collected her former child in a crushing bear hug and looked up at the woman in the white lab coat. Rachel cocked her head sideways and smiled, froth and spittle seeping between her clenched teeth.

"*Feeeeed,*" she hissed, and then bit her teeth into the little girl's neck. She savoured the moment, oblivious to the feeble struggles of the child, all uncertainty and worry now stripped from her. All that mattered now was the birth of the new species, and she continued to feast as the other humans turned and fled.

10.02AM, 16th September 2015, GCHQ, Cheltenham

GCHQ, the centre for Her Majesty's Government's Signal Intelligence, designated SIGINT. Through its listening posts across the country and across the globe, it monitored whatever it could monitor, often putting its own broad interpretation onto what was legal and what was illegal surveillance. From email traffic to web browsing patterns and telephone conversations, its software looked for patterns related to illegality and terrorism. And of course money, it searched for money. Part of the American Echelon surveillance network, put simply, it spied on the world. Friend or foe, its eyes and ears watched everything.

Sir Paul Crispin, the ageing GCHQ Director, was not in the best of moods, but then he hadn't been for several weeks now. He was shortly due to take medical leave to deal with a worsening case of Atrial Fibrillation, and there was a lot to be done before he handed over the reins to his, hopefully temporary, replacement. What he didn't know at that moment was that transition was never going to happen. The ever-intrusive intercom from his secretary beeped, and he pressed the acceptance button for the call.

"Sir, I have David Fairbank on the line. He says it's urgent."

"Thank you, Sandra, put him through." There was a pause. "David, what can I do for you?"

"Sir Paul, I'm down in operations and something is developing. The computers are sending us alarm pings about something happening in London and several other cities. We need you down here." "Fuck," Crispin muttered; every time he found a moment to himself, someone was there to take that moment away. But David was a reliable chap. If he said something was up, Crispin wasn't going to be the one to ignore him.

"I'll be there in five minutes."

Switching off his laptop, he stood up from his desk feeling the all too familiar flutter over his heart. He was almost used to it, and putting on his suit jacket, he left his office, pausing briefly to let his secretary know where he would be.

Actually, it only took him three minutes to walk there. Despite the image of the dark, secretive room Hollywood liked to portray, operations was well lit. One wall made up of a large bank of video screens, the room was occupied by over three dozen operatives, who each sat at an individual monitor. As Crispin entered, he noticed the main display showed a map of London with numerous red dots around the central area. "Somebody tell me what's happening."

"Director," Fairbank said rushing over to him. "We've got multiple 999 calls coming out of multiple locations in London, Manchester and Glasgow. We have direct contact with the Metropolitan police that their officers are engaged on multiple fronts with rioting. The satellite over London is showing massive engagements between the police and civilians around Canary Wharf and King's Cross. We also have word that live feed will be hitting the air shortly from Sky News and the BBC."

"What is it, riots?"

"Looks that way, sir, although it's all very random. We also have multiple reports of ambulance crews being attacked, and that the emergency services are having to deal with people biting and attacking them. And social media is on fire with stories of massed violence." A woman came over and handed Fairbank a clipboard, a concerned look on her face. He read it and handed it to his superior. "Sir, we have more reports of SO16 officers being involved in a live fire incident in Canary Wharf. There are also reports of panic at Euston station and on the Paddington Underground." Crispin read the memo and moved to the front of the room.

"Listen up, people. I want all eyes on this. I want to know what's going on, what caused it and how bad it's getting. David, get me the Home Secretary; put her through to me here."

10.04AM, 16th September, Houses of Parliament, London

The home secretary had just finished her infuriating conversation with Sir Peter Milnes, Commissioner of Police of the Metropolis, a man she didn't feel was at all competent for the job. Hell, she didn't think he was competent to direct traffic, but that opinion she kept to herself. She wanted to know why there had been a multiple SO16 involved shooting, and he hadn't been able to give her a satisfactory answer. Claire believed he didn't even know what was going on, which was unacceptable for the man in charge of the capital's law enforcement. She already had the press hounding her office for word on what was happening. Sir Milnes stated that he felt there was a possible breakdown in order in several areas of the city and that he was deploying units to counter this. Riot squads were already being assembled for deployment. He would let her know when he had more news. And then he had hung up on her. The nerve of the man. Her phone rang again.

"Home Secretary, I have Sir Paul Crispin on the line." There was a pause, and then the GCHQ head came on the line.

"Sir Paul, what can I do for you this morning?" Claire Miles asked.

"We have a live satellite feed over Canary Wharf and King's Cross. You've got what looks like riots developing in multiple locations." The home secretary's blood ran cold.

"Yes, so I've just been informed. What are we looking at?" she asked.

"I don't know; it looks very strange. We have a visual on the affected areas and there is just utter chaos. There doesn't seem to be any coordination. Part of Canary Wharf is on fire. And it's spreading. We are getting reports all over central London, as well as Manchester and Birmingham. I've seen riots in the past, and this looks different. I can't explain it. And neither can our computer analyses. It doesn't have the typical look of rioting. The only thing that comes close to it in the database is … is, well, an invasion." There was a knock at the door, and the aide to the home secretary walked in.

"Ma'am, we have word from Sky News. They are about to break the story." The aide walked over to the plasma TV on the wall and switched it on.

"Sir Paul, let me get back to you."

10.05AM, 16th September 2015, SKY NEWS Studios, Isleworth, London

The decision had been made not to report the first instances of the rioting in St. Pancras, and to only briefly report the Canary Wharf riots via the news bar at the bottom of the screen. The editor in charge that morning felt it best to get a reporter on the scene so as to actually have visuals of the events. In his mind, this would be more dramatic.

"… and I'm really not sure the opposition understands that their hostility to this proposal is only going to further damage the people they claim they want to help." The screen displayed on viewers' TVs was split. On the left, a concerned looking woman in the Sky News studio could be seen. On the right stood an obese, elderly man in a not so well fitting suit, with the backdrop of Parliament behind him.

"But, Minister, if I may, there are many in your own party who oppose this move. Really, as Conservative Chief Whip, surely if you can't convince your own MP's, how on earth do you expect to be able to convince the public?" She almost hid it, but the smugness slipped out before she could fully contain it. That was okay; the viewing public expected her to treat their elected officials with varying levels of contempt. And she was more than happy to oblige.

"As we have always said, on this matter we want the members of our party to vote with their conscience on the issue. That's why we are giving them a free vote. And if I might say ..."

"Sorry, Minister, we're going to have to interrupt you there. We've got some breaking news just in." The minister disappeared from the screen, his objection cut off, and a host of elaborate CGI was engaged. "We are getting reports of a police shooting at Canary Wharf, and further reports of rioting in the King's Cross region of Central London. We are going over live to our reporter on the scene. Jamie, what can you tell us?" The camera shot of the studio split in half again to show a balding man in his thirties holding a microphone. He was slightly out of breath, and the British Museum and St. Pancras Station could be seen about a hundred metres behind him. There was smoke rising from several buildings in the distance. and a sea of flashing blue lights strobed the scene. People were rushing past him, several displaying bloodied limbs. Everything was bathed in the sounds of human misery. The reporter himself looked harassed, fearful even.

"Thank you, Susan. Calls came in about thirty minutes ago reporting rioting on Pentonville Road outside King's Cross Station. We don't know what started it, but the scene here is complete chaos. First responders are on the scene but –" The reporter was cut off as the sound of semi-automatic gunfire erupted behind him, and he turned to the sound, obviously startled. The camera panned off the reporter and zoomed in down the road where armed police could be seen firing into the crowd that was massing towards them.

"Jamie, was that gunfire?"

"Christ," the camera turns back to the reporter and a ginger-haired police officer came into shot. He was ashen faced and obviously in shock. There was dark blood running from his head, and he staggered against a wall before attempting to compose himself. He failed and fell to his knees, collapsing on the ground in front of him. "Susan, we are going to have to get back to you; it's not safe for us here." There was brief panicked panning of the camera before the feed was cut, and just briefly, a woman could be seen attacking another woman, clawing at the flesh of her face with her nails. The onsite reporter disappeared from the screen, and the anchor woman took a brief moment to compose herself.

"Obviously disturbing scenes at London King's Cross. We will get you more on that story when it comes ... " She stopped and listened to someone speaking in her earpiece. "Sorry, we are getting reports of further rioting in Canary Wharf. Rest assured we will keep you updated as news comes in."

10.06AM, 16th September 2015, The Excel Conference Centre, London

Sixty minutes after the first infected was born as a new species, the Isle of Dogs was all but lost to humanity. Over one hundred thousand people worked in Canary Wharf, and by now, half of them were either dead and resurrecting or running manic with the infection that coursed through their bodies. Many of those carrying Abraham's gift split into small packs spreading to the outer areas; others hunted through the office buildings, seeking those who had escaped the growing army that wished to bring deliverance to the wicked. Many went into the underground station and followed the tunnels, spreading themselves out across the city. About a thousand, though, were drawn by instinct to London's biggest conference centre. What a banquet there was for them there. Was it instinct, or was it the collective wisdom of thousands of memories that told them this was the place to go?

Julie sat watching the surveillance monitors resigning herself to the tedium of another day as an underpaid and under-appreciated wage slave. She had the radio on in the background, but it was turned down low, so she missed the snippets that came across the brief news broadcasts about the growing contagion. One of the surveillance monitors in front of her was showing two halls that had been joined to accommodate an Australian self-help Guru and his thousands of adoring fans. She shook her head, not understanding how the ten thousand people in that room could be so naïve as to give the man their hard-earned money and their hard-earned time. Some had paid him thousands of pounds for him to tell them the wisdom that her late grandmother would have given them for free. This was the second day of his extravaganza, and they were all sat in rapt attention as they listened to the guy speak, words of enlightenment flowing from his lips into the ears of the worthy. Julie had listened to him when she was on security yesterday, and hadn't been impressed. The guy was a pompous idiot. It sounded like total New Age bullshit to her ears, and she'd heard plenty of it during her time working here. Other monitors showed other events ongoing, and Julie knew there were close to forty thousand people in the building. Her job was to keep them safe, despite how idiotic she thought some of them were.

She didn't see it at first, didn't see the mass of people in the Eastern Car Park, standing there, waiting. Nor did she see the hundreds running towards the centre from the west, small groups breaking off to enter the various hotels and businesses. But she saw the crowd, and when looking at the cameras monitoring the western entrance, she became concerned. There was a large crowd now at the bottom of the steps, getting bigger by the moment. There were no breaks scheduled from any of the events – why were so many people gathering there? She picked up her radio.

"Gary, are you at the west entrance?" she said into the black device.

"I'm at information, why?" the voice came back

"There's hundreds of people stood at the bottom of the Western Terrace. They just seem to be standing there. Go and see what's going on, will you?"

"Will do."

The infected stood, stirring and swaying in unison. They were all of one mind, one thought, intoxicated by the feast that awaited them in the large building. So much meat packed together, so many there for the infection to spread to. Every one of them was blood splattered, and the stench and the decay from soiled clothes and open wounds had attracted a mass of flies that buzzed and swarmed amongst them. The flies were ignored. Some of the crowd were naked, others missing fingers and teeth. Most could still be classed as human, but at the back, moving slowly, came the undead, the resurrected. Whilst most of the infected stayed still, several of their numbers broke off and began to run towards the sides of the huge building before them, enveloping, encasing it.

They hadn't encountered much foot traffic on their arrival, and those they had run into lay damaged and infested with the seed to swell their ranks. Some were already turning. Through the ether, they heard the instinct of their brothers and sisters at the other end of the Excel where a similar-sized crowd had gathered, drawing closer, sealing both major exits. They looked in unison as a single prey came into view at the top of the steps that led up from where they stood to the main entrance. They watched as he stopped well before the step's edge, startled by their presence. The all too familiar and pungent smell of fear evaporated off the man, and he took several hesitant steps backwards. Motion rippled through their numbers, and in unison, they took a step forward, then another. The prey ran, and the howl escaped them as their multitude surged forward up the steps, chasing the man down. The feast had begun.

Running wasn't something Gary normally did, which explained the large belly flopping around as he charged towards the automatic doors.

He was also slow, and the horror that he had seen had already reached the top of the steps. But he still ran, his heart almost breaking with the effort and with the terror that suddenly coursed through his veins and arteries. Adrenaline drove him on, away from the death that he had seen standing before him

"Gary, what the hell's going on?" the voice over his radio said, and he passed through the two sets of doors, both closing behind him automatically.

"Lock the outer doors, lock the bloody doors!" Gary shouted into his radio, now almost out of breath. Up in the surveillance centre, Julie could see it all and, hesitating for just a second, she pressed the buttons on her keyboard that locked all the doors at both ends of the Excel. Recently upgraded to be centrally controlled, the blast-resistant doors sealed themselves shut, just as the infected impacted against them. There was a cacophony of banging as dozens of fists and feet began to thrash on the half-dozen transparent outer doors. Bodies turned into battering rams, and they collided repeatedly against the glass. But the doors held, as they were designed to do. Gary turned to look at the mass of faces that stared at him through the barrier and backed away, visibly shaking. It was as if a thousand eyes were looking at him, and every eye's owner wanted to murder him.

A similar scene was being displayed at the eastern end, and many of the infected now streamed down the sides of the building, following their brothers and sisters who had forsaken the obvious entry route. Hundreds made their way down the dock's side, along the pedestrian route, and there they found their entry. Although normally locked, there were dozens of side doors, and it was inevitable that one was open. A small group of smokers, taking a break from the fashion event within one of the halls, was gathered at the dockside, the door they had exited not fully closed. The infected descended on them before they could flee, and the contagion found its point of entry before the conference centre employee guarding the door could close it. They forced their way in, opening other doors, and charged up the stairs to the halls above, the security guards tasked with guarding the stairs killed in moments. Smoking, it seemed, did indeed kill.

The Australian guru had them in the palm of his hand, as he always did.

"You are the creation of your own thinking," he said. "The world you live in is directly a result of the thoughts you hold in your mind. If you are poor, it's because you think poor. If you are depressed, it's because you think depressed." The crowd roared their approval at his words, although he could barely see them through the haze of his own magnificence. Oh, he was good, and today he was on fire. “If you are happy, it is because you have discovered that happiness comes from within, not from the external trappings sold to you by multi-national corporations and marketing firms who would sell arsenic to you as a children’s food additive if they could get away with it.” The crowd erupted in laughter. Well of course they did – that was why they were here. “All material goods are merely a distraction from who you truly are. You buy things you don’t need, with money you don’t have to impress people you don’t even know. And if you are successful in life, it is because you have decided NOW is the TIME for you to be a success.” The crowd cheered; they always did at that bit. “But you will never be successful until YOU believe you are worthy of that success. But most of you don’t want to succeed, not deep down.” Now a hushed silence as they took in what he was telling them, realising why they had wasted away so much of their lives. “You feel you aren’t worthy, and most of you don’t even realise it. The programming you received as children from your parents, your teachers, from your peers and from society in general is rooted deep within your mind. But today, my friends, today we are going to destroy that programming. Today you will learn how to unleash your inner dragon.” There was a loud roar of approval from the room, and he smiled his porcelain-enhanced smile, his face plastered across the countless video screens across the hall. There was a commotion at the back of the room, but he ignored it. But ignoring it didn’t help, because the commotion turned to shouts, and he felt the flow of his words destroyed. Irritation crept into his voice.

“Hey, at the back, can we keep it down?” the guru said, and thousands of heads turned to see what was now becoming something of a commotion. There was a screech, and then people started leaping from their seats. With the stage lights shining on him, the guru couldn’t really see what was happening at the back. But his security could. Stood at the side of the stage, they saw the dozens of people rush into the huge auditorium, saw them ravage the thin line of security that controlled who passed to hear their boss’ words, and then the humanity just gushed into the room. Rushing the stage, they ushered the guru off the back of the stage as thousands of people found themselves trapped in rows of plastic bucket seats, defenceless fodder as hundreds of infected attacked them.

“Terry, what’s happening?” asked the guru’s wife, who was sat in the green room behind the stage. She was smoking, which would have shocked the thousands who had paid their hard-earned money to see the guru tell them how to improve their lives. Her question wasn’t answered with words but with action, and the pair was ushered away from the stage towards a rear emergency door. The guru and his wife found themselves propelled along by their six-man security detail, and daylight hit them as they passed through the outer door where the guru's limo waited. Unfortunately,m the guru didn't get to escape in his vehicle, for it was surrounded by dozens of decrepit and manic human figures who swarmed him and those with him. For whatever reason, he was not chosen to join the spread, but was killed outright, his last minutes as a millionaire a time of pain and decapitation. His wife, bitten seven times and left defenceless on the ground, turned quickly and spent a good twenty minutes feasting on the disembowelled and headless remains of the man she had once secretly despised.

Locked inside the surveillance room, Julie and her subordinates saw it all. Calls to 999 went unanswered, and she was helpless to save those whose job it was for her to protect. It would be ten minutes before the pounding started on the door to her sanctuary, and by then, the tens of thousands present in the Excel were already well on their way to joining the army of the infected. She would never leave the room alive, for as the door to her sanctuary succumbed to the relentless onslaught of the damned, she was forced to join the army of the undead.

10.07AM, 16th September 2015, The London Eye, The SouthBank, London

Even at this time of day, the tourists were out in force. A large crowd had gathered to line up for one of London's star attractions, the huge Ferris wheel that overlooked the river Thames. The people swarmed and moved, intertwining themselves past each other. Prime pickings for Dorin, prime pickings indeed for his well-trained and well-practiced nimble fingers. At the age of 17, he had come to the UK, smuggled in a container with seventeen of his fellow countrymen. When they had reached their destination and were finally released by the people traffickers they had paid to get them into the Land of Milk and Honey, three of the people he was with were dead, including his brother. The stench of their death still lived with him in his mind.

Initially forced into a form of slave labour, housed with five others in a room big enough for just one bed, he one day fled and made his way to London. This was why he had come here. The promise of a better life, the promise of riches and iPhones and fish and chips. Unfortunately, being homeless in a city of ten million people was no better than his hometown poverty of Romania. In fact, it was worse, because he had no family or friends to fall back on, and the constant reminder of the riches available were thrust in his face every day of the week. So he did what he had promised his mother he would never do – he turned to crime. He became part of the growing problem of theft and violence on London's streets.

Presently, he was stalking a pair of fat and arrogant Americans, whose wealth was on display for all to see. In the crowded mass of humans, this would be easy pickings, and it would likely be several minutes before they even realised they had been the victims of his art.

The path for pedestrians was further choked by a man pretending to be a statue, a crowd gathered around him as he did absolutely nothing. And people paid him for this, thought Dorin. People gave him money to occasionally move and illicit a shriek from a surprised child? These people deserved to be robbed, they were so stupid. The two Americans, a prime example in his mind of this stupidity, were forced to stop, and his hand went into the open handbag of the female American. Within seconds, he was lost in the crowd, her purse now his property, another day of food and alcohol secured. And perhaps even enough to pay for a woman. These Americans, they were stupid, they were fat, but they were rich.

Not even London's notorious CCTV would have spotted that one, and he wormed his way to the wall that overlooked the river. Quickly, he stripped out the cash and the credit cards and deposited the purse into the bin next to him. His spoils went into his pocket, and he turned to find his next victim. That was when someone bumped into him.

"I'm sorry, I don't feel well," the man said and stumbled past Dorin, only to falter and fall to the ground, vomit spraying everywhere. Dorin hesitated, checking his own pockets as he always did when he suspected someone of using his own tricks against him.

"Sir, are you all right?" another stranger asked the fallen man, bending down to check him. A small crowd of onlookers began to gather, and Dorin retreated, moving away from the scene. If he didn't get up, there would be police, and he was known to them. He didn't want to spend the rest of the day in the cells. Ten metres away from danger, and that was when he heard the scream. Dorin didn't see what happened – his view was obscured – but in seconds, a madness took hold of the crowd. Like a living force, the people began to flee, and Dorin found himself swept away. He was not a strong man, and someone hit him hard in the back, sending him to the floor. A foot trod on his hand, breaking several bones, and then a boot kicked him almost casually across the bridge of the nose. Blackness threatened to take him, and he tried to claw himself up with his good hand. But another body tripped over him, sending him back to the ground, now winded and almost unable to breathe. And that was when the pain really hit, and through the tears and the stars, he turned his head to see the man who had originally fallen holding Dorin's leg, teeth firmly implanted into his ankle. The crushing pain threatened to bring blackness once again, but then the teeth released, and the attacker scurried up to Dorin's face, almost spider-like, so that their noses were a mere inch away. Dorin smelt a fetid exhale, and he gagged from the stench.

"*We will feed,*" the assailant said, almost smiling. He grabbed Dorin's face, licked him across the cheek, and then leapt up to fell another hapless civilian. Dorin lay back in disbelief, blackness still swimming across his eyes. The crowd around him had dispersed, and he propelled himself backwards with his hands and his good leg until his back was against a lamp post. The bastard had bitten him. What the hell? If truth be told, Dorin didn't even know what the concept of a zombie apocalypse was. Not being able to read meant his knowledge of the world was fairly limited. Wincing in pain, he brought his injured leg closer and pulled down his sock, examining the wound. The skin around the teeth marks was turning black, and the whole of his lower leg was starting to burn. His upper leg began to itch, and Dorin found himself crying with the pain. He pulled up his trouser leg and saw that the blackness from the bite had begun to spread like tendrils along his visible blood vessels, and he could see its advance. Dorin, for only the third time since reaching the UK, cried for his mother.

10.08A M, 16th September 2015, Euston Rd, London

Rachel walked out of the hospital main entrance, and her infected eyes looked around at the bedlam of humanity. Many of the cars had been abandoned now, and she saw her own kind working their way through the ever dwindling prey as they fled from the inevitable. One of her own kind ran past her, locking eyes briefly before he skid away after some fresh meat. In that moment, she felt as if she was as one with the owner of those eyes, and the voice demanding the birth of more of the virus' children roared in her mind. She licked her lips and raised her hand, biting into the entrails she carried, ripped from the innards of a helpless woman she had found hiding in one of the hospital's many rooms. Already she could hear that woman's voice join the thousand that already spoke as her dead body reanimated deep within the bowels of the hospital.

There was noise to her left, and her head shot in that direction. Her primal cortex recognised the gunfire as a threat, a possible weapon that could end her. Despite her strength, she knew she was not invulnerable, but she also knew her reason for being was for the greater good. If she had to die to propagate the species, to defend and further the spread, there would be no hesitation. She would happily sacrifice herself for her brothers and sisters. So she turned and ran towards the gunfire, no longer understanding what a gun was or how it worked. Only that the human wielding it needed to be killed, that her teeth needed to sink deep into its flesh. These were not conscious thoughts that formed in her head, but were more like basic survival instincts. She still carried the entrails. Her hunger, never satiated, would not let her relinquish that prize until fresher, riper fruit was handed to her. Face smeared in blood and faeces, she ran with muscles that now never grew tired, with lungs that now never burned and with a heart that could beat for an eternity. And dozens of her kind followed with her.

10.09AM, 16th September 2015, Glasgow Central Train Station, Glasgow

Jock awoke to the sound of shouting and the sound of screams. His head pounded from the previous night's (okay, let's be honest, previous day and night's) alcohol consumption, and his mouth felt like it was growing fur. Rolling onto his back, he slowly sat up, pushing the sleeping bag away. At first, he didn't know if the sounds of human peril were a remnant of a dream, or should that be nightmare? It plagued him constantly, waking him at night, his breath caught in his throat, his fist clenched ready to strike out at the demons that tried to possess him. But this time, the sounds were from the real world.

His head itched from the lice that infested him, and he scratched almost on automatic. Blinking the sleep out of his eyes, he looked out at the main street from the deep recessed doorway he had recently claimed as home. He wasn't quite sure he understood what he saw, but he understood what he heard. He knew screams; he had lived screams during twenty minutes of hell on the road to Baghdad all those years ago where his Land Rover had been blown off the road by what later turned out to be some idiotic Yank A10 pilot who couldn't distinguish a British flag from that of Saddam's cronies. He'd lost an arm in that friendly fire incident, along with a third of his platoon and most of his sanity. Of course, the sanity didn't leave him straight away; it bled away slowly over the years of PTSD. The alcohol he used to quiet the noise in his head took the rest. He lost his wife, he lost his kids, and he lost his mind all for Queen and Country. Only the Queen didn't give a fuck, and neither did the country. He recently read in a discarded newspaper that the country's prime minister had promised to have the ability to put ten thousand troops on Britain's streets in the event of a terrorist attack, and Jock had laughed out loud, earning stares and chuckles from the so-called normal folk around him. There were already nine thousand of Britain's finest living rough on the streets, so that was a promise the bastard might actually be able to keep.

The streets were his home now. Quiet begging with an air of respectful subservience kept him fed, and kept him in cheap booze, which kept the demons anesthetised. And his thousand-yard stare kept troublemakers away. Nobody messed with Jock, absolutely nobody. Even the police tended to leave him alone so long as he didn't get too drunk. He still found himself spending the odd night in the cells, but normally he behaved himself. And sometimes the cells were his choice, especially in the snows of winter.

And now the screams grew. In the darkened recess, he went relatively unnoticed by those experiencing the chaos of Scotland's largest city. There were people fighting, people running and people standing in obvious stunned shock as to what was going on. Instinctively, he rolled his sleeping bag up and gathered it together with his rucksack which contained his few meagre possessions. He needed to piss bad, but that would have to wait. Jock knew danger when he saw it.

This was more than a riot. Riots generally didn't have people lying bleeding out on the floor, didn't have children being grabbed from their parents and thrown through shop windows. He flinched as he heard a shot, and looking around the corner, he saw two armed police officers, firing off into a crowd approaching them. Jock smiled. This was what he knew would always come. He spent his days watching humanity, watching the human race slowly degrade into depraved beasts. He saw how people treated each other, how they raced through life chasing the almighty pound, trampling over their fellow humans for the slightest advantage to get that promotion, that new car, that pathetic shiny trinket. He saw how people reacted to him, mainly with fear, some with pity. Some with disgust. But he saw everything and found himself glad to no longer be a part of the rat race. He would sit and watch them, share stories with his fellow homeless, and drink himself into oblivion until the day he didn't wake up. That would be a blessing, but Jock now suspected that day wouldn't come. Because this was what he knew would come, and this was biblical. He had spent hours dreaming of this. Society had sent him off to fight and left him a broken ruin. And when they had deemed him unfixable, they had abandoned him to the streets. So if this was what he thought it was, it served the ungrateful fuckers right.

10.10AM, 16th September 2015, Whitehall, London

Funny, Croft seemed to remember sitting in a seat very similar to this some eight or so years before. He had been made to wait then, and he was made to wait now, which was actually a first for the COBRA committee. They had never made him wait before. He heard raised voices from conference room A, and a visibly shaken civil servant left, closing the door behind him. He walked off at pace, giving Croft a momentary glance. What the hell was going on? Well, Croft probably had the answer in his pocket. He took out his smartphone and went onto the internet.

It is a little-known fact that there is a countrywide WIFI network in place for people such as Croft. Using an encrypted network that piggybacks off all the conventional networks, reliable and secure 4G was a perk of the job. It was over this network that Croft accessed the BBC. Instantly, his alarm rose when he saw the reports of riots and police shootings. He hit the latest live feed video. On screen, the solemn-faced BBC anchorman was interviewing a reporter in the field. The reporter was stood behind a barricade, and a line of riot police could be seen about twenty metres behind him. Three armed officers ran across shot, and the reporter, who was looking behind him, turned back to face the camera. Just as he was about to hear what the reporter had to say, the door the civil servant had just left from opened, and the home secretary stormed in, a host of lackeys following in her wake. Croft switched the phone off.

"Croft, get in here," she said as the door to conference room A was opened for her. Always one to follow orders, he stood to follow, but was distracted as the other door opened again. Savage walked through, and he waited for her to reach him. There was a concerned look on her face.

"I don't think we will be having that lunch today, Major."

Croft was the last through the door, and he closed it behind him. He wasn't important enough to have someone to do that for him. The room was packed, and the wall display was showing the very BBC live feed he had brought up on his phone. There was nowhere for him to sit this time, the home secretary taking the last seat, so he stood to the side next to Savage, right next to the door he had entered by.

"Lucy, what the hell's going on?" he said bending down to speak into her ear. She turned her head and looked up at him, just the hint of fear glinting in her green eyes.

"Hopefully not what I think." As she said that, the prime minister stood up, and, holding the remote control, raised the volume so that the display screen could be heard by everyone. The voices in the room died down.

"... shooting just moments ago. There are dozens of wounded officers," the onsite reporter said. He had been full screen, but the CGI shrank him down and placed him alongside the studio anchor. The heading under the reporter showed his name to be Adrian Cunningham.

"What caused the rioting, Adrian? Has there been any official word?"

"No word as yet. We have been told the civilian shot was attacking a child and that the officer felt it was the only way to protect civilian life. The rioting isn't a result of the shooting from what I have seen – that was already happening." Behind him, an officer stepped into the shot and fired a projectile over the police line.

"Adrian, are they using tear gas?" the anchor asked visibly shocked.

"Yes, several canisters have been fired off..." The sound went mute. Behind Adrian, a woman was seen running at the police line from behind. She looked enraged.

"Can someone tell me what the FUCK is happening?" the prime minister shouted, slamming the remote on the conference table. The impact caused the battery cover to fly off, along with one of the batteries. Unseen by him, one of the home secretary's aides was taking a phone call, and he handed the mobile to his boss. She listened intently and put her hand over the phone, directing her attention to the PM.

"That was Sir Milnes; he says the situation cannot be contained. He wants permission to use baton rounds. And there's been more shooting at King's Cross."

"But baton rounds have never been used on the British Mainland." That was Mitchell Tanner, the Chancellor of the Exchequer. The PM turned to him. On the screen, the police line broke, and the crazed-looking woman charged at the BBC reporter.

"For fucks sake, Mitchell, they're shooting real bullets. Do you think the plastic ones are going to be any worse?" Osbourne said wearily.

"Oh Christ," Savage said loudly. Heads turned to her, saw her staring at the TV display. The enraged woman had been tackled by an officer, and the camera had panned down, running in close. Her eyes were bleeding, bulging from her head. As the camera got close, the woman bit into the police man's hand. The officer tried to push her off, but she was relentless. As fellow officers came to his aid, he started punching the woman in the face. All this live on one of the world's biggest international news channels.

Sir Andrew Kirslake, the Head of the Civil Service, had a very strict routine. Being an ardent Socialist at heart, he objected to the trappings of office, and whilst he accepted the huge pension that was one day promised, he did not believe in being ferried around by underpaid drivers. He was better than that, and was much more comfortable taking the train in to Waterloo Station. Kirslake always liked to walk across Westminster Bridge, no matter the weather. When asked, he always hid his true intentions behind a need to get at least some exercise for the day. The real reason was he liked to feel himself amongst the masses, the people he felt it was his duty to keep a check on the madness that was today's politicians. How he despised the Tories, but hid it well behind a veneer of officialdom. And of course, he always availed himself of a large chai latte from the same coffee house on Waterloo Road.

Alone in his office, nobody was there to see the infection take hold. They didn't see him collapse into his own faeces, didn't see him convulse and bite through his tongue. They didn't see him rip a chunk of his own hair out, or see his eyes start bleeding. The man that was five weeks away from retirement was reborn a new entity, with only one thought in mind. To feed. Pulling himself up from the soiled carpet, there was no sign of the arthritis in his bones, but there was also no real consciousness left to register that fact. A new pain lived in him now, a hunger that could never be fulfilled, could never be quashed. Kirslake looked around his office, his head moving in jerky movements. He could smell them, could smell their blood, their flesh, and he pounced onto his two-hundred-year-old antique desk, knocking over the picture of the woman he had loved more than life itself. He crouched there a moment, sniffing the air deeply, getting a sense of where his prey was in this fortified building. Leaping off the desk, he landed by the door to his office and licked it inquisitively. Residual memory, deep within what was left of his mind told him the thing on the door opened it, and it creaked as he snaked through into the outside office.

Fortunately for his secretary, she was not there, and he made his way out into the corridor which was also deserted. He smelt the air, hunting for meat, and a sudden spasm hit his neck and it cracked as the bones reset themselves. Kirslake grew several inches as his stooped posture corrected itself. "*We must feed,*" the voices said. He turned right. He knew where the flesh was.

There were five stages of grief, Croft knew. The first, denial, was being displayed by the majority of people in the room. Savage had just put forward the notion that the woman on the BBC news was displaying the symptoms shown by those at the Hirta disaster, but the majority in the room weren't having any of it.

"Captain," said General Marston, "perhaps it is premature to be making that determination based on one video feed."

"With respect, General, it is my professional judgement as a doctor and a scientist that we are looking at the virus that wiped out the research facility a year ago. And if that's the case, we need to get you and the prime minister out of here." Croft, standing by the door, heard something fall in the outer office, but ignored it due to the commotion in the room. He saw the home secretary's aide take another call, and again, she bent down to talk to her boss. The home secretary said something and leant forward, pressing a button on the speaker at the centre of the table. Sir Michael Young, not present at the briefing, came on the line.

"Sir Michael, what does MI5 have on this?" asked the home secretary.

"Through liaising with GCHQ, we have determined that the situation we are experiencing may be coordinated." Seconds later, his face appeared on the display, replacing the open melee that was now occurring in London's financial district. "We analysed facial biometrics and traffic cameras, and we have the same car and the same people cropping up in multiple locations across London." A map of central London came up on the screen, with a line joining up six dots. Two faces and a car registration appeared at the corner of the map. "Each of the dots represents a coffee shop where that car stopped and those two men got out. We've analysed the reported breakouts and as you can see," circles appeared around the dots, "those seem to be the epicentres of where this is all happening."

"You think this is a terrorist attack?" the PM asked.

"We don't know, but look at the map. Apart from Canary Wharf, they visited major transport hubs. Nobody needs to drink that much coffee. We don't know who the younger man is yet; the computer is still searching for him in its database. But the older gentleman is someone we have down in our inactive files. He was a radical preacher for a religious cult several years back. They called themselves the Children of the Resurrection, but we haven't had any intel on them for several years. We had assumed they had disbanded." Listening to this, Croft heard something impact softly on the door to the conference room. He turned his head, saw the door handle start to depress.

"They were seeding the virus," Savage said. "It's the only explanation that fits the facts." There was more murmuring and consternation at that. A Whitehall staffer passed across in front of Croft, just as the door to the conference room opened.

"Find me that car. I want those who caused this brought in for questioning," the PM demanded.

The man who people used to call Sir Andrew pushed up against the door, blood smearing its surface. The blood was from the body on the floor, a policeman who was bleeding out, his carotid artery severed by teeth. Kirslake heard the voices of his prey inside the room, could hear their hearts beating, the sweet nectar of their blood coursing through easily accessible organs and vessels. He inhaled deeply, savouring their narcotic scent like he had once savoured a fine wine.

"*We will feed.*"

His hand found the door handle, and he rested it there a moment, confusion seeping into what was left of his mind. He placed his forehead against the door, vestiges of memories and thoughts seeping into this waking moment. Where was he? What was he doing here?

"*WE WILL FEED,*" the voices roared, and the last of his humanity was stripped from him. He turned the handle, swinging the door inwards, and stood on the threshold for only a moment. A man in front of him turned, surprised by his dishevelled, blood-stained appearance.

"Sir?" Andrew Kirslake slanted his head to one side then launched himself at the man.

Croft took in everything and his training kicked in. Blood drenched, bulging eyes, teeth clamped on the arm of the hapless victim, the man who had just entered needed to be dealt with. He knew what this was; he had seen it over and over in the videos he had watched of the poor sods at Hirta. The attacker released the arm of his victim, flinging him to the ground with the strength of a madman and turned towards Croft, who manoeuvred quickly, planting a foot in Kirslake's chest. He kicked with all his might, sending the elderly man back out through the door, where he fell and sprawled for a second.

"We will feeeeed," Kirslake said, springing back to his feet with inhuman agility. Croft almost hesitated, surprised at what he was witnessing, but his brain wouldn't allow the training to be forgotten, and he slammed shut the door, putting his weight behind him. He heard the latch catch.

"Get diplomatic protection up here," he roared, jolting from the impact that suddenly hit the other side of the door. "And someone help me with this fucking door." There was an animalistic howl from outside, and a fresh impact, the wood of the door denting inwards. General

Marston leapt to his feet, and with the help of Savage, they both pushed themselves against the door. The wood splintered more, the impacts like a battering ram.

"How did he get so strong?" Savage cried over the noise. Nobody answered, and Croft thought he heard someone in the room authorising a kill order. Then the wood cracked in earnest, a hand coming through, clawing, searching. There was a commotion outside, and the hand withdrew just as the sound of semi-automatic fire filled the conference room. Crimson streaks were painted around the door's breach. Careful to avoid the blood, Croft peeked through the hole in the door and allowed relief to wash over him. He opened the conference room door, his hands raised, two dead bodies visibly painting the floor.

"Jesus," the armed police officer said, his gun pointing towards the new motion.

"Easy," Croft said, hands still raised. He stepped out of the conference room, closing the door behind him. The officer turned from him and pointed his gun back at the target he had just put four rounds into.

"Is that … is that Andrew Kirslake?" the officer said, visibly shaking. Croft knew that reaction well. He'd seen it many times; the shock of taking a human life for the first time could be devastating. "Did I just kill the Head of the Civil Service?"

"Looks like it. What's your name?" Croft said.

"Baker, sir, Jack Baker," the officer responded, but he continued to look at the body.

"Baker, look at me," Croft insisted. The officer did, although it seemed he was reluctant to take his eyes off his trophy. "What you did was necessary." There was the sound of running feet from the corridor outside. "You probably saved some very important lives today, mine included." Croft backed away, and Baker did also. Two more armed police entered. Croft turned to them just as Savage exited the conference room, closing the door behind her. She turned to one of the police officers.

"Whatever you do, don't touch the body. I need bleach, lots of bleach. And plastic sheeting if you can find it," Savage demanded.

"There are some plastic ground sheets in the cleaner's closet," Baker said. "It was going to be …" his voice broke off as the groan came from the floor. The corpse of Kirslake began to move, trying to push itself off the ground. Sprawled on its back, the zombie rose to a sitting position. It looked at those witnessing the spectacle, and hissed, blood bubbling from the four devastating chest wounds. The eyes that looked out at them, the eyes of the man who had been knighted by the Queen, had turned completely black.

"Shoot it," Savage said. "Shoot it in the head." Another shot rang out. Not the last to be heard in Whitehall that day.

"Looks like they might listen to you now," Croft said to Savage.

10.14AM, 16th September 2015, University College Hospital, Euston Rd, London

Holden sat, the half-empty bottle of water clutched in her shaking hands. She was suffering traumatic shock – she knew the signs. She had witnessed it often enough. But she knew she had to hold it together. At least she was with other people now, other than a scared new mother with a defenceless child. When she had witnessed the slaughter of the child by what was obviously its own mother, she had turned and fled again. This time, she held panic at bay, and minutes later had run into two other survivors. Both police officers, and both armed. Thank God. The relief she felt had quickly turned sour as they had been forced to run when confronted by half a dozen screaming banshees.

Now they were in a large staff canteen area, the provisions from various vending machines pillaged and collected on a central table. One of said vending machines was toppled over blocking off the door they had entered through, the loud banging of the damned a monotonous vile rhythm that taunted the living. The wood at the top of the door was already splintering. One of the officers, who had introduced himself as Brian, stood watch over the door. The other officer was called Stan, and he was filling a rucksack with as much water and sugar laden snacks as it could hold.

"How you bearing up there, doc?" Stan asked, giving her a sideways glance.

"I'll live. I just don't understand what's going on." She took another sip, trying her best to calm the tremors running through her body. Never in her life had she wanted gin more than this very moment. If there was a bottle before her, she suspected she would have downed the lot in the hope of bringing peaceful oblivion.

"Here," he said, tossing her a chocolate bar. "You need to get your blood sugar up." She tried to catch the projectile, but she fumbled it, and it fell to the ground. Holden picked it up, tears welling in her eyes, which she wiped away with her sleeve. Stan turned to the other woman, who hadn't said a word since they had met. She flinched as fresh pounding hit the door outside. "Ma'am," Stan said getting her attention. "Do you need anything?" She looked at him and just shook her head, cradling her newborn even tighter to her chest. The baby gurgled, and its mother made reassuring hushing noises. Holden looked at her and realised she didn't know the woman's name.

"Stan, try control again," his partner suggested from across the room.

"233SO to Sierra Oscar control, are you receiving me?"

"Sierra Oscar control to......3SO....garbled...say again?"

"What's going on? What is the situation, over?"

"Stan," the voice said, "It's Inspector Carver. I'm in operations." Static hit the radio mike that the policeman was holding. "... you still at the hospital, over?"

"Yes, sir. We are holed up on the third floor. We need to know what's going on, over." They certainly did need to know what was going on. They had been here guarding an important witness in intensive care. The star witness in one of the drug trials of the decade, the man had been gunned down on his front step, and the surgeons had only barely been able to keep him alive after eight hours on the operating table. What they thought was easy duty, spiced with cups of tea and plenty of biscuits from a mixture of flirtatious and curious nurses, their easy duty had turned into a battle for their own survival.

"We have word from Westminster. There is some sort of biological agent spreading through the city. We're losing ground on all fronts to people who just attack anything. There are thousands of them now. Over."

"I know, we've seen some of them, over," Stan responded.

"Stan, you and Brian need to understand something. If you can get out of there, head north. You are authorised to use lethal force on anyone who you suspect is infected. Don't fuck about. Head shots, it's the only way to stop them, over and out."

Holden listened to the conversation. She couldn't believe a word of it. There was no biological agent she knew of that could cause this. But how could she deny the evidence of her own eyes? How could she deny the violence and the carnage she had witnessed in the past hour? Her world and the world of those around her had been torn to shreds in a brief moment. Her head shot to the left as there was a loud cracking noise, and part of the door splintered inwards. An arm came through, the flesh gouged by the rough wood. The hand moved about wildly trying to grasp whatever was in the room. Then the arm withdrew and a face came to the hole, lips pressing up to it.

"*Feeeeed.*" Brian looked at Stan.

"You heard what the boss said, Brian." Both men put in their ear protectors.

"Shit," Brian said, shaking his head in resignation.

"*Feeeed, kiiiill you,*" the monster outside said. Raising his machine gun up, Brian clicked off the safety and lined up the shot. He paused briefly, looking back at his partner who just nodded solemnly. "Shit," he said again. "Ladies, might want to put your fingers in your ears." That being said, he put one round into the gore-stained head, the woman with the baby jumping at the deafening noise. The face disappeared from the door, only to be replaced by another one. Brian fired again. And again, and again. After a dozen shots, the faces stopped appearing at the door.

"Shit," Stan said. "I knew today was the day to phone in sick."

10.17AM, 16th September 2015, Horn Park, South London

"Mum?"

"Jack, what's up, love?" It was unusual for her son to ring. He was always too busy he said, but he came to visit once a week, so that was nice. Well, almost once a week. She was proud of him, though, guarding the prime minister like he did. Not many sons got to do that, not many sons got to serve their country like he did. Although, to be fair, she didn't care for the man who presently resided in 10 Downing Street, but you still had to respect the institution.

"Mum, you need to listen to me now. You can't argue, you have to listen and do what I say. I haven't got much time."

"But Jack ..."

"Mum, for Christ's sake, just shut up and listen. Get Dad and get some bags packed. Take only what you really need, passport, money, jewellery. You need to get in your car and go to the train station. Take any train south. Head towards the coast."

"But your dad's at work..." she protested.

"Mum, just do as I fucking say. It's all going to shit here, the whole thing's falling apart. You've got to go; you've got to go now." With that, the connection was severed, and Jack's mum was left standing completely confused.

There were dozens of such phone calls at first, then hundreds, then thousands. As the story spread through social media, across text messages, through emails and the news, some of the people began to panic. Some of the security forces began to abandon their posts, worried about their families. Others, torn between the safety of their relatives and their overriding sense of duty, resorted to warnings that they knew deep down were probably useless. The majority though, still living in a haze of denial, followed the orders handed down from on high not to contact friends and family members. But still the panic began to spread. Seeing the mayhem on the TV screens and the videos on YouTube and social media, the country began to wake up to the very real reality that the end of the world had arrived. But what did you do when your life suddenly became an R-rated horror film?

10.18AM, 16th September 2015, The London Heliport, London

The choice of the heliport was ideal. Minutes away from Clapham Junction, it offered the ideal way to escape the coming apocalypse. Sat in the comfortable departure lounge, Fabrice waited for the pre-booked flight to be readied for them. Brother Zachariah sat across from him, a huge smile adorning his features. It was the kind of smile often seen by those in the grip of religious madness. The departure board said they would be boarding in five minutes.

Fabrice couldn't believe the plan had been successful. He had been sceptical, had imagined that the security forces would have reacted quicker than they did. But no, here they were, minutes away from escaping the hell they had created. Five years ago, he would never have imagined he would be instrumental in destroying an entire country, that his actions would result in the death of millions. But five years ago, he hadn't known the truth, hadn't been blessed with the love of the creator. He had been a defiler, a fornicator, and an unbeliever. How meaningless and futile those earlier years had been. The drinking, the womanising, the drugs. The yearning for material possessions and significance. And then he had found salvation, had found and felt the presence of God in his heart. He had wept for hours, unrecognisable bliss just filling his soul.

And then he had become not just a believer, but a warrior of God. The new Crusade was here. Abraham himself had come to him, and embraced him and blessed him with the news that HE had been chosen to bring the Lord's wrath upon the wicked. Not the misguided Muslims that Christianity had fought against for generations. No, they were just puppets; there was a much more pressing target. Doubt had filled his mind at the prospect. Not the doubt that such a crime should be committed. No, doubt that he was perhaps not worthy of the task, that there were surely others more deserving, more godly. Those doubts had faded when his mentor and sponsor, Zachariah, had told him they had both been marked with this monumental mission. That had been six months ago, six months of waiting until the chosen day.

The departure time moved a minute closer, and Fabrice sipped the cool, refreshing water from the glass in his hand. He drew a finger across the condensation on the outside of the glass and placed it back on its coaster, trying to get the glass exactly on the ring of moisture that was already present. Fabrice, Zachariah, and the driver were the only three in the room when the flash bang was hurled into the room. His brain registered it, for a brief moment he tried to process what he was seeing, and then his vision whited out and a crushing deafness descended upon him with a searing pain. So shocked was he that he fell from his chair, consciousness suspended by the impact of the projectile.

"ARMED POLICE, ON THE GROUND, GET ON THE GROUND!" Through a haze of smoke and pain, men dressed in black appeared. He felt hands grab him roughly, felt his face being pushed into the plush carpet of the departure lounge. Still in shock, he was unable to resist, even when his dulled mind felt his arms pulled behind his back and his hands restrained.

As his vision cleared, he saw Zachariah looking at him, that same smile still there on his face. So the agents of Satan had found them after all. Dressed in black, the demons were here to make sure they remained to bear witness to the fall of the corrupt and festering empire. He lifted his head, only for it to be roughly pushed back down onto the carpet.

"I said stay on the ground, you fucker," a harsh voice said into his ear, and he felt a fist punch him in the right kidney. Another fist, followed by a kick to the ribs.

"We have the suspects in custody," Fabrice heard another man say, obviously communicating into a radio. From his limited vantage point, he saw six men with them in the room, all heavily armed.

"Get these bastards on their feet. We're transporting them to six." Fabrice felt his body rise as an external force lifted him. The zip tie holding his hands behind his back was too tight, and the roughness of his treatment caused pain in his shoulders. It was on his feet that the black canvas bag went over his head, but before it did, someone spat into his face. He felt another punch into his kidneys, and he was suddenly propelled forward. Outside, he couldn't hear it, but a helicopter was landing, and the three righteous men were forced from the departure lounge into the outside air, Fabrice feeling the September wind as they left the relative warmth of the building. So, soon he would be right in the heart of the belly of the beast. So be it. He would just get his reward in the afterlife.

10.20AM, 16th September 2015, Russell Square, London

Rachel found herself in a group of about two dozen infected. They had found each other through a deep animal intuition, and now stood outside one of the area's many hotels. She no longer understood what a hotel was; she just knew that it was full of what the voices told her to attack. The sounds of police sirens and repeated gunfire filled the air around them and several of her numbers flinched at the loud reports. There was still danger, despite their numbers. Although she wouldn't have described it as such (because she wouldn't know how), it was the sound of battle, a battle the human race was rapidly losing.

For some reason that only nature understood, Rachel had become the leader of her pack, and they followed her every move. Where she led, they followed, and she went where her nose led her, where the voices told her to go. She was now a lieutenant in one of the world's largest armies, and her instinct and the commands of the collective consciousness told her where to go and what to do. Although her vocal chords still had the ability to create words, she communicated through gestures and grunts because her brain had quickly forgotten all but the very basics of human speech. As a unit, they climbed up the steps to the front of the hotel, but found the doors locked, impassable. One of her kind head-butted the glass, but its toughened nature would not yield to his assault, and she found herself beating on the door's exterior in frustration. Inside, nobody was visible, and the urge to consume moved the group on to easier targets. Spread, feed, survive. With a gesture of her hand, they retreated from the hotel and scattered out into the streets, cars and people still trying to escape the madness that had descended onto the city. All were easy pickings, many still not understanding the true extent of the danger they now faced. The world that they knew was over, and the new world grew as the infection spread throughout the city's population.

Rachel watched as her brothers and sisters attacked all that they could find. This was her world now, the love of her daughter completely obliterated by the virus that coursed through her veins. The urge to go back to the hotel was strong, but her gut told her to move on. And there was a voice, calling to her, a powerful urge that told her there was a more pressing need that demanded her attention. She raised her head up to the sky and sniffed the air.

"*Come, join us*," the voice said. In a moment, she could see what her kind in other parts of the city could see, could feel what they felt, their urgency, their desire, their hunger. "*Spread, spread and join us*," the voices said. She howled into the morning air, and dozens of infected turned to face her. They too heard the voice, and as a unit they moved, attacking and maiming those they encountered, but no longer searching for the uninfected. This was the time to join together, to take the battle to the centre of the infestation that was humanity. She knew where they had to go. It was time to consume the heart of the human society.

"*Whitehall, come to Whitehall.*"

10.21AM, 16th September 2015, Whitehall, London

They were moving now. What many people didn't know was that the government buildings around Whitehall were all connected by a series of elaborate and well-guarded subterranean tunnels. Construction had been started in the late 1930's, but over the decades, the network had been expanded just as the infrastructure above ground had grown. It was along one of these tunnels that the prime minister and most of the people from the briefing room now moved, along with around a dozen armed police officers. Croft and Savage were at the back of the pack.

There had been other attacks in Whitehall, and the news had just reached them that the Speaker of the House had been found, by the Minister for Health, being eaten by his secretary. The secretary had turned on the shocked minister and attacked, biting a huge chunk from his hand and turning him within minutes. Both the secretary and the minister were reported shot dead after biting several dozen more people in the corridors of the Houses of Parliament. With over a thousand rooms, a hundred staircases and three miles of passageways, Parliament was being evacuated and abandoned on the prime minister's orders.

The group turned a corner and passed towards a door at the far end. Croft heard one of the police officers talk into his radio, and the door opened for the party to pass through. Croft heard the door close behind them, and the tunnel took on a slight upward incline. He turned to Savage.

"Do you think this can be contained, Lucy?" Savage looked at him as they walked, and then looked back towards the way they were walking.

"Probably not," she said. "There is no contingency for this. You don't plan to defend against what is supposed to be science fiction. It all depends on how widespread it is though." One of the officers escorting them overheard what she said and sped up so he was level with her.

"Is this for real? Are we really facing zombies?" the man asked, ashen faced.

"The word zombie is as good as any other, I suppose," Savage said, resignation in her voice.

"And you say we can't stop it?" the policeman asked. Savage ignored him for several seconds, obviously calculating a response.

"We will do what we can, but I don't know."

"But I have a family, what about them?" Savage looked at him with a pained expression, and Croft was the man to answer.

"Where do your family live?" Croft asked.

"Peckham."

"They should be fine for now," Croft said. Savage nodded her agreement, and the police office fell back behind them. Croft hated to lie, but he also knew what would happen if he didn't. If panic set in amongst those defending the city, then all was lost. The men with guns were their only chance.

10.22AM, 16th September 2015, Downing Street, London

Word of the shooting inside Whitehall had reached the whole security detail guarding the hallowed seat of British Government. Some were still in shock to hear that the prime minister had authorised the shooting of anyone even attempting to breach the security perimeter. That a civilised country like the UK could suddenly feel lethal force was needed as a first line of defence in such a short space of time was not what any of them expected to see in their lifetime. After all, this wasn't bloody America; these things just didn't happen here.

Smith stood looking out of the gate, his machine gun ready, safety off and finger on the trigger guard. He watched a skinny man wander drunkenly across the first half of the road, only for him to collapse in the street. In the middle of the road on the traffic island, the man just fell into himself. People were running, and no one stopped to help the fallen civilian. Smith resisted the natural temptation that came with the job, the temptation to help a member of the public in need. That wasn't his job, not today. Smith's concentration was broken as someone stopped at the pavement barrier and tried to push his way past.

"Sir, you need to stop that and step back," one of Smith's fellow officers said loudly. The officer raised his machine gun a fraction.

"You've got to help me. I've seen them. I've seen their eyes," the man pleaded. He sounded Scandinavian. An army truck drove past towards Westminster, briefly obscuring the fallen man. When the truck moved, the man was sat upright, looking around. Vomit was leaking from his mouth. The Scandinavian was trying to get past the barrier, gripping it, his knuckles turning white. He let go his grip, realising the futility of his efforts, and fled up the road, soon going out of sight. Smith ignored him, instead concentrating on the now not so well dressed man who was slowly pulling himself to his feet. The man vomited all down himself as if it was the most natural thing for him to do. Dressed in what was most likely a now severely soiled Saville Row suit, the slender man stood to his full height, sniffed the air and then his eyes seemed to lock onto Smith's. Smith felt a shiver run up his spine.

"Heads up. Back away from the gate!" Smith shouted, and raised his weapon. The skinny man charged their position, crossing the road and vaulting over the pedestrian barriers. He flung himself at the gate full on as the officers there stepped back, avoiding the clawing hand that thrust its way through the gaps in the bars. Smith watched as the attacker struggled for several seconds and, realising his prey were out of reach, the infected man howled in frustration, looked up and began to climb the black-painted metal that acted as the, up until now, effective barrier to Downing Street.

Smith didn't hesitate. He followed his orders and put two rounds in the skinny man's heart with a precision that would have delighted his now deceased shooting instructor. No warning, no attempt to take the man alive. The two bullets entered the man's flesh within a centimetre of each other, one perforating the right ventricle, the other punching a hole straight through the aorta.

The orders were clear, and the reason for the orders, although sounding insane, was even clearer. The machine gun round's impact flung the climber from the railings, and he fell to the street outside, thrashing on the ground for several seconds before falling still. Smith stepped forward and aimed up for a further shot, but one of his fellow officers put a restraining hand on his arm.

"Wait, Sarge. I need to see it. I need to see it with my own eyes." Smith looked at him, looked at the hand on his arm and then nodded to the man. He did not let his aim drop, however, but turned his attention back to the man he had just killed. The seconds passed by, and then after Smith had counted to five in his head, the body twitched and jerked. The head lifted itself off the ground, bringing the upper torso with it. They all saw the impossible, and they all saw the black eyes and look of pure evil in the now undead's face.

"Fucking zombies," someone said. Smith ignored the voice, and as the zombie began to rise from the ground, he followed the other order they had been given. Head shots were needed to stop them turning. The bullet went in above the right eye, and blew out the back of the creature's skull, sending brain and bone matter spraying into the street. The creature didn't get back up from that one. Smith had been the one to tell his men the new truth of the world, after being told said truth by a white-faced and almost panic-stricken inspector. Smith knew most of the men he told didn't believe him when he told them about the infected, about the zombies. They believed him now.

Smith put a finger up to his earpiece, apparently listening to something being said to him. "I'm being relocated over to Horse Guards Parade," he said. With a last disgusted glance at the corpse he had created outside the gate, Smith turned and walked away. He didn't look back at the men he was abandoning, many of whom he had known for over a decade. He had a job to do, a job more important than any he had ever been given in his entire life.

10.26AM, 16th September 2015, PINDAR, Military of Defence, London

The conference room had been abandoned for a more secure facility: PINDAR, the crisis management and communication centre deep below the Ministry of Defence. Joined to Downing Street by secure tunnels, the trip there had been mercifully uneventful. Croft found himself being ushered along with the rest of those who mattered, and now he sat in a room feeling like a spectator whilst those in the facility outside went about the unenviable task of trying to save the country. A task that Croft realised was not achievable.

There were seven people in the room in total. Croft, Savage, and General Marston made up the military side. The PM, the chancellor of the exchequer, the home secretary and Sir Peter Milnes made up the civilian side.

"So what do we need to do right now to contain this?" the prime minister asked.

"I've ordered the Grenadier Guards to deploy, and we are bringing in attack helicopter support. Unfortunately, we have very few military assets in the capital, although the SAS are en route, and we are trying to liaise with the other affected cities." General Marston did not look well. His skin was pale and clammy, and he massaged his chest. He saw Croft looking at him, and the sixty year old shrugged and withdrew something from his pocket. "Angina Major. I survived three wars only for my own body to give up the ghost." He placed the GTN spray in his mouth and took a hit. "It's why I was due to bloody retire shortly." Croft looked at Savage.

"You're the expert in biological agents, Captain. What do you think?"

"There's no containing this," Savage said. She hesitated slightly, aware of the fact that she was the lowest rank in the room, and one of only two women. Would her opinion even matter? Fuck it, she thought, it was past the point where ego mattered anymore. "The only way we have any chance of stopping this is with nukes."

"You can't seriously be suggesting we should use our own nuclear weapons on our own people," the home secretary responded, visibly appalled. "There would be no recovering from that. There would be no country left."

"Plus, there's no guarantee that would stop the infection. If this is a coordinated attack, we don't know what other cities might be next." Milnes sat back in his chair, removing a piece of fluff from his almost flawless police uniform. "I still think we can contain this," he said absently. The home secretary looked over at him and did well to hide her disgust. She wished he'd stayed at New Scotland Yard instead of rushing over here.

"You can't, it's too late for that," Savage persisted. "This is unstoppable, probably even if you use nukes if I'm honest." She didn't finish what she really wanted to say. That she knew the PM would never authorise nukes because he was a weak and feeble man. He was not a true leader; he was a man who happened to fall into a position of leadership out of pure luck. If Thatcher had been here, the nukes would probably already be flying … and she knew that the Iron Lady would have probably stepped out into the streets of her beloved capital so as to go down with the sinking ship along with the people she had led. But the present incumbent wasn't a patch on Thatcher. He was a fine example of that old British army saying, Lions led by Donkeys.

"Croft, what's your analysis?" the PM asked, turning to him. Croft paused, looked at Savage, seeing the almost pitying look she gave the prime minister. Croft looked at the general, who nodded approvingly.

"I don't have access to fancy computer graphics, Prime Minister. And I don't know enough about the virus to make a judgement on how fast it will spread. From what we've seen, though, it spreads quickly, and even when you kill those infected, they just come back. Savage, how many do you think are infected now?"

"Based on the initial sites that we think were the centres of infection, I would say around two hundred thousand are already infected in London alone. That's more than our entire front line armed forces. And spread across the country as it is, there's just no stopping it."

"Christ, this is madness," the PM said, exasperated. He was glad his family were at Chequers and not here to see him fail. "Is there even a protocol to deal with this?"

"No," General Marston said. "Nobody could ever envisage a zombie apocalypse. We need to inform NATO of the situation, and we need to contact the Royal Navy, get every ship in port to sea. I can phone the NATO Secretary General, personally. And now might be a good time to speak to the US ambassador."

"That dick head, Christ that's the last thing I need," the PM said. Croft looked at the man and could see he was close to losing it. Croft had never liked the man who the country had elected to lead them. He was a man of dubious character, and in his mind, not fit for office. He was not the kind of man the country needed in its present crisis.

"Prime Minister, let me tell you what's going to happen," Croft said. "I'll tell you what I know, because I have seen versions of it happen with my own eyes in several of the delightful countries I have been sent to in the name of Queen and Country. You will start off thinking you can stop this. You will think that martial law, that curfews and bullets and troops and tanks will keep the infected at bay. But they won't, because there are millions of people out there who are starting to panic. And many of those will be the people you are relying on to stop this. The police, the Army, most of them have families, and they will start dropping away in greater numbers to protect the people they love. If you don't cut off social media, the news will spread like wildfire, and people will panic. If you do shut off social media, people will panic even more as the rumours run rampant. Within a day, every corner shop and every supermarket will be picked clean. And the streets in every single city will be ripped apart. You will be fighting on two fronts. You will be fighting an ever-growing army of infected, and you will be fighting the very people you are trying to protect. I regret to tell you that you will just become overwhelmed. You don't have enough men, you don't have enough guns, and you probably don't have enough bullets. But more importantly, you don't have enough time. Forget the ambassador; someone needs to talk to the US president."

"We can't just give up," Claire Miles said, disgust dripping from her voice.

"I'm suggesting nothing of the sort, Home Secretary. I am merely stating the fact that we need to inject a dose of realism into this. We need a controlled retreat away from the infected zones, setting up areas of resistance where we can. I was employed by your predecessor for the task of making the difficult decisions in impossible situations. You all know what has to be done."

"Noah," Savage said softly, so softly that hardly anyone heard her.

"What was that, Captain?" asked General Marston.

"Noah, sir. Operation Noah."

"Has it come to that?" said a shocked prime minister.

"Yes, sir." She looked at Croft, who nodded his approval.

Operation Noah. Croft hadn't written it, but he had read it. Written twenty-five years previously as a theory document, it outlined a plan to save the brightest and the best of the country in the event of a national emergency. It was originally written with the scenario of an invasion, pandemic or bio-weapon attack in mind, but this present scenario seemed to fit the document rather well. Save what could be saved, sacrifice the rest. The document actually went into significant detail, outlining who could and should be saved, what resources would need to be allocated and where.

Events since then had seen the theory document made real, and as secrets go, it was one of the best held. Money had actually been allocated, and a network had been established to allow the top-secret plan to be implemented. It was the reason Croft had the job he had, he and those like him. Part of Noah was stopping the unthinkable before they became reality. The question was, would those in the room instigate the plan?

"What do you think, General?" the prime minister asked Marston. Marston removed his glasses, pinching the bridge of his nose. He looked at Croft, then at Savage, and then let his eyes rest on the TV screen. Shit, he was supposed to be retiring soon. He didn't want to be here; he wanted to be with his wife far away in their country retreat in the South of France. She was there now, visiting relatives, and he thanked whatever gods there were for small mercies. Marston put his glasses back on and looked the prime minister dead in the eyes.

"Prime Minister, if we can't get this under control in the next hour, I think it's the only real choice we will have."

Croft almost smiled. He knew Marston's reputation. The man was a competent leader, a military genius, and a living contradiction to the often heard saying that the British Army was made up of Lions led by Donkeys. But the military didn't run the country, civilians did, and it hadn't been since Thatcher that the military had really held any regard for those who ran the country. Croft prayed the present incumbent of Number 10 would for once do the right thing. Just as that thought left his mind, there was a faint tremor that hit the room

10.29AM, 16th September 2015, New Scotland Yard, Broadway, London

Geoff felt a mixture of elation and fear as he reached his destination. His stomach churned with nervous acid, and he had an almost insatiable need to pee. The dirty black Ford Transit van came to a halt in the middle of the street outside New Scotland Yard, the heart of the Metropolitan Police. Inside, the overweight middle-aged man turned off the engine and pulled the keys from the ignition. His left hand shook with a noticeable tremor, a side effect of the inoperable brain tumour that was slowly growing within his skull. He remembered sitting in the consultant's office, remembered being informed that the experimental treatment available in other countries wasn't available to him because the NHS didn't have the funds. Red tape and bureaucracy had signed his death warrant, and a slow and degrading death it was likely to be. He wasn't willing to accept that.

A red sedan drove up behind the parked van, and the occupant began agitatedly beeping her horn at the obstruction that blocked her path. Already late for an expensive Pilates class, she was unaware that she presently had twenty seconds left to live. Geoff sat for a moment, for there was nothing really left for him to do. Part of him was scared, but that was buried deep down under the overriding knowledge that this was truly God's work. Had Abraham not said as much? And was Abraham not God's messenger on this fetid and corrupted planet?

In the corner of his eye, he noticed two armed police officers exit the front of the police headquarters and head towards him. He ignored them, and ignored the horn behind him as it blared again. Even if they realised what his intentions were, they were too late to stop him. Sat beside him on the passenger seat, the red LED countdown stood at nineteen seconds. The counter was connected to the two thousand kilograms of C-4 plastic explosive that resided in the back of the van. Geoff had activated the device just as he was turning onto Broadway, and now he sat with the inevitability of his fate, a weight removed from his shoulders. Fifteen seconds. Geoff began to pray, letting his hands fall into his lap

"The LORD is my shepherd; I shall not want. He maketh me to lie down in green pastures; he leadeth me beside the still waters. He restoreth my soul; he leadeth me in the paths of righteousness for his name's sake. Yea, though I walk through the valley of the shadow of death, I will fear no evil, for thou art with me…"

The basic concept behind any explosive is very simple. It's just something that creates a lot of heat and a lot of gas in a very short space of time. The gas expands outwards along with the heat, creating an explosive blast wave that does structural damage. The heat just goes along for the ride, incinerating whatever can be incinerated. Geoff didn't feel the blast that killed him in a microsecond. One moment he was a thinking, breathing human being, the next he was reduced to ash. The truck itself, the casing for the bomb, simply disintegrated and turned into red hot shrapnel as the C-4 inside exploded. The blast wave spread out, slamming into the structures around where only a crater now stood. The red car behind the van was hurled into the air, its entire structure and contents incinerated. The iconic rotating sign outside New Scotland Yard vanished as it became part of the expanding shrapnel, and the two police officers who had come to investigate were ripped apart as their bodies were flung into the air. A micro-second later, the blast hit the Scotland Yard building itself. Although hardened against bomb attacks, no structure could withstand such an impact unscathed, and the whole front of the building was cratered inwards, the dozens of glass windows creating millions of tiny spears. In every direction, the blast wave hit buildings and people and pulverised them, decimating the built-up area for a hundred square metres. Within two seconds, over a thousand people were dead or injured.

The sound of the explosion followed behind the blast wave, and was heard for miles around. Some people realised what it was, others only realised when they were told by the news they were watching on their TV's and their smartphones. The nerve centre for the Metropolitan police, the brain for London's police force, had just been decapitated.

Moments later, there was a second such explosion on Milbank outside the MI5 building. Fortunately for those inside, it was a much stronger structure, and there were no buildings around it to contain the blast. Even so, the damage to the building was considerable, and the loss of life numbered into the hundreds. God's wrath had many ways to strike at the heathen for he would not be denied his vengeance on those who had forsaken him.

10.30AM, 16th September 2015, PINDAR, Military of Defence, London

"What the hell was that?" the prime minister said in alarm. Dust was still falling from the ceiling, a result of the shock wave when a second tremor ran through the room. A piece of ceiling plaster fell bouncing off his shoulder, and he brushed the residue off, his hands displaying he was close to panic. He looked around imploringly at those assembled in the room and found that only one of them had an answer.

"That, Prime Minister, was the shock wave from at least one explosion, probably two," said Croft. The door to the room suddenly opened, and a visibly distressed aide ran into the conference room and handed the home secretary a memo. She read it and her faced blanched. She passed it to the PM, who almost fainted when he read it.

"Someone has just blown up New Scotland Yard," Claire Miles said. "And Thames House."

"Good God," said the Metropolitan police chief, "I was there this morning."

"Then this is definitely coordinated," Croft said. "Someone's planned this down to the tiniest detail. There's no denying that fact now. Prime Minister, it's time to act." Croft didn't even try to hide the contempt in his voice now. Whoever had done this knew exactly what they were doing.

"We need to get you and the cabinet to a safer location," Marston said.

"I will not be seen to abandon my country in its gravest hour," the prime minister protested, although Croft detected he didn't really believe what he was saying.

"And you won't be. But as fortified as this building is, we need to extract you whilst we can. Your name's on Noah too, don't forget," Marston said, and he was insistent. He looked around the room for support. Most of those whose eyes he met nodded their agreement.

Croft leaned back against the wall. He listened as those in the room were formulating plans, watched as different people came and went, saw the frightened looks in their eyes as the rates of infection and violence continued to grow. It was at that moment he realised his government was probably no longer a viable employer.

10.31AM, 16th September 2015, University College Hospital, Euston Rd, London

"That definitely felt like an explosion," Stan said. A small tremor had just rocked through the canteen where they now all stood looking at each other. Moments earlier, they had made the joint decision that it was time to try and get out of the hospital. There had been no new assaults on the door to the cafeteria. Brian tried his radio.

"233SO to Sierra Oscar control, come in, over." All he got was static. He tried again, but still no response. "Looks like we are on our own for now," he said to his partner. Brian picked up one of the two filled rucksacks and handed it to Holden.

"I'll need you to carry that," he said, and she reluctantly took the offering from him. The makeshift barricades had been cleared, and Holden realised they were really going to do this.

"Where will we go?" Holden asked.

"Anywhere but here," Stan said. Brian stepped over to the lady whose name he still didn't know, and gently put an arm on her elbow to encourage her to stand. She flinched away, clutching her baby too tightly.

"Ma'am, we need to go," he said, but she shook her head vigorously from side to side. He looked back at Stan, exasperation visible on his face. Holden finished putting on the rucksack and stepped over to the woman.

"Come on, we have to go," Holden said gently. The woman looked at her, looked down at her baby, and shook her head again. Holden pulled up a chair and sat next to her, putting an arm around her shoulder. "You can't stay here. Sooner or later, one of those things will get in here and then there will be nothing you can do for your baby." The woman looked at her, anger suddenly visible in her face.

"Get your fucking hands off me," the woman almost screamed, leaping to her feet. Holden watched as she backed away into the furthest corner and sat down, trying to calm the baby that had just been awakened by its mother's outburst. Holden stood to try and continue her persuasion, but she felt a hand gently grab her arm. She turned to see Brian shaking his head.

"We can't just leave her," Holden pleaded.

"The only way to get her out is by force, and that means carrying her. And I can't handle that and whatever's out there." He looked to Stan for support. Was he saying the right thing?

"He's right," Stan said. "Look, I don't like it any more than you. But if she isn't going to come willingly, then we have to leave her.

"But she'll die," Holden said almost on automatic. She was trained to save lives. Brian released her arm and turned square onto her.

"If you were attending a massive RTA and you were the only doctor onsite, what would you do?" Brian asked. Holden looked at him then let her head drop in resignation.

"Save those that can be saved," she responded.

"Right now that's us. And now we are leaving."

10.32AM GMT, 16th September 2015, The White House, Washington DC, USA

"Mr. President?" The voice wormed its way into his sleeping mind. There was a faint movement as his shoulder was gently nudged, but at first, he refused to respond. His shoulder was nudged again, this time more forcefully by the ever-persistent White House chief of staff, as the subordinate tried to wake up the leader of the free world.

"Mr. President, you need to wake up."

"What time is it?" the sleepy voice said, and the first lady moved subconsciously, pulling the covers tighter up towards her neck. She let out a faint moan, trapped in whatever dream her mind was wandering in.

"It's five-thirty in the morning, sir. We have a situation." The president sighed deeply. We have a situation, how many times had he heard those words? How many times had he been woken in the early hours to be told there was a "situation"? Just once, he'd like to go a week without having his precious sleep interrupted, without having the weight of a thousand incidents dumped on his shoulders. Just once. At least he only had another year of this. That was probably why presidents were only allowed to do two full terms. Not out of some fear of a dictator coming to power, but more from the fact that any more than two terms would probably kill a man. Just look what happened to FDR.

So here we are again, he thought. Not wanting to wake his wife, the president pulled himself carefully out of bed, putting on the robe that Ben Silver, the White House Chief of Staff, was holding for him. Prior to becoming a senator and then president, he had always slept naked, but that ended with the knowledge that his bedroom was no longer a sacred place and could be invaded by armed men intent on his protection at any time. It was amazing he even got to have sex anymore, and he could understand why some of his predecessors had succumbed to that deadliest of sins. Sleepily, he donned his thousand dollar slippers and looked back briefly to the most beautiful woman he had ever known. Damian Rodney, the President of the United States, left the Presidential Bedroom and followed Silver along the corridor, for a moment briefly regretting his decision to stand for election. Life had once been so much easier, and power, as he had discovered, was completely overrated.

"So what's up, Ben?" the president asked. An aide appeared as if by magic and handed him a steaming mug of coffee, and the president thanked her for her kindness and consciously made a point of not eyeing up her very shapely rear as she walked away. 'Always treat those around you with respect' was the motto his father had beaten into him from an early age. Literally.

"We have a situation in London that has become evident over the last hour. General Roberts and Director Johnson are waiting for you in the Situation Room." Rodney sipped as he walked, following his Chief of Staff through the almost deserted corridors of the iconic building. So the Chairman of the Joint Chiefs and the Director of the CIA were already here. This didn't fill him with much hope. Hell, he'd not even had chance to brush his teeth. And his hair, Christ, he must look like hell. He stopped briefly as he passed one of the many ornate mirrors adorning the corridors of power, and cringed as he saw his decrepit reflection. He certainly didn't look like the leader of the free world.

"I'm meeting the South Korean Ambassador today at ten, Bill; don't forget that," the president said.

"I've already rescheduled that I'm afraid, sir. You'll see in a moment that London is going to take most of your day." They both turned a corner, and two immaculately dressed US marines snapped to attention where they stood outside what everyone called the Situation Room. The president and his chief of staff went inside, the guards relaxing after they passed. The Situation Room had a large conference desk running down the middle with seating for about twenty people. Those of utmost importance would sit at the table itself, the rest off to the sides, ready to hand their superiors whatever advice or folders were required. The seat for the president was reserved at the head of the table. Video screens lined the walls, and one huge screen was on the wall opposite to where the president always sat. There were five people in the room when he entered, and all of them rose to acknowledge their leader and the office he held.

"Mr. President," General Roberts said. It was five-thirty in the morning and the general, in his mid-sixties, looked like he'd had the best night's sleep a man could ever have. *He probably put in a ten-mile run before coming here*, the president thought to himself. Director Johnson also looked fully refreshed. *Did these people not need sleep*? the president thought to himself. They had both been watching a BBC news feed on a large screen on the far wall. The rolling news bar at the bottom of the screen told the president much of what he thought he needed to know, although he would quickly learn he was very much mistaken. He sat in his chair, allowing the rest of the room to sit.

"Fill me in, people." The people in the room all turned their attention to the CIA director who coughed nervously. He opened a folder in front of him, more a stalling tactic than the need for its contents.

"Mr. President, I have been in contact with my counterpart at MI6 in London, and they inform me that the UK is under biological attack." The image on the screen changed and the muted BBC program started to show video of the New Scotland Yard bombing survivors being helped by paramedics. The director noticed the president's attention had been drawn to the screen. "London has also experienced several terrorist bombings."

"A biological attack? How bad?" the president asked. There was hesitation in the room.

"It's difficult to believe what we are being told," the director said. Johnson turned to the man sat behind him who got up and left the room after the director whispered into his ear. "Perhaps it would be best if we get it from the horse's mouth." The screen at the end of the room flickered and went black for several seconds. "I am patching you through to Sir Stuart Watkins, the head of six." A second later, the face of the aged MI6 chief came online.

"Sir Stuart, good to see you again," the president said. They had met briefly during his state-sponsored visit of the UK two years previously.

"Mr. President, sorry to get you up at this hour, but we have a bit of a problem across the pond." *A bit of a problem*, thought Johnson. *The bloody English with their stiff upper lips.*

"I'm told your country has suffered a biological attack. What do you need from us?" the president asked. The man on the screen took a deep breath and looked off to the side briefly.

"As I am sure you will soon be briefed, we are facing the worst crisis in our history. Enemies unknown have released a biological agent across multiple cities. Those infected quickly become enraged and uncontrollable, attacking the uninfected, spreading their numbers rapidly. The disease is highly contagious and has a very short incubation period of just several minutes. The infection takes hold quickly and has spread through the heart of our capital and several other cities. Worse still, the infected seem to work together to spread the disease. The crisis is already threatening our seat of government." The MI6 chief paused to take a drink from a glass which looked a lot like scotch. "We have had to use lethal force to try and stop the spread, but we have an even bigger problem. The infected come back after death." The president blinked, processing what he had just been told. He looked at the people in the room with him, then back at the TV screen.

"You're serious, aren't you?"

"Yes, Mr. President, I'm deadly serious. And you asked me what we need?" The president nodded. "I have been authorised by Her Majesty's Government to request air support, and for you to liaise with NATO as to where we go from here. I have also been asked to advise you to consider recalling all your government and military personnel. I have briefed the CIA director as to the extent of our situation, and the twelve thousand US military personnel on UK soil will do nothing to help our situation. Best you get your lads home, Mr. President. We fear you might be needing them if this thing spreads."

10.33AM 16th September 2015, Her Majesty's Prison, Belmarsh

Chris Bryant had not had the best of luck when it came to crime. This was his third stint in prison, and it was to be his longest stretch, or so the judge had told him. That cunt with the wig had sent him down for fifteen years, all because he had felt the need to smack the guard across the head. Well, it wasn't his fault the guard didn't do what he told him to when he told him to. The fucker deserved a smack. Unfortunately, that added GBH to the armed robbery charge, and with his record, the judge had felt he had no choice but to make an example of him. Of course, as Chris was about to discover, the prison term wasn't going to be as long as originally planned.

Now he was locked in a cell in a prison that was in absolute uproar. Chris was alone, his cellmate being in the infirmary thanks to someone throwing boiling water laced with sugar in his face. Fucking nasty business that – those burns wouldn't be healing in a hurry. But that wasn't his concern, and that's what happened when you tried to muscle in on someone else's drug business. Chris had tried to warn him, but the guy hadn't listened. They never did.

What was his concern was the fact he was trapped in a room just big enough to swing a cat in, with a TV, a bunk bed, a sink and a toilet. And the TV was not making good daytime viewing. Somehow, a rumour had started that there were riots in the outside world, riots that were ripping the country apart. Somebody had then said he had overheard one of the guards saying something about zombies. Another fellow inmate had called bullshit on that story, which had started a fight, which had resulted in someone using a shank, which had started a mini riot. And now everyone was on lockdown. Chris walked over to the door of his cell and gave it a firm kick.

"Fucking bastards," he shouted at nobody in particular, but it started another wave of similar obscenities from the adjacent cells. So Chris was stuck here with a TV with a dodgy reception with seventy channels of bullshit to watch.

The thing was, Chris had heard another guard talk about zombies too. It was all over social media apparently. Facebook, only twats bothered with that. And Twitter, give me a break. Being at Her Majesty's pleasure, Chris didn't have the pleasure of such luxuries, not that he ever used them. He hated smartphones and everything they represented. He had a twelve-year-old daughter that was glued to the bloody thing. He could have done with an internet connection now, though, just to find out what was really going on.

At least his cell had a view, unlike most of them. He could see out over the perimeter wall, could see the streets and houses. Could see the people running and the traffic building up. Chris moved closer to the glass. What the hell? Cars were being abandoned in the middle of the street, and dozens of people were fleeing in one direction. There was a momentary lull, and then a large crowd swarmed down the road after them. He couldn't see them in detail, but there were hundreds of them. Was this a riot? Was this what everyone was talking about? Wow, for the first time in ages, Chris was actually glad to be behind those prison walls. He wouldn't have liked to be out on the streets with all that kicking off.

10.34AM, 16th September 2015, Hounslow, London

Clive, it seemed, had no objection to his employees using social media today. After all, he had been doing the same himself. He had returned from his doctor's appointment, fresh prescription filled and worry clearly visible in his eyes. He had paced around for several minutes and had suddenly told everyone that he was closing up and letting everyone go home early. To the great outrage of several customers, he had personally ushered everyone who didn't work there out of the building and put the 'Closed' sign up. His staff were amazed. Clive never shut the shop for anything. And their initial objections were cut short when he told them this was paid leave and that unless he personally rang them, they wouldn't have to come in tomorrow either. After he said that, they couldn't get out of the building fast enough.

As the security shutters at the front of the building descended, the only two people left in the building were Jack and his employer. Jack closed down the kitchen and joined Clive in the main body of the restaurant.

"You really think it's that bad, Clive?" Jack asked. Clive looked at him, massaging the pain in his chest.

"Yes, lad, I do. Sit down." The two of them sat down at one of the customer tables, Jack looking nervously at his surrogate father. "I made your dad a promise back in the day. In fact, we promised each other that if anything ever happened to either of us, we would look out for the other guy's family."

"Yes, I remember Dad saying that. He said I could always trust you."

"Well, you need to trust me now. We need to get your sister and your mom and we need to get moving." Clive turned and looked up at the clock on the wall behind him. "But we need to also go to my house. I need to get some shit." Clive stood. A siren blared outside as an ambulance raced along the road. Pedestrians stopped and stared, entranced by the nugget of excitement that had been briefly dropped into their lives. What a feat they would have from the real excitement that was merely hours away. "We'll pick your sister up on the way."

"Where do you think we need to go?"

"Jack, we are slap bang next to the country's biggest airport." He stood up and looked Jack square in the face. "We're going to get on the first plane out of here. But we have to move fast because I fear that flights won't be going for much longer."

10.38AM, 16th September 2015, University College Hospital, Euston Rd, London

They moved slowly. Holden followed the two officers, guiding them when she knew where they were. But it had to be slow progress. The infected could be around every corner, could be in any room. At least they weren't hard to spot. They had a tendency to scream loudly and run at you with manic force. And then there were the eyes, the red, bloodshot eyes. They managed to descend to the ground floor, and in the staircase, Stan listened to any sounds from behind the fire door.

"Sounds quiet," Stan said. Brian indicated for his partner to open the door, and he did a fraction. Nothing moving could be seen in the crack of the door, and he opened it wider, the door swinging inwards towards him. Stan shook his head into the corridor and did a full look around, and visibly relaxed. "Nothing," he said.

They moved into the corridor. Holden pointed down the corridor. "That's the way out onto Euston Road."

"Then that's the way we are heading," Stan said. As they moved forward, a door up ahead opened, and an infected stepped out into the corridor. It stood there for a moment watching them, then ran off in the opposite direction.

"That's new," Brian said, taking a further step forward.

"Stop a minute," Holden said. Both men turned to look at her. "What if it's not running away? What if it's gone for help?"

"Shit," Stan said. Holden had come to the conclusion that this was his favourite word. Brian pointed behind Holden, in the direction they had just come.

"Can we get out that way?" Brian asked.

"Yes, but it's a longer route," Holden answered.

"Then let's take the longer route." They reversed course and made their way back down the corridor, past the stairwell entrance. Considering it was the end of the world, the hospital corridor was virtually spotless. Stan heard a noise and looked behind him. At the end of the corridor where the infected had fled, he reappeared. Then another, and another, then three more.

"Shit," he said. "Run or shoot?" Four more infected appeared, and the mass began to creep towards them.

"Fuck this," Brian said, kneeling down. He trained his weapon on the first two infected and fired single rounds. One hit an infected square in the head, the other in another's chest. Only one of them went down. The infected stopped, roared, and Brian fired off three more shots, killing another infected. Five more joined them, however, and the numbers began to swell. "That answers that. Run."

The three of them turned and ran down the corridor, Holden quickly falling behind. She was a middle-class alcoholic doctor, not a fucking athlete. She wasn't built for this, and her lungs quickly began to burn. But she still ran, because behind them the howls of the nearly undead followed them as the noise of a dozen running feet echoed off the corridor walls.

10.39AM, 16th September 2015, US Embassy, London.

"Mr. Ambassador, we need to get you to a secure location." The US Ambassador for London, Benjamin Franklin Winchester the third, looked up from his briefing papers as the head of his protection detail walked in without knocking.

"Is it really that serious?" Winchester asked.

"Yes, sir. The CIA station chief has already ordered the evacuation of his staff. Helicopters are en route from our air base at Croughton. They will be here in 20 minutes." The head of his protection detail looked harassed, stressed even. Winchester had never seen him like that.

"Helicopters?" the ambassador asked.

"Yes, sir. The city is becoming grid-locked." Winchester nodded to his protector, who walked out of the room, closing the door behind him.

Winchester hadn't been alone in the room, and he looked at his startled secretary.

"Elizabeth, get me the Secretary of State. If I'm going to replay the fall of Hanoi, I want to know why."

"Yes, Mr. Ambassador," she said, standing and rushing out of the room, leaving her pile of paperwork on the seat she had just vacated. *What the hell is this?* the ambassador asked himself. First the rioting, then the British Prime Minister had stalled him on the meeting he had requested. Winchester picked up the remote control and turned on the news channel on his office's TV. The news was all about the apparent chaos in London. Headlining the news was the smoking crater that had been the centre of the Metropolitan Police's operation. There was a beep on his intercom, and he pressed the button.

"Mr. Ambassador, I have the Secretary of State for you." *That was quick*, thought the ambassador.

"Mr. Secretary, I've just been told of the evacuation order. Is there anything I need to know?"

"Ben," the voice over the intercom said, "you need to get your people out of there. I'm arranging transport for all your US-born staff. You're going on the first transport, and the rest of your team will follow."

"But why?" asked Winchester. "Surely rioting doesn't affect us. Hell this place is a fortress, and I've got sixty marines here to hold the fort, not to mention the Secret Service detail." There was a pained silence from the other end of the line.

"Ben, it's not just rioting. We have viable intel from the NSA and MI6 that this is a bio-weapons attack. The British are putting troops on the streets, but this is anything but simple rioting. This is turning into a full on war. The streets of London are already burning and we need you out of there."

"So where are you relocating me to?"

"We're not relocating you. We're bringing you home, Ben. All US military personnel are being recalled to their bases, and after a short quarantine period, they are being brought back to the states. From what we are seeing from the NSA feeds, the president has made the decision to airlift everyone home." Winchester sat back in his plush leather seat, personally selected to go in the office that had been his for over five years. "You're coming home, Ben. Your time in London is over." The phone went dead.

"Shit," Winchester said. He sat back in his chair, still processing the information he had just been given. How the hell does something like this happen?

10.40AM, 16th September 2015, University College Hospital, Euston Rd, London

They had bought themselves time. The double fire doors they had passed through had handles, and Stan had used his handcuffs to hold the doors together. As they ran, they heard the masses impact the doors, and they held. But straining as they were, they wouldn't hold for long.

"We need to get outside, find other officers. Or maybe military if there are any," Brian said through laboured breaths. The trio ran down a final corridor arriving in the main reception for the hospital. There were two infected there consuming the flesh from a dead nurse, and as they both looked up at the newcomers, Brian put three rounds in them, ending their existence.

"Getting low on ammo here, Stan."

"Hear you, Brian." The three survivors walked up to the glass doors and saw the carnage outside. There were bodies everywhere. Brian slapped Stan on the arm and pointed out the window across the road.

"Armed response vehicle," he said indicating the police car with the flashing lights. "That will at least have fresh ammo if we're lucky." He turned to Holden. "You think you can keep up?"

"Do I have any choice?" Holden answered. Brian smiled.

"That's the spirit, doc. Right, let's go."

They all exited the building at once, Brian fanning left, Stan panning right. They found no targets for their guns. In front of them was the dual carriageway separated by a central reservation. Past the reservation their potential armoury awaited, and with surprisingly few cars on this side of the road, they quickly made their way over to it. The road across the reservation was clogged with traffic, but again it was thankfully free of movement, infected or otherwise. The air was riddled with the sound of gunshots, but they were distant.

The driver's door to the police car was open, as was the passenger's. There was no sign of the officers, except for a policeman's hat that lay on the ground by the driver's front wheel. They could hear more gunshots in the distance, this time closer than before. Stan went straight to the boot and opened it. There were no weapons, but they found four clips for their semi-automatic machine guns, which they split evenly. There were another four clips for their side arms.

"Better than nothing," Stan said.

"233SO to Sierra Oscar control, come in please, over," Brian said, trying his radio again.

"*static*… to 233 …*static*"

"Hey, you got something," Stan said. "Try again."

"233SO to Sierra Oscar control, say again please, over."
"233SO, this is control *static*... overrun. Where are you?"
"Still at the hospital, over."
"Shit," came the response. Holden looked at Stan who was visibly surprised to hear the word. "You are right in the middle ...*static*... need to get to *static*"
"Say again please, over." But there was no response, just static.
"Shit," Stan said.
"Best bet, head for the nearest police station?" said Brian, doubt clearly evident in his voice. There was an eruption of gunfire up the road, and they could now hear a crowd roaring in the distance. A single infected emerged from the hospital and ran at them.
"*Feeeed!*" it cried as it crossed towards the central reservation. Stan dispatched it with a clean shot to the head. Even now, Holden jumped at the noise. The noise from the distant crowd seemed to go louder at the death of the infected, as if they were protesting the slaughter.
"Anywhere but here," said Holden.

10.42AM, 16th September 2015, Broadcasting House, The BBC, London

Peter listened to the scenes from around New Scotland Yard on his smartphone. Sitting at reception in the Broadcasting House foyer, he felt compelled to know what was happening out on the streets of the city he had lived in all his life. It was ironic he had to use a mobile device to find out the news when he was sat in the very building the news was coming from. And he thought this was just going to be another boring day sat at a desk.
The foyer itself was chaos, with at least a dozen police officers, some of them armed and a host of BBC employees who were coming and going from the building. There was a squeal of a braking car outside, and Peter saw an army Land Rover park up by the protective bollards. Two soldiers stepped out and entered the building, both brandishing machine guns. They stopped to talk to the police officer with the sergeant stripes, who pointed back outside. Peter couldn't hear what was being said, but he guessed the two soldiers had asked, "Where do you want us?"
"Reports are still coming in of riots across the city, and we have now heard of a shooting outside Downing Street," the earphone in Peter's ear said. This was madness; he needed to get out of here. He needed to get home. His wife would be worried sick. There were raised voices from the far end of the foyer, and two further police officers ran from the

elevators and went straight outside. He swore he thought he heard someone say "broken through", but he had no idea what that could mean.

"Attention, please. This is an emergency announcement." Peter pulled out the earbud and looked up at the ceiling, listening to the voice being relayed over the tannoy. "By order of Her Majesty's Government, we are evacuating the building. This is not a drill; I repeat this is not a drill. Please make your way to the nearest exit. I repeat, the building is being evacuated. Do not gather at your designated emergency zone. You are advised to head straight home." Peter couldn't believe what he was hearing, and sat dumbfounded until the sound of gunfire outside jerked him back into reality. The armed police moved as one, rushing outside. From his position, he could see directly outside, and saw a soldier kneel down, raising his machine gun. The soldier fired multiple shots, emptying his magazine, which he ejected, replacing it with another from his webbing.

What the hell was going on? Peter moved from his position behind the desk as the building's inhabitants began to descend into the foyer. It was his job to see them safely out of the building, but he was again distracted by the sound of shooting outside. The police had formed a line into the street, and had now joined the soldiers in what an innocent observer would presume to be a mass slaughter. But Peter couldn't see what they were shooting at, and he had to know. There was no denying his curiosity, and he joined the throng that, close to panic, was trying to get out of the confines of the building. He was one of the first dozen to exit the building, and what he saw would have frozen him to the spot if it hadn't been for the swell of people behind him, and he was pushed further into the street.

Ten metres down the road, there was a mass of almost a hundred people running as fast as they could towards the police and army line. The bullets ripped into them, felling them in their dozens, but they still came, some seemingly immune to the wounds that were being inflicted upon them. There was a fresh surge behind him, and Peter found himself being knocked to the ground, a boot catching him in the back of his head. At the same time, he hit the ground hard, and something in his arm snapped. He heard it, even over the noise and the uproar around him, and the pain shot through his body. Peter's brain couldn't handle the onslaught of such a sudden assault, and unconsciousness quickly descended on him. As he blacked out, the last thing he ever saw was a bloodied teenager, bringing a policeman down to the ground, clawing at his face. Her head exploded as a soldier fired at her at point blank range, covering the fallen police officer in her blood. Blackness took Peter, and when he finally came to, he no longer remembered the man he had once been. He no longer cared about his wife or his children. He no longer had pride in his job or his achievements. All he cared about was biting, and clawing and chewing and killing.

10.43AM 16th September 2015, Heathrow Airport, London

Patrick Stewart stood in the airport's control tower and looked at the chaos on the radar monitor. Moments earlier, orders had come in that all flights into the UK were to be redirected, and nobody high up would tell him why. Patrick had simply been told that nothing was to land, and there was a soldier stood next to him with a gun.

Nothing was allowed to land. Air traffic controllers were informing the agitated pilots who, low on fuel, had already begun to stack up in the airspace above the country's biggest airport. Most were being diverted to France, and across the skies of the United Kingdom, planes were banking onto new flight paths to take them to new, unexpected destinations.

And to make matters worse, his staff were deserting their posts. Despite a strict no phone or social media policy, the news of what was happening in the country was still filtering to everyone. They had responsibilities, but they also had families, and for many of them, family came first. He supposed it was understandable really. Stewart, however, didn't have that problem; he didn't have any family that mattered. He had no kids and the ex-wife who sucked money out of his bank account every month could go and fry her head in garlic for all he cared. And all his real friends worked in the airport. So as the person in charge of who landed and who didn't, he stayed at his post. He had been given a new mission to make things even more complicated. Get any planes sat on the tarmac fuelled, loaded, and in the air. The logistics of this were turning out to be a complete nightmare because he knew eventually the order would come to ground everything. And when that happened, the people in the terminals below were likely going to panic and rip the airport apart.

10.45AM 16th September 2015, Great Ormond Street Hospital, London

Rachel bent down over the body of her dead viral sister, briefly sniffing the bullet wound that had caused the back of her head to explode. She took a finger and probed the hole, scooping brain matter from around the hole's rim. She sniffed her finger and tentatively licked the gore that dripped from it, a ripple of ecstasy firing through her. The voices in her mind did not howl in the process, and she cleaned her finger with her tongue before discarding the corpse. As hungry as she was, the call to fight was stronger, and she stood, the body at her feet now of no importance. The battle for supremacy was all that mattered now. As strong as they were, their kind were still vulnerable, and she looked over to the man who had fired the shot, now in pieces as roughly twenty infected dined on his corpse. So many had been lost. But so many more joined their ranks as the minutes ticked past. Their numbers grew, and soon, they would become unstoppable. If the collective mind had any memory of religious lore, it might perhaps say it was legion.

The battle for the hospital had been bloody but short. The infected, through weight of numbers, had overwhelmed the dozen or so defenders who had taken it upon themselves to try and save the children who even now were defenceless inside. Only some had been armed with guns, and they had quickly run out of ammunition. And humans armed with axes and knives and pieces of wood were no match for an army of infected with enhanced strength and primal reflexes.

With the defenders subdued, the hoard could turn on those others that dwelled within. Many of the occupants of the children's hospital would be sick or crippled, but that would all change when the virus worked its way through their bodies, curing disease, bringing life and vitality to cancer-ridden torsos and lungs damaged by cystic fibrosis. Of course, the minds would die. The individuality, the essence of humanity and the vulnerability and innocence of childhood would be burned away. And the fire of the infection would take hold, turning the children into the ultimate warriors of the plague. Because even hardened soldiers might hesitate before killing children, many not even being able to fire.

Rachel jerked her head towards the hospital entrance. Three dozen infected who watched her and waited took that as a command to storm the building, and with an ungodly howl, they surged through the broken and shattered doors, stepping over carcasses and oblivious to the genocide they were about to unleash. As Rachel stood, eyes closed, head raised, she began to hear the sweet sound of slaughter, the screams, the aura of abject terror that just swelled her heart. Savouring the victory for mere seconds, she turned away, and fifty or so infected followed her. The voice in her head, the collective wisdom of hundreds of thousands of contaminated beings, told her where to go next. Why she was deemed worthy to lead such numbers she did not know. And she did not question, for she was the collective and the collective was her and her only goal was to serve, to feed and to spread.

10.45AM 16th September 2015, Sizewell B Nuclear Power Plant, Suffolk

For fucks sake, so much for his day off. The call had come in minutes ago. Sid had been sat at home, reading the newspaper when his mobile had vibrated violently on the table. He knew he should have switched it off, but he also knew that this wasn't allowed. You were needed, there was a problem at the plant, get your arse in gear the message had said. No doubt it was the usual drama that seemed to happen every time he was away from the place. The last time had been some bloody hippies trying to get onto the site by cutting the perimeter wire. Fucking idiots had almost gotten themselves shot for their trouble. Driving up to the imposing buildings of the Sizewell B Nuclear Plant, he drove past Vulcan Arms Pub where he had experienced many a beer-filled evening.

As a member of the Civil Nuclear Constabulary, it was his job to protect one of the country's nuclear power stations. Stationed at Sizewell for five years, he had risen through the ranks, and it wouldn't be long before he was in charge of the place, or at least in charge of its security. That meant a pay rise, and it meant more perks. He was still young, and he had plans to go onto regional command. But let's get the day's emergency over with first though. Sid still felt he had time to finish his coffee of course. Five minutes later, he was out of his house and driving to his workplace.

It was raining. Of course it was. It was one of those annoying drizzles that wasn't quite cleared by the lowest wiper setting, but which didn't warrant the higher speed, which is what they now squeaked at. And because the rubber was old, it scraped annoyingly across his windshield. Coming to the end of the private road that was the only vehicular access to the facility, he slowed and stopped at the imposing security gates. His ID was checked even though the guys on the gate knew him by sight. Hell, he drank with them regularly. But nobody got on site without valid ID, absolutely nobody. Sid exchanged pleasantries, and he was allowed access. As he manoeuvred his car into the staff car park, he was surprised to see two military helicopters flying low overhead. Big transport ones, obviously looking to land nearby. Sid parked his car and sat a moment, watching them slowly descend until they became obscured by the buildings all around him.

"What the fuck?" he said to himself. Exiting his car, he spied other military vehicles by the main entrance, which he made his way towards. Something was definitely up, and he made a decision to make his first stop the armoury. As a member of the CNC, he was authorised to be armed whilst on duty. As the days progressed, that was something he would become very thankful for.

There were soldiers in the building, some carrying ammo crates, and they ignored him as he made his way past them. He didn't like what he was seeing. Now fully kitted out, Sid headed to his inspector's office. The door was open, and he knocked upon entering. His inspector glanced at him, but continued to listen to a man in an Army uniform he was standing next to.

"We've acquisitioned some local building equipment and will have the tree line down by the end of tomorrow. I'll need your men to show us where the weak spots are, and we'll be doing what we can to strengthen the perimeter. If you have any suggestions, liaise with my sergeant, and we'll get this job done as quickly as we can." The man was a colonel, and he turned to leave the room, giving Sid a brief gesture of acknowledgment before he left.

Sid closed the door and turned to his superior officer.

"Inspector, what the fuck was that?"

"That was the shit hitting the fan. Have you seen the news today?"

"No," Sid said. "If you remember, I don't have a TV or a computer. I've always figured that if there's something I need to know, somebody would just tell me."

"There's something you need to know," the inspector said, sitting down, far too serious for Sid's liking. Normally, the man tried to inject humour into every situation, but not today. Sid followed his example. "The facility is now under martial law. The military has taken command of security because the country is being attacked. The powers that be have decided to keep the reactors going with a plan to shut down depending on how the situation escalates. We will have a full company of Her Majesty's finest stationed here for the foreseeable. As for why…" The inspector picked a folder paper off his desk and handed it to Sid. Sid opened it warily and slowly read the first page briefing paper.

"This can't be happening," Sid said after five minutes, shaking his head in disbelief.

"It is. I've spoken to my superiors. I believe that religious nutter of an ex-wife of yours would have called this The End of Days," the inspector said, no humour in his voice. They were both distracted by a change on the news channel which was playing silently on the large LED TV on the wall. The picture showed more scenes from a ruined New Scotland Yard.

"Shit," Sid said, "I used to work there."

10.46AM, 16th September 2015, Hounslow, London

"I'm sorry, but no you can't take Amy out of school," the stern headmistress stated. She looked disapprovingly at the two men who stood before her, her eyes staring out over the rims of her glasses. "There has been enough disruption in her schooling. We can't have anymore." Jack and Clive were stood in the main corridor of the school where they had encountered the headmistress on one of her many errands. She was not happy to see them on school grounds. She was not happy having to deal with interlopers when she had so much to do.

"But it's an emergency," Jack pleaded.

"Then her mother should be here." Jack felt the frustration grow in him. Most of the teachers at this school he liked, but this woman had always been a bitch. When he had been the one to tell her that Amy would be off due to the death of their father, she had been about as sympathetic as an SS camp guard. And here she was, seemingly oblivious to the chaos heading this way.

"My mother is dealing with the emergency; that's why I'm here," Jack tried to explain. He could hardly tell the woman the truth. Could hardly say, 'Oh no, Mum can't be here right now because she's probably already drunk'. He had done his best to hide this knowledge from the school, because that would mean a referral to social services. And that would most likely see Amy taken into care, which wouldn't help anyone. Jack felt Clive put his big hands on his shoulders. The older man stepped forward, using his size and bulk to intimidate the much smaller and frailer opponent. This was no time for social niceties.

"No, I can't allow it," the woman said. *For God's sake*, Jack screamed inside, *you know me, you know I'm her brother.* He was actually just about to say those very words when Clive pushed past him and stood towering over the thin, matronly woman.

"Madam, we are taking the child," Clive said, glaring down at the woman. "If you want to know why, I suggest you turn on any fucking TV channel or any radio." The headmistress visibly recoiled at the sound of the expletive. Clive pressed his advantage. "We are taking the child, and you would be wise to send the rest of the children home." He turned to Jack, no longer willing to waste any more time on the woman. "Which classroom?" Jack pointed and followed in Clive's wake as he stormed off down the corridor.

"I shall be contacting the authorities," the headmaster shouted after them.

"Yeah? Well, good look with that," Clive said over his shoulder.

10.48AM GMT 16th September 2015, CNN Studios, New York City

Despite the five hour time difference, CNN never slept. Gavin Rose, the early morning anchor for the CNN newsroom, sat in makeup finishing the last of his early morning coffee. He never minded the early mornings, never minded starting his broadcast at 6AM. He was a morning person, revelling in the relatively deserted streets and the breaking dawn. Little did he know that he would be working long into the evening and would spend tonight sleeping on his office couch.

Because he hadn't expected this when he had woken up this morning. Right now, he was watching a re-run of the Sky News broadcast, and around him in the production booth, madness ruled.

"We are running with this as our breaking story," his editor Brian Hawkins said animatedly. "This might be the biggest thing since 911, and we need to be the ones to bring this to the nation."

"Brian, isn't that a bit much for a riot?" Gavin asked.

"This is more than just a riot," Brian said. "We've got Simone Clemonts on the ground in London, and she says it's a full-scale war there. And you," he gripped Gavin by the shoulder excitedly, "you will be reporting it all live."

"Five minutes to air," a voice said in Gavin's ear.

"Get out there, Gavin. Get out there and win us some awards."

"This is CNN," said the voice on millions of TV sets across the globe. The compulsory computer graphics disappeared to show two people sat in a studio, with grim looks on their faces.

"Good morning, America, this is Gavin Rose, bringing you the news from around the world."

"And I'm Lucy Cartwright," said Gavin's co-anchor. He didn't like her, he never had. Mainly because she was smart, attractive, and had spurned his numerous attempts to get into her pants. Oh, he liked her in that way, and even now he would happily jump at the chance if she were to bend over and drop those sweet little panties he was sure she wore. But that wasn't going to happen. She somehow thought she was too good for him, even better than him. He could see it in the way she smirked at him, in the way she had rejected his proposals with a body language that just dripped pity and contempt. But such thoughts were for another day. He had a job to do.

"Breaking news from London, England this morning," said Gavin, "as

terrorists strike at the heart of London's police force. Live on the scene, we have a report from our London correspondent, Simone

Clemonts. Simone, what's the situation there?" The millions of viewers were transported to the heart of London, where a well-dressed and well-groomed African American woman could be seen holding a microphone.

"Thank you, Gavin. I'm here by the Houses of Parliament, the seat of the UK Government. It is absolute pandemonium here, as an everyday rush hour was disrupted by a series of riots that broke across the city in the early hours. Then moments ago, an explosion went off outside New Scotland Yard, the headquarters of the Metropolitan police force. No word from the British Government as to who is responsible for the attack at this time, but extraordinary precautions are being taken. Behind me, you can see a detachment of the Grenadier Guards, part of the British Armed Forces, are blocking off Westminster Bridge."

"There is a rumour that the riots and the explosion might be somehow connected. Are you able to confirm that, Simone?" Gavin asked, a fake look of concern plastered all over his face.

"Not at this time, Gavin, and the area around the explosion has been sealed off. Confidential sources have, however, told me the rioting has spread across the city, and as we know from earlier footage, there have already been police shootings in other areas." Three soldiers ran past her, but stopped as they were shouted at by an officer. All three turned and looked at the reporter and her camera crew, and then the world's millions saw them approach. Simone was relatively oblivious to this at first.

"Ma'am, we're going to have to ask you to stop broadcasting," one of the soldiers, a corporal, stated matter of factly.

"What's happening there, Simone?" The editor split the screen, and now Gavin was visible again to those watching. Simone could be seen talking off her microphone, shaking her head furiously, only for the soldier to become visibly more insistent.

"We are being asked to leave the area..." Simone answered, only for the camera to move off her and turn to the left slightly as the sound of gunshots rang out. The camera focused in on a lone soldier, machine gun raised, firing down the length of Westminster Bridge. One of the three soldiers came over and grabbed the camera.

"Alright, Sunny Jim, that's enough of that," the soldier said, and then the news feed cut out. The world's millions were left with Gavin looking gobsmacked.

"This just in, the British Government has just banned all live broadcasts from key areas of London. No word as to why though yet," Lucy said, reading the teleprompter. Gavin bristled inside at that. He was the lead anchor; he should have been the one to tell the world that. What the hell was the editor playing at?

"Shocking scenes there from London. Be sure to stay with us to learn the news as it happens. Only on CNN."

"You can't do that!" Simone shouted at the soldier who was wrestling with her cameraman. "The whole world is watching. I'm with fucking CNN."

"I don't care if you're the resurrection of the Queen Mother. My orders are no cameras in the combat zone. And you need to get in your truck and leave."

"Combat zone? What do you mean combat zone? And besides, I'm not going anywhere," she roared. "This country has freedom of the press, and I intend to tell the world what is going on here." She looked at the soldier defiantly. He looked at her for three seconds and then looked at one of the men with him.

"Private," he said, nodding towards the camera the private was now holding. The private had wrenched the camera out of the CNN employee's hand, and he now threw it hard onto the floor. The camera impacted, pieces scattering across the asphalt. The corporal took out his sidearm and put three rounds into the camera's body.

"Fuck me!" the cameraman shouted, jumping back in surprise.

"Orders are orders, ma'am, and you really don't want to be here. My advice … get in your truck and make your way out of the city as fast as you can." There was no pleasure in his voice, just resignation. "You really don't know what's going on. And you really do not want to test me on this. If you do not leave the area, you will be subject to immediate detention." An officer came over, captain's rank.

"Problem, Corporal?"

"No sir, just asking these civilians to leave the area." The captain looked at the CNN crew and then looked at the devastated camera on the floor.

"You, you're in charge here. You can't do this; I'm an American. I'll complain to my ambassador," Simone said weakly.

"Go right ahead," the captain replied. "But quite frankly, ma'am, I don't give a fuck. And neither will you when you finally learn what's going on here. Besides, from what I've heard, your ambassador is on a plane back to the States by now. Corporal," he turned to his subordinate, "carry on."

10.49AM, 16th September 2015, Fleet Command, Portsmouth Royal Naval Base, Portsmouth

It was bedlam. Portsmouth, home to much of the UK's remaining Royal Navy surface fleet, was the scene of absolute bedlam. Covering almost fifty square miles, there were over seventeen thousand people working at the naval base, and all of them were busting a gut to get the fleet to sea. Of course, not all the base personnel were present, and the emergency recall had gone out for those away on leave. By the end of the day, the numbers at the base would swell as permission was given for immediate family to join base personnel in what was to become a fully fledged evacuation of the mainland.

There were twenty military ships stationed at Portsmouth on that day. A collection of type 45 Destroyers, type 23 Frigates and patrol vessels. Getting all those ships to sea in such a short time scale was a monumental task, and it fell on the broad and experienced shoulders of the base commander, Commodore Nigel Rigby. He was in conference with his senior staff, and all he was being told was how impossible it was to get the job done.

"Commander Nelson," Rigby said addressing the Queen's Harbour Master, "impossible or not, it must be done. I am not privy to the why's and the how's, all I know is I have my orders from the chief of the defence staff. The fleet goes to sea, and it goes to sea today. We need anything that can float out there."

"My lads will do their best, sir."

"That's all I ask, Commander. As your namesake once said, all England expects is for every man to do his duty." Rigby looked up at the picture on his office wall of the man he was quoting. "Get my ships to sea, Commander."

10.51AM, 16th September 2015, Oxford University, Oxford

Professor McCann, head of Art History at Oxford University, sat at his open window, enjoying the morning breeze, his lit pipe a blessed distraction from the tedious assignments he would soon have to get around to marking. It had been a mistake to go into teaching – he realised that now. He just couldn't stand the mediocre minds that sat in his classes every day. Occasionally, there was one with promise, who showed a spark of true brilliance, but every year, it seemed he saw less and less of that. When he was a student, there was passion and rebellion, but he saw none of that now. All he saw was meek acceptance and an allergy in the young to discuss anything controversial. Gurdjieff was right; the masses were nothing but pointless machines.

He wasn't supposed to smoke indoors, but he was damned if he was going to abuse his arthritic hips with a walk outside. So damn the rules, and damn those who made the rules. And double damn those infuriating mindless drones who enforced them without even understanding why. They were everything that was wrong with humanity. He blew the smoke out the open window and wished for a mind that could challenge him instead of asking a question that bloody Google could answer. There was a knock at the door, and McCann coughed in surprise. He quickly knocked the remaining tobacco out of his pipe on the external window ledge and hid the pipe from view, his minor rebellion something he wanted to keep to himself today. Although part of him said he should just carry on smoking in open defiance – everyone knew he smoked in his office. The dean had even sent one of his bloody minions around to ask him, so very nicely, not to do so. McCann, not one to be told off by a lackey, had told the young man that if the dean wanted him to stop smoking, then the dean knew where his office was. Of course, the dean had never raised the matter. Probably because that very lunch time, an extremely annoyed McCann had wandered out onto the grass, and it being on the ground floor, had mysteriously found himself outside the window of the dean's office. Tapping on the window with the lighter his wife had bought him for their fifth wedding anniversary, holding a mischievous glint in his eye, McCann had proceeded to light his pipe and blow smoke through the open window.

"Come in," McCann said. The door opened, and his secretary popped her head in.

"Urgent phone call for you, Professor." She nodded to the landline phone that presently had the receiver out of its cradle.

"Am I never to get any peace?" McCann said half-jokingly. "Am I to be constantly hounded by jackals and ghouls?"

"I wouldn't know about that, Professor. All I know is the caller said it's urgent. I'll go and make you a nice cup of tea." With that, she left and closed the door. McCann sighed and picked up the phone receiver, pushing a button for an external line.

"Hello, Professor McCann here."

"Professor, please hold," the voice said.

"What? Now hold on…" But he was interrupted by an automated voice. Was this one of those bloody telemarketing calls? Urgent my arse, and he almost slammed the receiver down.

"Please hold for a message from the prime minister regarding operation codename Noah." There was a click and then a few seconds of silence and then the voice continued. “Please repeat your name for voice verification.” McCann sat confused for several seconds and then his blood ran cold. Noah? No, it can’t be; that could never happen. But still, he spoke his full name. There was another click, but this time, the prime minister’s voice came on the line. Obviously recorded, but still earth shattering, the professor sat and listened. When the recorded message ended, McCann put the phone back in its cradle and reached into his top drawer. He pulled out the half empty bottle of scotch and poured a decent measure into the empty glass that sat on his desk. Fuck the tea.

He still remembered the day the government official had come to see him at his home, uninvited and accompanied by two men who could have come straight out of a spy novel. The official had been courteous, but had refused to discuss why he was here on the doorstep. Sat in the professor’s lounge, the wife looking on, uncomfortable with the intrusion, the official had extracted a thick folder from his briefcase, as well as a clipboard. Only one of the other men had come into the house with them, the other staying outside, the front door now closed.

“What I have to discuss with you is highly confidential and is in the national interest.”

“The national interest? What is this? I’m a bloody history professor, not a spy,” McCann had stated bluntly, just a hint of fear starting to crawl into his mind.

“No, sir, you are mistaken. You are the best this country has in your field. Most of your peers say so, and that is the reason why I am here.” The official withdrew two sheets of paper and attached them to the clipboard. He passed it over to the professor.

“What the hell is this?”

“That document, when signed, states that you agree to abide by the Official Secrets Act. It states that if you discuss anything of what I’m about to tell you, you will have all your assets seized and will be arrested. Let me assure you, there will be no trial, and you will live out your days in a hole in a country most people haven’t even heard of.” The official pointed to the clipboard. “There are two copies there; your wife will need to sign one too.” McCann looked at his wife who was almost in tears, and he thrust the clipboard back at the official.

“I’m not signing anything. Get the hell out of my damned house.” The official looked at McCann for several seconds, ignoring the clipboard.

“Whilst I am not allowed to discuss the details, I am allowed to tell you the following. It is the government’s determination that, in the event of a national catastrophe, the best and the brightest should be saved where possible. You are one of those individuals, and you are being given the opportunity to live should the worst case scenario occur."

"You mean like nuclear war?" McCann said, shocked.

"That is one such scenario. I can't tell you any more until that document is signed. Signing the document also allows for your children to be added to the list of those to be saved. By not signing, should the worst-case scenario occur, you are likely condemning your children to die." The official reached into his inner pocket and extracted a Mont Blanc, which he passed forward. "Do you need a pen?"

McCann had signed and then put the incident away in the part of his mind where he kept memories of idle curiosities. And now the call had come. Across the country, hundreds of people on hundreds of phones were receiving the same message. Gather your essentials. Gather your designated immediate family – spouse and under eighteen-year-old children only – and proceed to the designated extraction point. Your communications are now being monitored. Failure to comply will result in a loss of your Noah privilege. Any attempt to contact anyone outside your designated group will result in a loss of your Noah privilege. Failure to be at the extraction point at the designated time will negate your Noah privilege. Arrival of the extraction point with anyone other than your designated immediate family members will negate your Noah privilege. Your Noah privilege? Life.

10.55AM, 16th September 2015, Marylebone Road, London

They had tried to reach the Albany Street police station just north of Great Portland Street, but abandoned that plan when they had seen it besieged by dozens of, as Stan called them, "those insane fuckers". Although they were at a distance, it looked like the police station had been overrun, and with the numbers of infected visible, the three of them were in no position to attempt any kind of a rescue. So they headed to Paddington, staying hidden where they could.

Humanity was all around them now, as well as the infected. Through the bedlam, they moved almost unseen, dispatching the occasional threat when it presented itself. They moved with purpose, the infected spread out and often isolated. Still in the distance, there was that noise, like an enraged crowd baying for blood, baying for vengeance. With all the traffic clogging the roads, it was almost impossible to see anything up or down the street, but as Holden noted on several occasions, the noise was getting closer, as if it was following them.

They reached Baker Street, smoke filling the road as flames billowed out of the windows of several of the buildings. The bodies of two dead officers lay under the protection of the bus shelter, gunshot wounds having shattered their brains. Stan had knelt down to inspect them, but the frantic voice of Holden telling him not to touch them had caused him to back off.

"They were shot for a reason," Holden had said. She didn't know exactly what was going on, but she had seen enough for her medical training to deduce what they needed to be avoiding. At the next junction, three frantic people ran across the road they travelled from north to south. Moments later, four obvious infected followed them, one glancing a look over at where Holden and her protectors stood. It was as if the infected looked right at her, and it held her gaze for a second, perhaps two, but then it continued its original pursuit. Neither officer moved to help the chased. This was no longer about protecting the public. This was now about survival, and they moved on past the junction.

They had received no further contact on their police radios. It was as if the whole system was collapsing around them, which was exactly what was happening. Stan stopped them in their tracks.

"Do you hear that?" he asked.

"What?" Brian asked as he turned on the spot once.

"I hear it, like a strong wind," Holden said. "It's the same noise that's been following us since we left the Euston."

"We need to get off the street," Brian added. "I've been wondering what that noise was and I remember now. It's the sound of people. We're slam bang in the middle of two huge crowds." They moved back to the junction they had just passed and stood briefly surveying the scene.

"There," Holden said pointing to the door of a fast food restaurant. The door was ajar, and they moved together, but Stan stopped them from entering. He opened the door, raising his weapon. He tried to ignore the blood trail that marked where someone had been dragged out into the street. He tried to ignore the dead body in the corner, and the single blood-stained child's shoe that sat almost artistically on one of the serving counters.

"Armed police, anybody in here?" he shouted through the open door. There was no response. "Show yourselves now or risk getting shot." Still nothing. "What do you think?" he said to Brian.

"Best we've got," came the reply, and the three moved inside, Holden closing the door behind her. "Look for the controls for the security shutters," Brian ordered as Holden flipped the lock on the very vulnerable glass paned door.

10.57AM, 16th September 2015, Wholesale Warehouse, Sheffield

It was the strangest phone call he had ever received in his time as manager of the warehouse. The call was from what was effectively his boss, telling him he needed to close the store down, get all the customers out and send non-essential staff home. Tell everyone it's a gas leak, tell them the Martians have landed, tell them anything. His anxiety raced when he was then told he had to seal it up tight, and he found himself reaching for his anti-anxiety meds. Within minutes of the call, two police patrol cars had arrived, and the security feeds playing on the screens in the main office showed four police officers entering the building. Two of them were armed. He had never seen an armed police officer in Sheffield before. He reached for the store intercom.

"Good morning, shoppers, this is the management speaking. Unfortunately, I have some bad news for you folks. The store is having to close early today as we have ourselves a bit of a gas leak. Now don't worry, we aren't all going to blow up, but safety has to come first with these sorts of things. Those currently at the checkouts, please finish your transactions and head for the nearest exit. As this is an emergency situation, we must ask that those not already involved in a transaction leave the store immediately. You will not be allowed to purchase anything, and police are here to ensure your safety to help you exit the building in an orderly fashion. There is no need to run; this is merely a precaution."

Announcements like that were being made across the country. Someone in government phoned someone else in government who arranged for the telephone tree to contact the national headquarters of all the main food distribution chains. They, in turn, sent the message down their networks. And the message? Close all the stores and lock them up tight because panic was coming. One by one, the larger supermarkets and wholesale stores were emptied of people and put under guard. As the day progressed, things didn't all go to plan. In some parts of the country, where the panic had already started, some stores were already being stripped clean. Some saw fighting and assaults as madness descended and the thin veil of civility began to tear. Once the chaos started, there just weren't enough law enforcement officers to deal with it. Any police that arrived did so too late to stop what had become basic fear induced looting, and in many cases, they just turned their cars around and drove away. In many of those stores, the staff themselves, realising what was happening, joined in the fray.

When the people began to realise what was descending on their country, they went into one of three modes. The first was denial; they didn't believe things were as bad as they were hearing. This was actually the majority of the people. They walked outside, saw cars on the roads, saw their TV was working and the lights were still on. They stayed at work, even when their friends and family started calling them, even when social media started to explode with the insanity.

The second was flight. Those individuals packed a bag and went to where they thought it was safe, but most of them didn't get anywhere, because their actions clogged the country's arteries. Most of them became trapped in a state of limbo, their cars barely moving, their nerves slowly disintegrating as they listened to the radio and the tales of the apocalypse it brought.

The third was chaos. Deciding to hunker down, they did what unprepared people always did – they panicked. Corner shops and grocers saw the same old pattern. First, it was five or ten people who arrived and loaded up baskets with canned goods, candles and bottled water. Then it was dozens, stripping the shelves bare. At first, the managers and owners looked on in wonder as their produce was sold at ever-increasing rates. Then hundreds descended, bringing chaos and theft and violence. Violence that spread onto the streets in the form of looting and flames, and in some areas, even rape. And sometimes murder. As the infection began to destroy the country's brain, its own people began to desecrate the rest of the now rotting carcass.

Rarely, however, there was an individual who was prepared. Gavin Hemsworth was such an individual. He watched the news with a growing sense of both excitement and dread, not knowing that the man who created the devastating virus was sat watching exactly the same TV channel just over a mile away. Excitement because it proved he had been right all along. And dread because he was presently alone. He had obviously not been expecting a zombie apocalypse, but he had been expecting the inevitable breakdown in civilisation. And here it was. Having no children, it made sense to him to plan for when the electricity stopped and for when the taps ran dry. His partner, James, agreed, and if anything, was even more convinced the end was coming. Several years of listening to Alex Jones and a library filled with David Icke books had convinced the pair that the New World Order was rapidly approaching, and that the only solution was to hunker down off the grid as best they could.

As a couple, they were well off through their internet businesses, but not anywhere close to being rich, so they couldn't buy a plot of land on an island somewhere to weather the eventual storm. However, they did the next best thing and moved as far away from humanity as was possible on the UK mainland, buying an old, run-down farm in the middle of Devon. They had moved here ten years ago, and had slowly made the farm self-sufficient. It had its own well, and a means of generating electricity through a combination of solar panels and wind turbines with an array of storage batteries. They had chickens, pigs and cattle, and a significant greenhouse that was growing a substantial crop. The farm, a thumb shape of sixty-three acres, even had its own natural defences, most of the property borders being bounded by a wide, rushing river. The only road that accessed the property could be easily blocked and easily hidden. With high hedges and thick layers of spiky plants, the rest of the farm's boundary was virtually inaccessible. Barbed wire and panel fencing had plugged any gaps. For anyone who managed to breach the defences, the five goats were the only alarm the pair needed, and the three German shepherds and the safe full of shotguns would make them regret the day they chose this plot of land to invade.

There were three accommodation buildings on the farm, and it was one of these, derelict on purchase, that Gavin had decided to upgrade for the apocalypse. With the help of his partner and his two brothers, who admittedly both thought the whole thing ridiculous and yet were more than happy to help their younger brother fulfil his dream, the farm was upgraded. The derelict was transformed into a fortress, basically rebuilt from the basement up. Six shipping containers had been purchased and precariously navigated through the winding country roads, only to be buried around the new building in an L-shape. Joined together, connected to the basement and covered in six foot of earth, the shipping containers formed a bunker that could easily house the couple and all their provisions. This was their ark, where they and their families could survive whilst the world around them went to hell in a hand basket. They could sit back, protected and hidden from the world, and drink red wine and eat home grown beef whilst the rest of civilisation burned.

The only problem was that James was not here. It was the classic scenario they had been warned about when they had joined the survivalist internet forums. Building a bunker and a hideout were all well and good, but what if you weren't there when the shit hit the fan? What if you were miles away or, worse still, trapped in another country? What if you were in the very city that was the epicentre of the problem, which is exactly where James was? Then there was the added complication that James wasn't answering his phone. And that's because James, intent on catching an early train back to Devon, had found himself in Waterloo Station just as the infection hit in earnest. As Gavin rang his lover again, hundreds of miles away a phone rang, ignored. It was ignored because the pocket of the person it was in no longer understood what a phone was. And even if he did remember what the phone was for, he wouldn't have answered. He was too busy, knelt down in the dirt of the street, his entire focus spent eating a dead child's liver.

11.00AM, 16th September 2015, Hayton Vale, Devon

The Children of the Resurrection – that was the name Brother Abraham had created. Waking one morning in his thousand-acre Texas ranch, he had had what he described as a divine revelation, a message brought to him by the very lips of God. The world was diseased, and he with his wealth and his charisma, he would be the one to cure God's children. For they had lost their way and had turned away from the Lord's wisdom. They were but petulant children who needed to be brought back under the protection of their father's wing. And thus, they were no longer deserving of his mercy, and all that left was for them to experience his fury. Abraham would be the Lord's hammer; he would smite the wicked and rid the planet of the heathen and the unbeliever. The defiler would meet death, and then stand before the Lord awaiting judgement and eternal damnation.

Delusions such as this in someone working a nine-to-five job usually resulted in a trip to the psychiatrist and high doses of medication. But when you ran a multi-billion-dollar private pharmaceutical corporation, with offices in seventeen countries and what amounted to your own private army, the psychiatrists were something you didn't really have to worry about. Because you owned the psychiatrists, and you could buy the politicians. And through them, you were immune from the laws that controlled the sheep.

There had already been several candidates when his agents had discovered Professor Jones. Abraham had been searching for someone to help fulfil God's plan, and God had delivered just when the first doubts had begun to sneak into Abraham's mind. Abraham had repented that sin, and knew that God forgave him. He still held the scars from his self-flagellation. After all, Abraham was only human.

The problems Professor Jones faced were twofold. How to create the virus, and how to disperse the virus. It had to reach maximum infection quickly enough that it couldn't be contained, but to a degree where it wouldn't make it out of the UK. Brother Abraham wanted an example, a testament to the power of the Lord Our God. He wanted a Sodom and Gomorrah, a warning to the world. Only then would the power of God be borne witness. The world would awaken to news that the doors of hell had been nudged open a fraction and that there was still time for them to repent. Only if the world did not awaken to the truth was the plague to be unleashed across the globe.

So it couldn't be airborne, which wasn't a problem because what Jones had in mind was too weak for that anyway. And the initial spread had to allow for those infected to become unknown and unwitting carriers first. Abraham also wanted it to be biblical. From his speeches, Jones had learnt exactly what Abraham had meant by that. He wanted the virus to cause the chosen country to rip itself apart, to create a media spectacle that would be talked about for generations. So a mere deadly flu really wasn't enough. Abraham wanted people driven insane, to tear out the throat of the very country that they called home. And so Jones worked, and it was by what he called blind luck (but what Abraham called divine intervention) that he discovered and created a virus that drove the human mind violently mad, and through that violence, precipitate its spread.

But there was another aspect to the virus that caused Abraham to rejoice in the obvious implications of its divine creation. Those infected developed a kind of hive mind form of communication. They could work together, could coordinate and engage in rudimentary strategy. As the number of infected grew, they even seemed to engage in some form of telepathy, some form of single consciousness. There was no Queen at the heart of the hive, of course; they themselves became the Queen. On reading the data on this Jones had given him, Abraham had wept with joy. He had called this telepathy the voice of God.

The choice of the coffee shops was perfect for spreading the infection. At major transport hubs, with roughly one to two hours for the ingested pathogen to take effect, most of those infected had spread themselves to other parts of the cities targeted. The two-hour time span also gave the disseminators of the virus the opportunity to use the city's transport network should London traffic become impassable, which was a not uncommon event in England's capital city. Whilst ultimately the plan was for the agents of destruction to escape the devastation by car to a private heliport and then by helicopter to Northern France, they were, however, more than prepared to go down with the doomed ship if that was what the Lord demanded. Likewise, those of the Lord's faith in the other cities had private planes booked to take them to safety.

Some of those who drank the tainted milk were in offices. Some were in cars. Some were on trains. Some were simply on the streets when the first symptoms hit. And wherever they fell, the infection spread, those attacked and bitten either dying from their wounds and resurrecting or turning within minutes to join the army of the infected and the undead. That was the design of the virus. Spread on by bites and bodily fluids, the initial infection was designed to allow the spread of those contaminated across the city. But the subsequent infections developed quickly, not allowing the emergency services time to quarantine and respond. Whilst it was theoretically possible to cordon off and quarantine a city of 10 million people, such operations took time, and such operations required a central brain to organise and plan and adapt. When the brain found itself under attack, any kind of quarantine would be ineffective and haphazard.

Jones sat in the living room of the farm, the BBC news playing on the TV in the corner. Beneath him lay the high-tech research facility where he had developed the virus that was known only as "The Horseman". He drank and savoured a cup of hot coffee as the nation's media exploded with terror on the large screen that was the focus of the room. How long before the coffee ran out? He knew his job was done, and he was now alone in the building, the others having left days before. There was no longer a need for guards and scientists. And yet he had stayed, despite the protests of those he worked with.

He would sit here and watch the corrupt decadent system die. Even when the terrestrial network went down, he could watch CNN, ABC and a host of other foreign news channels thanks to the large satellite disk on the roof. With five months of fuel for the generators, and its own water well, the converted farm made the ideal stronghold to ride out oblivion. But he knew he would never leave this place. Instead, he would sit as the world reacted with horror, grief, and blame. And there would be lots of blame, especially when Abraham gave the world God's message. Then he would wait, wait for the inevitable day when the infected came knocking on his door. And he would let them knock, the blast-proof structure he was in immune to their fists and their mass. He would sit, he would smile and when the time was right, he would take the vial he had kept especially for the end. He would inject himself and open the door to his new creations. He would lie down and become their next banquet of human meat. This very morning, he had turned off the defences that made this place such a death trap to the unwary.

Or perhaps the government men would come first. That was possible, and not without a certain degree of drama. Yes, he could see it now, soldiers storming the building, the futile attempt to find the cure. Futile indeed for there was no cure. As soon as an unauthorised person breached the laboratory's outer perimeter, the self-sustained Solid State Drives holding all the research data would self-destruct. There would be nothing left, nothing but what lived in his mind, and he would see to it that nobody would delve into that tortured abyss. Jones already had that scenario planned out in his mind.

"We are going to have to interrupt this broadcast as there is breaking news from Whitehall. We are going live to a press briefing about the growing crisis across the country," said the visibly distressed news reader. James picked up the remote and turned up the volume. He wanted to hear this. The scene on the TV changed, and a man in full military dress, adorned with ribbons, was seen standing behind a microphone festooned speaker's podium.

"We are about to hear an urgent news briefing from Sir Nicholas Martin, the Chief of the Defence Staff," a voice said off camera. There was a loud murmur and the flashes of cameras as the man stood rigid before the world.

"Good morning, ladies and gentlemen of the press. The prime minister has asked me to update you on what is presently happening across the country. I'm not one to mince words, so here it is in a nutshell. The country has been the victim of a bio-weapons attack. We do not as yet know the full extent of the attack, but emergency measures are being implemented, and the country is now under martial law, effective immediately. All civilians not engaged in essential work are advised to head home and await further instructions. Please ring 111 for up-to-date information in your area. That is all." With that, the general, to the great annoyance of the media hounds baying at him, turned and left the podium without another word. Jones turned the volume back down and smiled. That was one way to make people panic. That was just going to send a large number of them into a whirlwind of destruction. Excellent.

11.01AM GMT, 16th September 2015, Resurrection Ranch, Texas, USA

Abraham sat alone in his vast living room. There were four huge TV sets before him arranged in a square, and he watched their images whilst listening to the sound from a single set. He had planned this all out, just as he planned out everything. He would watch the BBC until the inevitable failure of their broadcasts, and then he would turn his full attention to the American networks. They had not yet picked up the true nature of the story yet. Even now, one of the American news channels thought the latest celebrity scandal was more important than the fact that London was burning.

But that was not the focus of the BBC news. The image of the British Chief of Defence Staff disappeared from his screens, and the talking heads started. Abraham wanted to be here when the story became biblical. He wanted to watch the world learn the true nature of how the world now was in the comfort and safety of his home. Although his part in the coming slaughter was unknown, his signature on this grand plan would be revealed eventually. He planned to reveal the secret on his death – the righteous should know the extent that man had to go to in order to appease an ever more impatient and disappointed God.

And there was always a chance that he would be uncovered sooner rather than later. If that was God's will, so be it. And he had planned for this eventuality. The ranch was a fortress, its perimeter a multi-million-dollar barrier of death. Claymores, mines and a host of other life-ending devices ringed his home, the structure of which could withstand a sustained assault. If they came for him, they would pay dearly. And he was not alone. Dozens of his most devoted followers were here, all trained to be his own private army. When you were worth billions, you could pretty much buy anything, and it was well known that one of his holdings was one of America's largest private military contractors. What wasn't so widely known was that most of the mercenaries who worked for said contractor would die for Abraham. Trained to the highest standards, fuelled by a religious zeal and armed with the latest and the best in military equipment, it would take a sustained assault by a sizeable force to breach his compound. Hell, he even had an air defence system. He did own several military contractors after all.

How far he had come since his days as an orphan. His earliest memory was also his most unpleasant. It stayed with him, haunting him and spurring him on to greater feats of wealth creation. When you had looked death in the eye at such an early age, you didn't really fear anything else, and he had known from that very moment that he had been destined for greatness. He couldn't explain how he knew this; it was just knowledge that was present, similar to the fact that he knew the sun would come up tomorrow. And the fact that he had reached greatness was proof of this. And then God had appeared to him and revealed the true reason for his being on this planet. Abraham had stared into the loving eyes of his Lord and had seen the truth of it. And the Lord had visited him often, an ever reassuring presence in his life. The very first memory sometimes came to him in a dream. It always started with the cold, and his eyes opening to a shattered world. Smoke filled the air and burnt his lungs as his three-year-old body tried to escape the weight that was pinning it down. He was in a crashed truck, the vehicle toppled over onto its side; the body of his dead father had fallen free of its seat and was crushing him to the bottom of the truck's cabin. But that hadn't been the worst. The worst of it was the blood. When the explosion that had sent the truck careening off the road had hit, a piece of shrapnel had lanced through into the cabin slicing his father's neck open. Lying underneath him, the blood had washed over Abraham, painting his face and bathing him in the life-preserving juice that Abraham's father had needed to live. It had taken several minutes for the man to die, and the groan that escaped his body, along with the waste and the smell, had etched themselves into Abraham's soul.

He could move an arm, but he had no strength, and for days he had lain there, kept alive only by the rain water that had fallen in torrents through the open driver's window. Lying there trapped, knowing only fear and the smell of the decaying body of the man he idolised, his young mind slowly began to break. And then, close to death, Abraham had been found by the enemy. Of course, Abraham didn't understand what an enemy was then; he was only three. But he had learnt the meaning of the word as he grew into a man. As his power and wealth grew, he spent his resources investigating how his family had been killed. And he learnt that his father, fleeing the Russian advance, had been killed by artillery fire from the very lines he had been trying to get to. British lines. And within his sick and twisted mind, a hatred had grown.

A tired and almost emaciated British soldier found Abraham. Rummaging through the wreckage, hoping to find the elusive German Luger he had been determined to acquire since landing on D-Day at Sword Beach, he had found the much-desired weapon strapped to the corpse of his dead father. But he had also found Abraham and had rescued the child, handing him over to the nuns at the nearest aide station, not wanting to be burdened with the safety of a frightened and starving child. He remembered the nuns all too vividly, their coldness, their cruelness. He had hated the face of that soldier ever since. The face of the almost skeletal man – worn down by years of war, weary and devoid of empathy – became distorted by Abraham's decades of hate and undetected insanity. That face, to Abraham, became the very face of Satan. And by association, the British had become everything he despised about the world.

11.02AM, 16th September 2015, Westminster Bridge, London

It would be known in the international media as the Battle for Whitehall. Captain Grainger, a hardened veteran of the Grenadier Guards, had never thought he would see this day come. He had trained for it, run scenarios and helped create systems and plans for how to deploy and how to defend the seat of government. But he never believed he would actually find himself following through on those plans. The original idea had been developed in the Second World War. Fearing a

German invasion, it was decided to make the invading army fight for every step, fight for every speck of dirt, for every house, for every street. Seventy years on, things had been significantly modified and adjusted. It was no longer considered realistic for an invading force to threaten this 'Green and Pleasant Land'. That was no longer the world anyone thought possible. Now, the most realistic threat was a direct assault by either insurgents or by an uprising of the masses. And that's what Grainger trained for.

And now, here he was. Stood behind barbed wire, behind machine guns and tanks as the unthinkable massed around him. Zombies had never even entered his head, and up until now, he had been glad about that. He didn't read about them, didn't watch those ridiculous films his brother loved. No, his thoughts were on Jihadists and home-grown revolution. And there had been classic examples of what the plans to defend Whitehall were for. The student protests several years ago, complaining about the implementation of oppressive student loans, had almost turned into a full-blown riot. Thousands had massed in Parliament Square, and although only minor skirmishes occurred, those in the know were well aware they had dodged a bullet. If a determined force had descended on Parliament, it could not have been defended without the use of lethal force. And even then, it would be touch and go. Because of that analysis, plans had been made to extract the top brass should the need arise.

And yet here he was, ordered to hold the western end of the Westminster and Lambeth Bridges. And he didn't have enough men. There just weren't that many troops stationed in London, not any that would be effective at least. From his vantage point by the Boudiccan Rebellion monument, he could see smoke rising from St. Thomas' Hospital across the river. Westminster Bridge was a natural choke point, and he was in direct communication with the other officers on the other bridges. But holding the bridges wouldn't be enough. There were other forces engaged directly with the threats to the North, and now there were reports coming from all over the city. The army and the police were now in open conflict with an enemy that spread its numbers rapidly, that killed without mercy, that could be man or woman, adult or child. It was Grainger's opinion that they should pack up everything in one great armoured column, tanks in front, and just bust themselves loose from the city before chaos descended like a death shroud. Unfortunately, the generals and the civilian leadership didn't agree with him when he had voiced that opinion. He was after all just a captain, and he knew that further comment was pointless.

His present orders had come direct from Downing Street. Hold the bridge whilst the military brass and the political leaders decided what needed to be done. He looked around at his men, men he had commanded for five years, and knew they were the best for this job. An hour ago, they had been talking about the weekend's football, their girlfriends, their wives. Now many of them had a look of shock and disbelief that their whole world was about to crumble around their ears. Some were close to panic. Grainger would not let that happen. They were British soldiers; they had a job to do, and he was going to see that they did it. He saw two men setting up the last of the razor wire and shouted some last minute orders at them. He hoped that he had enough firepower to hold off what was on the other side of the river. And he hoped he had enough leadership to keep his men from breaking ranks.

From what he had been told during his earlier briefing, he prayed the defences were enough. Zombies, fucking zombies. Stood beside an FV10 Warrior, he noted the positions of the three Jackal reconnaissance vehicles with their 12.7mm heavy machine guns. A transport lorry had just arrived, unloading crates of ordnance. Fifty men in total manned the defences on this bridge, fifty men with families and fears who stood between chaos and control. Grainger spotted one of his corporals and called the man over.

"Corporal, I want a look out on each side of the bridge. I don't know if these things can swim, but let's not get caught with our pants down." The corporal saluted and rushed off to fulfil his orders. Due to the walls on this side of the river, there were limited ways someone could climb out of the water, but those ways were there, steps down from Parliament to allow the important to come and go via the water.

A private came over and handed him an iPad. "Video feed from the drone, sir." Grainger looked at the display which was being remote operated. There were hundreds of them massing on the eastern side. The drone banked, and he saw dozens more leaving the hospital that sat on the banks of the Thames. Some of them moved quickly, more agile than humans should be, almost ape-like. Others were slow and cumbersome, some missing limbs, some crawling.

The captain looked up. Overhead, the sound of rotors increased as an Apache attack helicopter flew overhead, positioning itself over the middle of the bridge, and began to strafe the gathering crowd with its machine gun. That's when he truly knew this was all for real. Bodies fell, and the gathered infected scattered into the side streets and buildings. "Christ," Grainger said. The things had intelligence. The mini-cannon on the attack helicopter fired again and chewed up tarmac, chewed through walls and flesh and cars, its bullets hunting for those that threatened the leadership of the country.

"Captain, we have contact in the tunnels." The voice over his earpiece was from the sergeant he had sent with two platoons to secure the underground. Grainger swiped the iPad, and camera feed from the bowels of Westminster tube station came up. The view over the display showed a tube tunnel lit by flares. Humans could be seen at the end of the tunnel running towards the camera. In the sky, the minigun ran dry, and the helicopter banked away.

There were a series of explosions visible on the display as the infected charging down the tunnel set off the M8 claymores. Grainger swiped the iPad again, creating a different view, this of one of the platforms. Westminster tube station was quite rare in that it had automated barriers on the edges of the platform, to stop the insane from pushing the rich and powerful under oncoming trains. Whilst they were strong, he had no illusion that they would keep the infected out of the station for long. He had learnt long ago that making assumptions got you killed. So the staircases and escalators were all mined with further claymores. All the access gates were locked tight, welded shut and reinforced, with men positioned outside every conceivable way out. He had flamethrower units and machine gunners on every major exit. Any and all fire doors in the stations had been closed, but Westminster was poorly designed. It was actually difficult to seal it off.

He had hopefully turned the underground station into a kill box. The captain looked over to the nearest exit, right by where he stood, and noticed the two L7A2 general purpose machine guns crews set up there. Firing out 7.62 NATO rounds, they could turn what had once been human flesh into mincemeat. There were more explosions as more claymores were set off by remote, throwing more lethal ball bearings into the meat grinder, but still the infected kept coming. Some that had fallen could be seen getting back up, staggering forward with shambling determination. Several were seen hitting the live rail, but most seemed to avoid the danger. Did they hold residual memory?

"Contact, we've got contact in St. James's Park, over," another voice came over his headset. And then he heard it, a howl from across the bridge.

"We have contact in the water; I repeat, we have contact in the water, over." Grainger ran over to the railings and looked out at the Thames. Over on the far bank, dozens of human forms could be seen jumping into the water, the unmistakeable blueprint of people swimming following the impacts. Grainger cursed and backed away from the railing. He couldn't defend this position with confidence. There were too many enemies coming from too many directions. There was the sound of automatic fire from the west, and with that, Grainger ran to the Warrior light tank. He went round the back and motioned for the corporal inside to pass him the radio handset.

"Put me through to Colonel Bearder."

"Putting you through now, sir." The wait seemed like hours, all the time the sound of gunfire increasing. Grainger could hear single rounds also being fired in the distance now. The rooftop snipers most likely.

"Bearder," a voice said over the radio.

"Colonel, Captain Grainger. I cannot hold this position without air support. I have infected swimming the river. I'm not able to create a choke point."

"Captain, you need to hold. Wildcats are en route with Apache support. ETA 5 minutes. We are most likely evacuating the cabinet and the chief of the defence staff from PINDAR. The Wildcats are bringing you a few friends from Hereford." Hereford. That meant SAS. "I need you to give me time, Captain. Can you do that?"

"Yes, I can, sir." He said the words, but he wasn't sure he would be able to fulfil his promise, even with elite forces backing him up. Up above, he heard the first close-up sniper round from the nearest rooftop and looked up. So this is how the country dies.

"We have contact on the bridge; here they come." Due to the curve of the bridge, Grainger couldn't see, so he climbed up onto the Warrior. And that was when he saw them, thousands.

"Open fire!" he bellowed into his headset. "Do not let anything cross that fucking bridge."

10.55AM, 16th September 2015, Baker Street, London

The three of them looked out of the third-floor window at the road below.

"Fuck me," Brian muttered to himself. On the road, they had been travelling on minutes before, hundreds of infected had gathered, formed from two groups they had merged into one large mass, and seemed to move with a uniform coordination. That had been the noise they had heard, the hum that seemed to hang over them, the combined noise of vast numbers of infected moving as one. There was almost a ripple that moved through them, the crowd seeming to twitch and sway as one unit. It was as if the crowd itself was alive, the individual's mere cells in a greater, more powerful organism.

The trio made their observations secretly, through closed blinds, mindful that discovery by this ravenous throng was not the best plan for survival. Holden looked at the individuals in the group. She saw men, women, children. Children, Christ. How could this be happening? How could everything collapse so quickly? Hours ago, she had been worrying about a hangover, and now everything that she had known as a foundation for her life had been destroyed. And then she realised something. She hadn't even tried to call her partner. In the madness and the urgency, she had forgotten about the person she spent her life with. Pulling away from the window, she took out her phone. No messages, no missed calls. Part of her wanted to call him, but part of her had visions of him hiding in a closet somewhere, infected hunting him, only for them to find him as his phone rang loudly. Tears began to form. She began to feel the last of her sanity slipping, the phone dropping from her hands, its screen cracking as it hit the marbled floor. She suddenly found herself lost in despair and sorrow, and the blackness of the new world quickly threatened to envelop her. And then she felt herself being grabbed gently, felt arms encasing her – strong, protective arms. She felt them gently hug her, and she surrendered herself to the embrace.

"Let it go, doc, don't hold back," Brian said. And she collapsed into his arms, sobs running riot through her body, the tears flowing. She hugged him back, needing the connection, needing the humanity, needing something, anything to cling onto. Brian rocked her back and forth, her head buried in his chest. "You'll be alright," Brian said. He looked at Stan, "What are they doing now, mate?"

"They are moving off, heading south."

"We'll stay here, see if the road clears." He turned back to Holden and let go of her, stepping back. He took her face in his hands and looked down at her. "You've held it together well so far, and I'm going to need you to stay with us for a while longer. Can you do that?" She looked into his piercing blue eyes, saw nothing but concern and compassion there. No judgement, no disappointment.

"Yes, yes I can," she said, and she straightened herself up. Because she could do it. She could tell mothers that their children had died of meningitis, and she could tell husbands that their wives were in a coma that they were unlikely to ever come out from. And she could do this. So help her, she would survive this.

11.04AM, 16th September 2015, Westminster Bridge, London

Rachel hid behind a car and watched as one of her brothers fell. One moment, he was standing in the street, the next, his head exploded as the sniper round entered just above his right eye. The brains exited through the back of his head, and he collapsed in a heap, forever lost to the collective. Rachel felt pain at the loss, and felt anger at those who caused it, although the feeling was purely visceral, there were now no words to describe it. Her human vocabulary had now been reduced to just three words.

Kill
Spread
Feed

She looked at those around her, many cowering from the precision rounds that were being fired from across the river, and for the first time, she saw the true enormity of what she was part of. There were thousands of her kind here now. And their numbers grew every minute. They filled the buildings, they filled the side streets, and they filled the tunnels beneath her feet. And deep within her mind, she felt thousands more of her kind converging on this part of the city. Their numbers were legion, and as the battle for the city progressed, their numbers swelled. Despite the losses they experienced, the army grew. And the voice inside her urged her to move, the collective wisdom telling her where she needed to be. It wasn't here; the bridge was too well defended. So she, and thousands like her, readied themselves to move, to swarm north where the defenders were thinner, already being overrun. By sheer weight of numbers, they would bring their prey down. She looked up, sniffed the air, felt the voices of the collective, felt the whole calling. More were coming, so many more.

There was movement beside her, and she turned to see one of the resurrected shambling past her. Its left shoulder was in bloody tatters, and the arm hung held only by slowly decaying sinew. The eyes, black as coal, saw everything and saw nothing, and she felt awe at the creature's presence. But she felt no connection with the zombie. Its mind was vacant, completely disconnected from the collective, and it moved with its own purpose, its own vision.

11.05AM, 16th September 2015, Over Shepherds Bush, London

The fourteen helicopters travelled at near top speed. Eleven Wildcat transports escorted by three Apache, they flew over a city filled with panic and despair, a city dying from a cancer ripping it apart from within. Fires could be seen everywhere, the smoke rising into the sky like beacons to destruction. Below, the roads were clogged with gridlocked cars, people trying to get away from the centre of a city that was now gangrenous, rapidly spreading its infection to the rest of the country's organs. A gangrenous limb could be amputated, but you couldn't amputate the head, and that was where the contagion had taken root. The rot was spreading quickly, made worse now by actual rioting as order began to break down and the thin veneer of civility ruptured, letting loose the darkest aspects of humanity.

The British Government, mindful that their actions on the international arena made their country a target for terrorism, always kept one squadron of SAS on standby in case of the unthinkable. Sixty-four men ready to combat any perceived terrorist threat, trained to be the best, trained to fight against those who cared little about innocent human life. But never before had a whole squadron been deployed at once on the British mainland. This was B squadron, with its four specialised troops, each led by a hardened, ruthless captain, giving orders to hardened, ruthless men. There were none better. This was the best humanity had to offer … but it wouldn't be enough.

Captain Hudson, leader of number 7 troop, B squadron, looked down at the mayhem below him. They flew through the smoke of multiple fires, and he could see the blue flashing lights of emergency vehicles that were trapped in the mass exodus, their owners below bravely trying to contain and control the growing chaos. His father had always said the end would come. He always said one day civilisation would crumble from the inside out, and only those who knew how to fight would make it through the chaos. And he had followed his father's example and joined the military, learnt what was needed to survive and to thrive in times that would kill ordinary men. In fact, he did one better and became a leader in one of the world's most elite fighting forces, pushing himself to the limit of human endurance. He thought he was ready for anything.

But a biological contagion that sent the living mad? He still had difficulty believing the briefing he had been given, but there was no slack-jawed perplexity on his face or the faces of any of his men. They took their orders and did what they were told. They would fight and die for their country. They would do their duty, because that was all there was for them to do. There was no other purpose in their lives but to do what they were trained to do. Their friends, their families, all were secondary to the life they had signed up for. Below, the scenes of carnage and panic on the ground disappeared as they flew over Hyde Park.

"8 troop breaking off, Captain." Hudson looked as four helicopters banked right. They would not be going to Whitehall. They had the easy duty, rescue and evacuate the Royal Family whose Royal Protection team had rounded them up and was even now delivering them to Buckingham Palace. There had been no reported attacks on the palace yet, but the Queen and her family were top priority.

"Three minutes, Captain," the pilot said.

"Time to earn our keep, lads," Hudson said, and he rechecked his weapon. He would die for these men, and he knew each one of them would do the same for him. For an officer, he had proven his worth.

11.06AM, 16th September 2015, Shepherds Bush, London

With the underground trains now no longer running, the tube network became nothing but tunnels for the infected to run through. And they were fast, no longer seemingly restrained by stamina or muscle aches; the virus coursed through their bodies pumping out adrenalin like they were on PCP. Thousands descended into the network, some semblance of memory knowing that eventually all the tube networks came out into daylight and tracks that had little more than flimsy wire fences to seal them off. It was the perfect way to spread quickly throughout the city, and to bypass the cordons and the armed soldiers that still threatened to end the dawning of the new species.

Dave got out of his Aston Martin Vanquish and looked at the line of traffic that led off as far as he could see. Far off in the distance, he could see the blue lights of emergency vehicles. *Probably either an accident or the plod are arresting some terrorist scrote*, he thought. Directly to his right, he could see the Shepherds Bush Market tube station and noticed that the barrier gates were down. There was honking far behind him, and he turned to see a similar situation to the rear. Both lanes of the road were stopped solid, and he realised that nobody would be going anywhere for the foreseeable future.

"Any idea what's going on?" he asked a guy in the opposite lane who had his window down.

"I think it's the riots. They're all over the place apparently." The man paused hearing something on his radio. "Hold on, mate," he said, turning up the radio. Dave looked at the decrepit white van the man was driving and thought to himself, *I'm not your fucking mate.* But he didn't say it out loud – the guy's van might have been rusty and not long for the scrap heap, but the guy he was speaking to looked like a walking advert for steroids.

"... moments ago that Sir Nicholas Martin, the Chief of the Defence Staff, told us that the country was now under Martial Law. And now the shocking news that has been released to us by Whitehall that the country is under terrorist attack..." the radio stated.

"Fuck me," white van man said and punched his horn. Dave got back in his car and turned on his own radio. He never listened to it, preferring instead to listen to his motivational MP3's. With the amount of miles he had done over the years, he reckoned he'd acquired the equivalent of a university education, which had helped make him the success he was. And for the first time in his life, not listening to the radio had been to his detriment. The guy in the van beeped his horn again. Dave watched as he got out, gesticulating to someone out of his line of sight. Turning his head, he looked to see a much smaller man shouting at him two cars up.

"... and is it true that those infected become incredibly violent and attack those around them?" the voice on the radio asked.

"Yes, that does seem to be an aspect of this contagion. That is why the government are advising everyone to stay inside." *Fuck me,* thought Dave.

Dave's head spun round to look back out of his windscreen as an almighty crash grabbed his attention, and he jumped in his seat. At first, he couldn't tell what had caused the noise, but then he saw a woman frantically get out of her yellow Ford Escort. Just as her other foot touched the asphalt, a body fell from the railway bridge above, evidently following one that had already fallen onto the bonnet of the woman's car. Then a third body fell, this one hitting the road in-between the two lanes. Then a fourth, then a fifth. The bodies twitched, moved and began to stand upright. One collapsed straight back down, but the others got to their feet and span round as they surveyed everything around them. Three more bodies fell, and Dave found himself locking his doors. The woman from the Escort backed away, but the one closest to her pounced on her.

"Fuck me," Dave heard himself say, and in the periphery of his vision saw the steroid monster run past his car to help her. White van man grabbed the attacker, pulling him off the woman, who collapsed as the infected released her. White van man began to rain blows down on the woman's assailant, but this just drew a howl from the rest of the infected, and they converged on him. Dave saw the projectile before it hit the bonnet of his car and came to rest against his windscreen. An arm, torn from its muscular body, blood splattering across his vision. And then more bodies fell, dozens of them, and they spread throughout the trapped cars, and the trapped people. Dave ducked down, taking his phone out of his pocket. He manically dialled 999.

"All operators are busy. Please hold and we will connect you to the first available operator." *This is ridiculous*, he thought. *How could 999 be engaged?* He looked up from the phone to see one of the infected jump up onto his car and place its face up against the window. It stared at him almost quizzically.

"*Feeeeed,*" it hissed and licked the blood off the glass, a shiver of pleasure rippling through its frame.

"*Spreaaaad,*" it said, its eyes bloodshot and bulging. Drawing a fist back, the creature punched the windscreen, breaking through on the third attempt, and a bloody shattered hand thrust through, hooking Dave's hair with the non-crippled fingers. There was a cry of rage, and the attacker dragged Dave forward out of his chair to the steering wheel where his face was repeatedly smashed, the horn blaring as his cheek impacted on it. The ruined hand released him, and Dave collapsed into his seat. He did not see, and he only vaguely felt the hot liquid splatter on his body as the infected vomited through the hole in the windscreen.

"*Spreaaaad,*" the creature roared and pounced off the car in search of more prey. Dave, dazed and traumatised, not knowing that the infection now poured through his body, felt consciousness slip away. He would awaken without the memories of his former self.

*

It seemed that even the end of the world didn't stop people shopping. Viraj Mendis sat at the table in the food court and waited for his coffee to cool. He had no smartphone, believing such technology to be nothing more than a distraction. And whilst he had a cheap mobile phone, he did not have it on him. After all, why would he need it just to go shopping?

The Westfield shopping complex seemed quiet today, and he looked around at the reduced throng of people. A man ran past in definite agitation, people cursing him as he clipped them. Viraj looked the way he had come, down the full length of one of the shopping lanes. He liked to people watch, liked to sit and judge and criticise those who dwelled around him. Look at that fat bastard; how could he let himself get in that state? And what the hell was she wearing? She looked like a slut. Probably a drug addict and a whore. Let's not even talk about that man's dress sense. Why the hell would you wear a baseball cap indoors?

He came here about once a week to shop, and always did it when most people were at work. And whilst he himself was self-employed and worked from home, he was always surprised by how many people didn't seem to be gainfully employed. Benefits scum and layabouts. At the far end of the shopping alley, a good hundred metres away, shouts rose. Viraj brought his coffee to his lips and took a sip, scrutinising the commotion. What was this, a fight?

He felt it before he saw it. It was like a wave that rolled over him, a feeling that something in the air had changed. He returned the cup to the table and stood. An avid comic book fan, if asked, he would say his Spidey sense was tingling. Although he wouldn't be asked, because there would be nobody to ask him. There was a scream, and then the people at the end of the shopping aisle began to run. As they ran, the people closer to where he stood began to run, and a ripple of humanity propelled itself towards him. Viraj stood mesmerised as the crowd surged closer. He noticed people around him standing, commenting on what was occurring. Somewhere, he heard someone say zombies, and he felt someone push into his back as they pushed past him.

"Watch it, you idiot," Viraj said angrily, turning to his brief assailant. Viraj was a big man and liked to use his size to intimidate people when they crossed him. But the person who had banged into him was already too far away for it to be a real issue. He turned his attention back to the crowd, to the bedlam. Something inside him said run, but having no knowledge of the present state of the country, he instead took a step forward. There were more screams, and he now saw people being assaulted. Viraj saw a young man tackle an elderly lady to the ground. A child ran past, tears streaming, six years old at most.

"Mummy, where's my mummy?" Well, that was it. Viraj had no time for rioting scum, and he walked purposefully towards the brawling mass. It wasn't until twenty paces into his advance that he realised his error.

"What the fuck?" This wasn't a riot. The people weren't fighting; they were being ripped apart. People were running because they were being chased. He should have listened to his inner voice, and he stopped dead in his tracks and began to back up. Ahead, he saw a nightmare, now not obscured by fake foliage. A woman fleeing, baby in hand, was felled by two elderly gentlemen who ran with a speed that defied their arthritic age. The baby went flying, landing with a sickening thump. Its mother, now sprawled on the floor, reached for it, pleading for its safety, but one of the elderly attackers jumped on her back and bit deep into her scalp. It ripped off a piece of hair and flesh with its teeth, reached up and cast the morsel aside. Its partner abandoned the mother and looked straight into Viraj's eyes.

"*Feeeeeeeed,*" it howled and flung itself at him. Viraj ran every day, did weighted uphill sprints, but as he turned to flee the blood-stained abomination, he knew he couldn't outrun it. His burst of speed was no match for his pursuer, and he felt a hand grab his sports jacket. Even with his powerful forward momentum, he felt himself yanked back and powerful arms encased him. There was no moment to pause, no lull where he got to contemplate his fate; the teeth were into his neck instantly, and he felt a searing pain as a huge chunk of flesh was ripped from him. The scream that formed in his throat was just one of many that now echoed through the shopping centre. Warmth spread down his right side, and the arms released him. Viraj staggered, a hand going up to his slaughtered neck, blood spurting from the severed artery. He managed to turn, saw the ghoul that stood chewing savagely on its prize, and in his faltering mind, he could have sworn the creature smiled at him. Viraj stumbled and landed on one knee, the pain of the impact almost unnoticed as a blackness began to creep into the periphery of his vision. The creature watched him briefly and then its head darted to one side, and it ran off after another prize.

Every second, his neck spurted red out across the shopping centre floor, and bleeding out, Viraj collapsed fully to the floor, his arms saving his face from the impact. He lay there, the life pouring from him, the virus worming its way into his every cell. He passed out and died on the floor whilst hundreds around him were turned to the new cause.

But death, it seemed, meant nothing these days. It wasn't the end. Enough of the virus had entered his system and enough time had elapsed for the heart to pump the contaminated blood to the brain. Even with the carotid artery partially severed, some blood still flowed past the injury, and after several minutes black eyes opened to look at the world with a dead mind. There was only one thing that mind wanted, the taste of fresh human flesh. The figure rose, imposing in life, terrifying in its reanimated from. It stretched, testing out the already decaying muscles and tendons. Its balance faltered momentarily, but it took a hesitant step nonetheless and then another. Shambling forward, the monstrosity made its way through the carnage on pure predatory instinct. There was no food here – the tsunami had already passed, and most of those attacked had merely been infected. They were now off, hunting, devouring, feeding. It could hear them, in the vestiges of its mind, the chatter of a collective driven by the power of the virus. It cared not about the strategy; it was beyond that now. All it wanted was uninfected flesh. And on automatic it headed for a likely feeding ground.

Jen couldn't believe how empty the cinema was, and that was exactly why she liked to come at this time of day. Most people went at stupid times, packing themselves in the uncomfortable seats, gorging on overpriced chemical food and sugar laden drinks. Not Jen, she was smart – she brought her own food with her, organic, from Waitrose no less. She had to look after herself, because nobody else in this world was going to do that for her. When she had entered, she had been alone, and now there were perhaps only two other people in the entire room with her. *Perfect*, she said to herself and she melted into her seat as the film captivated her. Only in her peripheral vision did she notice the shambling figure that entered the cinema room, staggering slightly as it started up the steps. Christ, was he drunk? He couldn't even walk in a straight line. She ignored the new arrival, concentrating on the hero who was presently blowing bad guys away with what seemed to be magical accuracy. Yes, she ignored him, at least until he chose her row to sit on, walking past the row of upended seats as he shambled towards her.

"You've got to be kidding," she said under her breath. The last thing she needed was to deal with a creeper like this. And he was a big guy too. It happened occasionally, pathetic men thinking they could somehow impose on her solitude. She expected him to plonk himself down in the seat next to her, but he didn't, and she looked up at the hulking figure. In the flash from the cinema screen, she saw something more horrific than her lifetime's addiction to horror films had ever shown her, and she screamed, a more realistic scream than she had ever heard on film. The body of Viraj fell on her, all fists and teeth, unfeeling and unrelenting. It was not concerned with spreading the virus, all it wanted was flesh.

11.07AM, 16th September 2015, Westminster Bridge, London

"We have them contained in the underground, General, but they are swimming the Thames in large numbers," Grainger said loudly into the radio. He was having difficulty hearing the person on the other end, as everything he had was firing at the swarm hurling itself across the bridge. "I'm spread too thin to contain this. And the spread through the tube network cannot be stopped. Any station we seal off, they will just bypass. I cannot hold them."

"Captain Walker has had to retreat from Russell Square. I've told him to come and reinforce your northern flank, but he has lost a third of his men. Understand this, Captain, the city is most likely lost. The only way to save it now is to destroy it, and our political masters aren't going to agree to that in time." There was a loud noise as a mortar team fired off at the bridge. The resulting explosion sent body parts into the air. The attacking infected weren't making progress across the bridge, the fire being laid down on them too strong. But those that fell just got back up, hardier and more resilient than their former selves. "The politicians aren't listening to us yet, so all we can do is consolidate and try and save what we can." That was General Marston. The news sent a knife through Grainger's spine. They were admitting defeat so easily. That was when he heard the helicopters, and he looked up to see the black shapes approaching in the sky. "Marston out," said the voice on the radio.

One SAS troop had diverted in order to land at and secure Horse Guards Parade. The rest came into view overhead, hovering above Grainger's position. One by one, the Wildcats manoeuvred into position, and then their side doors opened. As the ropes fell out, men dressed in black began to descend. The first man to hit the ground unbuckled himself and quick marched over to the Warrior where Grainger stood. The captain stood with a look of awe on his face. As the newcomer with the presence that indicated a thousand wars came towards him, he was massaged by the ghosts of gun smoke that were being whipped up by the rotors above.

"Hudson SAS," he said, shaking Grainger's hand. One of the Apaches began to strafe the hoard on the bridge. "I was told you needed a bit of help."

"*We will spread, we will feed, we will kill.*" Thousands of eyes looked at the carnage on the bridge, thousands of linked minds thinking as one. They didn't really understand what they were attacking or why, just as a wolf didn't intellectually understand why it killed its prey. But the infected kept pushing, weight of numbers being their primary weapon. From all around Waterloo, those carrying the virus converged on the heart of the damned, adding thousands to their ranks with every passing moment. As they fell beneath the impacts of bullets and mortars and rockets, their bodies changed, mutated. Resurrected, they stood, they crawled, and they lumbered towards those guarding Westminster purely on instinct. They were relentless, merciless and their hunger grew even when they bit into the flesh of the living. With their internal organs rotting within their very bodies, there was no mechanism to digest that which was consumed. Many of the zombies found they weren't even able to swallow, and merely spat out what they bit off, only to fill their mouths once more. The mutation in the brain told them to. It was their essence for being. Nothing else mattered except the wet, slick, coppery taste of human flesh and the need to make more of their kind.

There were ten million people in London, and by now, three hundred thousand were carriers of the deadliest disease man had ever known. That number grew by the minute, for as the people fled, they became easier targets, bunched together as they became trapped in bottle necks. Some didn't flee, but hid behind locked doors, hoping that the infected would pass them by. But they never did, and the contagion forced them to damage their own bodies to get at the living. Because death was irrelevant – it was just another form of life now. And so the infected began to converge, to combine and to swarm. All the bullets in the world couldn't stop such a force, not over such a wide area, not when they recruited new soldiers from the very army they fought against.

*

Hudson looked at the opposite bank, saw the hundreds of infected now throwing themselves into the river. Whilst there weren't many ways to get out at his side of the Thames, there were further up and down, so eventually the enemy would be massing against them on multiple fronts. The sound of machine gun fire was all pervasive. He turned to Grainger.

"Can you hold them?"

"Maybe for a while, but we will be overrun," Grainger replied.

"Then let's see if we can buy the politicians time to pull their fingers out of their fucking arses." Hudson smiled, and Grainger felt the corners of his mouth turning up too.

"Fuck it," Grainger said. "Let's get this done."

11.09AM, 16th September 2015, Hounslow, London

"Bloody hell, Clive, where did you get that?" They were in the somewhat decrepit kitchen of Clive's semi-detached house, somewhere Jack had never set foot before. His sister, nervous of the new environment and the strangeness of the day's events, clung to him. He put a protective arm around her.

Jack suddenly realised he had never been in the man's house. He looked at the older man with wild, excited eyes as he took the automatic pistol out of the box he had brought down from the attic moments earlier.

"A little souvenir from my time in the para's, Jack," Clive said, working the action. "I keep it oiled regularly." Clive put the gun on the kitchen table the box sat on, and extracted three magazines from the same box, placing them alongside their future home.

Clive and Jack's dad had served in the same parachute regiment, going through basic training together. As the only two black men in their company, they had formed an instant bond and became lifelong friends. They had fought off the racism they knew would be thrown at them to test their resolve, and had both broken jaws and arms in proving their worth. The bigots that shared their barracks soon learnt they were not to be fucked with. They had fought together in the Falklands at the Battle of Goose Green, earning medals and respect. Eventually, they had both left the services together. Although married, Clive hadn't followed his friend's example and hadn't had any children, and his wife had died ten years ago through cancer. The death of Jack's dad had hit Clive hard.

"Why do we need a gun?" Jack asked naively. Clive looked at him patiently and indicated for him to sit down. He turned behind him and switched on a TV set that was on the kitchen counter. Although the sound was off, the picture told a story of a thousand words. Clive pointed at the screen.

"That is why we need a gun, Jack. I've seen violence before; I know how it spreads. We need this for our protection. And we need this," Clive said extracting several thick bundles of twenty-pound notes out of the box, "to get us on a flight out of here."

"So we are definitely leaving the UK?"

"The shit you see on the screen is coming our way. We might just have time, but we have to move quickly." Clive put the cash in his jacket inside pocket, and put the gun in the waistband of his trousers. Picking up a case he had also brought down from upstairs, he turned to walk out of the kitchen. "Time to go and pick up your mother."

11.11AM, 16th September 2015, Baker Street, London

The crowd of infected moved. Their numbers had swelled, doubling, tripling whilst Holden spied on them. And then, as if called by some unseen force, they ran. Mere humans would have fallen and been trampled, but the infected moved with a coordination and a stamina that would have taken her kind years of training. Packed together, they moved south away from the junction that Holden's vantage point overlooked.

"Looks like they have a mission," Brian said. "We should wait till the road clears and then make our move."

"Where to?" Stan asked.

"Well, they're heading south, so let's go in the opposite direction," Brian responded. He looked again out of the window. Most of the crowd had left the street now, their numbers dwindling. His attention was drawn to a noise in the sky, and an attack helicopter came into view. It hovered above the street high above the buildings, and followed the crowd. Suddenly, its Gatling cannon erupted, strafing the hundreds of infected, who, pre-warned by the noise of its approach, had already begun to scatter before its onslaught hit them. Like ants, they disappeared into buildings, beneath cars, some falling as parts of them were blown apart by the high-explosive rounds. Holden watched mesmerised, amazed that this wasn't a movie, amazed that this was real. The helicopter banked right and headed off to its next target. Holden looked and despaired. Its attack had seemed devastating, but in truth, its impact had been negligible. The infected paused and then the crowd reformed, the swell surging it south again. There was no way the three of them, here in this room, could survive against that. So yes, north was the only real way to go.

11.20AM, 16th September 2015, PINDAR, Ministry of Defence, London

General Marston and the prime minister were arguing.

"It is the only way to contain it, sir. If you act now, we can have the instructions relayed to the submarines and have the missiles flying within hours."

"You want me to order our own forces to nuke our cities. I can't do that – it will kill millions," the prime minister protested.

"Millions are already going to die, Prime Minister," Marston said. "You sacrifice the few to save the whole. At the very least, we need to inform the submarine captains of our situation. We don't want to start a World War." Croft new exactly what Marston was referring to. Every nuclear submarine captain had a personal letter from the prime minister in his cabin safe. These 'Letters of Last Resort' gave instructions if all contact was lost with the mainland. The last thing anybody needed was the UK nuclear deterrent being unleashed in the mistaken belief that the UK had been attacked.

"He's right, David. We are losing the battle." The PM turned to look at the home secretary who had just spoken. There were tears in her eyes. "Shit," she said, "I can't believe I just said that." The prime minister looked around the room. Some people nodded their approval, others looked away, afraid to be seen as complicit in the contemplation of killing whole cities. Osbourne sat down, defeated. He put his head in his hands and said nothing for several seconds.

"I need time. I need time to think," he said, almost sobbing.

"Time is something you don't really have," Croft said from the corner of the room.

"But what about the men and women out there fighting? We will be condemning them to certain death," the PM pleaded.

"They are already dead, Prime Minister," Croft said matter of factly. "Every one of them should have accepted that when they put on the uniform. They aren't your concern. You need to decide whether you want cities to die, or an entire country."

"Could you do it, Croft? Could you order the death of millions?" the prime minister shouted, hurling a folder at him. Croft looked at the man, who was close to breaking. He looked sideways at Savage, and then back at the prime minister.

"Yes," Croft said. They were interrupted by someone entering. An officer walked over to General Marston and handed him a note. The general read it, nodding solemnly. The people in the room watched him. On the one hand, they wanted to know more, on the other part of them wanted to just run and hide. After about a minute, Marston looked at the officer standing next to him.

"Pull it up on the main screen," Marston said, indicating the large TV that was presently playing CNN. The officer nodded and left the room. Within moments, the live news broadcast was replaced by a satellite live feed over the streets of London.

"What the hell's this?" the prime minister asked.

"This is live from over Baker Street. GCHQ have re-routed a satellite to give us as much intel as possible. This is the latest swarm gathering."

"But there's hundreds of them," the prime minister protested.

"Yes, Prime Minister. All civilian forces in that area have been overwhelmed. And according to GCHQ predictions, they are heading straight here."

"You said swarm," Croft said standing, looking briefly at Savage. She raised an eyebrow.

"Yes, the brains at GCHQ have identified something. It seems the infected are working together, almost like insects. They move and attack in a combined fashion. Rarely do they act alone, and rarely do they kill outright."

"So," replied Savage, "they are growing their numbers. Creating an army big enough to overwhelm anything we have left."

"So it would seem," said Marston. He flung the paper he was holding onto the conference table in front of him. "And there are dozens of swarms like this now across the city."

11.25AM, 16th September 2015, Westminster Bridge, London

So far, he hadn't lost any men, which was a blessing, but he was running low on ammunition, especially for his heavy machine guns. And there was another problem, one that was clear and present in his mind. He saw no way to get his men out of this. The SAS, Grainger expected, could climb back into their helicopters, but he would have to get his men out via ground transport along streets that would be clogged with fleeing civilians and infected alike. He signalled his corporal to give him the radio handset.

"Patch me through to Colonel Bearder." There was a pause, and Grainger's superior officer came on the radio.

"I'm running out of ammunition, Colonel."

"Everyone is, Captain," the voice replied. All of a sudden, a huge explosion erupted north of their position. Although it was far enough away that he couldn't see it, smoke began to rise into the air. He climbed to an elevated position, and from where he was, he saw several soldiers running up Victoria Embankment. Over his earpiece, he heard chatter from the conflict in other parts of the city.

"Colonel, I'm hearing that the infected are being engaged at Trafalgar Square. I need more air support. I need more men." As he spoke into the radio, he noticed several more attack helicopters fly over his position. But they did not unload their ordinance on his immediate threat as he had hoped. Instead, they carried on north.

"Captain, there aren't any more men. In fact, you need to prepare your men to head out. Get ready to abandon your position on my order. We are evacuating the capital." Grainger let the knowledge sink in.

"How am I going to get my men out, Colonel?"

"By boat, Captain. Your ride will be with you shortly."

Hudson and his men had headed north up Whitehall, and within minutes, had found themselves firing their weapons into a crowd of a dozen blood-soaked infected that had broken through the army lines. Some of those they shot were in army uniforms, which was not the news Hudson wanted to see. Despite this very recent engagement, it was now relatively peaceful in this part of the city, the distant gunfire muffled by the surrounding buildings. They reinforced the army position at the intersection of Whitehall Place and Whitehall, the last line of defence if the infected broke through from the north of the city. Around them, dozens of Grenadier Guards ran past them to the north, to reinforce the main defence closer to Trafalgar Square.

"Boss, do you see a way of getting out of this?" his sergeant, a man called O'Sullivan, asked.

"That's what the helicopters are for, Sarge. They are ours after all," he said with a grin. He put his hand up to his ear, raising a finger to his sergeant as he listened to a message being relayed to him. He walked out in front of his men to get their attention.

"Get ready to pack it up, lads. We've had new orders; we'll be in the air in fifteen minutes. We are to reinforce Horse Guards Parade."

"Bloody hell," the sergeant said, "we've only just got here." Hudson just shrugged. The SAS didn't need telling twice.

11.29AM, 16th September 2015, PINDAR, Ministry of Defence, London

"General, Captain Grainger reports he will most likely be overrun. Forces are already in retreat from Charing Cross, and they are engaging the infected in Trafalgar Square. We are losing personnel at an alarming rate, sir," Colonel Bearder said over the intercom. "Civilian forces are all but gone."

"Thank you, Colonel." He turned to his prime minister. "Prime Minister, we have to leave, and we have to leave now. This position is lost."

"Yes, yes but how?" Osbourne asked.

"We have helicopters waiting at Horse Guards Parade. We will evacuate you and the cabinet first, and then as many other personnel as we can. We will travel under SAS escort to the evacuation zone." The general turned to Croft. "Need a ride, Croft?"

"Why thank you, General. Awfully decent of you." Croft watched as the general stormed out of the room, bellowing to someone in the control centre outside.

"Get me MI6 on conference call. We need to start this evacuation."

11.35AM 16th September 2015, MI6, Albert Embankment, London

Normally, MI6 was not involved with operations on UK soil. That was the job of MI5 and the police. However, the decision had been made to change all that for one very simple reason. The MI6 building was a fortress. It was built to resist terrorist attack and was considered impregnable to anything but a hardened military assault. It could also be evacuated by helicopter, which would be required over the coming hours and days. Many of the candidates for Operation Noah had gathered here, as well as much of the surviving staff from the MI5 building, which had been abandoned after the bombing. Although nobody in MI6 could see it, the MI5 building still burned.

Throughout the building, the offices and hallways teemed with life. Deep in its basement, several of its subterranean holding cells were also occupied with recent acquisitions. Fabrice shifted uncomfortably in his bonds, saliva dribbling from his mouth which had been clamped open. They wanted this one alive, and restrained as he was, there was no way for him to commit suicide the way Brother Eli had. He had been stripped naked and examined from head to toe. Even his teeth were tested in case – like out of some bizarre spy novel – he had cyanide capsules secreted away in his mouth. Unfortunately for him, he had no such devices. Strapped to a metal table, the cold metal slowly warming to his body heat, he found that he was almost completely immobile.

So this was to be his fate, thought Fabrice, amazed at the calmness that dwelled within him. His mission had been a success, but escape to live in the new world would not be gifted him. The agents of Satan had him now, and his mind ticked over the torments that lay ahead for him. Did not Abraham always say the worthy would have their faith tested to determine their piety and devotion to the One True God? Fabrice was determined not to let these bastards break him.

He heard the door open, and it was several seconds before a figure came into his peripheral vision. The woman was blonde, shoulder-length hair tied back into two pigtails. She had pale skin and deep scarlet lipstick, matched by the colour of her obviously long and sharp fake nails. The woman was dressed in a black, skin-tight leather that was cut short at her arms and legs, barely hiding her modesty. She moved with a grace rarely seen in this day and age.

"Fabrice Chevalier, 32. Born in France, but nationalised to the UK at the age of 3. Father English, deceased. Mother French, deceased." Fabrice moved his eyes to watch the figure, who was reading off what looked like an iPad. "National Insurance Number NX 374627 D. No employment history or taxes paid in the last 18 months. Most recent employment with Apollyon Incorporated for a six-month period, for which it seems you were paid most handsomely." The goddess paused and pressed a button under the metal table. Fabrice heard it click, and the table moved ever so slightly, raising the head of the table about thirty degrees. "Prior to that you were known on the 'Player' scene by the name Genji after the infamous Japanese seducer." Fabrice tried to say something. The woman looked him in the eye and smiled. "I would have liked to see you try your game on me, boy." She chuckled to herself and shook her head. She held a finger to her lips briefly before continuing. "There is no need to speak now – that will come later, of that I am certain. You will speak, you will beg to tell me everything you know. You see, we know a lot about you. Whilst your file is not overly large, you are a British subject, and as such, we have substantial data on you. What we don't know is why you did what you did." The woman turned and walked over to the wall, returning dragging a metal cart on wheels. She discarded the iPad on top and ran her eyes down his captive's body. She seemed to be almost appraising him.

"We know a lot about you, but I'm being rude." The woman crossed her arms and tipped her head to one side. For the first time, Fabrice noticed a scar that ran down across her left eye and down her cheek. It did nothing to diminish her beauty, which was only matched by the seductive aura she carried with her. "So let me tell you a little something about me." Fabrice's eyes followed the woman as she moved down to the foot of the table and round to the other side. She ran her fingernails along the table as he did so, making the barest contact with Fabrice's skin only once, sending an erotic shiver through him.

"My name is Davina. I am a woman in possession of a very specific skill. It is, in fact, rare for me to operate on British soil. Usually, I find myself in much warmer places, where the local customs and laws are more … tolerant to my way of thinking and to my activities. The fact that I am a woman helps in the breaking and the interrogation of those who live in such climates." The woman came to a stop by the head of the table and, putting both hands on it, she bent her head down so that her lips were by Fabrice's ear. She licked him briefly and then whispered. "I am an extractor. When people wish to know what an individual refuses to divulge, I get to practice my art." The extractor lifted a hand and carefully placed it under Fabrice's chin. She gathered some of the spittle that had run there and wiped it over her victim's face. "You are fortunate I was in London to be debriefed about my latest assignment. If you had committed your crime two days earlier, I would still have been in Pakistan, and the next few hours would be a lot more pleasant for you. How fickle fate is." Davina stood upright and walked away from her victim. "We will get to know a lot about each other, you and I. You will learn why I am so good at what I do. And I will learn your every secret. Of that, you have my word."

Through the surveillance feed of the room, Sir Stuart Watkins watched the beginning of the interrogation. This was not something he liked to do, but time was short, and the normal rules no longer applied. This was not a time for the good old British sense of fair play. Now, normally a woman like Davina would never be allowed to operate on UK soil, because, being a liberal Democracy, torture was somewhat frowned upon, especially the kinds of torture this woman was a master of. Her speciality was sexual torture, lasting days, breaking the very soul of the men she inflicted herself upon. But they had no time for that today, so she would resort to the standard tortures taught her by the clandestine services which employed her. When Stuart had informed her of the time constraints, he could tell she had been disappointed. Fabrice was a fine male specimen, just the sort of man Davina liked to get her teeth into.

The Liberal classes hated it; the bleeding hearts who believe that terrorists had rights and that the West deserved what the Jihadists threw at it. But Sir Stuart reckoned he didn't have to worry too much about them right now, because most of them were probably running amok in the streets trying to eat people.

This was to be nothing so amateur as waterboarding or pins under the fingernails. No, this was indeed an art. Torture was usually a very poor way of getting information out of a subject, but that's only when the woman called Davina didn't do the torture. Nobody knew just where she had acquired her sadistic sexual skills, but MI6 had, on occasion, found her to be a useful asset. In fact, she was so good, she was often contracted out to the Americans.

Whilst the British population would declare outrage at her actions, and the fact that she was sanctioned by MI6 and thus Her Majesty's Government, she was incredibly effective and had retrieved information that, to date, had saved thousands of lives. And now it didn't matter anyway. There probably wouldn't be a populous left to complain for much longer.

Watkins remembered well the first time he had seen Davina work. That wasn't her real name, of course, and very few people in MI6 knew that she wasn't even British by birth. She was Ukrainian, and had been born into violence and death. The first time he had seen her torture someone had been through a monitor such as this. Every word said had been recorded, every scream and every plea for mercy noted and logged. That had been on a radical fundamentalist, a hard-core terrorist who had known the whereabouts of a Dirty Bomb somewhere on the streets of Brussels. Until her arrival, the Jihadist had withstood four days of interrogation and torture. Davina had acquired the information in under twelve hours.

11.40AM, 16th September 2015, Swiss Cottage, London

Was it wrong for it to seem normal for her to see people get shot? They had made it to Swiss Cottage almost unscathed, Stan only having to discharge his weapon three times. But each of those times his aim had been precise, and the madness rushing them had been felled by a shot to the head. Brian brought up the rear, sandwiching her in a protective shield.

When she had awoken this morning, her body had told her to stay in bed. It would have been so easy. Just pick up the phone, feign sickness, bring the covers back over her head and spend the rest of the morning in careless bliss. Who better to phone in sick than a doctor? But she hadn't done that, had she? Her sense of duty had told her to get out of bed, to get to work, to do what she was being paid for. Even though she hated it. Even though the thought of it sometimes made her ill, made her dread the career path she had chosen. And now look at her. Trapped in a diseased city, moving further and further away from the man she told herself she loved.

But did she? Did she love him, or did she just stay with him out of convenience? Had she just let herself settle for a mediocre man in a mediocre career, living a mediocre life? Well, it was far from mediocre now, engulfed in a zombie apocalypse. Her only emphasis now was on surviving. The patient she had resuscitated yesterday didn't matter. Her mortgage didn't matter. The fact that the stress was triggering a craving for alcohol didn't matter. Living mattered. Living and maintaining her sanity.

The streets were strangely deserted, and they walked down the middle of the road, abandoned cars rarely obstructing their path. Holden thought she saw the odd curtain twitch, heard the distant cries of battle and slaughter, but the bulk of the infected were behind them it seemed. She had asked about taking bikes, to speed their retreat, but the two officers had said that wasn't an option now. They needed to be guns ready, and they couldn't do that on the back of bicycles. So they walked.

Living south of the river, this was not a part of London Holden was familiar with. But Google Maps was, and she had been given the job of directing them via her smartphone. They had to get as far north as possible to be out of the infected zone and join up with reinforcements. But could they move faster than the infected expanded?

She didn't know where the officers lived; she hadn't asked them. This was not the time for mindless chatter. This was the time for caution, for concentration, a time for mere animal existence. Humanity was being hunted, and the hunters were everywhere. Following Stan, she stopped behind him as they came to a corner, the three of them hugging the brickwork of the building that hid their path. He held a hand out indicating his companions to stop, and he peeked around the corner briefly.

"Shit," he said under his breath. He poked his head back and looked at Brian. Stan shook his head in rejection. "Infected," he whispered.

"How many?" asked Brian.

"Too many." Brian snaked past Holden and took a peek around the corner himself. Twenty metres up the road, six figures could be seen crouching in the street. They were unmistakably infected, their fingers ripping into the fallen bodies of their latest victims, their mouths gorging on flesh. One of them, an elderly lady in her former life, was nibbling on the fingers of an arm she held with both hands. From where he stood, Brian couldn't see who had once owned that arm.

"Not good," said Brian when he pulled his head back. He looked at Stan. "Go through them or around them?"

"Shit." Neither asked Holden, and she didn't expect them to. She was alive because of them, and she was going to do whatever they said, when they said it. "Okay, we go through them."

"Make sure you don't miss," Brian said, smiling.

"Fuck you," Stan said. Holden stood, an observer to the stress-relieving banter of friends. Then there was a scream. If it had been close to them, it would have been ear-splitting. As it was, it was far enough away to just be loud. She could tell that the infected were between the three of them and the owner of that agonising cry. Brian looked around the corner again and saw that all six infected were already moving away.

"Fuck these things are fast. Okay, let's go." Given another reprieve, they made their way up the road past the remains of three dead people, and after several metres turned right, following the arrow on Holden's phone. They heard the scream again, closer this time, and the three of them felt the unquenchable urge to run. And run they did.

11.45AM, 16th September 2015, Heathrow Airport, London

Jack was still surprised at how lucid their mother had been, and how willingly she had accepted what Clive had told her. She had been stood in the kitchen in her dressing gown when they had all entered, pouring vodka into a glass. She had looked at Clive, a sad look on her face coloured by a tint of guilt, and she had not resisted when he had walked over to her and gently removed the bottle from her grasp. Despite his size advantage, he had shown nothing but tenderness, and after he told her what needed to be done, she had simply responded with, "I'd better get dressed then." Jack had almost burst into tears at how easy it had all gone.

Now they were all sat in Clive's car. Living a ten minutes' drive from the airport would be considered by many to be a curse, but right now, with the city quickly deteriorating, there were millions who would have given everything to be sat where Jack was, up front in the passenger seat. His smartphone played the live news broadcasts that every minute reinforced Clive's decision. Social media was on fire with tales of zombies and police shootings.

"Mummy, where are we going?" the little voice said from the back seat. Jack turned to see her sister being comforted.

"We're going on holiday, dear," their mother said. "Won't that be nice?" Jack's mother smiled at his sister who nodded agreement. She cuddled her daughter and winked at Jack, who turned back to look out of the front. It was then that the car stopped. All up ahead, the traffic was gridlocked.

"I think we walk from here," Clive said. Jack saw the wisdom of it, and he could see the airport's perimeter fence at the end of the road. There were other people with the same idea, and the pavements and roads were filled with a mass exodus of hundreds of people all heading to the same destination. Clive kept his hand close to his weapon at all times. Although he would prefer not to shoot anyone if possible, just wielding it would be a significant deterrent should trouble arise.

It had taken them a further fifteen minutes to reach the departures area of Terminal 5. There were people everywhere, and a good dozen armed police officers could be seen away from the doors. One of them had a bullhorn.

"There are no more flights. You will not get on a plane if you stay here. Please return to your homes." There were howls of protest at the policeman's words, and several missiles were thrown from within the crowd. The crowd itself was pushed up against the airport entrances, hundreds of them banging and slapping the reinforced glass of the automatic doors. Because the doors wouldn't open. To Jack's eyes, it was obvious that they had been locked.

"You are ordered to disperse." More missiles flew towards the officers, who backed off from the crowd. One of them raised a handgun into the air and let off three shots. The tone of the crowd changed. Where it had been tinged with desperation-inspired anger, now it was overcome with fear, and scores of people began to break away. A large group turned and ran towards where Jack and his family now stood, and they pushed themselves up against a wall to avoid being swept along in the panic.

"Shit," said Clive angrily. "We need to get back to the car." Jack took out his phone. He was going to go on the BBC website, but nothing came up.

"Clive, I'm not getting a signal anymore."

*

"But I have tickets for Miami," the grossly obese American woman demanded.

"I'm sorry, madam, but this is a state of emergency. You have been allocated to flight EO135 to Paris, which leaves in 45 minutes." The check-in lady was stressed. Even with the announcements and even with the fact that these people were being given a chance to get out of a country that was on the brink of ruin, still some argued. Still some thought they had rights, that they had some sort of consumer power. Hadn't they seen the news? Didn't they know what was happening here? Hell, the only thing keeping her here was the fact she had been promised a flight out herself.

"But I want to go to Miami. I demand to speak to your supervisor."

"Well, hard fucking luck. You either accept this ticket or get out of the way and I will give your seat to somebody else. You're lucky to get a seat, you ungrateful bitch." The American gasped in surprise at how she was being spoken to. Nobody spoke to her like this, nobody. She stammered, unable to find the words to express her outrage. She was an American, she paid her taxes, and this sort of altercation just didn't happen to her. For goodness sake, she raised money for her church. Behind the airport check-in desks, a policeman calmly walked over and addressed the American.

"Do you have a problem?" he asked, his hand flexing on the handle of his machine gun.

"I … I want to go to Miami. I paid to go to Miami." The policeman looked at her with disdain. "Please, I have to get home."

"So do I, love, so do we all," said the policeman. "Look, love, I know you're scared, and I know this isn't how you wanted your day to go, but believe me when I say that if you do not accept what you are being offered, you will regret it for the rest of what will likely be a very short life." The check-in lady held out the ticket, which the American reluctantly took off her and sauntered off, muttering to herself. The policeman put a reassuring hand on the airport employee's shoulder and bent down to whisper in her ear. "You're doing fine. Remember, any trouble and I'm here for you." She looked at him and nodded her thanks, then turned back to allocate more seats. Shit, she had lost it there. If she had spoken to a customer like that any other time, she would have likely been fired immediately. But such trivial things as customer service didn't matter anymore, and if she was honest with herself, it felt good to get that out of her system. Five years she had been doing this job, five years of grumpy fuckers giving her shit for stuff that wasn't within her power to change, or even her fault. Still, she only had another fifty seats she could give out. After that, all the planes would likely be full, except for the ones set aside for those who worked at the airport, the ones who had remained after the reality of the situation had landed on them like a two-hundred-pound bomb. Many had left, rushing home to be with family and friends, blindly abandoning the very means of their escape. Others rang loved ones, urged them to come to the airport, to bring passports and documents and money. Then the phones stopped working, the cell tower system around the airport knocked out on the demands of someone, somewhere.

Things would really get interesting. When the police and the staff started drifting away, it wouldn't be long before those left behind would react. That had been the promise. Stay and you get a way out of the madness. Or you can leave and take your chances. It was surprising how many chose to stay. A voice boomed out over the tannoy.

"Attention. Please remember that when you get your boarding pass, please head directly to the departure gate. Remember only one piece of carry-on luggage is allowed per person."

*

The tunnel was dark. His lungs worked overtime as he ran as best he could, given the unevenness of the rails and the danger of the electrified rail. His mind didn't understand what electricity was, or how to now even say the word electricity. But something primal within him told him it was dangerous, told him it would cause pain and maybe even death. So he avoided it, as did the three dozen others with him. Lit only by the occasional side lamp, the underground tunnel was the perfect means for them to spread themselves throughout the city.

He had once been called David. A plumber by trade, he had been one of the originals, one of the Founding Fathers of his new race. He had drunk the tainted coffee and had transformed into a superior being. David had been reborn into pain and confusion. Only as the numbers grew did the voices whisper in his mind. And now he ran at the head of his pack, others following his lead, all following the commands of the growing global consciousness. Hundreds of thousands of minds all joined as one, sharing an overwhelming desire to feed and to spread and to kill. David didn't even understand what a plumber did anymore, that part of him stripped away, memories just vague ghosts in his predator mind. All that mattered was the hunger – the burning, unquenchable hunger deep in his gut that just couldn't be satisfied. He was the hunger; it was all consuming.

Up ahead, a light began to show, becoming brighter as they ran. The group became excited, running faster as the smell of meat began to reach them. Within seconds, they had reached the underground platform. If their minds could still read, they would have been able to decipher the sign that said "Heathrow Terminals 1,2,3". It didn't matter; they knew where they were, the collective having sent them here. One by one, they vaulted onto the platform and headed for the escalators. A man in an orange and blue outfit appeared. Why he was there, they didn't know. He stood shocked as the crowd of slavering beasts rushed towards him. One took him down almost silently, teeth finding his neck, biting down hard and slicing through the carotid artery. The rest of them carried on, letting their brother briefly drink the blood they all so desperately craved. On the edges of their minds, they felt a semblance of his pleasure, and the pleasure of the thousands of their kind who were at that moment biting, chewing, gnawing and slicing into human skin.

They all bore the uniforms of recent slaughterers. Their clothes dirty and blood-soaked, mainly from the injuries inflicted on others, they looked like the survivors of a natural disaster. Except for their eyes of course. Bloated and blood red, their eyes were the eyes of monsters. David led the group up a flight of stairs, an escalator that had been turned off. At the top, they saw that the security gate was locked, and they grunted in frustration.

"CONTACT!" a voice shouted from above, and David looked through the gate to see three men clad in black appear. There was a loud noise, and one of David's brothers fell backwards as the back of his head exploded. The group roared in outrage and fled back towards the escalator, unable to reach their attackers due to the barrier. David felt something punch him in the left shoulder, and he flew sideways, losing his feet and landing hard on his right side. At the top of the escalator, his momentum sent him tumbling down. Something in his left arm broke, but the pain was meaningless to him, just as meaningless as the fresh bullet wound that had shattered his left collar bone. His brothers and sisters clambered over him, moving with grace and inhuman speed away from the bullets. Several of their numbers fell, but most weathered the bullets that struck them, and soon were out of range from the threat. David picked himself up, his body broken but still useful. So the main way in was blocked, the collective mind registered. Very well. They would just head back through the tunnels to where they came out into the light. More of their brethren were coming and soon they would spread their seed into this mass of humanity. There were too many of them to stop now.

11.46AM, 16th September 2015, Jubilee Railway Bridge, just North of Westminster, London

"Hold them, just fucking HOLD THEM!" Grainger roared at his men. He had moved his position further up Victoria Embankment, the Golden Jubilee Railway Bridges crossing the road in front of him now his last line of defence. The infected were swimming the river in their hundreds now, impossible targets to hit in the undulating water, even for the dozens of skilled snipers on the rooftops all around him. Even when the shots hit, the infected barely seemed to notice. The Westminster Bridge was no longer the issue; they could hold them there, and it was still burning from the last napalm strike which an American jet had dropped. The issue now was the thousands of infected that had just begun to charge at them along the northern end of Victoria Embankment. No matter how many they killed, they just got back up and kept on coming. Their weight of numbers was slowly pushing forward against the awesome but dwindling firepower being rained upon them.

"Head shots, men, it's the only way to stop them," he said over his helmet microphone. Another attack helicopter flew overhead, this time in the wrong direction. It was obvious its ammunition was spent.

"Sir, it's Colonel Bearder," a corporal said, handing his captain the radio handset.

"Colonel?"

"Captain, we are evacuating the cabinet and the prime minister from PINDAR. Your orders are to hold until the helicopters are in the air, and then do a rolling defensive withdrawal to Westminster Pier. Boats are already arriving to take your men away to a safer location. I am heading there myself now."

"What about the infected in the water? There are hundreds of them," asked the Captain. He could barely hear his commanding officer over the biblical onslaught being rained on the attackers.

"We will just have to do the best we can. The river is the only way you are getting out. There aren't enough helicopters, and the roads are grid-locked. Oh, and Captain ...?" There was an eruption as three of his men fired off anti-tank rounds to try and bring the bridge infrastructure down to block off the tunnel.

"Yes, Colonel?"

"I am advised to tell you to abandon any of your men who become bitten or contaminated. I am told it would be the ultimate mercy if you put a bullet in their heads first. Bearder out." Grainger handed the radio handset back to his corporal, his face blanched. He felt sick. He knew he was the right man for the job, but he didn't want to be. At this moment, he wanted to be anything but.

"Are you okay, Captain?" the corporal asked.

"No, lad," Grainger said putting his hand on the young man's shoulder. "No, I'm far from okay, but we've got a job to do, and I'll be damned if we don't get it done."

11.47AM, 16th September 2015, RAF Fairford

Major Douglas Potter the Third stood on the runway tarmac and watched the loading of his B52 Stratofortress. Stood well away from the fuel lines, he allowed himself the luxury of smoking one of his diminishing stock of Cuban cigars. His wife would play merry hell with him if she saw this transgression, but she wasn't here, and by the time he next saw her, the smell would have long left his person. Even the most successful marriages required secrets, and his cigars were far from the worst thing he kept from her.

He didn't like this, he didn't like it one bit. But he had his orders, and he had his mission, having been briefed thirty minutes ago. Doug was still reeling from the information that had been crammed into him. The thought of abandoning civilians did not rest easily with him, but watching the video footage had convinced him there was no other option. He knew his crew felt the same way, and suspected they had experienced the same level of nausea at the truth that was given to them all. His crew knew what they were being asked to do was distasteful, and yet they all knew they would do as they were ordered. They had little choice – those orders had come from the president himself. There was no ignoring that. All across the airbase planes were being loaded with the bare essentials so that as many personnel as possible could be shipped back home or to Europe. It was like the retreat from Saigon all over again.

If only there was something that could be done. The noise of a C-130 super Hercules plane reached him as it taxied onto the main runway. He turned to watch it, the huge bulk moving forward towards take-off. It would be full of civilian personnel and their families from the neighbouring area, over ninety in all. Their lives would have been wrenched apart by the day's events, but at least they were heading to the home of their birth. The civilian staff from the local indigenous population had already been told that; regrettably, they were to be left behind to face whatever fate life threw at them. Even marriage hadn't helped. If you didn't hold a US passport, there was no place for you on the plane, and he knew personally several US personnel who had refused a seat on one of the planes. They had chosen love over duty. Doug couldn't fault them for that.

If only he had some decent ordinance, he might be able to put it to good use. Whilst he knew it was unlikely the politicians would authorise the use of nukes any time soon, if at all, there were other options available. At least there would be if they had been back home in the US. His plane could carry a thermobaric bomb to any city in the UK and cut the infection off at the source. Otherwise called the Mother of All Bombs, the MOAB could kill everything within its significant blast radius. Of course, there were two problems with that. Firstly, there would be thousands of civilian deaths, and secondly, they didn't have any MOAB's in the UK. So his B52, designed to level cities and carpet bomb whole regions, was not being loaded with weapons of war. Instead, it was being loaded with vital equipment and people. His beloved plane was being turned into a glorified passenger jet. Major Potter could almost weep at how useless he felt.

11.48AM 16th September 2015, Horse Guard Parade, Whitehall, London

More tunnels. More steps. At the back of the pack again, armed now with a semi-automatic machine gun and a sidearm, he felt like a soldier again. To be honest, though, he had never stopped being a soldier in his heart. There was another mini tremor followed by a muffled explosion. Before they had abandoned PINDAR, he had heard General Marston authorising the use of air strikes on the city. Savage was by his side, because where else was there for her to be?

"Do you have family, Captain?" Croft asked as they walked at a brisk pace.

"My mother is in Newquay, well away from all this. I have no other close family worth speaking of. What about you?"

"No, no family to speak of." He looked straight ahead, uncomfortable with the line of questioning. Croft wasn't a man to let people into his private thoughts. Savage seemed to sense his unease.

"It won't work, you know," Savage said, changing the subject.

"What won't?"

"The nukes, at least not in London. The infected in the tube network will be shielded, and the radiation won't allow ground forces to mop up. Even if the radiation does kill them, there's nothing to say they won't reanimate. They will just come to the surface after the blast and attack the survivors. And the fallout from hitting so many cities will kill half the country. Not to mention the damage done when it spreads to the continent."

"So it's a lose-lose situation, no matter what we do," Croft said, irritation in his voice.

"We're fucked, Croft," Savage said. The final door stood before them.

Then they were out in the open, the cool morning air refreshing. A light drizzle was falling, and Croft found himself walking onto Horse Guard Parade, helicopters waiting for them, more hovering above waiting to land and rescue as many people as possible. And in the distance, the incessant rattle of sustained and lethal gunfire.

Sergeant Smith stood far enough from the helicopter that the rotating blades were not a threat to him. Despite the noise and the bedlam around him, he felt strangely calm. Those around him thought they were containing the threat, thought they were buying time so that the country's leaders could make their escape. But they didn't see the greater threat. No, they just didn't see it. Ordered to abandon his position guarding Downing Street, he ignored his redeployment orders and made his way to Horse Guard Parade where in the chaos he just became another uniform. Here he waited for the ruling elite to make their escape. This was where he was needed; this was where he was supposed to be.

There were three helicopters on the ground, and they waited patiently for their latest passengers, dust whipped up into a storm by their presence. The infected were in the park to the east of their position in large numbers now, and the soldiers, backed up by the SAS troop, formed a line of death to keep them at bay. Heavy machine gun fire and the shouts of men fighting for their lives could be heard. With police snipers on the surrounding buildings, their advance was being held back, but it wouldn't be long before the position got overwhelmed. The infected had two major advantages: they spawned their soldiers from their enemy, and they were very difficult to kill.

There was a motion at the periphery of his vision, and Smith turned to see the prime minister and half the cabinet emerge from a guarded doorway. They were being escorted towards the helicopter next to where Smith stood. It was also the spot near to where Her Majesty the Queen would sit every year to watch the Trooping of the Colour … something that was unlikely ever to happen again. Smith withdrew the magazine, checking how many rounds he had in place, and slammed it back into his weapon.

The prime minister did not look well. As the man grew closer, Smith saw that he looked pale and ill. *So this is who we have to lead us in our time of crisis*, he thought, relieved that he had arrived here in time to do his duty. So this was the man the people elected to keep them safe, to keep their country safe. The home secretary looked more up to the task. She had that aura of resolute determination. That's what a leader needed. It didn't matter if your world was falling to shit. Those who followed you needed to see that you were the rock for them to depend on. You needed to be the example. Smith felt his finger move off the trigger guard and onto the trigger, and he moved to intercept the party, mindful of his job to protect those he served. The protection detail saw him and nodded. He nodded back, showing his mutual respect. Smith knew most of them, drank with some of them. He stood guard as they passed, his shoulder patted by several of the officers he knew personally. Even the home secretary gave him a look of thanks as she passed, although true to form, the prime minister didn't even seem to see him. And as the prime minister passed, a mere five metres away from the welcoming safety of the helicopter, Smith knew that the time had come. He raised his semi-automatic machine gun and emptied the magazine into the party, the prime minister, chancellor of the exchequer and home secretary falling to fatal wounds. General Marston fell to the ground with a wound in his lower abdomen.

Smith killed five people, and his gun clicked empty before the shock of what he had done registered a response. The soldiers and the protection detail were so focussed on the external threat, the fact that one of their own had become the enemy was completely alien to them.

"The prime minister is down, the prime minister is down," Smith heard over his own earpiece, and then he felt the impacts as bullets smacked into his Kevlar vest. Huge iron fists barrelled into him, one after the other in quick succession. One round entered just above his left knee sending him to the floor, and his last thoughts before a sniper round went through his skull was how honoured he felt to do God's work. Brother Abraham had chosen wisely in his selection.

Croft was in the third group that left the exit to Horse Guard Parade. He saw the prime minister pass the policeman, saw the officer raise his weapon, saw him fire a full magazine into the country's leader and his entourage. But was too far away to do anything to intervene. All he could do was stand and stare and bear witness to the traitorous act. There was no defence against that. There was no way to defend the leaders of a country when those tasked to defend them were the very assassins one feared.

11.49AM, 16th September 2015, Swiss Cottage, London

They were encountering people now. Refugees fleeing the slaughter. Holden had the urge to stop and try and help those that she saw were wounded. But this was about survival now, and besides, many of the wounds she saw looked like bites. How long after being bitten did people turn – was that even how the infection spread?

"We need to keep moving," Brian said. "This still isn't safe."

"Some of them are bitten," Holden said, indicating the people around them.

"I know. And I know you want to help, but we all know what that means." She nodded, and she looked at Stan.

"Shit," he muttered to himself.

"Officers, can you help us?" a voice said. Brian shook his head in despair, knowing it was the right thing to do. But the voice came from an elderly lady who was helping an equally elderly gentleman navigate the pavement.

"Sorry, can't," Stan said and they picked up the pace. He looked at Holden hoping not to see disapproval. He didn't. She just nodded to him, and they made their way further up the road.

"If we carry on up the Finchley Road, we can be at the M1 in about an hour. I suspect there will be military there," Brian said.

"Then what happens?" Holden asked.

"Then, doctor, you will most likely be drafted to help with any wounded, and we will most likely be drafted to help kill these things."

"But first we've got to make it there alive," said Stan. "And whilst I hate to say it, the more people we put between ourselves and those things, the more chance we have of making it." He looked at the two of them and then reproached himself. "Shit, I'm sorry, that sounded harsh."

"You don't have to outrun the bear," Holden said, more to herself than anyone.

"What's that, doc?"

"Something I heard once. If your camp gets attacked by a bear, you don't have to be faster than the bear. You just have to be able to run faster than the other campers."

11.52AM, 16th September 2015, Victoria Embankment, London

"Colour Sergeant," Captain Grainger shouted over to his subordinate. Standing at the back of his fortification, he could see how hopeless his position was now. The sergeant – a big, burly man with a handlebar moustache – was probably one of the most respected men in the regiment. He ran over to Grainger, seemingly oblivious to the noise and the mayhem around him.

"Sir," Colour Sergeant Vorne said coming to his commander's side. He didn't salute.

"We are retreating to the Westminster Pier. Form the men into three lines for fire and movement with the vehicles leading the way. I want their heavies laying down covering fire as we make out retreat."

"I'm on it," the colour sergeant said and moved off. Grainger motioned to the corporal who was crouched by his side.

"Corporal, all units are to retreat towards the Westminster Pier. Make sure the snipers on the roofs have already left their positions as per my previous orders." His corporal nodded and began to shout into the radio he was carrying on his back. Grainger stood, momentarily mesmerised by it all. He had walked down this river embankment several days earlier. It had been a peaceful Sunday night, a cloudless sky, the stars vibrant in the cool air. He had felt safe, walking the streets of what was still one of the world's most powerful countries, and the crisp air had invigorated him. And now everything was blood and smoke. The cordite fumes from the thousands of rounds being fired drifted across the battle, and the howls of the undead spilled out across the city.

He quick marched it over to the river and looked over the wall that stopped the Thames flooding the city. With no way for them to climb out due to the steepness of the artificial river walls on this part of the Thames, the infected thrashed and bobbed in the water. There were hundreds of them, fighting against the current, searching for a way to escape so they could sink their teeth into the living. The captain looked to the south to the proposed escape route for his men, the Westminster River Pier, right by the Westminster Bridge. Two Apache attack helicopters hovered over the pier, laying withering minigun fire into the river and onto the bridge itself. Below them, several boats bobbed almost gracefully, awaiting owners that would never again return for them.

They would stay there until nature reclaimed them, their wood eventually rotting and submitting to the power of the river. Grainger hated the water. His father, a marine, had been almost devastated when he had learnt his son was joining the Army. He had half-joked that it had almost felt like betrayal. Across the river, the city burned.

Further up the embankment to the north, the infected massed. Their initial surges had been stopped, and the railway bridge infrastructure had partially collapsed due to mortar and tank rounds. But the contaminated were coming from all directions now. His air drones showed thousands descending on their position from all over the city. The grenadiers were retreating on all fronts, and in some areas, were even being overrun. There just weren't enough troops available at such short notice, and with a disarmed population, the viral spread just couldn't be contained. Word had reached him moments earlier that Captain Walker had been killed when his retreating forces had been outflanked. Where Grainger stood was part of the last defensive position, and with less than a hundred men, there was no way to hold out. His colour sergeant came over to him.

"Sir, the men are ready to get the fuck out of here." Just as he said that, there was a roar from the enemy's position, and they began to charge. Fifty metres away, they moved with frightening speed, even with heavy machine gun fire being laid into them.

"Very good, Sergeant. Fire and move." Vorne nodded to him and turned to face the backs of his men, who were now in three lines. He spoke into his helmet microphone. "Fire and move to the pier, lads. I repeat, fire and move."

The front line of men crouched and fired off full magazines into the surging mass of infected and undead. Magazines depleted, they retreated, running between the two lines behind them, putting the second row in front, forming a new line ten metres behind. Each man at the new front fired off five rounds and followed their fellow soldiers, taking up fresh positions. This way they could do a leapfrog retreat whilst still maintaining suppressing fire and, more importantly, discipline. Grainger knew if the line broke, the infected would be upon them.

"Hold them," Grainger roared, walking amongst his men, showing his presence as he retreated with them, the colour sergeant doing the same. The sergeant held a fearsome presence, and Grainger suspected some of the soldiers held more fear for him than they infected.

"If any of you bastards die with a full magazine," the colour sergeant bellowed, "I will rape your fucking corpse." Shit, even Grainger was afraid of the man at that instant.

"Sir, Colonel Bearder," the corporal said, holding out the radio handset. They walked backwards as Grainger spoke to his commanding officer.

"Sir, we are retreating to the pier, over," Grainger said.

"Yes, I can see you. I'm there now. Horse Guard Parade is being evacuated. The infected are now in Downing Street. Over." There was a loud boom as one of the retreating Warrior tanks fired off at the bridge, and the structure finally collapsed blocking the road from the north. It didn't seem to stop the assault as, like enraged ants, the infected just swarmed over it. The infected was what they were now called. An hour ago, these had been people with lives, with hopes and fears and dreams.

"Is there any word on General Marston? Over," the captain asked.

"I hear he's going to be okay. He's a tough old dog. Over."

"Yes, he is, sir, thank you, sir. Grainger out." *Thank God*, thought Grainger. He had met the man several times and knew that the general was the kind of man the country needed right now. A friend of his fathers, he was a man who could make the hard decisions and not flinch from his responsibility. Not like that prick of a prime minister. The news of the PM's death had spread quickly through the ranks and, although Grainger hadn't heard it voiced, the opinion was that the man's death was probably a blessing in disguise. He hadn't been the kind of man a soldier respected.

"Head shots men, head shots," one of his lieutenants commanded. The rolling retreat continued. Grainger stayed near the front with his men. At this rate, they would run out of ammunition. The air rocked from the shock wave as one of the Warrior tanks fired off another shell, and despair began to form in his heart. There was a tug at his sleeve, and his corporal stood there holding out the radio handset.

"Sir."

The captain took the offering.

"Grainger here. Over."

"Good morning," a loud American voice said over the handset. "Sorry we're late to the party, Captain. Thought you could use a hand. Over."

"Who is this? Over," Grainger said, putting a finger in his other ear.

"This is the AC-130 Spectre gunship, call sign Sunray, that is now over your position. Feel free to mark any areas you want obliterating. We'll cover your retreat so you can get the fuck out of Dodge, over." Grainger looked up into the sky, but wasn't surprised when he didn't see anything. Typical Yanks, always late to the fucking party.

*

The AC-130 Spectre gunship. A glorified Hercules transport plane loaded with a huge amount of armaments. For some reason, the Americans had developed a fetish for sticking big guns on big planes. Two M61 Vulcan cannons each with a magazine of three thousand 20mm rounds. Mounted behind them, a pair of 7.62x51mm NATO calibre GE GAU -2B miniguns, capable of firing up to six thousand rounds a minute. And, of course, if that wasn't enough, the Spectre also sported two howitzer cannons capable of firing two-pound brassed-case shells at the rate of one hundred per minute, each round capable of penetrating 5cm armour plating and making the asphalt presently below it look like the surface of the moon. It was about to do exactly what it was designed for.

Grainger's men continued their withdrawal, faster now as he wanted them out of the blast zone. They ran in full retreat. As their suppressive fire stopped, the advance of the infected swelled. And for a moment, Grainger thought he had made a catastrophic error, for a moment he thought the Americans would fail him, that the speed and the great weight of numbers would overwhelm his position. But only for a moment. Then the ground to the north of him just disappeared as a mass of ordinance was dumped on such a relatively small area. Dozens of infected were pulverised in the first wave. Dozens more in the second, flesh and bone disintegrated and ripped apart by bullets the size of sausages. And then the howitzer rounds hit, creating a deadly impenetrable wall of death that nothing living could penetrate. He actually saw corpses flung into the air. It gave Grainger time, precious time to get his men to the docks, to get his men out and away. He ran with them, as hard and as fast as he had ever run in his life.

*

Rachel. Had her name been Rachel? The thought passed through her mind so quickly it was as if it hadn't even been there. Her mind filled with a void as it tried to process, tried to reset itself. Dazed and confused, she looked up at the sky, her mind swimming with what had just happened. She blinked several times, realising her sight was different. She didn't know it, and her infected mind didn't care, but her right eye had been shattered, and her right arm had been severed at the elbow. Scorch marks scarred her skin, and the debris from the blast that had hit right next to her still landed all around.

She had been in the crowd storming towards the soldiers when the heavens had unleashed fire upon her. Groggy, even with her infected strength, she tried to sit up, and it took several attempts before she managed it. She looked down at where her arm had been, blood pouring from the wound, and groped at the emptiness with her other hand. Pieces of concrete and tarmac spat at her flesh as bullets landed all around her. She didn't understand what this meant, and she grunted in confusion. The smell of burning was so strong it blocked out the smell of the meat that she so desperately craved. Even with her injuries, she wanted that flesh, to dig her teeth into the warm, vital tissue that would bring her so much pleasure and yet do nothing to relieve the clawing hunger. There was pain from her injuries, but it was far away, blocked out by the virus that needed to keep her agile and mobile as long as possible.

Looking around, she saw debris and body parts. Her fellow kind ran past her, and more fire rained down from above. To her right, a body flew backwards and warmth hit her directly in the face. Rachel tried to stand, and something clipped her scalp as a bullet nearly put an end to her. Back, back, the collective mind cried, and she followed its command, turning and staggering back the way she had come. A second explosion hit near her, and the shock wave took her off her feet again. She landed face first onto fresh rubble, lacerating her face, her good eye fortunately spared. But there was a new sensation, and she pushed herself up off the ground, only to feel a tearing in her chest. A piece of rebar that had been embedded in the shattered concrete she had landed on had penetrated her left lung. It came free with her effort, and she got to her knees, only to find she could no longer breathe. Sarah frowned, lacking the consciousness or the logical powers to understand what had happened. Still she tried to stand, but her injuries were too great. The strength finally left her now failing body and she fell back to the ground, her world now a gasping, bleeding ruin. As strong as she was, she had no life left to give and her eyes closed. Something in her told her not to fight it, to just let go, some instinct that was wordless and formless.

Nobody came to help her. No hands grabbed her and pulled her to safety. She was left to die in a cratered street by her own kind. They gave her that gift. As she bled out, and unable to oxygenate what blood she had left, her mind switched off, the last of her consciousness dwindling to nothingness. One last feeble attempt to breathe was matched by a final beat of her heart, and then her system shut down. Within seconds, she was clinically dead, the cells beginning to break down through lack of oxygen and nutrients. And there she lay, the assault by the Spectre gunship slowly moving away from her as it moved to other targets. Her fellow infected rushed past her, walked over her; she was now invisible to them. But inside her mind, something changed. Although everything that had made her human was already dying, something in there began to fire. Synapses reformed and reignited. Dead for less than three minutes, her good hand twitched, then twitched again. It rose into the air, the hand opening and closing as if clawing for an invisible enemy. And then her right eye opened, and the world around her was swallowed up into its blackness. This was Abraham's ultimate vision, for the wicked and the sinners to be born again.

7.43PM 7th July 2013, Hotel Suite, The Sheraton, London

"You understand what you will be expected to do?" Abraham asked. He sat in a leather recliner, looking at the man who may one day be instrumental to his plan. The man sat in a similar chair, within touching distance. The look of awe in the disciple's eyes was palpable. "Will you be able to do it? Will you be able to be God's Holy Messenger?"

"If I'm there, and if things go down as you say they will, I can get as close to him as anyone." Smith picked up the beer he had been served by one of Abraham's minions, the server now absent from the room. He still felt blessed to be in the room, to be in the very presence of the man whose message he had discovered several years before. Taking a long swig, Smith relished the coldness as it entered his mouth. His foot shifted, and he again wondered why the carpet was covered in plastic sheeting.

"God's will requires your devotion. It requires your faith. And you understand that it will also require your life?"

"My life is his," Smith said. "I am here to serve him through your counsel." Abraham reached over and grabbed Smith's hand. He smiled, and Smith felt warmth spread through him. Yes, they had selected well with this man.

"This will be the last time you will see me. And you will have little warning when the time comes. Also, I cannot tell you WHY I need you to kill this man, but you will see the message and know that the time to act is upon you."

"What message?" Smith beseeched.

"You will not mistake it," Abraham said patting his hand. "I am bringing God's justice upon the world. His message will be biblical." Abraham released the man's hand. "But first, you must prove your love for the Almighty." There was a noise behind Smith as a door opened, and he heard somebody enter. There was the sound of a struggle, as if someone was being dragged into the room. Smith didn't turn around.

After several seconds, a bound woman was thrown to the floor in his direct line of sight. From behind Smith, a hand appeared holding a knife.

"As you can see by the ridiculous Hijab, this heathen is a follower of another faith. Her kind will also face God's wrath in the goodness of time, and I will bring fire and brimstone upon them. But that is not for today." Smith grabbed hold of the knife, and the hand vanished from sight. He looked down at the woman, whose mouth was gagged and whose eyes pleaded for mercy whilst being infected by terror. He guessed she was about seventeen and looked Caucasian.

"You can spare this woman a life wasted to a false God. End her, Smith; send her to be judged before she taints her soul anymore. Show our Lord the warrior that you are. Show me that you can be trusted with the task I have given you." Smith had hesitated, but only for a moment. For weeks after, he felt like he couldn't get his hands clean, and scrubbed them red raw every day. The blood, although no longer visible, was still there – it just wouldn't come off.

When Smith had left, Abraham sat alone in contemplation. The pieces were slowly falling into place. He had always known why he had been chosen to hear God's message. It was because he had the will and the resources to bring God's will to fruition. If he had been asked why God himself didn't just smite the planet as he had so viscously done according to the numerous stories in the Old Testament, Abraham would have smiled knowingly, shaking his head at the naivety of the questioner. It was all part of God's test. He was giving mankind a chance to prove their devotion, to give Abraham a chance to prove his worthiness to sit at his son's right hand.

And Smith wasn't the only disciple within the ranks of the UK government structure. There were dozens of them, working away behind the scenes to prepare for the day of atonement and making sure that the Lord's plans were kept secret from the huge behemoth that was the UK's surveillance and counter espionage network. But Smith was particularly key to the overall plan. Abraham's one fear was that the apocalypse he intended to unleash would be snuffed out by nuclear fire. So dealing with the individuals who could order such a strike would be essential. But he knew no plan was ever foolproof, so if Smith failed, if the head of the snake lived and the missiles were sent flying, Abraham would still have the satisfaction of seeing millions die at the hands of humanity's scientific insanity. It would still send a message, but deep down, Abraham wanted the island to be a living hell, not a radioactive wasteland. It was this that was in his dreams. He would wake in the dead of night, not from a nightmare, but from a dream so compelling and enticing it was almost erotic. A dream of death and of viral induced rebirth. The creation of a new species who followed only the word of God.

11.55AM, 16th September 2015, Heathrow Airport, London

Despite his injuries, David led his pack of infected out into the daylight. They had easily traversed the fences, and had combined with other infected that had been sent to reinforce their numbers. The collective mind knew everything that they knew, and they knew everything the collective knew. It worked as one, it spread as one and it fed as one. Devoid of everything but the most basic emotions, devoid of everything but the most rudimentary language, the collective concentrated on satisfying the relentless hunger that gnawed at its individual soldiers. Even when they got to feed, the collective hunger forced them on, abandoning the banquet that was all around them. There was no sleep, no respite, just hunger or death, which for some led to mindless resurrection.

Now a hundred strong, the pack – registering David's disability – appointed a new leader. David did not object, for he had no words with which to object to. His virus-infused mind just accepted what the collective demanded. No resentment, no remorse at his failure. For there was no failure when you had no concept of what the word meant. His only concern was to feed and to spread. He joined the group as it headed towards the airport, the perimeter fence now in view.

Strength was returning to him, and he could feel the wounds on his body beginning to heal. Another of Abraham's gifts, the virus sped up the body's healing process. His arms would be useless for many hours yet, maybe even days, but already the bleeding from the gunshot wound had stopped. It almost felt like the collective approved, and he heard the roar of the victories across the city as fresh minds joined with his.

A half a dozen infected broke off from the larger mass, and David found himself following them. The roads to the airport would be clogged with prey, prey that was likely unarmed. *Let us spread, let us feed.*

*

Clive led the group back to the car. Where else were they to go? There were even more people now, and they found it difficult to go against the flow as most were heading towards the airport. Of course, some were taking the day's events as an opportunity, and several shops on the roads they travelled were already being ransacked.

They turned a corner, and the car was now in sight. The road was clogged, however, and Clive knew that they wouldn't be going anywhere in it. Some of the cars in the street were even burning. He had hoped that some of the traffic had cleared, but if anything, it was even worse. Even the pavements were blocked. So their choices were limited. A child, an alcoholic and a man whose heart was about to explode at any minute. Only Jack had any real hope of making it out of this, and Clive knew he would never leave his family.

"Jack, come here," he said, walking away from Jack's mother and sister. Out of their earshot, he grabbed Jack lovingly by the shoulder. Neither of them saw the bloodied figure that was skulking towards them, hiding between the cars as it wormed its way towards where they now stood.

"We have to consider what our next move is," Clive said. "I'm going to lay some painful truths on you, and you aren't going to like what I have to say." Jack looked at his mentor and nodded.

"I already know, Clive. The only way out of here is on foot."

"That's right, and there's no way I can make that, not in my condition. My heart's already threatening to burst out of my chest just from walking to the airport and back." Clive pointed at Jack's mother who was sat on the curb hugging his sister. "And your mother's already knackered." Jack turned to where Clive was pointing, a sad smile hitting his face.

"Then we go back to your house and hold up till this all blows over," said Jack. Clive shook his head.

"Lad, this isn't going to blow over. If anything, it's only going to get worse. We need to..."

"Well look at these two black cunts," a voice boomed out from behind them. Clive turned, and Jack moved to look in the same direction. Owen Paterson stood outside a pharmacy not six metres away, a rucksack in hand. Behind him stood three of his minions. "Oh, this is perfect. I told you I was going to have you, son," Owen said pointing at Jack, "and look how you fall right into my lap." Owen dropped the bag and reaching behind his back, he pulled out a hunting knife. Jack took a step back.

"Are you kidding me?" Clive said, a sarcastic smile spreading onto his face.

"No, old man, I'm going to cut your balls off in front of your boyfriend, and then I'm going to feed them to him." There was a cackle of laughter from one of Owen's gang, and two of them high-fived each other.

"Oh, is that right?" Clive said. Clive took a step backwards and pulled out the gun from its holster. He raised it and pointed it towards the group. They stilled as they realised their target was now actually a significant danger to them. "Just for the record, this is a Sig Sauer P226," Clive brought his hand up and chambered a round in an exaggerated fashion. "This particular one is outfitted with a fifteen-round magazine, and I personally put the hollow-point Smith and Wesson rounds in it this morning." Clive pointed the gun at the thug who had laughed moments ago. He certainly wasn't laughing now. "You know what a hollow-point round will do to you, don't you, boy? Of course you do; you watch movies."

"You haven't got the balls to fire that gun, you black shit," Owen said.

"Really? You mean like when I fought in the Falklands and killed three men in close-quarter combat, one by sticking a bayonet blade into his throat? You mean those kind of balls?" Clive turned the gun back towards Owen and lowered his aim towards the young man's crotch. "Speaking of balls, guess where my first bullet goes?" One of Owen's gang grabbed him by the shoulder.

"Come on, man, this old dude's crazy." Owen shrugged the hand away and pointed to Jack.

"This isn't over, you hear me?"

"I hear you," Jack said. Own pointed the knife at him menacingly for several more seconds, then he turned and looked back at his now cowering friends, and together they ran off down the street. Clive watched them go, sweat now breaking out on his forehead. He didn't lower the gun until they disappeared from sight. And then with his free hand, he fumbled frantically in his pocket for his GTN spray.

"Christ I'm too old for this shit," Clive said. It was then that Jack's sister screamed.

*

"That fucking cunt," Owen steamed under his breath. Everything in him wanted to turn around and go back at that bastard, to stick his knife right into the guy's balls. But the man had a gun, a fucking gun. How the fuck did the manager of a fast food dive get a gun? Even worse, how was it that he so obviously knew how to use it? *Jesus*, thought Owen, *I've been fucking with a trained killer*.

"Yeah, fuck him, man. We'll get him next time," one of his cronies said, and the others with them muttered their agreement. Owen didn't pay any attention, but continued to walk at a fast pace, gripping the rucksack full of alcohol to his shoulder. His other hand still held the knife, the knuckles white with how hard he gripped it.

The road they were on was shrouded in smoke from several burning cars, and the revelation that Owen and his crew were not perhaps the top predators here was seeping home to him. There were dozens of others their age running rampant around them, and there were screams travelling on the sounds of destruction. They needed to get off the street and get inside. Owen didn't like how this was going, and he figured his mates liked it even less. So they moved swiftly, knowing that they were not far from the place they could hold up in.

Owen leading the way turned the corner first, and was the first to stop dead in his tracks. The side street was riddled with bodies, some on the ground, some fleeing, some chasing. Social media had hinted at there being some kind of zombie outbreak, but nobody had really believed it, not until now, not until they had witnessed it first-hand. They stood mesmerised as metres away a young boy, surely no older than ten, rode on the back of an overweight woman who was frantically trying to throw him off. His arms were wrapped tight around her neck, and his teeth were finding purchase wherever they could. Another child, this time a girl, was ripping into the abdomen of another woman who was either dead or unconscious lying on the ground. The fat woman collapsed to her knees, still sporting her rider, and the girl, seeing the motion, abandoned her kill and leapt upon this new prey, helping to bring the woman's weight fully to the ground. Her pleas went unheeded – in fact, if anything, they seemed to spur the attackers on.

"We have to get out of here, man," someone said grabbing Owen's arms. "Man, this is fucked up." Owen shook off the grip and took a step forward. He couldn't believe this. He couldn't believe how good this was. This was epic. This was the world he could live in.

11.56AM 16th September 2015, MI6, Albert Embankment, London

Fabrice screamed, his mouth still gagged. It was all he could do. He had sworn to himself that this woman would not break him, that he would be resolute in his resistance. But that had lasted all of 5 minutes.

"It hurts, doesn't it?" Davina said. She pushed on the fine needle that was sticking in Fabrice's neck and moved it in a fine circular motion, disrupting the nerve bundle that lay beneath. It felt like hot lead was being dripped into Fabrice's neck, and violent stabbing pains shot throughout his bound body. "I won't go into the finer details of what I am doing to you," Davina said. There was little emotion in her voice, and she could have just as easily been talking about last week's weather. "What I will say is I have been working on you for less than 10 minutes, and you already have experienced more pain than you have ever imagined. Worse than when you had appendicitis. Worse than when you broke you right leg at the age of nine." Davina removed the needle and placed it back on a metal tray that was to her side. Made from fine copper, there were three dozen other needles. "Imagine your surprise when you realise that this isn't even an appetiser." Fabrice felt a hand rest on his lower abdomen. The hand was cold. Then he felt the table he was on moving, and his body began to tip back so his feet were raised above his head. "We can't have you fainting now, can we?" the woman said. And she actually winked a seductive wink, a smile appearing on her face. "Now I give you an opportunity to talk to me, to tell me what you know. All you have to do is nod your head twice, and I will remove your gag. Men will come in, and you will bear your soul to them. If you decline my offer," Davina began to move her hand down Fabrice's abdomen, "it will be an hour before I will make you that offer again. And by that time, you will be missing one of these." Davina grabbed her captive's scrotum and yanked sharply causing Fabrice to yelp under his gag. "And rest assured, the pain I inflict will never go away. So do you wish to speak?"

Fabrice hesitated a moment and then shook his head. Davina released his balls and gave his chest a playful slap. She ran her fingernails tenderly up and down his chest, and pinched his left nipple playfully. "Good," Davina said. "I hate it when they break so easily." She turned to the tray and picked up a fresh needle.

Fabrice lasted seventeen minutes before he was begging to bare his soul, his pleas barely audible through the rubber stuffed into his mouth. There were seven needles in him at that point, all connected up to a pulsating electric current. Travelling along the needle to the tip, the electricity was directed straight into the various nerve bundles that the woman had selected. However, the one that had broken him was the needle she had slowly inserted into the head of his cock. The current suddenly stopped, reducing the pain to a mere agony.

"I told you it would be an hour, and an hour it will be," Davina said looking up at the surveillance camera. "But there are people here who wish to know what you know, so I will do you a deal. Tell them what you know, and I will stop the pain. I will end your torment, and release you from my care." Davina looked down at the helpless man. "Do you agree?" Fabrice nodded. Davina sighed in disappointment. She unstrapped and pulled the gag from the man's mouth, saliva stringing from it.

"Yes, anything, just stop the pain."

"Very well," Davina said, and began to remove the needles, slowly, ever so slowly. She liked to take her time with this part, which caused Fabrice to yell and scream from fresh agony, but also in relief that it was about to end. Torture could be unbearable, but what was worse was the belief that there would be no end. Davina knew this, had seen many a man (and woman) beg for death just to end their pain. Of course, Davina never killed them – where was the fun in that?

Within minutes, men entered the room and the questions started. Davina did not leave, and they did not unstrap him. She stood within sight of Fabrice's eyes, twirling one of the tortuous needles between her fingers. There was a sly smile on the torturer's face. What she had forgotten to tell Fabrice is that she always followed through on a promise, and very shortly, she would renew his torture with fresh vigour. Davina would leave Fabrice broken, in permanent pain and without any teeth or genitalia. And all with the blessing of the agents of Her Majesty's Secret Service who, it seemed, no longer gave a fuck about the rule of law. Because, with the information acquired, she had permission to torture him the way she liked, the way she adored. She was a sexual sadist who had managed to make a living doing what she loved for Queen and Country. And despite how handsomely they paid, she loved the torture more than she did the money. Besides, she had nothing better to do at the moment.

11.57AM, 16th September 2015, Westminster Pier, London

Grainger was the last to step onto the Thames Clipper. That was always his motto – first on the battlefield, last off. The boat slowly moved out into the centre of the river, the waves buffeting it slightly, Grainger holding onto the railing to steady himself. Further up river, he could see the other boat that contained Colonel Bearder. All his men were accounted for, and he looked over the exhausted troops with pride. They had lost the war, but they had come out alive, and they had done their duty. But what of their families, their loved ones? Grainger knew that his wife was already on her way out of the country. She had been visiting family in Portsmouth, and he had managed to get a message to her after the morning's briefing, told her to pack up the kids and leave.

His father-in-law owned a yacht, and hopefully, they were already at sea. Her dad was a stubborn old soul, but he wasn't an idiot – after all, he had been military too.

Sergeant Vorne walked through the troops, praising them and encouraging them. The man was like a father to most of them. Admittedly a grumpy, sometimes violent father, but every one of the men on this boat had nothing but respect for him. Most of them would die for the man because they all knew he would die for them. He would willingly lay down his life for the men he took into battle if it was called for. And so would Grainger, truth be told. That's what it meant to be a soldier.

They had no fear of the infected in the water; the boat was moving too fast for that. Flanked by one of the Apache helicopters, it sped through the water, leaving the artistry of the Spectre gunship behind. Grainger looked back at the pier and saw the last boat loading the remnants of the civil forces that had been helping in the defence of Parliament. London was no longer a human city now. It belonged to the infected.

*

Rachel pushed herself up off the rebar, freeing herself from her temporary restraint. There was no coordination anymore, just brute force and animal instinct. With no circulation, her body had already begun the process of decay. She stood, mindless eyes surveying the scene. Spotting the boats on the river and drawn to the noise of the helicopter, she staggered over to the river bank, where she clawed at the sky, moaning deeply. The virus wanted flesh, and she reached into the sky to try and reach it. She did not register the renewed assault behind her as the gunship did its final flyby, didn't register the explosion until its blast wave propelled her over the wall that was a barrier to the river. She fell into the water, and with no oxygen in her lungs, sank slowly to the bottom.

*

"This is Echo 3 Sentry to Tango Lemma 47 attack wing, over."

"Go ahead Echo 3 Sentry, over."

"Ground forces have evacuated the target area. NATO Command has authorised your bombing run. You are green to approach attack vector. Over."

"Roger Echo 3, we are starting our attack run now."

The city was lost; there was no denying that fact. The decision had been made to make the environment for the infected as harsh and as inhospitable as possible. There were too many of them to stop the spread, but the hope was they could be slowed down. Of course, there were still hundreds of thousands of non-infected individuals in the city, but without the military to defend them, they would only swell the ever-growing ranks of the infected hoard. There was still talk of nukes, but nobody alive could or would authorise that. And by the time somebody would, it would be too late.

The six A-10 Thunderbolts came in from the north, each having a designated target for the unconventional ordinance they held. Napalm was an old weapon, going back to the Vietnam War. But it was still stocked for use, despite the denials by the talking heads at the Pentagon. The A-10's came in hard and came in fast, each dropping their bombs on the largest groups of the infected.

Grainger recoiled from the explosion that spread the length of the Victoria Embankment. The great wall of fire mushroomed into the sky, incinerating everything it touched. Jesus Christ. A second explosion hit the other side of Parliament, and all across the city, he saw fire rising up into the atmosphere. Napalm, shit he didn't even know the Yanks still used napalm. He heard the murmuring of his men, as several of them rose out of their seats to witness the spectacle. The powers that be truly had abandoned the city.

"Calm down, lads, just the Yanks getting their own back for us burning down the White House in 1812." Sergeant Vorne again. Nobody laughed, not at this. Moments later, the whole riverside section of Parliament exploded, the iconic building being reduced to rubble and ashes. Nothing was to be spared the scorched earth policy it seemed. Not even history.

11.58AM, 16th September 2015, MI6, Albert Embankment, London

Another set of eyes watched with fascination as the city further up the river burned. Davina stood looking out of a top floor window of the MI6 building, a hot cup of organic coffee in her hands. She had brewed it herself, extracting the coffee powder from a chilled compartment in the cases she had brought with her. She had refused to put that cheap processed shite they served in the canteen here in her body. She had even supplied her own distilled water. A coffee break was just the thing. Down below, she had left Fabrice to answer the questions posed by the agents. They would let her know when they were done, and she would return to restart her manipulations.

Another explosion hit by the Parliament, and the muted sound reached her a brief moment later. She was fascinated by the power on display here, fascinated by how quickly the whole flakiness and falseness of society had been stripped away. Humanity had been complacent for too long, thinking its technology had put it to the top of the food chain. That was no longer the case; now there was a new predator out there, one that would use humanity's own weaknesses against it. It didn't have the technological superiority of man, but it could swell its number rapidly, taking its soldiers from the very forces it pitted itself against. It was nature at its most extreme.

Davina smiled. She had always considered herself separate from other people, almost as if she wasn't actually the same species. So few of them could inflict the pain and the suffering that she was able to, and fewer still could do it in a controlled fashion. Most of those that society labelled as violent sociopaths were controlled by their sociopathy; they enjoyed it too much. It wasn't a gift to them despite what they thought. It was a curse, an addiction. Eventually, they succumbed to their desires in a way that showed their true colours.

Davina was different. She used her skills in a controlled way, living her dream of actually maiming and ruining people with the sanction of government. She never did it without that sanction. And she charged a heavy price, which funded a very opulent lifestyle. Fortunately, that lifestyle was situated outside the United Kingdom, and soon she would join the exodus from this building. Those fleeing the country were being shipped to Ireland where camps were already being set up to take the hundreds of thousands already en route. The Irish didn't like it, but it was the logical choice. Nobody wanted the infection getting to the European mainland.

She took another sip of coffee. This was good, too good. Watching civilisation burn whilst caffeine coursed through her veins. This was turning out to be a very good day. Even better was the news that shortly she would likely be gaining another "client". Apparently, the creator of the virus had been located, and a team had been dispatched to secure him. There was a whole army of scientists ready to pour over the information she could extract from the man's mind. Good. She liked the clever ones; it added an extra dimension to the psychological cruelty she could inflict. And her enhanced fee had already been approved. Yes, this was indeed turning out to be an excellent day. For her at least. She didn't care about the millions dying on the country's streets.

But there it was again, the little gremlin in her mind. She had never read her MI6 file, so she wasn't privy to the fact that psychologically she was considered a broken and damaged individual. If she hadn't been so good at what she did, if she hadn't obtained the result her paymasters demanded, she would probably be locked in a padded cell somewhere, mind crushed by numerous medications. But she was free, and yet there was that gremlin again, the memory that haunted her. The memory of pain, of torment and of the birth of her true self. Over the years, she had come to accept it, just as someone with arthritis accepts the burning in their joints. And it did seem to come less and less as the years progressed. But always in her moments of true satisfaction, it seemed to appear in the back of her thoughts, reminding her that life was a dark and nasty beast that would willingly take her to her knees given any opportunity.

That was why she demanded such control over her environment. If she was a film star instead of a torturer, she would have been labelled a Diva. Davina the Diva, it had a certain ring to it. But she deserved the life that she lived, had earnt it through blood, sweat and an ocean of tears. When she was six, she had been abused by her father and his mother. Head of a Ukrainian underground paedophile ring, her father had farmed her out to others in the group relentlessly. Living in a household that had the veneer of an upstanding Catholic family, for years she had been molested and defiled by hundreds of men, and even a few women. The women were the worst, relishing in a form of sadism that few humans could understand or comprehend.

Some of her abusers were even famous, members of Parliament, powerful leaders of industry. Whereas some people would break and recoil into themselves, Davina managed to retain her sense of identity, and began to develop a sense of purpose. But the abuse also saw part of her die, her empathy. When she looked back upon those times now, she considered that a good thing. She learnt to numb herself to the pain and the humiliation, and slowly, relentlessly, a hatred grew within her. And at the age of 14, she killed her first victim, although the word "victim" was perhaps a misnomer considering the reason the man died at her then amateur hands.

Suspecting that his control over his daughter was nearing its limit, and perhaps sensing the danger that was growing within her, she was sold. One morning, hands grabbed her emaciated form and a bag was forced onto her face. The chloroform acted quickly, and she drifted into sweet oblivion. When she came to, she was in complete blackness. No sight, no sound, and her limbs immovable. Her mouth, her cunt, and her anus were filled and, looking back, she was surprised she hadn't choked to death. Despite all that, she could tell that she was being moved, most likely by truck. Hours passed, and she drifted in and out of a sleep that more resembled unconsciousness. That was where she finally mastered the power of going into herself, of encountering a mind that thought of nothing. To cancel all thought, to exist in a realm of nothingness created a place where no pain could reach her. It was a skill she used when the memories of her anguish threatened to overwhelm her.

When light eventually hit her eyes, she was in a stone walled room with no windows. The lid had been removed from what was obviously her transfer box, and three middle-aged male faces looked down at her.

"Such a sweet little thing," one of the men said. "Such a sweet little mouth."

Lifted out of the box, she had suffered for a day and a night. Man upon man raping her mouth and her bleeding anus. Strangely, they didn't touch her vagina. There was no time down here, only pain and misery. Only endless torment. Except the misery had long since departed. What replaced it was determination. When she had seen them, gaping in at her, Davina had decided that she was going to kill as many of them as she could. Even if it meant her own death. Then they were finally finished with her. The larger of the three men had looked down at her, zipping up his jeans and said, "Tomorrow, we should remove its teeth. We can grow this thing into the perfect fuck toy." One of the other men had laughed at that, the man called Rob.

"That's a good idea," said Rob. "And by the end of the week, I intend for her to take my whole fist in her tight little ass pussy. I'm going to work her till she begs me to kill her." But how ironic it was that Rob was eventually the one who did the begging.

They had left her alone to sleep. But she did not sleep. On a dirty, stained mattress, she plotted, knowing that human nature would play into her hands very soon. Davina had waited, eyes shut, feigning sleep, feigning weakness. She pretended to ignore the sound of the key in the lock, the sound of the door to her prison opening as Rob walked in.

"Hey little slut, I just wanted one more go at that pretty little mouth before we take the plyers to you tomorrow." Rob roughly grabbed Davina by the hair and slapped her across the face to wake her up.

"You are going to suck me, and you are going to take your time. I want plenty of tongue, and I want you to show me that you enjoy it. So you look me in the eye whilst you're down there little piggy, you hear?"

"Can I …?" Davina said, pretending to trail off into shyness.

"What's that, you little cunt?" Rob said, yanking her head back.

"Can I show you what my father taught me? He showed me how to suck cock real good. Can I show you?" Rob's eyes lit up at this.

"Yeah, you better, piggy, you better show me. And if I feel any teeth, I'm going to take an eye." So Davina had shown him what her father had taught her, but just as the man reached the brink, Davina showed him what her father had created. Standing there, his prey kneeling before him, Rob's world turned from pleasure to the blackest of pain as the centre of his world was bitten clean off. Rob collapsed in near faint, only for Davina to pounce on him, thumbs worming their way relentlessly into Rob's eyes. After blinding him, she stood and spat out her captor's most prized possession. Bile rose in her throat in response to the taste of another man's blood, but she swallowed the vomit back. She would not let her enemy have that power over her.

Davina stood for several minutes watching the man who writhed and moaned in near unconsciousness. She felt something she had never felt before. Achievement. She was watching a man die, at her hands, a man far bigger and much stronger than her scrawny, malnourished frame allowed. There was no remorse, no pity, no anger. Just release. Davina smiled for possibly the first time in her life. And as Rob bled out, she waited for the other men to respond to the man's earlier screams. Davina resigned herself to death. But nobody came.

Exiting her new prison, she ascended steps with sore and scarred feet that had been tortured only hours before. At the top, she found a farmhouse, dark and deserted. She found food and warmth. But then she found something that pleased her even more. With a knife she found in the kitchen, she returned to what she now realised was the basement, and finished off her tormentor. That was the moment – the smell of mould, blood and faeces lingering in the air – that was the moment Davina found her life's purpose. She took her time with him, and she revelled in her new discovery.

Her phone rang, dragging her out of her memories. How easy it was to slip into nostalgia and let the mind rebel. Every time it happened, every time she lost control of that part of her, she hated herself. It was not that she had been abused as a child – that had been necessary to create the woman she was now. No, it was that her mind would wander to those memories against her wishes, which meant she still wasn't a master of it. But she would gain that mastery, she was determined, and every year brought her closer to that goal.

Davina looked at the phone. The caller ID showed a number, 101. No name – she didn't put names on her electronic devices, even ones with such secure encryption as this one. She pressed the accept button and held the phone up to her ear. She forced a smile on her face.

"Assistant Director, how are my friends at the CIA this morning?"

11.58AM, 16th September 2015, Heathrow airport, London

Patrick Stewart was running out of planes. With nothing landing, most of what was on the ground at the beginning of his shift was already on its way out of the country. But there were still a dozen jets to get up. He watched his people work and was ripped from his almost meditation-like state by the door to the control room slamming open. Three armed officers stormed in. They didn't point their guns at anyone, but Patrick had a feeling it wouldn't take much for that to happen.

"Listen up," the one in charge said. "I regret to inform you that no more planes are to be allowed to take off. As promised, helicopters are waiting to take you all to a safe location. If you will follow us, we will escort you there."

"But we have planes lining up. They need to take off," Stewart protested.

"Not going to happen. The infected have breached the airport. If you want to save yourselves, you need to come with us, now." The people in the room didn't need telling twice. Nor did Patrick. He was the first out the door.

Shelley had worked at passport control for twenty years. She liked her job, but she hated her life outside work, which was why she volunteered for whatever overtime she could get and sometimes seemed to 'forget' when her holidays were due. Truth was, she no longer loved her husband, and often found herself despising the man and his selfish behaviour. And the kids were all grown up and moved away. And they never called; they didn't care and even seemed to resent the annual gathering at Christmas time. So when she learnt what was happening in the country, she had chosen duty over the option others had chosen. Now she waited, the line to one of the last planes slowly moving forward. She looked around her, noticing the collection of airport staff, police and civilians lucky enough to get through the passport control area she had once defended. Now that was closed by steel grilles, thousands left stranded on the ground side of the airport. She could choose to feel bad for them, or choose to accept the gift life had given her. A way out and a possibility of a new life. It was almost exciting.

She wasn't the first to hear the scream, and she only turned towards the noise when she heard the gunfire. No, I'm so close, please let me on the plane. The crowd pulsed and lost any semblance of civility. She felt herself picked up in a wave of humanity as it swarmed towards the entrance to the jet bridge. Being short, she felt her feet lift off the ground as she was crushed in the mass. And then the crush parted and she dropped, catching her footing and falling to the ground. Nobody helped her, and legs buffeted her, feet kicked her. A knee caught her squarely in the face, shattering her nose, and she felt blackness descend as consciousness slipped away. Now flat on the floor, feet trampled her, and she cried out as three of her ribs cracked. Another foot kicked her hard in the temple, and the last she saw through the mass of legs was a police officer being brought down by three infected. The crowd screamed.

They had come over the fences, dozens of them at first, then hundreds. They swarmed across the runway tarmac, attacking ground staff whenever they encountered them. But mainly they headed for the terminals, climbing stairs and getting entry wherever they could. There would be no more flights, the promise of rescue to those who stayed behind mainly broken by the inevitable arrival of the hoard. The hoard that spread out through the airport, decimating the assembled humanity. The collected mind roared in triumph.

*

Clive and Jack turned to see Jack's mother being attacked by a man in a ripped business suit. The savagery of the attack took them both by surprise, and Jack's heart froze when he heard the terror in his sister's cry. Where the hell had he come from? There was a roar behind the horrendous scene, and Clive saw two more demon-like figures running towards them. He didn't hesitate; he raised his gun and fired off three rounds into the oncoming attackers, one shot in the head, the other being hit twice in the chest. Both fell to the ground as Jack ran to help his mother.

Clive trained the gun on her attacker, but couldn't get a clear shot; they were thrashing around too much. He took a step forward, finger easing on the trigger, lining up the shot. Easy, easy. Just as he was about to fire, Clive felt someone grab him from behind, felt his gun arm being swung down, the gun erupting as the bullet went wide of the mark. Spinning around, he landed a fist with his free hand into whatever was there, and saw a young woman drenched in blood fall to the ground beneath his assault. He didn't hesitate and put a bullet in her head. He heard someone shout "NO!" Was that Jack?

Turning back towards Jack's mother, he saw the attacker had abandoned her and was charging at Jack, who stood motionless. He had the shot and he took it, the body being stopped dead as the bullet entered the skull via the left eye, its motion bringing it to rest at jack's feet. Clive moved forward, the pain in his chest now a tight band that was making it hard to breathe. The pain was bad, the worst ever. He knew what it meant. He knew what the doctors had warned him.

"Jack?" Jack didn't answer. He was looking at something on the ground behind a car out of Clive's line of sight. His mother lay groaning, blood pouring down her neck and out of her mouth. He took another step forward, the pain now crushing and vice like. Clive fumbled in his pocket and withdrew the GTN spray, giving himself two good hits. It didn't help, it didn't help at all. One step closer, and he saw the girl's foot sticking out from behind the car. No, God no.

Staggering over to where Jack stood, gun dangling by his side, he dropped the spray as he saw what had happened. Jack's sister lay on the ground, a red bloom growing from a chest wound. The shot that had gone wide had hit her in the centre mass. She wasn't moving; there was no way a body that size could survive such trauma. Jack turned to him, tears in his eyes, disbelief washing over his face.

"You killed her," Jack said.

"I didn't …" Clive started defensively, but he had. He might not have been responsible for the shot, but he had been wielding the gun. He felt all the energy fall out of him, and he collapsed to his knees, the gun falling from his fingers. It clattered onto the ground almost unheard. His left arm had gone numb, and someone was beating an invisible fist into his jaw. *I'm having a bloody heart attack*, he thought.

"You killed her," Jack said again, and moved towards him. Clive tried to reach up to him with his good arm, but Jack just swatted it aside. Jack bent down next to him and picked up the gun. Clive couldn't breathe, and the world around him started to shrink into tunnel vision. He was dying, and there was nobody here that could help him. Jack looked at him, the boy's face twisted and broken with anguish. Everything he loved was being torn from him, and insanity tiptoed around the edges of his mind. Jack turned away from Clive, ignoring his now obvious plight, and walked over to the small body, picking it up, sobs wracking his body. Clive saw him look over at his mother, saw that she wasn't moving. And then his heart exploded in his chest, and the last thing his conscious mind saw was the ground rushing up to smash his face. And in the distance, he thought he heard a thousand voices howl.

12.01PM 16th September 2015, Above Whitehall, London

Croft was now airborne. He had witnessed the massacre of government and had watched what remained of the country's leadership take to the skies. General Marston was stable at least, and there was already word that he had taken control. None of the remaining government ministers had been foolish enough to argue. The UK was now under military rule, reportedly with the express permission of Her Majesty the Queen.

Croft had chosen to leave in one of the SAS helicopters, along with Captain Savage. He figured the best chance for survival now rested in being around men and women who were the best in the business. The faces of hardened men surrounded him in the now cramped helicopter, and he looked down at the city landscape below him. Soon, he would be travelling over areas that were yet to face the infected, areas that had been abandoned to their fate.

And they had left behind so many. How do you evacuate so many people in so short a time? As the noose of the infected grew ever tighter, thousands of government personnel would become trapped. Even in their secure bunkers, they could not last indefinitely. It was only a matter of time before the underground network became compromised. Croft had to admit he had a level of respect for whoever had organised this. It was a brilliant plan, using the country's own population to destroy itself. And now with the heads of the government gone, there was nobody in the immediate future to order the nuclear strikes. With their launch being under civilian control, it would take time to transfer their command to NATO. And as he had already said, time was something they just didn't have.

"Major Croft, I have MI6 for you." Croft, sat near the front of the helicopter, turned and acknowledged the co-pilot who had just spoken to him. Another voice came over his headphones.

"Actually, technically I'm MI5, but I'm not sure it even matters anymore. How you holding up, Croft?" Arnold Carver said, the static making it difficult for Croft to hear.

"Pretty well actually, considering I feel like I've failed in my mission," Croft said in return.

"David, I hear you have a few SAS chaps with you. How would you like to go on a fishing trip?" Hudson looked over at him solemnly, listening in on the conversation. Croft could tell he felt the same way.

"Go on," Croft said, intrigue in his voice.

"One of the chaps who started this whole mess that we grabbed in the heliport has started singing. He seems to know a lot about all this, including where the virus might have been manufactured. Apparently, the maniac who created it might still be there. It would be awfully decent of you if you could go and fetch this man for us. There is a lady here who would like to have a chat with him." Savage tugged on his shirt sleeve, and he looked at her. Sat next to him, she indicated he should remove his headphone.

"If we can find his research, we might be able to find a cure," she shouted.

"And let me guess, you're the only one who will know how to find it?" Croft replied, smiling slyly at her. She was a bio-weapons specialist. Despite the carnage this thing had caused, this was her mission in life, it was her calling. He could see she was excited by the prospect of getting her hands on the raw strains, perhaps even a vaccine. Croft put his headphone back on.

"Consider it done, sir," he said.

12.11PM, 16th September 2015, Hounslow, London

Jack ran. Carrying his sister, panic and anguish ripping him apart, he fled through streets that were now awash with carnage and chaos. Tears streamed from his eyes, and he mumbled to himself a mantra, "You'll be okay, you'll be okay."

Eventually, fatigue took him, and he tripped over something. It could well have been his own feet. Stumbling forward, he landed hard, his sister's body spilling from his arms. There was no sound from his sister's body, no shout of pain or whimper of protest, and she flopped uselessly on the ground. Getting to his knees, he shuffled over to her, ignoring two men who ran past him laden with their recent spoils from the off-licence whose alarm was blaring out across the street.

He grabbed her head gently, propping it off the ground, pushing the hair from out of her face. Deep down, he knew she was dead, the bullet wound in her neck no longer pulsing blood. The eyes were lifeless, but still he cradled her.

"It's going to be okay, sis," he whispered in her ear. "It's going to be okay."

But it wasn't. It wasn't going to be okay, and he was shocked out of his trauma by the sound of a shop front window exploding. The brick that went through it was followed by half a dozen looters who were intent on acquiring the electrical goods that lay uselessly inside. He looked around at the stupidity of mankind and wept fresh tears.

He looked back down at the body of his sister, fluid dripping from him onto her face. He knew he had to leave her, and he placed her head back down onto the asphalt. He kissed her tenderly on the forehead. Jack didn't want to leave. He wanted to sit here and let the ground swallow him up, to curl up and die next to what was left of his family. But something inside him didn't want to give up. Something inside him wanted to live, and he found himself standing to his feet. It was then that he noticed he was still holding the gun in his blood-soaked hand. Jack looked around and for the first time truly saw how the world had collapsed. What had Clive said on the way back from the airport? He had to head west.

Looking back down at the corpse he had carried for what seemed like forever, he was wracked by fresh grief. "I love you, sis," he said to her dead corpse. "I love you, and I'm sorry." She didn't answer back, her lifeless eyes just staring off into space. "I have to go now, sis," he said and took a step away from the body. He took another step, his hand tight on the handle of the gun. For a moment, the thought of putting that gun to his own head and pulling the trigger leaped at him. It was so inviting, so seductive that the hand actually moved halfway towards its target. But he rejected the siren call, his hand falling back down to his side.

"Goodbye, sis," he said. Turning, he made his way off down the street, repositioning the backpack straps that he only now noticed were digging into him. He still held the gun, still clung to it like it was a part of him. Someone shouted in celebration behind him, and he heard another window smash. Jack began to run again. The infected were coming, and he had to get away from them. But also, he ran from the torture he left behind.

*

David followed in the wake of his new pack leader. They turned into a new street, and he saw it all in an instant. Even with useless arms, he was still useful, and with a roar, he joined into the attack. There were dozens of people in the street, most oblivious to the new threat they faced. They were too intent on wanton looting, and many of them carried boxes and trinkets that would very shortly be useless to them. As a pack, they charged, taking down seven individuals before the crowd reacted. Most of them ran, but several turned to fight, armed with a host of weapons that were effective against a human enemy. But they were no match for the infected, and one by one, they fell to bites.

David charged at one, who threatened him with a long knife. David didn't care, didn't even register the supposed danger, and the wielder panicked at the last moment, turning to try and flee. But he fell over his own feet, falling to the ground, the knife clattering away. David fell on him, vomiting all over his back. And then he was up, after more prey. Without working arms, he found it difficult to contain the humans long enough to get his teeth into them, so he just used his waste. He went for another, who punched David in the face. David staggered, falling onto his backside, his lip cut and bleeding. He looked up at the astonished teenager, sniffed the air, saw that he was infected by the virus in the blood that smeared his hand. The teenager wiped the violence away on his hooded top, but it was too late; the contagion was already starting, boring its way through his skin painlessly, infecting the blood stream, the body pumping it towards every organ, to the brain. Lurching to his feet, David paid the teenager no more attention and went off after other prey. He stopped briefly at the body of a black child, sniffing it. Dead. Dead was good to eat, and the hunger took him to his knees. He licked the corpse's face and put his teeth to its lips. Biting down, the flesh separated, and he chewed with teeth no longer designed to consume raw flesh. Something in his mouth broke, but he ignored it and swallowed hard, the jolt of pleasure ripping through him. Taking another bite, the body moved as he shook his head violently to detach another morsel, this time an ear. David's body quivered with ecstasy, but the voices demanded he stop.

"*Spreeaaad now. Spreeaaad. Feeeeed later.*" For a brief second, David almost rebelled, almost went for a third bite. But despite the hunger, the collective mind was stronger, and he stood reluctantly. He saw movement through a broken shop window and, face freshly bloodied, he charged through the shop's shattered frame, a scream announcing his arrival.

*

Owen was briefly alone. He stood outside the door of his flat and looked down into the courtyard of the housing block. One hand clutched the edge of the safety railing, the other clutched the beer bottle he had liberated from the off-licence. Down below, a woman was being eaten by two of what the news called 'infected'. Owen watched them, feeling safe five floors up. All around him he could feel curtains twitching as those without means did the only thing they could do in this situation. They hid. Well, Owen wasn't going to hide. This was his world, a world where law and order no longer applied. And he was going to make the most of it.

The bottle was nearly empty, and he flung it down onto the diners below. The glass shattered close to one of them, who jumped backwards away from his meal, searching around. Then he looked up, spotting Owen looking over the bannister at him. The infected looked at Owen and hissed. This drew the attention of the other infected, and they both stared up at him.

"Come on then, fucks," Owen shouted. This drew the desired response, and they both ran towards the staircase that led up to where Owen stood. Somewhat drunk, Owen didn't contemplate whether this was wise or not. He wasn't afraid of these fucks; he wasn't afraid of anything. Hadn't he proved that? Taking several steps back, he reached into the open door of his flat and picked up the crossbow that rested against the wall. He also picked up the bolts, and stepped out into the centre of the passageway. Loading the crossbow, putting the rest of the bolts on the floor, he knelt down and aimed at where he knew the infected would come from.

He heard them before he saw them, their footsteps resonating up the stairwell. Then the first of them appeared, then the second. He was a good shot with this thing, had put in the hours to make sure he was a good shot. Of course, he wasn't going to be using target bolts here. No, these were proper bolts, for proper killing that he had acquired off a source. They were sharp enough to do the job.

The first infected appeared. It paused at the sight of Owen, sniffed the air, and then shambled towards him. Whoever this had been, he was only dressed in stained underwear. And blood. He was dressed in blood. Owen paused, and loosed off a bolt that took the infected just below the right shoulder. His attacker stumbled but didn't fall, and then came right on coming. Owen quickly reloaded and fired another shot. This one just grazed the infected's leg. Less than twenty metres away now, and Owen found himself fumbling, panic starting to set in. This was stupid, what was he doing? He fired off the third shot, and it went straight into the infected's head, sending it crashing to the floor. It was a lucky shot more than anything, penetrating the left eye and entering the brain. The infected twitched for several seconds and then lay still.

The second infected was already coming at him. It didn't even seem to register its fallen comrade. Was that what he had to call these things, thought Owen as he searched around him for another bolt. 'It', should he call them it? His bolt took the second in the upper thigh and it fell to the ground, the bolt snapping off. It lurched back to its feet and hobbled towards him, the injury having slowed it down. The next bolt took it in the lower abdomen, and that didn't even seem to register. Ten metres away now, and Owen realised he only had one bolt left. He fired, and it penetrated the ribs to pierce right through the heart. The thing came to a stop, a look of bewilderment on its face. It reached a hand up to the projectile sticking out of its chest and pulled. The bolt came free, followed by a gush of blood. The infected fell to its knees, reaching out to its vanquisher.

"*Feeeeed,*" it said.

"Not today, fucker," Owen said in response. The hand dropped as life left the viral carrier, and it collapsed forwards, the abdominal bolt being forced through so that it poked through the infected's back. Owen put down the crossbow. It was not as effective a weapon as he had hoped. It had taken his entire stash of bolts to deal with the threat, and it almost hadn't been enough. He needed a gun. If he was to live and thrive in this world, Owen realised he needed a big gun and ammunition. And whilst he knew there were places someone such as him could get a gun, those sources would likely not be up for relieving themselves of what now amounted to life or death. Shit. This might be his world, but he wasn't prepared for it. There was movement to his left as Gary came out of the flat.

"What's all the noise, Owen…shit," Gary said noticing the two cadavers on the floor. Gary was the only one who had stuck around, the others running off to their fucking parents. The problem was Gary wasn't up to much. Gary was weak, both in body and mind. And he was already balding. Who lost their hair at fucking eighteen years of age? Gary was holding a backpack filled with alcohol and snacks, and Owen grabbed it off him. He pulled out another can of beer, and put the backpack on.

"Fucking infected, innit," Owen answered. "Crossbow ain't worth shit. It doesn't have the stopping power." He pulled the tab on the can and took a long pull of its contents.

"You need a shotgun, Owen," Gary said. Owen looked at him.

"No shit, Sherlock." He tapped Gary on the back of the head in admonishment. "But do you see any shotguns lying around here?"

"My uncle has one," Gary said, a huge shit-eating grin painted across his face.

"Your uncle has one? Your uncle that lives twenty minutes from here?"

"Yes," Gary replied. "He uses it for clay pigeon shooting."

"Well, what the fuck are we doing here?" Owen grabbed his cheek and gave it a playful pinch. "Good boy, Gary. See, I always said you would come in useful." Gary smiled even wider. It had taken him this long, but he finally had his opportunity to prove his worth. Owen started to move.

"Mind the blood, Owen." Owen stopped and looked down at the pools that were spreading from the bodies. "Before my phone went down, I read on the internet that the blood was infectious or something, that you could like catch the shit just by touching it." Owen backed up and turned around. He gave Gary a friendly slap on the arm and ran off along the walkway in the other direction. Gary followed as best he could, his gangly legs not able to keep up with Owen's athletic form. Neither of them saw the second body move and lift itself up off the ground. Neither heard its low moan as it pulled itself upright by the barrier. It, however, saw them, but they were too far away, and with its black eyes, it went off in search of fresh meat, shuffling with the bolt still stuck in its thigh.

12.31PM GMT 16th September 2015, CNN Studios, New York City, USA

Even during the end of the world, there were still ad breaks. This one was an enforced break brought on by the interrupted transmission resulting from an attack on a CNN camera crew in Birmingham city centre. One by one, the reporters on the scenes in Britain had either fled, been arrested by security forces or had succumbed to the infection ravaging the now dying island. Contact with CNN's head office in London had been lost over an hour ago, and communications with other news agencies throughout the country was sketchy at best. The BBC was still relaying information, but it had been over thirty minutes since the ITV news network went off the air, and Sky News was reporting that they would shortly stop broadcasting from their UK studio as the military were demanding their evacuation. Rose, who normally would have finished for the day by now, was still on the air, editors determining that he was now CNN's face of the crisis. All normal programming had been suspended, and the world sat and watched from the safety of their homes. Rose, not one to give a fuck about the fate of fellow human beings, couldn't believe his luck, and deep down he revelled in the once in a lifetime opportunity he had been given. Sitting in his studio seat, he got the signal that he was going back on air.

"This is Gavin Rose, reporting for CNN. As you are no doubt aware, we have abandoned normal programming to bring you the latest news on the crisis in Great Britain. Moments ago, news broke through Reuters that the British prime minister and several other senior government officials may have been assassinated. We are still trying to get you confirmation on that report…" There was a voice in his ear which distracted him.

"Goddamnit," the voice said, "we aren't broadcasting."

Across the USA, the face of Rose and other reporters disappeared, and a blank screen momentarily hit the nation. The TVs remained blank for only several seconds, but for many of those watching, those seconds seemed like an eternity. In 2012, it was discovered that the United States Emergency Broadcast System, designed to relay important messages across every TV screen and radio in the nation, was hackable. Despite attempts to correct the blatant flaws in its security, the problem was unsurprisingly never really fixed, which was why Abraham's anonymous message was allowed to play across every television set in the country. It wasn't just CNN; it was on every terrestrial and satellite channel, on virtually every screen across the Land of the Free. After those agonising several seconds, the blankness was replaced by the face of an anonymous figure. Before a black background, the seated man could be seen from his shoulders up, wearing a blank white face mask.

"Good morning, America. Good morning people of the Earth," the computer distorted voice said. "Today, you witness the death of a country. Today, you witness God's wrath and will see that his vengeance and his justice is swift and decisive." The face disappeared to be replaced by scenes previously aired on various news channels, all showing the infected attacking the uninfected. Then the face returned.

"This is only the beginning. For too long, you have rejected the word of the Lord Our God. For too long, you have worshipped false idols … or perhaps more disturbingly, no idols at all. Your greed, your sin and your decadence have blinded you to the teachings of the faithful, and the Lord Our God grows tired of your debauchery. Now you reap what you have sown."

"Your leaders will be tempted to act. They will be tempted to rain nuclear fire down upon the Necropolis we have initiated, to try and stop God's plan with their technology and their weapons of war. But they will not do that, for we need Great Britain to be an example, and we cannot have God's canvas spoiled by a nuclear winter just as his masterpiece is nearing perfection. So they will not interfere, or we will unleash similar devastation on their own lands, for we have the power to do as such. We want the world to learn, we want the world to witness, we want the world to repent. But we are also quite prepared to let the world suffer and die in God's name. And you must ask your leaders where this virus came from. For we did not create it, merely acquired it. The British Government secretly created it, so it is only fitting man's manipulation of nature be unleashed upon the British. Take to the internet, my friends. Let it tell you the secrets of the Hirta Island disaster, and know that the government of the United States was complicit in its creation."

"And to you, dear listener, we have a message. You have seen God's anger. But he is merciful. To you at least. Take him into your heart, and he will show you his love. Accept his son, Jesus Christ, as your Lord and saviour. By your devotion, you set yourself free. The truth will be revealed to you shortly via Satan's own instrument, the internet. And to you who bow down to false gods – to Krishna, to Allah, to Buddha and perhaps to Satan himself – I say this to you. Renounce your heresy. For the One True God is watching, and he will judge you, in this life and the next. And we, his emissaries, are watching too. Repent your ways or reap the whirlwind of his anger." The image of the face flickered, and then was gone.

Across the planet, millions punched in the words Hirta Island Disaster into Google. Seeded by Abraham's minions, the world wide web threw up a host of websites, blogs, and videos. Most disturbing of all was found on YouTube, a recording of the Hirta Island disaster itself. The stunned masses watched as the silent security video recordings showed the scientific personnel being attacked by their own friends and workmates. And most of the websites made damning claims about the involvement of the US government in the creation of what people were informed was a bioweapons virus that had either escaped containment or been deliberately released. The gullible and those who despised and distrusted the federal government believed what they wanted to believe. And across the world, eyes turned to the United States, eyes brimming with mistrust and suspicion.

12.33PM GMT 16th September 2015, Resurrection Ranch, Texas, USA

Abraham felt elated, complete. Things had gone better than he could ever dream. Even now, the country he so hated was removing itself from the map. In an ideal world, he would have had a nationality-specific virus that killed only the English, but that wasn't possible. So he had resorted to this, the next best thing. Turning down the volume on the TV, he groaned as he pulled himself off his leather chair, and got down to his knees. The rug beneath him cushioned his weary bones, and he had put it there for that specific task. Sometimes, he just needed to get on his knees and thank God for showing him the light, for showing him the blessing of the Creator. He had made the United Kingdom a modern day Sodom and now prayed that the rest of the world would heed the words they had just heard.

It was the Lord who had told him to do this, in his visions, in his dreams. It was the Lord that had given him the plan. How else had the thoughts popped into his mind but from God's will? Abraham was merely a vessel, a channel for the wisdom of the ages. The Lord Our God was the inspiration to make the British government complicit in their own destruction by releasing the virus on Hirta. And it was the Lord's inspiration to tell every living American that their government was complicit in the construction of the virus. If there was distrust in the federal government now, that was nothing to what was coming. And with the money he had filtered to certain right-wing paramilitary groups, he was hoping chaos would descend on the so-called Land of the Free. Let the people rise up and overthrow their oppressive government, for who better than a billionaire to help fill the void and restore order in the name of God? In Abraham's insane mind, it was all part of God's plan.

12.34PM, 16th September 2015, Hounslow, London

Gary's uncle didn't answer the door. And strangely for London, the door to the semi-detached house was unlocked. Gary opened it and went inside. "Uncle?" he shouted. No answer, but there was noise from the TV coming from the other room. Owen followed him in, and found himself having to squeeze past stacks of magazines and newspapers. The house smelt, smelt of damp and rotting food, and the carpet he walked on was sticky underfoot. Owen had only met the house's owner once, and the man was a fucking disgrace. A slob, someone who probably didn't bathe. He definitely wasn't someone who could be respected. And now he saw the utter squalor the man lived in, and that smell, Jesus. Owen wasn't going to feel any remorse about stealing the man's shotgun. Fully through the threshold, Owen closed the front door behind him, mindful of the danger that lurked in the world outside.

"Where's the shotgun, Gary?" Gary had disappeared out of the entrance corridor into the kitchen at the end. He was obviously looking for his uncle.

"It's in the basement." Oh of course it was. That's just what every zombie horror needed, a fucking basement. Owen had been in houses like this before, and the basement entrance was always under the stairs, which were right in front of him. He walked boldly over to the door and pulled it open, easily finding the switch to turn on the basement lights. It really didn't smell good down there either. A hand landed on his shoulder, making Owen jump.

"Fuck," Owen cried.

"Sorry, Owen. Owen, there's blood in the kitchen." That wasn't good. Gary made for Owen to follow him, and he did, abandoning the basement for the time being.

The kitchen was a wreck. Not through anything zombie related; it just didn't look like it had been cleaned in a decade. The sink overflowed with unwashed plates and pots, and there were multiple black bags full to brimming with garbage. Flies buzzed throughout the room, and Owen couldn't believe there were maggots crawling out of several of the bags.

"Doesn't clean up much, your uncle, does he?" Owen said sarcastically.

"No, he has a bit of a problem. He feels he can't throw stuff away in case it might be useful. You should see upstairs."

"No, I shouldn't. I've seen this on TV. We're not going to find him dead under a pile of newspapers, are we?" Owen said half-jokingly.

"That's not nice, Owen. Not with that." Gary pointed at the kitchen table. A dusty, blood-spattered first aid box was open on it, and there was blood smeared all over the table's surface. Owen suspected there was blood all over the floor too, only he couldn't see it because of the dirt.

"How the hell did your uncle get a shotgun licence with all this?" Owen asked. He knew the police came round to check the integrity of both the owner and the property. Gary half smiled.

"Don't be silly, Owen. You don't think he got it legally, do you?" *Even better,* thought Owen, *no gun cabinet to deal with then.* He looked around the kitchen.

"Well, I'm sure he'll be alright. He probably just cut himself making a sandwich or something." He stepped up to Gary, putting just the right amount of menace into his voice. "But Gary, I need that shotgun. I need it now."

"Of course. Sorry, Owen. I'm just worried is all. It's this way." Gary led him back to the basement entrance, Owen giving the kitchen one last disdainful look. Gary went first down the steps, and Owen followed behind. The basement was surprisingly well lit considering the circumstance, and when they reached the bottom, Owen was surprised to see it was relatively barren. The hoarding, it seemed, didn't extend to down here. At the far wall, there was an old wooden desk. The shotgun rested on it. Owen pushed past his friend and picked up the gun.

"He just leaves it lying around, does he?"

"I guess so," Gary said. Holding the gun in one hand, Owen started to hint through the drawers of the desk. He found two boxes of shotgun shells, one of them half empty. That was less than a hundred shells.

Would that be enough? There was a thump from upstairs. Gary spun round and made for the stairs.

"Uncle, is that you?" Owen worked the action, figuring out quickly how this particular shotgun opened. He had shot one before. He knew what to do, where to put the shells. He heard Gary going further up the stairs and dug into the half-empty box for two shells.

"Uncle?" Owen put the first shell in and then he actually heard Gary squeal. Grown men didn't make noises like that, or at least they shouldn't. Obscured from his sight, Owen couldn't see what Gary saw, but the secret soon became evident. Just as Owen slotted the second shell into place, there was the sound of a commotion, and two figures came tumbling into view at the bottom of the basement steps. Gary was now screaming, trying to fight off the attacker he was now entangled with.

"Uncle, stop, it's me, Gary," Owen heard him plead, but it did no good. Owen watched in morbid fascination as Gary's uncle bit down onto his ear and ripped it clean off. Owen snapped the rifle shut, the noise causing the infected's head to spin towards him. He leapt off Gary and stood metres away from Owen. Owen didn't hesitate; he fired at point-blank range, the shotgun blast taking Gary's uncle clean in the face.

"Fuck," Owen shouted, the noise of the shotgun painful in the confined space. The body was propelled backwards with the blast, hitting the wall opposite Owen, the body then falling into the shrieking form of his nephew. The uncle twitched, most of his face and jaw gone. Owen took a step forward and fired again, unconcerned that Gary might be caught in the blast as a large part of the infected shoulder was blown away. Gary howled in pain as some of the shot hit him. Quickly breaching the gun, Owen replaced the shotgun shells with two fresh ones, and he lined up for a third shot.

"Don't shoot me, please, Owen," the voice came from beneath the now deceased former owner of the shotgun.

"You've been bitten, Gary. You know what that means. I'm doing you a mercy," and he fired again, aiming at Gary's head that was sticking out from beneath the cadaver. The impact did much the same damage that had been inflicted by the first round. He fired a fourth time for good measure. *Damn, this is more like it*, thought Owen, and he shook his head to clear the disorientation caused by the noise. Looking at the scene before him for a moment, Owen turned and began to stuff his pockets with shotgun shells. The rest he stuck in his backpack. He did one last search and found another box and a kit to clean the shotgun with, and he deposited these in his backpack also. He put two fresh cartridges in the gun and snapped it closed. He liked the feel of the gun, and liked even more the damage he could inflict. This had real stopping power

"Now then, let's go fishing."

12.35PM 16th September 2015, Hayton Vale, Devon

Gavin watched the hacked CNN broadcast over the satellite link and felt a cold chill encase his body. He had been right. He had been fucking right. His family had mocked him, some had even stopped talking to him. But here he was, safe and isolated in a natural fortress with enough food and provisions to last him over a year. Gavin removed the phone from his pocket, saw the dozens of missed calls, knew there would be answer machine messages and texts from those who had ridiculed him. He paused momentarily, and called his mother. They weren't close, but the least he could do was say goodbye. The phone rang, but wasn't answered. You should have listened to me, Mum – you all should have listened to me.

He had been busy the last few hours. In one of the storage sheds were dozens of large water containers, which he had dragged to the outside tap and filled, putting one or two drops of water disinfectant in each. Not to clean the water, but to keep it clean. He knew that as the madness spread the water supply would eventually shut off. This and his stored mineral water would see him through several months. And when it ran out, well, he had the river. He had everything he needed to hold out indefinitely, everything except the one thing that had made the whole idea worthwhile, his lover.

The fact that his partner was probably dead hadn't really hit home yet. He had been too engaged in preparing for the end for it to really sink in. He watched as the normal broadcast came back, watched the harassed and upset faces of those presenting the news channel. Watched his namesake try and explain to his viewers what had just happened. Flicking through the channels, they all talked about the same thing. Fucking religion. Was humanity still at the stage where the belief in an invisible friend caused them to kill men, women, and children? It was madness, and it should have been treated as such. Gavin turned off the set with the remote and left the living room in disgust. Out in the farm's hallway, he put on his heavy coat and stepped out into the afternoon air. It was time to close off the road, to make it invisible to all but those who lived in the area. Because, like it or not, the infected would be here soon, and although this was not the apocalypse he had planned for, he hoped his precautions would be enough to keep them at bay.

12.38PM, 16th September 2015, Windsor

Jack had found a bike lying in the road and had taken it. Now on the Windsor Road, he knew there was only one place he could go. At some point he would need to sleep, to rest – he was presently running on the last of his adrenaline. But if he did that, then the infected would reach him. He was ahead of them now, he knew that, and now he was just part of a mass exodus. The roads were jammed, so everyone was either on foot, or like him on a bike. The occasional motorbike wormed its way through the crowds, but it seemed the days of mechanised transport through much of the country were probably at an end. The roads just weren't designed for everyone to take to them at once. It just took one to break down, one accident for the whole thing to grind to a halt. It wasn't like the RAC were going to come out to the rescue.

Strangely, there was a semblance of order here. He had not only left the infected behind, but the looting and the violence too. This was the scared face of the civilised, the educated, those with children and those with a sense of duty and an understanding of right and wrong. And as he peddled, Jack bit back tears, realising that his family should be here with him. He had failed them, just as Clive had failed them all. No, that wasn't fair; he had seen what had happened, knew that it wasn't Clive's fault, knew that it was an accident. But that didn't change the fact that the man had killed his sister, the man his father had considered almost a brother. It was perhaps best that Clive had died of a heart attack, for how the hell could he live with that on his soul?

The number of people in the road ahead thinned out, and he put on a burst of speed. That was another thing he noticed about the people around him, the people he passed. They were carrying so much shit with them. Suitcases and backpacks filled with stuff. Didn't they realise there was no need for this material shit anymore? Your Rolex, your bank account, your share certificates were all meaningless in the world of the undead. Your Porsche and your Aston Martin all worthless, left to rot on roads that would slowly decay and crack through lack of maintenance. What mattered now was speed and the will to survive. What mattered now was being able to leave it all behind and do what needed to be done. Jack didn't know if he had that in him, but he was certainly not going to give up. He was going to fight, because he had nothing else to do.

12.40PM GMT, 16th September 2015, The White House, Washington DC, USA

"We are still getting live feeds from GCHQ, Mr. President, and we have re-tasked several satellites to give us more coverage." General Roberts, the Chairman of the Joint Chiefs of Staff, was briefing a man he didn't like, but a man he respected. The man the secret service called POTUS had proven to be a competent leader, a man who had been able to make the hard choices. But he wasn't a man the general would want to sit down and have a drink with, wouldn't want to spend an evening sharing stories or going fishing with. But that wasn't really relevant right now.

"Can someone fill me in about this Hirta Island?" the president asked.

"We don't have much on it, Mr. President," said the CIA director. "We've asked the British for information, but I don't know if it will be forthcoming."

"Do we have any intelligence that suggests the British created this, or is this just to blow smoke up my ass?"

"We have nothing, sir," Johnson said. "And we definitely had no involvement. I can give you that as a cast iron guarantee." The president looked at him, his eyes searching for deception, seeking the lie that he suspected was there. He didn't see anything, so either the man was telling the truth, didn't know the truth, or was a damned good liar. One out of three was terrible odds. Rodney turned to General Roberts.

"How long until the British will be able to give us intel?" the president asked. He was looking at computer simulations showing the entire United Kingdom. The dozen or so people in the room all looked at the same thing. Every minute, the red blobs encompassing several cities grew larger, displaying the reported extent and the computer predictions of how far the infection had spread. That had been a rare job for someone in the Pentagon's IT department. "*Hi there, we just need an algorithm to plot the spread of a zombie contagion.*"

"GCHQ is outside the initial infected zones, but they are already evacuating. The listening station at Menwith Hill is already silent; it was deemed too close to one of the infected zones." The general put his hand on the map which joined Bristol to Southampton. "Everyone west of this line is going to be fleeing into the southwest of the country. We need to decide whether we want to help get them out." The general paused. He looked at the CIA director who was sat next to the president, and then looked back at his commander-in-chief. "Or do we quarantine the whole island and stop anyone leaving?"

"Does NATO have a view?" the president asked.

"Yes. They want to quarantine. Our continental allies are scared of the infection getting onto the mainland. The French are already taking measures to fortify their coast. They say they will shoot down any planes leaving the UK. And the Irish are not happy about our commandeering their Shannon Airport to route all our assets through. They are even less happy about the British evacuating their best and brightest there."

"Operation Noah, we briefed you on that earlier," Director Johnson said to the president, who nodded his thanks.

"What would you do, General?" And there it was, the question that only a certain breed of men could make. Did they try and save what they could and risk the infection getting off the island, or did they leave millions to perish?

"We know the infected can only travel by foot," Director Johnson said, "and we can project how fast they will spread based on that. And the short incubation period works in our favour in that those infected manifest the symptoms quickly."

"And how certain are we that all the infected cases transform within ten minutes?" the president asked. There was silence in the room as he looked around at them all. The silence was the answer he needed. Nobody really knew anything about the virus. What if it lay dormant in some hosts? What if some who came in contact with it acted like a biblical Typhoid Mary? "So I ask again, General, what would you do?"

"I would salvage what military and government assets we can. Salvage the Royal Navy and the Royal Airforce, and evacuate what's left of their ground forces, most of which have already abandoned their defence of the infected zones. But I would use Ireland as a containment and buffer zone."

"And the rest?" the president pressed.

"We don't have the resources to save but a handful, and that would represent an unacceptable risk of the infection getting off the continent." The general knew this was the only response that made sense. It was the response of a military mind whose sole job was to defend the integrity of the United States of America. The president sat back in his chair and flung the briefing paper he was holding onto the table.

"Ben," he said to his White House Chief of Staff, "get NATO on conference call. We are going to implement a blockade of the United Kingdom. Military and government personnel presently en route to Ireland will be able to land. I want the bulk of their military assets salvaged, but it all goes to Ireland. If the Irish kick up a fuss, remind them who has the aircraft carriers. I want the CDC on site at Shannon, and I want a quarantine order implemented by NATO." He looked at General Roberts. "I want you to contact MI6 and General Marston and let them know if they want to salvage anything, they have three hours to do it. I want that," the president pointed at the map on the screen, "locked down before I have my lunch with the first lady today." The president looked at the CIA director. "And Keith, you bring me the fucking heads of the people who just removed my country's most important ally from the political map. And you do it quickly. I don't care what laws you have to break and what letters of immunity I have to sign. Bring me these fuckers and do it yesterday." That was what General Roberts didn't like about his commander-in-chief. The man was the most ruthless son of a bitch he had ever met. He was even more surprised by what his president said next.

"And if we can somehow use this for our political and strategic benefit, well then we might even be able to use this crisis to our advantage."

12.46PM, 16th September 2015, MI6, Albert Embankment, London

The wind buffeted her coat, but her hair tied back as it was stayed in place. Standing on top of the MI6 building, she looked off across the cityscape, seeing the smoke rising up in the distance from multiple locations. This would be the last time she would see this great city, but honestly, she didn't think she would really miss it. It was just a city after all. There were others that she would one day get to see again. But her immediate future was Ireland, and that's where she would be heading now. First out of the infected zone, and then on a flight out of the quarantine zone. Many in the building below wouldn't get that privilege, duty forcing them to stay behind to try and keep some semblance of humanity going in this death pit.

She turned and walked to the helicopter, climbing aboard. She took the last seat, and ignored the smile of the man who sat across from her, instead putting her attention out of the window that appeared when the side door closed. Men did that a lot. Some smiled, some glared, transfixed by her presence. Others cast her with subtle side glances that they hoped she wouldn't see, as if they needed just a glimpse of her to somehow survive. But that was men, and she didn't mind. They amused her, weak as they were. There were very few she encountered who even interested her, and when she did find one of those rare breeds, she made it her mission to break and destroy the mind of that man. How she loved to do that, to take their ego and their strength and twist it.

Of course, she didn't use her torture skills on these men. No, that she reserved purely for paying jobs. Instead, she used more subtle techniques, making them crave her, making them regret the day they ever encountered her. She knew how to manipulate, make them feel like only they had been able to tame her, and then she slowly ripped them apart from the inside, and in doing so, watched with great amusement as they destroyed their own lives. She was a sociopath, after all. As the rotors began to start up, her thoughts went briefly to the man strapped down to the surgical table in the bowels of the MI6 building. She had returned to him, as promised, his interrogation over. The MI6 men had left her alone in the room, and she had looked at her captive with a wicked smile.

"You did well," she had said to the naked man, sitting next to him. She ran a fingernail across his chest, and looked at his face. Despite his restraints, he did what he could to avert his eyes from her.

"Look at me," she had said softly, and when he didn't, she had gripped his left nipple in between two sharpened fingernails and dug them in harshly. "I said look at me." He did, they always did.

"I'm leaving, you know, but before I do I have a promise to keep." Standing up, she walked over to her instrument table and began to pick up the copper needles one by one. Slowly, she walked back over to him and held them in front of his face.

"No, not that. I did what you asked. I told them everything."

"Yes, I know," Davina had said. "But you took too long. You should have taken me up on my offer when I gave you the chance. You see I made you a promise about what I would do to you, and I always follow through on my promises." The next five minutes were spent to the soundtrack of his screams as she slowly reinserted the needles and connected them back up to the electric current.

"I'm leaving you now. I've connected you up to an IV to keep you hydrated, and that should allow you to live for at least the next five days. Five days for you to enjoy the stimulation from my little toys. And I'll be locking the door behind me so that none of those nasty infected can ever get in." She smoothed his hair across his head. "No, you don't have to thank me. It's the least I could do." With that, she had turned on the power, sending his body into violent convulsions. Davina left him down there to spend his last few days in total mind-rending agony.

12.48PM, 16th September 2015, Hounslow, London

Owen Patterson was having the time of his life. So much so that he had to take his pack off and acquire more shells as all the ones in his pockets were used up. This gun was just what he needed, although he had so far been fortunate in that he had not met any infected in groups of more than two. Because the gun only had two shots, and he was still getting the hang of opening the breach and reloading it. It was a bit stiff at times, and Owen found himself wondering when the last time the thing had been cleaned was.

And although he told himself he was killing zombies, he knew that some of those he had shot were not infected. They had just become inviting targets, victims of his blood lust. This was the most fun he'd had in a long time, and he often found himself whooping with joy when he managed head shots.

Loading up his pockets, he put the backpack on again and slipped two rounds into the chambers. Flicking the gun closed, he headed off back down the road, in search of fresh prey. It was fifteen steps later when his luck ran out. He turned a corner into a side street and was faced with a mass of at least a dozen infected. He stopped dead in his tracks, just as they did, looking at him with that dog-like tilt of the head he had seen so many times. They swayed and moved in front of him, an apparition of hell on the streets of Ye Olde London Town.

Owen froze. He had two rounds against twelve of them. *Shit, so this is the end of the party,* he said to himself. "Fuck it," he said loudly and brought the gun up. That sent the infected off, and they charged him with a howl. At less than ten metres away, he still managed to get both shots off, blasting the face off one and taking another in the hip. But then they were on him. He tried to turn the gun around as a club, but it was ripped from his grasp, and he felt his nose explode as he was punched in the face. Their combined mass brought him to the floor, and they pinned him down, insane faces hovering above him.

"Come on then," Owen roared. "Do it, do it now." He struggled with all his might, but hardly moved as they kept him pressed to the tarmac of the road. Then he felt one of them lifting his left arm, bringing his hand up to its mouth.

"*Feeed,*" it said softly, and held his fingers splayed as it bit off his left little finger.

"Oh, you fucker," Owen cried, and then the hand was passed to another infected who sucked on the wound, its eyes bulging from its sockets with delight. The second infected bit off another of his fingers, one of its teeth cracking off at the gum line with the extent of the force it bit down with. Owen cursed again, and then he felt himself released, and the crowd of infected moved away from him.

"*Spreeeaad,*" he heard them say and then as a unit they moved off, leaving him bleeding and alone in the middle of the street. Cradling his hand, he sat there for several minutes, realising the fate he had been dealt.

"You bastards, oh you fucking bastards. I'm going to kill every last motherfucking one of you," he bellowed. In response, he thought he heard the city roar.

13.03 PM, 16th September 2015, M1 Junction, London

The M1, the country's primary motorway. Many people had also had the idea of fleeing north from the city, but they had soon abandoned their cars due to the gridlocked roads leading up to the motorway. And why was it gridlocked? Because of the multilayer metal fencing and concrete road block that had been put across it.

Holden had been the first to see the crudely written sign about twenty minutes earlier. It had been written on large sheets of plywood. She suspected there would be others on other routes.

NORTH LONDON EVACUATION ZONE
ABANDON YOUR VEHICLE AND FOLLOW THE ARROWS TO THE PROCESSING SECTION

MILITARY AND LAW ENFORCEMENT PERSONEL USE THE BLUE CHANNEL. FOLLOW THE BLUE ARROWS.

The arrows in question had been crudely spray painted on the sides of buildings, billboards, and bridge supports. There were thousands of people here, and the crowd moved slowly. Whilst they received mild protests, their weapons and the ingrained British respect for law enforcement allowed Holden and her protectors to push their way through the crowd. Holden was constantly on the lookout for those who had been bitten. She didn't see any.

Closer to their destination, they saw another sign.

PREPARE FOR PROCESSING
ONLY 1 BAG PER PERSON
NO SUITCASES
YOU ARE ENTERING A QUARANTINE EVACUATION ZONE
PREPARE FOR MEDICAL EXAMINATION

That was also when they saw the first blue arrows, and as they turned onto the North Circular Road, the crowds of people got even thicker, and they could see the signpost for the slip road that led to the M1. They continued to worm their way through the crowds, soldiers now visible at the side of the road. Brian led them to where two of them stood their vigilance.

"You don't know how good it is to see you guys," he said as he offered a hand which was accepted. "We saw a sign that said take the blue channel?"

"Yeah, keep to the right of here," he said indicating. "You'll be going up the M1 off ramp." The soldier looked at Holden. She had long since abandoned her not so white medical coat, so she just looked like everyone else in the crowd. "She a civilian?" the soldier asked

"She's a doctor." Holden held up her hospital medical pass which was still around her neck. The picture didn't actually really resemble her present dishevelled appearance, but the soldier didn't even look. The soldier looked tired, broken.

"Okay, she will be able to go with you. We need every doctor we can get our hands on." In the distance, they could hear someone speaking on a loudspeaker.

The three of them walked in the direction indicated, and as they got closer to the off ramp, the loudspeaker voice became audible.

"Civilians keep to the left. Military, police, and medical personnel, move to the right into the blue channel. Be prepared to show proof of identity for the right-hand lane."

"Thank God you kept that, doc," Brian said. "I'm not sure our word would have been good enough here." Despite herself, she smiled.

Passing through a security cordon, they shortly found themselves separated from the rest of the mass of humanity by temporary wire fencing topped with vicious looking razor wire. Holden couldn't help but notice the looks of resentment and disgust that were sent her way by the trapped populace. She didn't feel guilty. Why should she? Her years in medical school hadn't given her much of an advantage in life recently, so she wasn't going to pass up life giving her a break for once.

13.12PM, 16th September 2015, Hounslow, London

Owen didn't remember passing out, but he must have. Why else was he lying in the middle of the road covered in his own vomit? His head was killing it, and moving only made the pain worse. But it wasn't just his head, it was his whole body. He felt hot, and yet he was shivering, sweat soaking through his clothing. Managing to get to his knees, he realised he still had the shotgun with him and he used it to help him get to his feet.

Owen staggered, but he didn't fall. He felt nauseous, like the last time he had the flu. Only worse, much worse. He didn't want to move, wanted to just lie back down and let the ground swallow him up, but that's not what he was going to do. No, fuck that.

"Come on you fucking cunt," he said to himself, and took a step forward, then another. He was shaky, unsteady, his sense of balance seemed off, but he didn't fall. Looking around through blurred vision, he realised he knew where he was. Not far from his squat. That's where he needed to go; that's where he could go and rest. Owen looked at his hand, noticed the crude bandage that had stemmed the bleeding from the stumps of where his fingers used to be. He didn't remember doing that. When had he done that? Fuck it, got to move, got to get off the street before any more of those infected fuckers found him.

Infected? Oh shit. What had Gary said? The virus could be passed on by bites? Owen looked at his damaged hand, flexed it, felt the fire rip through as the muscles of his limb protested the motion. Was he infected? Was he going to turn into one of them … one of those things?

"You bastards," he seethed through gritted teeth. No, that wasn't going to happen. Not to him, not now. So he moved, stumbling and nearly landing face first onto the road surface, but the shotgun saved him, and he managed to right himself, and carried on walking. It wasn't far, just a little further.

He didn't hear them come up behind him, didn't see them until one stepped right in front of him and grabbed his chin. Owen stood wide-eyed, his bladder opening as one of Satan's minions sniffed him, moving Owen's head from side to side with its blood-stained fingers. He heard the other one behind him, sniffing, felt something lick the back of his neck. Then a voice whispered into his ear.

"*Spreeaad.*" He felt the hot breath as the creature exhaled the words, and then the one in front of him let go of his face. The infected in front of Owen took a step back and then flicked its head to the left as if it had heard something. Its companion joined it, and the two viral carriers ran off down the road, leaving Owen confused and amazed at the same time. He watched them run off out of sight, only for their departure to be met with a scream in the general direction they had run. Owen turned around, noticed nothing else moving in the vicinity and got moving as fast as his body would let him.

13.24 PM, 16th September 2015, SAS Base, Hereford

Croft stood by the helicopter that would shortly be delivering them to a location in the middle of Devon. Its rotors were quiet, the only noise the sound of fuel filling its tanks. Captain Hudson held a computer tablet showing the map of the area they were going.

"How do you want to do this, Croft? You're technically in charge here." They both looked at the screen as it zoomed in via a live satellite feed.

"You're the expert here, Captain," Croft said. "These are your men, and you know what they are capable of." He gave a tired smile. "I wouldn't dream of telling you how to do things."

"Awfully decent of you," Hudson said. He turned and looked at the three helicopters that were being refuelled. "We should be in the air in 45 minutes. I suggest," Hudson said, indicating a point on the satellite image, "that we land here and go in on foot. The compound we are heading to has a helipad, but with the way things have been going, I wouldn't be surprised if they had some form of air defence system. We will use drones to survey the situation once we are on the ground."

Croft was also holding a tablet, and it bleeped at him, indicating data had arrived over the secure network. He lifted it up and opened the package that had just arrived over the ether. "Looks like we have the satellite imagery GCHQ promised us." Croft passed the tablet to his subordinate who used his fingers to zoom in and out. The pictures were incredibly detailed. "They had to re-task a satellite to get these," Croft said.

"So we have a three-storey building in grounds of around two acres of flat terrain. The perimeter is double-wire fencing. That's going to be a lot of open ground to cover. This might get interesting," the captain said.

Croft knew what Hudson was talking about. Nobody would be able to approach the house without being visible. There were no trees or ditches to hide behind. And the intel they had from the guy presently suffering in an MI6 cell was that this place was a fortress. He looked from the tablet just as a corporal came over to them.

"Boss," the corporal said addressing Hudson, "Captain Savage is ready to give her briefing." Hudson nodded and indicated for his subordinate to lead the way. Croft followed in their wake.

*

Ma'am Hottie. That's what the lower ranks had called her behind her back, whispering to each other what they would do to her if only the posh bitch was willing to learn her place. Of course, they had never disrespected her to her face – none of them wanted a stint in the glasshouse after all. But she saw their glances and occasionally caught the nudges and the winks. It was something she had struggled to get used to, not experiencing it in her medical career before the military. She had initially put up a shield to protect herself, a cold, no-nonsense approach to her leadership, which had actually made things worse. That just added 'frigid bitch' to the things they called her. With so few women in the military, the armed forces still had a long way to go on the road to equality. Coming from a medical background, where equality had been accepted and discrimination almost obsolete, it was definitely a wakeup call.

And still she managed to rise through the ranks, despite the fact that she suspected the officers were just as bad. There had been incidents where she clearly hadn't fit the mould that those around wanted of her. She was attractive, but she was also damned good at what she did, better than most of the men around her, and she wasn't going to let the prejudice of mere men, men who should know better, get in the way of that. And despite the contempt and envy that many held for her, her determination had led her exactly where she wanted to go, to her passion for researching infectious agents. And now, in charge of her own facility, the whispers and the murmurings had finally stopped to a degree that they were no longer there on the peripheries of her interactions with her subordinates. She actually found it amusing now, and knew that when she got her next promotion, her nickname would change. Major Hottie.

Stood at the front of the briefing room, she looked out at the forty or so men present and saw none of the old sexism. All she saw was respectful attention. These men were here to do a job, and they were the best at what they did. They knew that their lives would probably rest on the information she gave them. For one of those rare moments, she felt the respect that her position demanded, and she realised that this was why she did what she did.

"What we know so far is this. Sometime this morning, a biological agent was released across several cities, including London." She pointed to a map that was being projected on the wall behind her that showed red circles around the affected areas. "The initial outbreak we believe occurred about an hour after initial infection, those affected becoming violent, attacking those around them. Those who become exposed to bodily fluids or who are bitten undergo the same infection process, only much quicker. Our data shows these secondary infections cause the transformation within ten minutes." Savage pushed the remote which moved her PowerPoint projection on one page, displaying a still of the riots broadcast on the BBC. “From our observations, we can see that the infected have no concept of fear and lack any kind of empathy. They are much stronger, faster and seem to have much greater endurance than the average human. The infected become agents with one goal, to spread the infection to others as quickly as possible. It would be very easy to describe them as mindless, but reports from the ground show that they have the ability to coordinate their activities, working together to overwhelm and attack the population and defensive positions. Some have described it as being almost insect like.” There was silence from the crowd in the room.

“The infected seem to show little response to pain stimuli, and gunshot wounds that would incapacitate an adult male seem not to stop them unless the wound is fatal. They can be killed, but this is where the science fiction part comes in. Death by anything but a head shot allows for them to come back from the dead.” That got a response – even hardened SAS soldiers were going to react to the news that zombies were real.

“Let’s call a spade a spade here,” she said. “Zombies are real. So far as we can tell, when an infected is killed and reanimates, the only way to stop it is to destroy the brain, or remove the head from the body. Unlike the infected, the zombies are slower and somewhat uncoordinated. And whilst we have not seen many of them so far, they represent a threat the human race has never encountered before. To engage with either an infected individual or a reanimated is to deal with something that cannot be reasoned with, that cannot be bargained with, and if at all possible, needs to be dispatched at a distance. We have first-hand experience of what happens when one of these things gets near you.” She changed the screen’s image again, showing a still of an infected projectile vomiting over several police officers. “If they get any kind of their bodily secretion on your exposed skin, you will become contaminated. And gentlemen, there is no cure. Now that I’ve put a dampener on your day, I’ll hand over to Major Croft who will go through today’s planned operation.”

Savage stood to one side and watched Croft walk up from the back of the room. She noticed the slight nervousness he kept under the surface. Even this man, who had endured so much, who had killed countless times and had been forced to order the deaths of dozens of people, even this man had his insecurities. That was something else to like about him. Strange that she was letting her hormones get the better of her when the whole world around her was going to shit. She handed him the PowerPoint controller and stepped to the side, giving his arm a slight squeeze, not caring that the killers in the room would have registered the fact, would have instantly twigged the romantic interest between the two. Who were they going to gossip to?

"Gentlemen." Croft stood before them, Savage a ghost in his peripheral vision. "We have an opportunity to apprehend the man responsible for all this. Intelligence from MI6 states that the creator of the virus is still in this country. Here, to be exact," he said pointing at the screen which showed an aerial view of a farmhouse, with an inset map of where in the UK the farmhouse was. "We do not know what assets are on site here. What we do know is that we need to take this individual alive, because if he indeed created this fucking fiasco, he may well have the cure. And if he has the cure, you may well get to spend Christmas with your families." Croft looked out at the men he spoke to. Every one of them could have deserted their post. Every one of them had the skill and the training to disappear, to run and gather those they held dear. But they didn't; they stayed and they did their duty, just as Croft did. He put the PowerPoint controller down. "Let's get real here, guys. Two nights ago, I was eating quail and drinking wine so expensive it would pay my rent for a month. The luxury our so-called betters enjoyed is gone. There is no more Queen and Country. There is only vengeance and survival. You are the best this country has, and you are its one chance of redemption. And despite my rank and my training, don't for one second think I'm going to be telling any of you what to do. I know how much you all despise officers." There was a chuckle from the audience.

"Damn fucking straight," someone shouted, which got more laughs. Even Captain Hudson got caught out by that one.

"Whilst officially I am here as an advisor, I am also here to set out the rules of engagement." There was a mild groan at that one. The rules of engagement, the restrictions soldiers found themselves fighting under. "The rules are there are no rules. You do whatever you need to do to bring this fucker down, and more importantly, you do what you need to do to stay alive."

13.38PM, 16th September 2015, Windsor Castle, Windsor

The Queen was not in residence. *She's probably on her way to some tropical island she owns*, Jack thought. He stood outside the castle walls, amidst the throng of people that were also gathered there. The fortification was designed to keep people out, which was just what you needed when the zombie apocalypse was upon you. But for that to be of any benefit, you first had to be let in, and that didn't seem to be happening. The crowd was hundreds strong and bad tempered. Jake kept to the edge of it, not wanting to get swallowed up should it turn nasty. He could hear someone shouting over a megaphone. Someone in uniform, glimpses of him visible from where Jake stood. And there were soldiers everywhere, heavily armed soldiers. Above, a large helicopter flew overhead and began to descend into the castle grounds. "Let us in, you bastards," he heard someone shout.

Jack's dad had been in the Royal Marines. Because of that, when Jack was younger, he'd learnt everything he could about the British military, had even considered joining up until his dad had point blank stated that this would be a bloody stupid idea. "No lad of mine is going to make the mistake I made," his father had said. "Besides, it would break your mother's heart. She had to live with the thought of me not coming back from deployment. She couldn't cope with the thought of losing you." Although he had possessed a rebellious streak back then, it was a mild one. He couldn't ever go against the word of the man who had been his living hero.

Not living anymore. But because he had been fascinated by the military, he had learnt the insignia of the regiments, and he knew that Windsor Castle was defended by troops from both the Coldstream Guards and the Household Cavalry. And both forces were out in force today. The helicopter he saw land took off again, and in the distance, he saw another approaching. Were they reinforcing or evacuating? His intuition told him they were evacuating. Jack moved further away from the crowd and followed the road that ran outside the castle walls. How the hell was he going to get in?

13.41PM, 16th September 2015, Hounslow, London

Owen felt like he was dying. He was sure this was what it must feel like. This wasn't the flu; this made the flu feel like a mild sniffle. Lying face down on the mattress, he just let the agony sweep over him. He had already wet himself again. Making it here had taken everything out of him, and he just couldn't face moving to use the bathroom. What was worse than the pain was the delirium. There were voices in his head. Well, voices were perhaps an exaggeration – it was more like noises, but there were words within the cacophony. And the words enticed him, enthralled him. And despite his agony, despite the bolts of electricity that shot along every nerve ending, he was hungry, felt the gnawing ache deep in his midriff.

But he didn't do anything about the hunger, couldn't. He groaned and rolled onto his side, bringing his knees up in a foetal position as a fresh wave of torture tore through him. Was this what it was like? Was this how becoming one of them felt? Why had he been so foolish? Why had he gone on a killing spree instead of hiding out until the infection had burned itself out? Because he was an idiot, that was why. He had always been an idiot. That was why his father had left, that was why there was no love in his life. Because he was diseased, corrupted, and those who loved him smelled that corruption on him and wanted nothing to do with his diseased mind.

"What?" he said to himself, fighting through the delirium. Where the hell was this all coming from? Was this what he actually thought? No. No, that was bullshit. His father had left because he was a selfish cunt. *It wasn't my fault. How could it be? I was too young.* An image floated into his mind, a fantasy that he had dwelled on many times in the past, of finding his father. Of hurting him, demanding answers.

"Why did you leave?" he roared. "Why don't you love me?" Tears welled in his eyes, and the sobs stormed through him in competition for the pain. *I deserve better than this, I deserve to be loved. Why did you abandon me? I loved you, why did you take that from me?*

Owen coughed, blood splattering the mattress. *No*, he thought, *I will not go out like this. I will not let some fucking disease get the better of me.*

"Join us, feed with us," the voices demanded.

"No, I won't," Owen roared lashing out with his damaged hand, hitting the wall and sending an arc of pain into his brain. "No, you fucks, I won't let you have me!" He shouted with such force that the veins in his neck stood out, and he thrashed as a spasm rippled through him. And then his body, overwhelmed by the stimulus, allowed his brain to pass out, his bowels loosened and his mind switched off into sweet oblivion.

13.47 PM, 16th September 2015, M1 Junction Quarantine Zone

Holden quickly learnt the reason everything was moving so slow. They had walked up the off ramp, and onto the M1, only to see more fencing and more people. The blue channel took up the hard shoulder of the motorway, and they walked along the edge separated again from the rest of humanity by more fencing. Ahead, tents were visible, along with hastily erected watchtowers topped with men with machine guns. The one thing she also noticed was how few soldiers there actually were.

But the reason things were taking so long was that everyone had to filter through a limited opening. It was different for her and her companions – they were the only ones in the blue channel – and she made it to the new sanctuary quickly. That was, however, when the fun began. Through the initial makeshift gates in the fencing, she was directed at gunpoint to a tent where a female nurse did a full head to toe check of her. Which meant she had to get naked. "I'm looking for bites," the nurse had said, almost apologetically. The intelligence those manning the place had about the virus wasn't much, and they had no test for it, so physical examination was the best they could do for now.

Things got better after that. She was treated almost like royalty. As a consultant in accident and emergency medicine, she had more experience than any of the other medical personnel there, which was a mishmash of paramedics and a few GP's. She soon found herself put in charge of running the triage tents which the general populace were filtered through. There were too many of them to do full physicals. Her job was to organise the treatment of those with debilitating injuries. Everyone else was directed through the tents to a holding area that had been set up on the motorway behind them. There they waited for an assortment of buses that had been organised.

"Where are they taking the people?" Holden had asked a military police officer who was guarding one of the tents.

"Luton Airport, ma'am. I don't know where they go after that." Holden stepped out of the back of the field tent and looked at the penned-in civilians. They were scared; she could see it in their eyes. Holden felt she knew what they were thinking. There were very few in today's world who hadn't, at some time in their lives, witnessed scenes from the Jewish Holocaust in World War Two. Either in films or in photographs. Lurking in the back of their minds, many of them would surely be thinking about concentration camps and mass executions. At least, she assumed that was what they were thinking, because that was the image that kept popping into her mind. Perhaps she was too morbid. Perhaps all the people she saw were worried only about survival. All the scene needed to make it complete was rail box cars and snow.

All around the saved were scattered armed police, and in the distance, she heard the approach of another returning bus. A ripple went through the masses, a current of excitement. Salvation, one step closer to salvation. Looking around her, Holden was amazed this had been set up so quickly and had nothing but praise for whoever had organised it. Someone had told her that most of the fencing had been salvaged from a nearby building site, and she could see that the watchtowers were made of wood and scaffolding poles. The army unit that set this up had requisitioned most of what they needed from the local area.

She saw Stan. Given the medical all clear, he now found himself guarding the civilians. He spotted her, and she gave a slight wave. He gave her a smile and turned back to watching the civilians. She went back into the tent.

"I still can't believe you made it out of Euston. That was the heart of it." Holden stood next to a civilian paramedic called John who was taking the blood pressure of a recently arrived police officer. The officer had a deep gash to his forehead, and Holden was stitching the man up. He didn't wince once, just stared out the back of the tent, staring into the void of his own approaching insanity. The officer had been non-communicative since his arrival, almost catatonic, and was clearly in a state of shock.

"I had help," Holden said. Finishing up her suturing, she put a hand on the officer's shoulder. "There you are, you're all done." John took off the blood pressure cuff and gave Holden the thumbs up. "Why don't you lie down, officer? You need your rest," and she gently pushed him backwards on the bed. He didn't resist, and lay his head down onto the pillow. Suddenly, the officer grabbed her hand, not firmly but gently. There were tears welling in his eyes.

"I saw them. I saw them eat children," the officer suddenly said.

"I know," Holden said, caressing his cheek gently. "I saw that too."

"How could they eat children?" Holden carefully eased his hand away and placed it on his chest.

"You get some rest, you've earnt it." She moved away from her patient and told John that he needed a sedative.

"Don't we all," John half-joked.

"Where were you when this happened?"

"I was attending an RTA just off the main junction onto the M1 at around half past ten. That was when the army turned up in helicopters, abseiling right onto the hard shoulder." John turned and picked up a syringe and a drug vial from the medical cart he was stood next to. "Sedative," he said indicating the officer.

*

She could smell them, she was so close, so inviting. With a few steps, she could reach out and touch one of them. There were thousands here, all ripe with fear and sweat. Something had sent her here, some instinct she didn't have the capacity to understand. The understanding of her surroundings had changed. Whilst the names of things around her drifted in and out of her thinking, much of her mind was spent thinking about one thing. Feeding the hunger.

She didn't want to be seen, not yet. Some animal cunning told her not to spook the herd, not to send them running. Because that would bring the guns, and she was the only one of her kind here, and they might kill her before she could do what the voices commanded. But now that she had seen what she had seen, so had her brothers and sisters. And they would be coming, running at full pelt, coming to help her feed. Then she saw the soldier with the gun, and she hid herself even more. Wait, should she wait? No, she would not wait; she would spread, she would infect.

With an agility she had not possessed in her former life, she grabbed a drain pipe next to her and climbed, her small child's frame easily supported. The building she stood next to had a flat roof, and she easily made it up onto it. Scuttling so as not to be seen, she peered over the roof lip. With a few jumps, she could make it across several rooftops she saw, and she executed her plan, the spaces between buildings not enough to hamper her progress. On the roof of the third building, she looked down on the dozens of people who milled below her. She felt the bile rising, felt it flowing up her throat. Leaning her head over the roof edge, she opened her mouth wide, and rained viral vomit down upon those below. Shaking her head from side to side, she sent droplets flying far and wide, and she heard the cries of disgust and surprise from those below.

"There, up there," came a voice that she barely understood. But she understood the bullets, understood how to hide as they impacted into the brickwork. She ran further along the rooftop, the vomit rising again. But this time, she didn't lean her head over the edge. This time, she backed up and ran, leaping off the roof edge, her mouth disgorging the contents of her stomach as she fell. She landed hard on the floor amidst the crowd, hitting bodies, felt something in her leg snap. She ignored it and grabbed a leg that was close to her, her arms pulling her mouth onto it, biting through the thin material into the flesh – the joy, oh the bliss at the taste. It was exquisite, it was her whole life. But then she released and was on another, and then another.

"Move, get out of the way," a voice said, but she used the crowd to hide in, crawling between legs, slashing and biting, ignoring the feeble blows that were rained down on her head and shoulders. And then the crowd parted, and she was in the open. She turned and saw the man with the gun. Saw two of them. The first one hesitated, lowering his weapon.

"It's a child; it's a fucking child." He didn't shoot, and she ran at him, only for something hard to hit her in the chest multiple times, and she was flung backwards, pain irrelevant to her. She tried to get back up, but more bullets hit her, and then her world went dark as a bullet entered her left eye, exploding the back of her head, sending infected brain matter all over the road.

"She's not a child now, none of them are," the second soldier said, hitting the first soldier lightly on the arm. "Get your fucking act together, Corporal." He activated the radio on his shoulder. "We have infected on the perimeter; I repeat, we have infected on the perimeter." And then both soldiers ran. They had their orders. There was no way to tell who here had now been contaminated. They knew they were alright though. Surely they were alright.

Holden heard it over the radio one of the police officers was wearing. "*We have infected on the perimeter; I repeat, we have infected on the perimeter.*" She looked up from the leg she was dressing, a deep laceration caused by falling in the street. She looked around, saw the look of horror and resignation on the faces around her.

"How many did we save?" she heard someone ask.

"Not enough," came a response. A soldier ran past her, and she finished dressing the wound, and made her way out the back of the tent. She saw Stan running towards her.

"Time to go, doc," he said.

"Go, but I'm needed in there," she protested.

"Not anymore. The infected will be here within minutes, and we are leaving."

"But what about all those people?" Holden wanted to scream. She had fooled herself into thinking she was safe, that she could go back to doing what she did best, healing people. And now they were going to run again. "There's thousands of them out there."

"I know," said Stan, "and there's millions of them in London. Millions in Manchester, millions in Glasgow. But you are here now, and you have a chance." He pointed at a bus several metres away. "Get on that bus. You did what you could. They need you; they need doctors more than anything."

"But …" she tried, she really tried to counter his argument. But there was nothing she could do here. There was no way she could help those outside the barricade. "Fuck!" she shouted, looking back into the tent. "At least help me get these injured onto the bus. Can you do that for me at least?"

"Yes, doc," he said. "I can do that," and he followed her back into the tent. Brian appeared moments later.

"I bet my ex-wife is regretting divorcing me now," Brian said. He didn't smile.

13.48PM, 16th September 2015, Windsor Castle, Windsor

Jack suspected what was going on. There were trucks parked outside the castle, surrounded by soldiers. He had come across them as he walked around the castle's perimeter. The trucks were being loaded full of boxes. Indeed, the castle, was being evacuated, but not so much of people. It was being evacuated of treasures. No doubt those boxes were filled with paintings and shiny things, precious heirlooms and the spoils of British conquest. It was not an exaggeration to say that Jack had never been a fan of the Royal family. He saw them as an elite inbred ruling class that leeched off the hard work of the people. That's the kind of thing fathers tell their sons when they become disillusioned about fighting in another country for wars that don't make sense. Jack crossed the road and made his way to where the small convoy was being loaded.

He knew this was his only way out, so had to try something. As apparently safe as the castle was, there was a reason it was being abandoned. The castle would soon enough become a death trap. Either the infected would get in, or those inside would die of thirst or starvation. You could only hold so many supplies. And then there was the risk of disease. Packing so many people into such a relatively small area risks all kinds of contagions to spread throughout the masses. Two soldiers noticed him and made to intercept, one holding an SA80 machine gun. The soldier's finger was on the trigger guard.

"That's close enough, lad," one of them, a sergeant, said.

"I want to help," Jack said, looking past the man briefly. "The more people you have helping load those crates, the quicker you get out of here."

"And you think you can help, do you?" the sergeant asked, almost mockingly.

"I think so, Sergeant. And I won't give you any shit. All I want is a place on one of your trucks." The sergeant squinted at him. "I know you might not think the son of a Royal Marine would be of any use, but I might surprise you." Jack kept his face blank, but the sergeant smiled.

"Your dad was a marine?" he asked.

"Yes, and he's probably turning in his grave at me offering to help army grunts," Jack said, shrugging his shoulders, but he held a little twinkle in his eye.

"Ballsy little cunt, isn't he?" the other soldier said sounding annoyed. The sergeant said nothing, just looking Jack up and down. And then he laughed.

"Aw, what the fuck. None of this matters anymore. Looks like you've got your ride, lad."

13.58PM, 16th September 2015, M1 Junction Quarantine zone

The infected swarmed through the packed in cattle. They hit the crowded refugees in waves, relentlessly infecting everyone they saw. Some of the humans tried to fight back with fists and blunt instruments. Some even with knives, but their attempts were futile against the new species. The fists only infected those who struck, the blunt objects only sent infected droplets flying, contaminating those it landed on. And the knives, the knives just send torrents of infected blood onto the very hands of those who wielded them. And there wasn't a single soldier in sight.

Not in the bulk of the crowd anyway. There were plenty of soldiers behind the fences. The crowd surged, clattering against the wire, demanding entry, demanding a chance, just a chance to escape the infection. The fence rattled, groaning against the load it was being put under, and it began to buckle. It was a makeshift effort, not a high-security fence. As the last soldier boarded her bus, Holden felt the vehicle move, just as one of the watch towers began to tumble. Sitting at the back, she looked out of the rear window and saw the people swarm over the downed fences and through the tented area, hoping that just one bus would stop to let them on. But that wouldn't happen. The buses were full, and to stop now would see them swamped, meaning their escape might not even happen. So they sped up, and the faces she saw receded from her sight, but would always be etched in her memory. Thousands condemned to be infected and to die.

16.36PM, 16th September 2015, Hayton Vale, Devon

The satellite feed was good enough for him to watch live streaming video. Gavin sat watching the latest web stream from his favourite conspiracy website. The figure of Andrew James, host of the show and long term champion of truth, was waving some papers at his internet audience.

"... and the truth is here in the government's own documents. For years, they have been putting cancer viruses in the vaccines and poisoning you with genetically modified crops, but now they have implemented their master plan." The thin man on the screen glowered at the studio cameras and pointed out at his audience. "I've been warning you about this day for over twenty years, and now it's here. Remember the mysterious Georgia Guide stones that appeared almost overnight, with their dedication to reducing the human population to only half a billion. This is happening right now in Great Britain, and before the week is out, you will most likely see martial law in this country. They will come for your guns, ladies and gentlemen, you can take that to the bank." Gavin took a sip of the tea he held, riveted by the man's performance. He was intoxicating, his charisma having helped his radio and internet show reach ratings that exceeded most of the mainstream media news channels. Right now, almost seven million people were tuned in to what he had to say, and he was going to say it like he saw it.

"We have the documents, ladies and gentlemen. Our inside source has given us the lowdown on the Hirta Island experiment, and we have proof that this so-called zombie outbreak will be used to bring in the One World Government and the cashless society. Not only are they coming for your guns, but they are coming to force you to take the implantable microchip, which means they will be able to track you every second of every day. And if you remember the information from last Tuesday's guest speaker, you now know how those microchips will be used to control your thought processes by manipulating your body's electromagnetic field. This is not a drill, ladies and gentlemen – this is it. This is their power grab, and you need to ask yourself if you will be on the side of the oppressors or if you are willing to stand up and fight for what you believe in."

This was the most passionate Gavin had seen his conspiracy guru since the events of 911. This was why Gavin believed what he believed. This was why he was here now, safe from the plague that was eating through the heartlands of the world's fifth largest economy. But was he safe? When you believed in such conspiracies, it often came hand in hand with a dose of paranoia. But, of course, you weren't paranoid if they were actually out to get you, which is why the noise from outside sent his blood cold. He stood up from his desk where he had been watching the computer monitor, and turned the volume down on the speakers. The noise was getting louder, and it was unmistakeable. Helicopters.

Gavin ran from his office into the kitchen. Picking up his shotgun from the kitchen table, he opened the stock and inserted two cartridges. Snapping the gun shut, he quickly made his way out through the back door of the kitchen. In front of him lay open and flat grazing fields, and it was here that he stood and watched the two transport helicopters land. Every fear about government and oppression surfaced within him then. But surely they wouldn't waste such resources on just him. He was insignificant. And he had kept himself to himself. He had never voiced his beliefs to anyone but family and friends, hadn't started blogging about the New World Order, and hadn't inundated his MP with letters and complaints. He was a nobody, so why the hell were they here?

The helicopters hit the ground and the engines cut off. The side doors opened and soldiers stepped out, heavily armed soldiers. Gavin knew instantly that the shotgun he held was pointless, and he let it drop from his hands. So this was it, this was how it ended. He let himself then drop to his knees and watched with growing dread but an almost resigned acceptance as one of the soldiers and a civilian walked towards him. He couldn't speak. The civilian looked quizzically at him, and the two men stepped within talking distance.

"Good afternoon," the soldier said, smiling. "Sorry to drop in on you unannounced, but this was the best place for us to land." Croft stood next to him and wondered why the hell the man they were talking to was on his knees with tears in his eyes.

16.45, 16th September 2015, Hounslow, London

Owen woke up and lay there motionless for several minutes. The room was dark, and there was a disgusting taste in his mouth and a dampness from his lower regions that meant only one thing. He needed to move, but there was confusion as to where he was and why he was here. There was still a grogginess to his mind, and the dull constant thud from his damaged hand helped to remind him of the traumas he had been through. He had been bitten, but he was still here.

Sitting up, he expected a wave of nausea to hit him, but it didn't. There was no longer any signs of the fever that had threatened to take him, and he looked at his watch, amazed to see that he had been out for several hours. The gibbering voices in his head were also silenced, and he felt himself again. No, that was wrong – he felt better. But the room stank or, more realistically, he stank and was just infesting the air around him with his own stench. He needed a shower, and a fresh change of clothes. And a drink, by Christ he needed a drink.

Propping himself up against one of the walls of the small room he found himself in, he looked at his damaged hand. His makeshift bandage had long since been lost, and the chewed stumps of the lost fingers were open to the air. He looked at them, expecting to see seeping blood. But he didn't see that, only dried blood. He tried to flex the hand, and although he felt pain, it was not as severe as his mind remembered from earlier. Still, he'd probably need to take some antibiotics, and was sure that he had a stash somewhere in the kitchen of the squat. They always kept a stash of medical supplies for the unexpected. In his line of business, avoiding doctors meant avoiding unwelcome questions and often the annoying glare of the police.

Owen stood and stripped off his clothes. That was an act so disgusting he felt himself shiver in disgust. His jeans were soaked through with his own piss, and his legs were smeared with his own faeces. He wouldn't be wearing those clothes again, and he gingerly picked his wallet out of the jeans' front pocket. But, holding the leather in his hand, he realised that there was no point. There was no use for money now, not in this world. There was no need for him to prove his identity, and he very much doubted he would be stopped on the streets by the rozzers anytime soon. In fact, he was unlikely ever to see another police officer ever again, except in the infected variety.

Owen walked shivering into the bathroom and switched on the shower. It had been ridiculously easy to have the water restored to what was supposed to be an abandoned council flat, and the regular bills that came through the letter box were so minimal as to be easy for him to pay. He hadn't bothered with the gas and electricity, though, which was why the shower he took was arctic. But he felt clean, and the cold water seemed to invigorate him. As he stood under the water, letting it run over his head and his body, the filth sliding off him, he looked again at his hand. He carefully used the water to remove the dry blood and examined the two wounded digits. Both had been bitten off at the second knuckle, and were all but useless now. But he had seen wounds before, and these looked different, almost as if the injuries had been received several days ago. Whilst tender, the tissues at the edges had a healthy pinkness to them. What the hell was this?

He dried himself on a clean towel, and delved into the first-aid kit in the bathroom cabinet to dress his hand properly. He smeared the wounds with antibiotic ointment and then used safety pins to hold the bandage he wrapped around his hand in place. It would have to do for now. Looking at himself in the mirror, he saw a face he hadn't seen in a long time. Not the face on the surface, but the secret face that lived below the mask. It was the face of the man he had always wanted to be. The face of the man who could achieve anything and who was entitled to everything.

"There you are," he said to himself. "There you are at last."

16.46, 16th September 2015, M4 Motorway

Jake sat in the back of the truck he had been allowed on. They had left Windsor hours ago, but the going had initially been slow due to the congested traffic. Everyone was understandably trying to flee London and the surrounding areas. Sat next to crates and equipment, he was near the back of the convoy, at the front of which was a Warrior infantry fighting vehicle. Most of the troops stationed in the two barracks servicing Windsor were being evacuated in this column. Jake didn't know where they were heading, and frankly he didn't care.

The traffic on the London inbound lane of the M4 was almost non-existent. Nobody, it seemed, wanted to drive into an infected zone, and once the convoy had traversed the log jams around Windsor (with a little bit of help from the Warrior tank pushing immobile vehicles out of the way), they had swapped to the London-bound lane. It had been pretty much plane sailing from then on.

The convoy, it seemed, had no intention of stopping, and Jake felt he needed to piss badly. The two soldiers he presently shared the back of the truck with had both taken leaks off the back of the truck, one flicking the V's when the driver of the truck blew his horn mockingly. Jake wasn't sure he could do that, wasn't sure he could take a piss in front of other people so blatantly. But with the other two soldiers now asleep, he had a plan. He would piss into the empty bottle that lay on the floor next to him, and would pour out its contents out the back of the truck. It would have been easier to just throw the bottle, but he suspected he would need it again. There was no telling how long this journey would take. But he was with soldiers, and that was all that mattered now.

17.34PM, 16th September 2015, Hayton Vale, Devon

There were no infected here. It would take days for them to reach this part of the country. So there was time, time to do what needed to be done. Hudson looked around at his men, looked at Savage, who surprisingly didn't seem out of place amongst the hardened killers. Fifteen of the hardest, bravest and fiercest warriors the planet had ever created. And every one of them armed to the teeth, and she seemed to just fit right in. The cloudless sky looked down on them as they approached the fence that marked the boundary to where the creator of the virus was supposed to be hiding out. The building was a good five hundred metres away over open terrain. There was absolutely no cover, as if the land had been artificially flattened.

"Sergeant, send up the drone."

"Right boss." O'Sullivan turned and indicated to one of his men. Within seconds, the small surveillance drone was aloft and heading up over the fences. Hudson watched the display on his tablet as the drone's video feed was relayed to him. Croft stood by his side.

The drone flew on to the house, circling it several times. Nobody was visible, and the drone moved in closer, buzzing the windows so that its cameras could see inside. It saw nothing – the windows were all curtained.

"Switching to infrared," Croft heard the drone operator say. The image on the tablet changed, but again the tell-tale heat signatures of humans were not visible.

"Nobody home?" Croft asked.

"Only one way to find out," Hudson answered. He switched off the tablet and stowed it in his pack. "Move it out, people, let's get this done." He turned to Savage. "We'll try and get your guy alive if we can, but the lives of my men take precedent. We are going in hard and fast."

"The research on the virus is more important," Savage said.

"Good job," Croft said with a smile.

Two SAS moved up to the fence line. There were two fences at the perimeter, and it had been spotted almost immediately that the inner one was electrified. There was also an abundance of surveillance cameras on posts inside the fences.

"Pretty obvious whoever is in there knows we are here," Croft said.

"Yep, no sneaking up on these fuckers. Figured as much when I saw the original satellite feeds. Which is why we have those." Hudson pointed at the hand-held ballistic shields eight of his men carried. The idea was to use them for cover as they approached the house. It wasn't great, but it was a hundred times better than just walking up to the house.

In the house, Jones had been warned of the soldier's approach by the various electronic sensors that surrounded the property. He abandoned the living room and walked to a smaller room with over a dozen monitors. All showed images from outside the house, three showing the gathering of Special Forces outside the fence. No surprises that they were here, thought Jones, only he hadn't expected them to get here so quickly. No matter, he was already bored with the news channels and had abandoned the alcohol. Despite the carnage he had created, he felt virtually nothing. He had expected to feel elation, at least satisfaction. But if anything, he felt disappointment, because it wasn't enough. The millions that had died and the millions that would die meant nothing to him. He wanted the world to burn. He wanted to step out into the clear morning sun knowing he was the last human being alive on the planet.

Walking over to the wall, he took a key that hung from a chain from around his neck, and inserted it into a glass case at chest height. Inside were a series of twelve switches, and he flipped six of them. There was no immediate reaction, but he knew the property gates would shortly be opening, their controls on timers. Those gates led to tunnels, which led to exits all around the property. What the gates held captive would very shortly be released. Jones turned back to the monitors and saw the explosion. Moments later, soldiers began filing through the hole blown in the electric fence.

If they had been in possession of an armoured vehicle, that would have been Hudson's preferred way of breaching the fence and approaching the building. But there was nothing like that here. The farm they had landed at had an old Land Rover, but that would be no use here. So they went in on foot, their current position a twenty-minute walk from where they had landed. Once they had secured the area, the plan was for the helicopters to lift off and pick them up from potential killing fields they were now about to try and traverse.

Six SAS went through the breach in the fence first, spreading out, shields before them, moving low and slow. Behind them, two sniper teams watched the grounds and the building for any threats, the drone doing constant circuits of the building.

The six men walked forwards, mindful of threats ahead of them and at their feet. "What if the grounds are mined?" Croft had asked.

"There are no anti-personnel devices. Look at the grass – it's cut regularly, well looked after. That's not something we have to worry about." Croft shook his head in disgust; he should have spotted that. He'd been too long out of the field, too long chasing ghosts and filling out reports. But he still didn't like this. He watched the six men move closer to the building.

It smelt the meat. Its sense of smell was enhanced by the virus over and above what nature had already provided for it. Food was coming. It walked over to the gate and sniffed at the ground. Even with its genetically enhanced vision, all it could see was the small patch of light far off behind the gate. That was where the smell was coming from, that was where its meal was coming from, and it growled deep within its throat. Behind it, five other growls joined in forming a low-threatening chorus. They sang together as there was a mechanical beep. The gate, the thing that had kept them here since their conception, here in the darkness and their own waste, the gate began to move. It backed up slightly, apprehensive at what this meant. But the gate continued to move, and the virus in its mind forced it forward. Its brothers followed as it stepped further past the threshold of the gate. Although the word didn't mean anything to it, freedom was there, and it began to run. They all began to run, and the light got closer and closer as they headed out to deal with their prey, virus-riddled saliva dripping from their elongated jaws.

Of the six men, four had stopped a hundred metres from the house, whilst two had continued on. Croft watched as they reached the actual building. All of them wore standard gas masks.

"Sierra one three at destination. No hostiles," the voice over Croft's earpiece said.

"Roger Sierra one three. Team two, move up," Hudson commanded. Six more men moved past where Croft crouched and made their way through the breach in the fence. They fanned out and sprinted to where their four colleagues were camped out. There was no sniper fire, no explosions. It was as if the whole building was deserted.

"This is going too easy," Sergeant O'Sullivan said over the radio. He had gone in the first batch of men, and was presently crouched down behind his ballistic shield. As if to prove that he had spoken too soon, there was a howl from somewhere behind the building. Another howl echoed from somewhere else on the property. "Shit, me and my big mouth," Croft heard the sergeant curse.

Jones watched his pets charge towards their prey. They were infused with a slightly more primitive version of the virus, but it still made the Dobermans faster and stronger than they had been before his needles had pierced their bound flesh. He had no illusions about them dealing with the threat his stronghold now faced – the attackers were undoubtedly too well-armed and too well-trained for that. But it would slow them down, and might even remove several of them from the equation. What he also noticed was that two of the dogs had chosen their own path, and had run off into the wooded area away from where the soldiers were. The dogs had originally been trained to guard the perimeter of the farmland, but the virus had impacted on that training. The first trials, with them released into the space between the two fences, had seen them repeatedly charge the electrified inner fence to try and get at the observers watching them. Their training obviously destroyed, and with the risk that they might find a breach in the fence and escape into the outside world, those original test subjects were put down. *They seem to go after anything living, so what the hell were those two strays after?* thought Jones.

The drone saw them first. "Contact, we have contact," shouted one of Hudson's men. He had his own tablet, and he thrust it at the captain. The drone had picked up heat signatures on the periphery of the property, outside the fence. They were moving fast, and closing in, and almost a dozen were now visible.

"Everyone, inside the fence now," Hudson commanded. Nobody second guessed him. The fence became a natural barrier to the new threat, and only the hole that had been blown was the weak spot. Croft saw the movement first. Swift, almost silent, and with a speed he hadn't seen before.

"Attack dogs?" Croft questioned, unconsciously manoeuvring himself in front of Savage. He raised his machine gun and let off several rounds through the fence towards the oncoming abomination. There was a squeal as one of the dogs was hit. Those around him began firing also, but only at targets they could see, their training too ingrained to waste valuable bullets on mere spooks and shadows. They backed up away from the fence, heading towards the house. There was another yelp as another dog was felled. And then those that remained were at the fence.

"Fuck me," Hudson said to nobody in particular. The dogs were larger than normal Dobermans, and looked almost as if they had been skinned. Their bodies seemed to glisten with moisture, and drool dripped from their snarling mouths. The beasts paused for only a moment, surveying their prey. The soldiers paused their fire briefly also, stunned by what they were seeing. Then the dogs charged through the holes in the fence towards the onslaught of bullets. One dog got electrocuted as it touched the fence metal, but it recovered quickly, seemingly only stunned. Its recovery was quickly quashed when its head exploded. Croft thought it had been his shot, but he couldn't tell for sure.

The men under Hudson's command didn't need telling when to open fire, and they continued to rain hollow-point rounds into the oncoming savage beasts. None of the dogs made it to their prey – most were dead in seconds, several lay mortally wounded, panting as death crept towards them.

"Remember, head shots are the only way to finish them. We can't be sure, but they might turn," Savage advised.

"Looks like they've already turned," Hudson commented.

"Fuck me rigid, zombie pooches," one of the SAS men said. Hudson turned to Croft.

"Do you get the feeling someone is playing with us?" Hudson asked

"Do you get the feeling someone is playing with us?" the voice over the speaker said. Jones stood, a slight grin on his face.

"Oh my friend," he said to himself, "I haven't even begun to play." Jones turned to the panel. He knew that if he did this, there was no getting out of the building he stood in. And he also knew he didn't care. He flicked the last six switches on the wall box. He had two minutes before something far worse than devil dogs was released, this time inside the house. Moving quickly, he left the room and made his way to the basement entrance. Pressing his hand against a palm reader in the door itself, a green light washed over him and an electronic voice spoke.

"Access granted." The door opened, sliding sideways into the wall itself, and Jones stepped through, the lights beyond coming on automatically. He moved quickly down the stairs, ignoring the first and second subterranean levels. At the third level, the stairs ended, and he made his way through another security door and followed the signs that said 'Main Laboratory'. On the two levels above him, a claxon sounded briefly and several doors opened. The occupants of those rooms, locked up since their conception, stirred.

Croft watched as the SAS sergeant, along with one of the other soldiers, fired RIP tear gas rounds through the windows of the building. From where he stood, he could see the sergeant reloading his Remington shotgun, most probably with Hatton breaching rounds. "Gaining entry," O'Sullivan said over the radio. The sergeant stepped up to the main door after a brief check for booby traps. Raising his shotgun, he stood to the side; another SAS stood at the other side of the door. This was precision, they had done this hundreds of times before. O'Sullivan blew off the hinges and the lock of the front door, the second soldier kicking it in, only to throw something in. Both men took cover as an explosion erupted in the front lobby, smoke billowing out of the now decimated entrance. Clouds of tear gas began to billow out of the doorway, and the two soldiers stormed in, followed by four more. At the back of the building, Croft could hear a similar entry being gained.

"Do you miss it, Major?" Hudson asked, referring to the adrenaline of what they were witnessing. Croft looked at him.

"Of course I fucking miss it," Croft answered.

It took only minutes for the ground and upper floor of the seven-bedroom farmhouse to be cleared, the constant metronome of explosions going off as each room was cleared with flash bangs echoing through the afternoon air.

"Building secured. There's a security door to the basement," the voice said over the headsets they all wore. Hudson nodded, and Croft followed him as he entered through the devastated front door. Savage followed with two more SAS men flanking her. They had all donned standard issue gas masks, as the rooms were still infused with noxious

CS gas. Savage noted that it was more comfortable than the ones they had at Porton Down. The sergeant met them and guided them to the room that Jones had used to view their arrival.

"Whoever's left here had plenty of warning of our arrival," he said pointing at the video feed monitors. Croft looked at the unlocked panel with the switches, not really recognising its significance.

"You said you had found a security door?" Hudson said to his sergeant.

"Yes, boss. This way." They followed the sergeant. He led them down a hallway, through mist and debris.

"Looks secure," said Croft.

"Not to worry, Major, I've got just the thing to get through that." Croft could tell that the sergeant was smiling, and he watched as the SAS man took his backpack off.

The door blew inwards, off its tracks and bounced off the wall. As the smoke cleared, Croft was thankful that technology had advanced enough to take down the door without taking down the whole building. Before the smoke even cleared, four SAS men entered and went down the stairs. The lights didn't come on until halfway down the stairs, most of the bulbs having been shattered by the force of the blast. The communication continued as they descended, but began to become garbled, infused with static.

"First floor, more stairs going down. One door off." Croft listened without interfering to the communications that were being relayed to Hudson. These guys knew what they were doing. "Entering door." Savage watched as the sergeant followed four more men down. They would take the structure floor by floor. Controlling and clearing each level before descending to the next. He would stay here with Hudson and Savage until the job was done.

"Clearing first basement level." That was followed by a series of muffled explosions. The same tactic as before, flashbangs followed by sweeping the rooms.

"Room clear."

"Room clear."

"Contact." There was a succession of gunshots. "Be advised there are infected in the building." More gunshots, more explosions.

"Fuck, get back." Croft watched Hudson, saw no reaction in his body posture. Having been in the field, having been in command, Croft knew what the man was going through. Every man under his command was his responsibility.

"Shoot that fucker."

"Three infected down. Moving to the next room." There were more explosions, louder this time. Those weren't flashbangs. Those were grenades.

"Room clear, two infected down."

"Bob," Hudson said to the corporal next to him, "have the drone do a sweep of the perimeter. I don't want any surprises."

"Yes, boss," the corporal responded.

"Room clear."

"Room clear, two infected down. Christ, these things are fast."

"First sub-level cleared, boss. Proceeding to second sub-level."

They went on like that for a further twenty minutes. The substructure was vast compared to the surface building. Despite the presence of infected, none of the soldiers had been contaminated from what they could tell. But hey, they'd know in ten minutes or so.

"Third sub-level cleared, boss. All ready for you. Looks like we've found the main lab too." Savage's ears pricked up at that. She grabbed Hudson's arm.

"Is it damaged? Have they found anyone?" Hudson relayed the question.

"No. We ran out of grenades on the second sub-level, so have had to do it old school," the voice said, now heavily distorted.

"Wait for us, we are coming down," Hudson said. Leaving the two SAS soldiers behind, Hudson, Croft, and Savage descended into the bowels of the research facility, passing soldiers on every level. On the third level, Croft noticed that the SAS present had all removed their gas masks. They hadn't used CS gas down here, and the facility's air filtration unit had kept the air here clean. It was good to have that thing off his face, and it felt easier to breathe. Savage was visibly relieved. O'Sullivan led them to the main laboratory, where another security door barred the way. This one, however, had a green light on the entry panel, and Croft gave it an experimental pull.

The door opened. Croft was surprised that it wasn't locked, and he was apprehensive as to why it wasn't. He had seen many doors like this in recent years, all designed to keep things in, but sturdy nonetheless. No doubt a breaching charge would have gained access, but there was no need. Hudson followed him through, Savage waiting for O'Sullivan.

The room Croft entered was well lit and large. Clean and white, it looked sterile, like some laboratory from a cheesy science fiction movie. Instruments and equipment littered the room, and Croft paid them little attention because he didn't even know what most of it all did. And his attention was on something far more important. At the end of the room was an isolation chamber, and inside was the man they had come to secure, the man that had nearly destroyed a planet.

Jones stood looking out of the chamber through a large window. He saw Croft raise his pistol, but knew he wouldn't fire. And even if he did, Jones wasn't concerned. The window was blast resistant. The explosive force needed to shatter it would be enough to bring the whole chamber down on those planting the explosives. The only way in was the door to the right of the window, and a big red light above it indicated that this door was locked. Jones walked up to the reinforced glass and put a hand onto its cold surface. His left arm ached slightly from where he had injected himself, and he looked at his watch. In ten minutes, probably sooner, the watch would be meaningless.

Croft lowered his weapon. He knew ballistic glass when he saw it. He stepped up to it and thumped it with his fist lightly, never once breaking eye contact with the man inside. The man didn't smile, which wasn't much but at least it was something. Strange how those who were insane often looked completely normal. The man casually jerked his head towards something and Croft followed the motion with his eyes. Croft walked over to the intercom panel and pressed the button.

"You can't stay in there forever," Croft said. Behind him, O'Sullivan and Savage entered, Savage walking over to where Croft stood. O'Sullivan went over to the chamber door, inspected it, inspected the entry controls, and turned towards his captain and shook his head. 'We aren't getting in here anytime soon' that head shake said, and he moved back to where Hudson stood. Jones took a step over to the intercom and pressed the button.

"I know. I know I'm not getting out of here."

"Why did you do it?" Croft asked, genuinely curious. "Why did you kill so many people?"

"I didn't kill anyone. I merely created the means. I wasn't the agent of its delivery. That comes later." Jones smiled this time, and chuckled quietly to himself. "Everyone thinks this is bad. This so-called apocalypse is nothing. That idiot thinks he can control this, but he hasn't got a clue."

"Who are you talking about?" Savage asked. "What did you do?"

"Not telling, that would spoil the surprise," Jones lectured, wagging a finger at Savage. He felt a chill run down his spine and looked at his watch. "But you'll see soon enough. Why not grab a chair and get ready to enjoy the show?"

"You can still make this right," Croft said. "If you made the virus, surely you made an antidote, a vaccine."

"Of course I made a vaccine. The great Brother Abraham demanded it. Of course, it won't do him any good. It's useless against the virus." Jones twitched, and his neck spasmed briefly. That was when Savage saw the injector gun lying on the table behind Jones, and her eyes went wild with realisation. "Yes, Dr. Savage, now you know."

"Wait, you know her?" Croft asked, pointing at his partner.

"Of course I know her. I have a whole dossier on her provided by my most generous benefactor. You though," Jones said with feigned confusion, "you I don't know. But I suspect you are the mystery man who flies around the country putting out fires that Abraham has been so interested in. Failed with this one, don't you think?" Croft was about to respond, but Jones was enveloped in a sudden coughing fit that doubled him over. The man spat blood onto the floor, and everyone took a step back from the viewing window, even though it was obviously secure.

"He injected himself," Savage said. Why would he do that, why would he expose himself to something so painful, so deadly? Jones stopped coughing, although his face was now a deep red. He looked like he was going to have a stroke.

"I did indeed inject myself. And I destroyed all my research. There's nothing left for you here. Nothing left at all."

"Bastard," O'Sullivan spat. "I've got enough Semtex to bring this whole building down. Let's bury the cunt and make it his tomb." Without breaking eye contact, Croft put up a hand to silence the sergeant.

"But still, there is something you want to tell me, isn't there, James?" Croft asked. Now the man smiled and nodded. He coughed again, but it was only to clear his throat.

"Oh yes. I'm not giving you the cure, and I'm not telling you the surprise I have in store for you, but getting here proves to me you deserve at least something." Jones pointed to the wall by the door Croft had come through. "There's a USB stick on the counter over there. On it, you'll find everything I know about who funded this little charade."

"Why would you give up your boss?" Savage asked.

"Because he's not my boss. He's just a self-centred, greedy megalomaniac who thinks his billions give him immunity. He thinks he can shape the world in his image, but I'm afraid he is very sadly mistaken. He thinks he has used me to do his bidding, but I have actually used him to do mine."

"Your bidding?" Croft asked.

"Yes. The world let the only people I ever loved die, and did nothing to punish the person responsible. So I became my own vengeance. I killed my family's killer," Jones ran a hand across his forehead, noticing the sweat that was beginning to pour.

"So this is why you turned off the building's defences, to tell us this?" Croft asked.

"Of course. But you had to earn your prize, which is why I unleashed my little pets. Did many of you die?" Jones said mockingly.

"Twat," Hudson said quietly.

"Indeed I am. I killed thousands, and now I will kill the world." A pain hit Jones in the stomach, and he stumbled against the glass. Despite this, despite the agony, he still smiled, blood now visible as it began to pour from his gums. "Here I go."

Savage and Croft watched as their mad scientist collapsed to the floor. They saw him vomit, saw him convulse, his head impacting off the ground several times. They both got closer to the glass, to get a better view of him as he underwent his transformation. Savage looked at Croft, who caught her glance and met it.

"This isn't right," Savage said. "This is different." Indeed it was. Jones wasn't just becoming infected; he was changing. His skin was rippling, his muscles swelling and deflating. Croft backed up from the window.

"Sergeant, I want this room sealed," he said. "I don't want anything to be able to get in or out of here." As he said this, he caught hold of Savage's arm and pulled her backwards with him. The sergeant disappeared from the room, and Croft raised his pistol, putting three well-aimed bullets into the control panel for the door that allowed access to where Jones now writhed and buckled. Sparks flew and the door mechanism malfunctioned. From where they now stood, nobody could see the man in the chamber. But was man the right thing to call him?

"I've got the USB stick," Hudson informed them. A bloodied hand smacked onto the bottom of the window, and smacked it again. The hand was bigger than it should have been. Then a head appeared, the scalp and facial skin split into great fissures as if the head was growing.

"Time to go," Croft said, and he ushered everyone else out of the room. Before he left himself, he saw the hand reach to the intercom. Jones had something to say one last time.

"This," Jones said through laboured breath, "this is what I wanted for the world. Total annihilation." He half stood now, and pointed to himself. "This was my vision…" Jones vomited all over the window, then wiped it away with an already drenched sleeve. "But don't worry. This is my baby. I'm not unleashing this onto the world. It's far too quick." One of Jones' eyes exploded, and the man screamed with pain. Still he continued with his lecture. "No, I've got much better things in mind." With that, he reared back as blood cascaded out of his throat, and the blood vessels of his face and neck exploded. There was no arm to wipe off the window's blood this time, and Croft left the man to die, closing the door behind him.

They stood outside the old farm house, a good safe distance away, knowing that underneath them a maze of subterranean chambers lurked. The SAS sergeant held the detonator, looking at Hudson. The captain turned to him and nodded. O'Sullivan pressed the button, and there was a brief pause before the whole structure before them shook. The sound was muffled but still loud, and the ground beneath the house seemed to implode, the structure falling into a crater.

"Nobody's getting in there anytime soon," O'Sullivan said, visibly pleased with himself. Hudson patted him on the shoulder and then removed his backpack. Taking out the tablet, he powered it up and put in the USB stick.

"So let's see what we can see." She swiped her finger across the files, opening them up. "Fuck me," she said.

"I think that's the first time I've heard you swear," Croft said, feigning shock.

18.30PM, 16th September 2015, NATO Headquarters, Brussels, Belgium

"I see, Major; that is disappointing." General Marston sat in the plush black leather chair, the injury in his shoulder patched up, the pain now a distant throb. He had refused the offer of painkillers. The ones he would have to take to have any effect would dull his senses. He wasn't having any of that. And he was far from happy. He had just been informed that the research needed to create a cure for the virus had been destroyed.

"It would seem the scientist who created this virus was crazier than the people funding him," the voice of Croft said on the telephone handset that the general held to his ear. "We know who the mole is, however, and we know who funded this whole thing." The general's eyebrows raised in delight. Finally, some good news. He listened, his poker face hiding the revelations that were being relayed to him. It took Croft several minutes to relay all the information. "I've sent it to you by secure uplink. But that's everything you need to know."

"You've done well, Major," said the general. "And now I have news you're not going to like." Marston felt himself go cold. He was abandoning men in the field, leaving them to their fate, outnumbered and without support. He told Croft about the quarantine, about the position taken by the US and NATO.

"I see," was all Croft said.

"Goodbye, Major, you will be in our prayers," Marston said putting the phone down, carefully, mindful to hide the anger that was bubbling up inside him. He looked across the conference table at the other people who were present in the room with him.

"Did they find the cure?" a man to his left said. The general turned to him.

"No, Sir Michael, but they did uncover some other useful information." Marston looked over at the door to the small conference room where two armed soldiers stood, and with a flick of his head indicated for them to come over. He turned back to the MI5 head. "For example, we now know who the traitor in our midst is." Both soldiers walked up to where the general sat. Without looking at them, he said, "Corporal, put Sir Michael under arrest. He is to be held pending interrogation and trial for charges of sedition."

"What? This is preposterous," Young shouted, fear not yet finding its way into his voice.

"No, dear boy, this is treason. And you have a lot of explaining to do. Get this fucker out of my sight."

18.36PM, 16th September 2015, Hayton Vale, Devon

"Those pencil-necked bastards," O'Sullivan roared. Hudson had gathered his men, and was giving them the news that they had been abandoned in a doomed country. Most of them didn't take it very well. Savage was pale with shock and disbelief. She had always believed that there would be a way out of this, and now she finally knew what it felt like to be utterly betrayed.

"So what do we do, boss?" one of the SAS soldiers asked Hudson.

"What do you think, Croft?" Hudson said turning to his superior.

"We get as far away as we can from the virus, buy ourselves time. Load up with as much gear as possible, and try and make a fight of it. It's the only choice we have."

"Any suggestions?" O'Sullivan asked.

"South Western tip of the country would be my best bet. So why not Newquay." Hudson nodded and looked at his men.

"Lads, every one of you is now freed from your obligation to me and to the uniform. You have my blessing if you want to skip out on your own. I know some of you have families, and you are free to go and collect them and if you can make it to where we are heading you can join us." There were murmurings amongst the men, and Croft could tell from the faces that at least a third of them wouldn't be coming.

"Newquay it is then," Croft said. "Let's get back in those helicopters and get the fuck out of here."

18.45, 16th September 2015, Hounslow, London

Owen stood outside his flat, listening to the sounds of the coming night. There were no police sirens, hadn't been since he had woken up. That was unheard of for this part of London. There should have been the sound of at least some kind of emergency vehicle. Nor was there the sound of traffic. All he could hear was things in the distance being broken, the occasional scream and the call of the infected. Looking down into the courtyard, he saw that it was empty. He wondered how many people still hid out behind their doors on this estate. Should he go knocking on doors, should he see how much of humanity was left? Fuck that and fuck humanity. He had more important things to do. There was something he needed to figure out.

Owen remembered being bitten now. He remembered being examined by the infected after that, remembered them leaving him alone. Would they still leave him? Would they look at him as one of their own, or had his body ridden itself of the virus? There was only one way to find out. Wearing fresh clothes he kept stored here, he had filled his pockets with more shotgun shells. Grabbing the shotgun, he made his way over to the steps that led down to the courtyard, and out into the streets below.

It was five minutes before he encountered any. A lone infected, a child, was sat chewing on someone's foot. In the failing light, he walked up to it, shotgun ready.

"Hey," Owen shouted. The infected child looked up at him, eyes blood red. They seemed to pierce into his very soul, and the child sniffed deeply. Seemingly of no interest to it, the infected looked away from Owen and continued chewing on the foot. Owen wasn't satisfied. He boldly walked up to it and prodded it with the barrel of his shotgun. The infected ignored him at first, and when he prodded again, it batted the shotgun away, only to then carry on with its meal.

"Fuck me, it's like it doesn't even see me." He walked past – no point wasting a shell on something. Five minutes later, he encountered two more infected, and again, they paid him little to no attention. This new discovery excited him, but not as much as the discovery he made on walking into the main street.

There was an abandoned police car in the middle of the road. But not any old police car. It was an armed response vehicle. Lying next to it was the headless body of a police officer, his machine gun discarded at the side of the body.

"My day just keeps getting better," he said to himself. He strolled over and picked up the gun, felt the handle was sticky with blood. No worries, he could clean it later, and he slung it over his shoulder. The boot of the car was open, and inside he found a treasure trove of ammunition and weapons, as well as a bag to put them all in. Never one to look a gift horse in the mouth, Owen didn't discard the shotgun. Instead, he broke it down and placed this in the bag also. With the bag on the floor, he unslung his new toy and examined it. It took him a good minute or two to figure out how to work it, how to fire it, the shot booming through the deserted streets. There was movement in a house to the left as a curtain twitched, and he briefly saw the petrified face of an old lady in an upstairs window.

"King of the world, Grandma!" he shouted, and whooped with delight. At the end of the street, a pack of six infected appeared, drawn by the noise, and they made for him quickly. Owen tensed. *Oh shit, what if I was wrong?* But as they neared him, their manner changed. They stopped, sniffing the air, no longer even looking at him, and turned around and went back the way they had come. Owen smiled.

"This calls for a fucking celebration," he said to himself, and made off in the same direction. He would find the nearest off-licence and get himself some quality hooch. And then he would go and see if any members of his gang were still alive. No point being fucking King if you didn't have any subjects.

21.45PM 16th September 2015, London, Manchester, Birmingham, Glasgow, Nottingham, Leeds

The world watched the fall of a nation. With the government evacuation of London, the terrestrial and satellite TV networks went dark as the infestation reached their doors. Only the BBC still played, broadcasting from the secure emergency bunker in Evesham. BBC1 relayed information to the so far unaffected parts of the nation who were glued to their sets, and Radio 4 broadcast to the country a sombre message that the land was dead, and for those waiting for the zombie hoards to descend, no help would be coming. Some people fled their homes, but where was there to flee to? The country's motorways seized up as people tried to get away from the growing infected areas, and fights broke out in railways stations as thousands rushed to get on trains going anywhere but where the infected were. Only the infected were everywhere, and most of the trains weren't running, those tasked with driving them abandoning their posts. Who could really blame them? Within hours of the start of the outbreak, the transport infrastructure was broken, blocked and no longer functioning. So people returned to their homes where they hoped their locks and their barricades would save them. But all they were doing was waiting for the inevitable. The infection would find them, and it would consume them.

Others took to the streets, fear and confusion sending them on a whirlwind of destruction and chaos. Law and order evaporated as the police went to protect their families, no longer willing to defend those who could not control themselves, and any residue of the armed forces found themselves ordered to evacuation zones. Only some went. As the carnage grew, the non-infected towns and cities burned and the streets ran red with the intoxication of anarchic release. As the hours passed, and as the contagion spread in ever-increasing circles, the initial illegal desire for TVs, designer clothes, and other consumer goods changed as reality dawned on the lawless. What use was a 40-inch plasma when very shortly there wouldn't be any electricity? What use was a Rolex watch when millions of ravenous, blood-thirsty horrors were descending on you, intent on biting and ripping and gouging your flesh? So the gangs and the mobs turned on the supermarkets, on the corner shops, and then on each other. And all the while the law abiding hid behind their doors and prayed to whatever gods were left to listen.

Outside the UK, the world shook on its axis. In Wall Street, the Dow Jones Industrial Average plunged down a thousand points on opening as some of the world's largest companies became worthless. Banking stocks collapsed as the loss of the UK's financial hub, the City of London, rocked them to their core. And at the realisation that there was now no chance Britain's massive debt would ever be repaid, the system went into meltdown. The world's stock markets closed shortly after opening as trading was suspended, panic wiping out trillions of dollars in mere hours. Commodities and FOREX markets across the globe suffered similar fates, and the British pound plummeted in value to near worthless paper. On Wall Street, suicides skyrocketed as fortunes were decimated and people hurled themselves into the street below.

All international flights to the UK were cancelled and every sea border with the country was closed. Before the order came, hundreds of private jets and helicopters took off and left UK airspace as the rich and the connected fled. Except for the earliest flights, all were directed to Ireland, which was to be the world's buffer zone. The United States went to DEFCON 2 and NATO began to mobilise forces in two directions. Firstly, to the northern border of mainland Europe, and secondly to Eastern Europe in case a recently empowered Russia saw this as an advantage to claim back former glories. Now with no mainland government to control them, the remaining UK forces, including its nuclear submarines, were taken under NATO control. But even with its losses, one of the world's most powerful militaries had escaped relatively unscathed, most of its personnel and heavy equipment overseas. Queen Elizabeth II may not have had a country left, but she was still the sovereign of an effective fighting force.

Fearing an influx of infected, the Channel Tunnel was sealed at the French end, and demolition charges were set midway through. In the Mediterranean, the United States Navy Carrier Strike Group 2 was ordered to the Atlantic to coordinate the naval blockade of a country that had once used the sea to conquer a quarter of the globe. En route from America, Carrier Strike Group 8 was redirected to help with the blockade. NATO instructed Britain to deploy every ship it had out at sea to help quarantine their own home. Despite the fact that their families were being left to die, very few of the remaining service personnel refused their orders. There was, after all, nothing they could do, no homes for them now to go to. With the certainty that their families, their friends and loved ones back on the mainland were most certainly doomed, all that was left was duty. And suicide, there was plenty of that.

Operation Noah was deemed a success. Over four hundred individuals were extracted from the mainland, with very few no shows. Scientists, doctors, industrialists, authors, and artists all found themselves whisked away from a dying country, in planes and helicopters also laden with precious art and rare trinkets, mainly from private collections. Any initial resistance to abandoning the country was quickly countered by the horrific news coming out of London that was broadcast across every available channel. People watched in horror as a country of sixty million people burned and tore itself apart.

EPILOGUE

David, his name had been David. He still remembered that on occasion, but it meant nothing to him now. The brief spark of memory hit him again as he wandered down onto the beach, the sky slowly beginning to darken as the sun began to disappear from the cloudless sky. Then the thought was gone, replaced only by the hunger and the churning of millions of voices. The voices drove him on, urged him, forced him to continue what the virus demanded. Somewhere along the way, he had lost one of his shoes, and he walked lopsided, the wet sand soaking through his sock. He barely registered the chill of the ground or of the air around him, his attention fixed on the distant horizon. The abrasions on his foot and the glass embedded in it were of no consequence to him.

His arm no longer ached from the gunshot wound and broken arm, the virus having partially repaired the ripped muscle and shattered bone, knitting him back together over the days it had taken him to make the journey from London. He had been in the vanguard, spreading the contagion through the towns and cities that surrounded the nation's capital. At first, he had found nothing but abandonment and desertion, but eventually, his kind caught up with the fleeing humanity. The motorways, the trains and the airports all clogged with frightened, defenceless beings with nowhere to go. It had been a slaughter. Deserted by the government whose armed forces had all but fled, those caught by the infected were easily converted and swelled the ranks. By the time he had reached the beach, there was an army of over thirty million infected. And now he was at the edge of the island's humanity, and yet the hunger spurred him onwards. Ever onwards. Never stopping, never sleeping, his body a wiry, emaciated mass that fed upon itself to feed the viral hunger.

He walked into the surf as it came in to paint the sand, the sun visible in the clear sky above. There was movement to his left, and his head briefly turned to see dozens of his kind walking towards the ocean's edge. They were all of one purpose, one mind, one vision, the virus wanting to spread, to seed itself further and further. David looked back at the horizon, and although he could not see it, he knew there was more land out there. In his human days, he would have called this the English Channel, would have known that people had swum it countless times. He stepped further into the water, oblivious to it as it came up over his knees, then up to his thighs. He could hear more infected behind him, and knew that there were hundreds, no thousands doing as he was doing.

The water, now up to his waist, held no threat for him. The currents and the cold would not end him. Should his life be taken, then would he not merely be transformed? Now the water was up to his chest, and he paused briefly. David knew where he had to go, where they had to go. On that horizon, the enemy waited, and he and his kind would bring to them the new order of things. He looked around him one last time, and felt the cry rising in his throat, heard his brethren join him in the chorus of the damned.

"*SPREEEEAAAAAD.*" With that, a thousand voices were silenced as they submerged themselves under the water and began to swim towards the French coast.

Coming soon……….

The Contained

Book 2 of the Necropolis Trilogy

By Sean Deville

"They're coming to get you, Barbara"
– Johnny, *Night of the Living Dead*

The Washin

Friday, September 18th, 2015

Great Britain Quarantined

The world woke up this morning, still reeling from the horrific events of two days ago, when the world watched a once proud and great country brought to its knees by what is now believed to have been a Bio-weapon terrorist attack. News is coming out that a religious death cult is being held responsible for the outbreak that saw Great Britain quarantined and abandoned. The YouTube video presently circulating across the internet that claims to be from the perpetrators of the attack has still not been verified by the authorities. With over a billion views to date, its claims have left the worlds governments in turmoil. Although multiple government sources will neither confirm or deny this, rumors continue to circulate across the internet that the cult released a pathogen that resulted in an outbreak that has resulted in mans worst nightmare coming true. Zombies, it now seems, are real. Millions are now believed dead, and the United Nations Security Council are still in emergency session.

Rer
foll
imp

The
that
rela
the
beh
of a
exp
in l
its
beh
con
or v

It m
tota
thir
dec

TOP SECRET

THIS IS A COVER SHEET

FOR CLASSIFIED INFORMATION

ALL INDIVIDUALS HANDLING THIS INFORMATION ARE REQUIRED TO PROTECT IT FROM UNAUTHORISED DISCLOSURE IN THE INTEREST OF NATIONAL SECURITY OF THE UNITED STATES.

HANDLING, STORAGE, REPRODUCTION AND DISPOSITION OF THE ATTACHED DOCUMENT WILL BE IN ACCORDANCE WITH APPLICABLE EXECUTIVE ORDER(S), STATUTE(S) AND AGENCY IMPLEMENTING REGULATIONS.

UNLAWFUL VIEWING, REPRODUCTION OR TRANSPORT IS A FEDERAL OFFENCE UNDER 18 U.S. Code § 798 AND CARRIES A TERM OF A MINIMUM OF LIFE IMPRISONMEN

(This cover sheet is unclassified)

TOP SECRET

703-101

NSN 75690-01-21207904

NSN 75690-01-21207904

The Office of The Secretary of Defence

A confidential report to the President of the United States from the office of the Secretary of Defence

11.17.2015
To: The President of the United States of America
From: Carl McGruber, Secretary of Defence

Mr. President,
Through liaison with the Director of the CIA and the Joint Chiefs of Staff, we have collated the information regarding the events in the United Kingdom and have concluded that the terrorist threat to this country is real. It is our recommendation that we take no action at this time to suppress the biological threat on the UK mainland, and instead concentrate on finding the culprits that we believe reside on our own soil.

Our present understanding of how the contagion works is this. Initially spread through contaminated milk in coffee shops, the pathogen is spread by bites and by direct exposure to bodily fluids. From analysis of the information forwarded to us by the remnants of the UK government and MI6 still holding out in their London headquarters, we know that someone exposed to the virus, even via skin contact, will turn within, on average, ten minutes. They will then become violent, with immense strength and stamina, similar to someone on PCP. They will be immune to most painful stimuli and can sustain injuries that would kill most humans. If they are killed by anything other than brain trauma, they will resurrect as – what you will know from popular horror fiction – the undead. Of the samples captured by MI6 agents on the ground, we have been told that the undead display no vital functions. They have no heartbeat, no blood pressure and show only the faintest of brain readings on MRI or EEG. Although dead, the isolated virus seems to kill all other pathogens in the body, slowing decomposition considerably. The reanimated can move although they cannot perform fine motor functions. It is understood that they can climb and open doors. It has been shown that they can only be stopped by destroying the brain stem. This explains why the UK forces had such difficulty killing anyone infected.

The NSA were able to salvage much of the data from their UK counterparts at GCHQ upon the facility's evacuation. That combined with the MI6 interrogation of the captured terrorists has led us to believe that, whilst the laboratory used to make the virus was on the UK mainland, and that the chief scientist behind the virus was still at that lab on its destruction, the main perpetrator of this atrocity is still at large. We have as yet no knowledge of how the lab was funded or whether further samples of the virus have been smuggled out of the country. We have been advised that we will be kept appraised of any developments brought forth from the data seized at the laboratory, but we have not, as yet been given access to it. Due to the biological hazard presented by this contagion, the Joint Chiefs rejected the initial proposal to send our own Special Forces to aid the operation to seize the laboratory.

Regarding the threat made via the uploaded YouTube video, which, despite our attempt to suppress it, has reached almost one and a half billion views, the original upload was done through a host of proxy servers, and it is impossible to determine even which country it originated in, never mind who created the video. We believe, however, the video is real and that the threat posed to our nation is possibly the worst since the Cuban Missile Crisis. We advise that all Federal and State law enforcement agencies be put on high alert and that operation Clean Sweep be implemented. We have confirmation from the Justice Department that Clean Sweep is legal under Executive Order and that FEMA can have the detention camps ready for detainees by the end of the day. The first stage of Clean Sweep should see half a million radicals, terrorist suspects and undesirables taken off the streets within 24 hours. The NSA will begin blocking alternative media sites, and the main news broadcasters and print news have confirmed they will push the narrative we give them. All it requires is your approval, Mr. President.

Regarding the quarantine of the UK mainland, this is now complete. There is a twenty-five mile naval exclusion zone and all air traffic is banned from going anywhere near the UK in a three-hundred-mile radius. This has obviously impacted on European air travel, but no country has yet objected. Any vessel trying to breach this quarantine will receive one warning, before being either shot down or sunk. We have confirmation from NATO and the Russian Republic that they will aid in this quarantine. The Russians have assured us that they will not use this crisis to further their territorial demands. The only fear at present is if infected individuals try and swim the UK channel, or if reanimated corpses fall into the ocean and get swept away.

We will brief you further as and when developments arise. We do not at this stage recommend declaring martial law, and do not advise suspending the Constitution at this time.

Carl McGruber,
Secretary of Defence

Carl McGruber

CHECK OUT OTHER GREAT ZOMBIE NOVELS

ZBURBIA
by Jake Bible

Whispering Pines is a classic, quiet, private American subdivision on the edge of Asheville, NC, set in the pristine Blue Ridge Mountains. Which is good since the zombie apocalypse has come to Western North Carolina and really put suburban living to the test!
Surrounded by a sea of the undead, the residents of Whispering Pines have adapted their bucolic life of block parties to scavenging parties, common area groundskeeping to immediate area warfare, neighborhood beautification to neighborhood fortification.
But, even in the best of times, suburban living has its ups and downs what with nosy neighbors, a strict Home Owners' Association, and a property management company that believes the words "strict interpretation" are holy words when applied to the HOA covenants. Now with the zombie apocalypse upon them even those innocuous, daily irritations quickly become dramatic struggles for personal identity, family security, and straight up survival.

ZOMBIE RULES
by David Achord

Zach Gunderson's life sucked and then the zombie apocalypse began.
Rick, an aging Vietnam veteran, alcoholic, and prepper, convinces Zach that the apocalypse is on the horizon. The two of them take refuge at a remote farm. As the zombie plague rages, they face a terrifying fight for survival.
They soon learn however that the walking dead are not the only monsters.

CHECK OUT OTHER GREAT ZOMBIE NOVELS

900 MILES
by S. Johnathan Davis

John is a killer, but that wasn't his day job before the Apocalypse.
In a harrowing 900 mile race against time to get to his wife just as the dead begin to rise, John, a business man trapped in New York, soon learns that the zombies are the least of his worries, as he sees first-hand the horror of what man is capable of with no rules, no consequences and death at every turn.
Teaming up with an ex-army pilot named Kyle, they escape New York only to stumble across a man who says that he has the key to a rumored underground stronghold called Avalon..... Will they find safety? Will they make it to Johns wife before it's too late?
Get ready to follow John and Kyle in this fast paced thriller that mixes zombie horror with gladiator style arena action!

WHITE FLAG OF THE DEAD
by Joseph Talluto

Millions died when the Enillo Virus swept the earth. Millions more were lost when the victims of the plague refused to stay dead, instead rising to slaughter and feed on those left alive. For survivors like John Talon and his son Jake, they are faced with a choice: Do they submit to the dead, raising the white flag of surrender? Or do they find the will to fight, to try and hang on to the last shreds or humanity?

CHECK OUT OTHER GREAT ZOMBIE NOVELS

VACCINATION
by Phillip Tomasso

What if the H7N9 vaccination wasn't just a preventative measure against swine flu?
It seemed like the flu came out of nowhere and yet, in no time at all the government manufactured a vaccination. Were lab workers diligent, or could the virus itself have been man-made?
Chase McKinney works as a dispatcher at 9-1-1. Taking emergency calls, it becomes immediately obvious that the entire city is infected with the walking dead. His first goal is to reach and save his two children.
Could the walls built by the U.S.A. to keep out illegal aliens, and the fact the Mexican government could not afford to vaccinate their citizens against the flu, make the southern border the only plausible destination for safety?

ZOMBIE, INC
by Chris Dougherty

"WELCOME! To Zombie, Inc. The United Five State Republic's leading manufacturer of zombie defense systems! In business since 2027, Zombie, Inc. puts YOU first. YOUR safety is our MAIN GOAL! Our many home defense options - from Ze Fence® to Ze Popper® to Ze Shed® - fit every need and every budget. Use Scan Code "TELL ME MORE!" for your FREE, in-home*, no obligation consultation! *Schedule your appointment with the confidence that you will NEVER HAVE TO LEAVE YOUR HOME! It isn't safe out there and we know it better than most! Our sales staff is FULLY TRAINED to handle any and all adversarial encounters with the living and the undead". Twenty-five years after the deadly plague, the United Five State Republic's most successful company, Zombie, Inc., is in trouble. Will a simple case of dwindling supply and lessening demand be the end of them or will Zombie, Inc. find a way, however unpalatable, to survive?

CHECK OUT OTHER GREAT ZOMBIE NOVELS

DEAD PULSE RISING
by K. Michael Gibson

Slavering hordes of the walking dead rule the streets of Baltimore, their decaying forms shambling across the ruined city, voracious and unstoppable. The remaining survivors hide desperately, for all hope seems lost... until an armored fortress on wheels plows through the ghouls, crushing bones and decayed flesh. The vehicle stops and two men emerge from its doors, armed to the teeth and ready to cancel the apocalypse.

TOWER OF THE DEAD
by J.V. Roberts

Markus is a hardworking man that just wants a better life for his family. But when a virus sweeps through the halls of his high-rise apartment complex, those plans are put on hold. Trapped on the sixteenth floor with no hope of rescue, Markus must fight his way down to safety with his wife and young daughter in tow.

Floor by bloody floor they must battle through hordes of the hungry dead on a terrifying mission to survive the TOWER OF THE DEAD.

CHECK OUT OTHER GREAT ZOMBIE NOVELS

RUN
by Rich Restucci

The dead have risen, and they are hungry.

Slow and plodding, they are Legion. The undead hunt the living. Stop and they will catch you. Hide and they will find you. If you have a heartbeat you do the only thing you can: You run.

Survivors escape to an island stronghold: A cop and his daughter, a computer nerd, a garbage man with a piece of rebar, and an escapee from a mental hospital with a life-saving secret. After reaching Alcatraz, the ever expanding group of survivors realize that the infected are not the only threat.

Caught between the viciousness of the undead, and the heartlessness of the living, what choice is there? Run.

THE DEAD WALK THE EARTH
by Luke Duffy

As the flames of war threaten to engulf the globe, a new threat emerges.

A 'deadly flu', the like of which no one has ever seen or imagined, relentlessly spreads, gripping the world by the throat and slowly squeezing the life from humanity.

Eight soldiers, accustomed to operating below the radar, carrying out the dirty work of a modern democracy, become trapped within the carnage of a new and terrifying world.

Deniable and completely expendable. That is how their government considers them, and as the dead begin to walk, Stan and his men must fight to survive.

Printed in Great Britain
by Amazon

75773673R00180